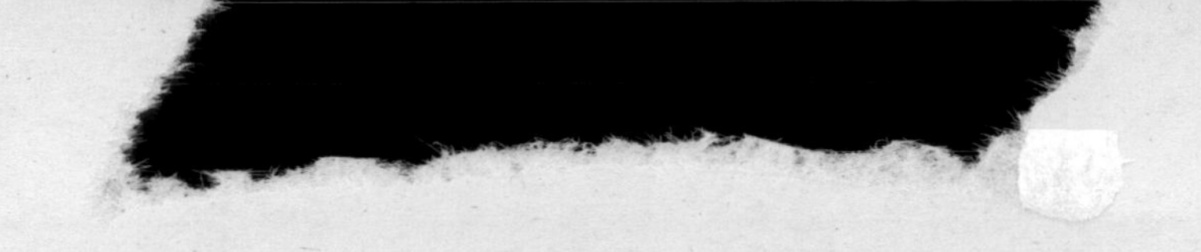

John Lescroart is the *New York Times* bestselling author of twenty-three novels, including *Damage*, *Treasure Hunt*, and *A Plague of Secrets*. His books have been printed in sixteen languages and published in more than seventy-five countries. He lives in northern California with his wife and two children.

Praise for the novels of John Lescroart:

'The master of the legal thriller' *Chicago Sun-Times*

'John Lescroart is a terrific writer' Jonathan Kellerman

'Unusual in his ability to combine courthouse scenes, action sequences and well-drawn characters that come together in a fast-paced text' *Wall Street Journal*

'John Lescroart is one of the best thriller writers to come down the pike' Larry King

'A master' *People* magazine

By John Lescroart

Sunburn
Son of Holmes
Rasputin's Revenge
Dead Irish
The Vig
Hard Evidence
The 13th Juror
A Certain Justice
Guilt
The Mercy Rule
Nothing But the Truth
The Hearing
The Oath
The First Law
The Second Chair
The Motive
The Hunt Club
The Suspect
Betrayal
A Plague of Secrets
Treasure Hunt
Damage
The Hunter

JOHN LESCROART

THE HUNTER

headline

First published in Great Britain in 2012 by
HEADLINE PUBLISHING GROUP

First published in paperback in Great Britain in 2013 by
HEADLINE PUBLISHING GROUP

1

Cataloguing in Publication Data is available from the British Library

ISBN 978 0 7553 9316 9

Typeset in Granjon by Palimpsest Book Production Ltd, Falkirk,
Stirlingshire

Printed and bound in Great Britain by
Clays Ltd, St Ives plc

Headline's policy is to use papers that are natural, renewable and
recyclable products and made from wood grown in sustainable forests.
The logging and manufacturing processes are expected to conform
to the environmental regulations of the country of origin.

HEADLINE PUBLISHING GROUP
An Hachette UK Company
338 Euston Road
London NW1 3BH

www.headline.co.uk
www.hachette.co.uk

To the memory of my parents,
Maurice Eugene Lescroart and Loretta Gregory Lescroart;
and again, forever, and always,
to my wife and true love,
Lisa Marie Sawyer

[The Under Toad] was the color of bad weather. It was the size of an automobile.

John Irving
The World According to Garp

1

THEY WERE HAVING the special, wings and tuna wontons, in a window booth at Lou the Greek's, two guys in their early forties, talking over the lunchtime noise.

The good-looking one, Wyatt Hunt, said, 'Gina and me, we're both reluctant to commit.'

'Reluctant,' Devin Juhle said. 'I like that.' He was a San Francisco homicide cop, and relationship issues, even those in his own life, weren't his main concern. He'd been with Connie for fourteen years and didn't think about that stuff too often. They just worked, had their three kids, did their jobs. Loved each other. Committed.

Juhle picked up a wing, held it out between them. 'What is on this thing?'

'Skin.'

'No, Kemo Sabe. What spice?'

'Peanut butter, I think,' Hunt said. 'And garlic and cayenne and probably soy sauce. Pretty good, huh?'

Juhle nodded. 'For Lou's.' He took a bite and chewed. 'So you guys are done?'

'Pretty much, I'd say.'

'I can't say it breaks my heart, you know.'

'Yeah, well, you and she had kind of a different thing.'

'She's a ball-buster.'

'Not to me.'

Gina Roake, the woman in question, was a lawyer a few years older than Hunt who'd had occasion to fillet Juhle on the witness stand in a murder trial a while ago. It hadn't been his finest moment.

'I don't want to hear any trash talk about her, Dev. We had a good run and she and I are still going to be friends, okay?'

Juhle shrugged. 'It's your life.'

Hunt nodded. 'Damn straight.'

But they weren't there to talk about Hunt's love life. This was a job interview.

And Juhle was holding up his hand. 'Before you get too far, Wyatt. I appreciate the offer, I really do. I'm surprised and flattered, honest. But I don't see how I could.'

'You reach your hand out over the table, we shake on it, the deal's done.'

Juhle shook his head. 'Connie would kill me.'

'Connie wouldn't even maim you. She wouldn't care if you changed jobs. You could push a hot dog cart and she'd dance ahead of it, hawking sales in her cheerleader outfit.'

Juhle nodded in acknowledgment. 'Well, okay, so maybe not Connie. But there are other reasons. My retirement, for example. Health insurance. Being in homicide, which puts me at the top of the food chain. Besides which, I actually like what I do.'

'Yeah, but the bureaucracy, the union stuff, all the rules . . .'

'Hey, rules are my life. I love the rules. Why do you think I became a cop? I'm a rule guy.'

'That's what Ivan said, too.' This was Ivan Orloff, one of Hunt's new hires. 'And guess what? That whole rule-guy thing – it turns out, not so much. He loves the freedom of being on his own, plus he turns out to be an amazing investigator, which he didn't even know until he stopped being a cop. Now he sees stuff even I miss on the first pass. Not to mention we get along great together, which I'm hoping might even happen with you. Although that's a bit more of a long shot.'

'And getting longer every minute.'

Hunt leaned back and crossed his arms. 'Twenty-five percent.'

Another head shake. 'It's not the money. Twenty's fine if I wanted to do it. But I'm not even slightly tempted. Besides, I've got some pretty severe reservations about the whole boss thing between you and me . . .'

'I wouldn't be your boss.'

'You'd be paying me, am I right? Wouldn't that make you the boss?'

'Technically, perhaps. But you know me, I wouldn't ever pull rank.'

A small smile. 'Yeah. Until you did. And then there goes twenty years of you and me getting along, such as we do.'

Hunt stayed hunched back against the wall of the booth for a moment, then came forward, his elbows on the table. 'Come on, Dev. Don't you think we could have us some real fun?'

'We're having fun now, dude. Eating great wings. No hierarchy between us. Just two guys out living the high life on a weekday afternoon. It ain't broke, so we don't need to fix it. That's a main life rule, and as I said, I'm a rule guy.'

Hunt was in his bedroom, having changed into nicer clothes for his next appointment, sitting on his bed, talking to his receptionist/secretary/assistant Tamara Dade on his cell phone, telling her the disappointing news about Devin Juhle. He heard the little ping telling him he was getting a text message, but as usual when he was talking to someone, he ignored it.

'It was a long shot anyway,' he was saying, 'but I figured worth a try.'

'Definitely, but I can't believe he didn't jump at it. Was it even close?'

'He stopped me before I'd even finished the pitch. No interest.'

'Could it be that fun being a cop?'

'I guess. Who would've known? Or here's a thought – maybe he thinks it's not that much fun being a private eye.'

'That couldn't be it. He's seen us at work, where the fun never stops. Now, for example. Are we having fun now or what?'

'Fun. No question.'

'QED, right?'

'Well, there is one other theory.'

'What's that?'

'You.'

'What about me?'

'He finds you too attractive to deal with and is afraid if he works around you every day, it'll impact his marriage to Connie.'

'Right, Wyatt.'

Again he heard the tone indicating a message, and again he ignored it.

'No, seriously,' Hunt continued. 'He's worried he'll become addled with wild sexual fantasies, unable to concentrate. Eventually turn to drink, despair, and divorce.'

'He mentioned this to you, did he? Used the word *addled*?'

'Not exactly. I read between the lines, though. It was kind of sad.'

'I'd imagine,' she said.

He said good-bye and touched the 'End' bar on the face of his cell phone. The latest text message – the second message, the one that showed on his screen – was from Tamara's brother, Mickey, but to Hunt it barely registered. The messages could wait. Hunt didn't want any interruptions at the moment and he held down the button to turn off the power and then slipped the cell phone into its holster.

Frowning, he swore under his breath.

Why did he bring up that lame attempt at humor to Tamara?

That Juhle thought she was too attractive to work around? Distracting? Addle making?

When it was he who was having the problem.

Since 1912, the Mission Club has made its home in the Kearny Mansion, an enormous yet gracious four-story stucco structure on Nob Hill Circle, just around the corner and a little downhill from the Fairmont and Mark Hopkins hotels. Its membership includes 183 members – never more, sometimes less – making it the most exclusive private club in the city.

The club employed a male butler, Taylor, a chisel-faced, strongly built African-American in his late fifties or early sixties. Taylor was leading Hunt back to his meeting room when Hunt touched his arm and stopped their progress to check his reflection in the foyer's mirror.

He was wearing his best slacks and sports coat, but as always when he came here, he felt inadequately turned out.

'You look fine, sir,' Taylor intoned.

Taylor was in a tuxedo. Hunt looked him up and down and couldn't keep a smile off his face. 'Easy for you to say.'

Because of his assignment here, Hunt had gotten access to some of the club's statistics, such as the average age of sixty-seven, the average net worth around sixty million dollars. What wasn't in the stats was the average cost of what the women wore. Hunt figured, what with the designer dresses and shoes and handbags and other accessories – and oh, let us not forget the jewelry – nobody walked around with less than twenty thousand dollars worth of *stuff* clinging or hanging or otherwise attached to their bodies.

And then they were at the doorway to the room where the three members of the Membership Committee sat chatting in Queen Anne chairs that surrounded the lace-covered table on which rested a selection of pastries, cookies, coffee, and teas.

Taylor intoned, 'Mr Hunt.' The door closed behind him.

'Ah, Wyatt.' Dodie Spencer got to her feet and crossed over to him, offering her cheek for him to kiss. She was a distractingly beautiful woman reminiscent, Hunt thought, of Grace Kelly or January Jones. From his background research, he knew that she was forty-two years old and married to Lance Spencer, owner of Execujet. 'So good to see you again,' she said. 'It's always good to see you.'

'And you,' Hunt said, then added, 'all of you.' He included the other two women who remained seated. 'Mrs Wren, Ms Hatcher. Good afternoon.'

Deborah Hatcher nodded politely. Hunt knew that she was seventy, that she had never been married, that her father had made their fortune in mining salt out of the bay.

Gail Wren, eighty-four, observed Hunt with her glacier-water eyes. She wore ornate gold and emerald earrings, several rings, and a multistrand necklace that Hunt thought probably contained forty carats in diamonds, maybe a thousand carats. She was old, old money, with somewhat obscure equity ties to the first years of the Bank of America.

Deborah Hatcher reached forward to take a cookie from the tray while Dodie kept a light hand, possessively, on Hunt's arm, as she turned back toward her two comembers. Gail fixed Hunt with an impatient cold eye. 'Since you're a little late, we may as well get right to it. Does that suit you, Mr Hunt?' The elderly dowager pointed with a bejeweled, arthritic finger. 'Take that chair. Pour some coffee if you want. And, Dodie, for God's sake, quit mushing, would you? And sit down.'

'Judith Black,' Hunt began, 'is not exactly who she appears to be.'

'I *knew* it!' Gail Wren slapped the side of her chair. 'I knew something wasn't right with that woman.'

Deborah Hatcher turned her head, reached a hand across to

her neighbor's chair, and spoke in a calm tone. 'N
said that exactly, Gail dear. Not yet.'

'Oh, nonsense. Of course he has.'

'Maybe we could just let him go on,' Dodie Spencer s
'Wyatt?'

He nodded. 'Thank you.' He came forward, elbows on his knees. 'She is in fact on the payroll at Abbot-Cantor Securities and has been for the past five years . . .'

'She's a *broker*?' Gail might as well have said *hooker*.

Dodie glanced her impatience at the older woman as Hunt pressed on. 'Not exactly a broker, Mrs Wren. More like a finder, although Josh Cantor called her a business development manager. I was up front with Cantor and told him that I was helping with Judith's membership application background check here and he made no bones about her role in the firm.'

'Her role in the firm?' Deborah asked. 'Which is what, exactly?'

'She cultivates clients and funnels them to Abbot-Cantor.'

'Cultivates,' Gail said. 'Charming. *Funnels.* And sends them to our city's very own Bernie Madoff, only he hasn't been caught yet.'

Again, this got a small rise out of Deborah. 'Now, Gail, we don't know that.'

'Hmph! Would either of you work with him, with what we already know? He's been dodging indictments for the past decade.' And then, back to Hunt. 'How much does he pay her?'

'We didn't get into that, and I don't think he would have told me if I'd asked.'

'Never mind that,' Dodie said. 'The point is, she lied on her application.'

'Well, not exactly. Under "Employer," she put "not applicable."'

Deborah huffed at that. 'She's working for Abbot-Cantor. That's applicable.'

Hunt spread his hands. 'That might be a matter of interpretation.'

'Nonsense. It's purposefully deceptive,' Gail said. 'Do any of us doubt that she wants to become a member so that she can – what was your word, Mr Hunt? – she can *funnel* our members into Mr Cantor's funds? When the rules explicitly forbid soliciting other members in business matters . . .'

Dodie reached across and touched Hunt's knee. 'Did you find any evidence of that? Specific solicitation?'

'Well,' Gail put in, 'I don't think we're going to need that. Not after this.'

'Nevertheless,' Hunt said, 'I did contact each of her three sponsors and, yes, two of them have moved their money to Abbot-Cantor within the past two years, and the third one, Florence Wright, is thinking about it right now. None of them seemed aware that Mrs Black worked for that firm, and I asked all of them specifically as it came up. And then when I asked if they thought the monthly dues would be a problem for Judith, they all volunteered that she was one of the most astute investors they knew, with close ties to Abbot-Cantor. In fact, the results she was getting with that firm were why they'd switched or were thinking about switching.'

'*Funneled*,' Gail rasped out in disgust.

Hunt nodded. 'Funneled. I tend to agree.'

Dodie let out a disappointed little sigh. 'Well.'

'It's such a shame.' Deborah's eyes were downcast. 'She should have known she wouldn't have been happy here if she really wasn't who she's pretending to be.'

'She doesn't care about happiness, not in the same way you do,' Gail replied. 'Happiness to her is money. And she just wanted to make money off of us, plain and simple. You're such a *believer* in the goodness of people, Deborah. You'd think you'd have grown a little more realistic by now.'

'It's just that I've always liked Judith,' Deborah said. 'She seems so sweet.'

'Con men don't succeed if they're not sweet,' Gail replied with her usual asperity. 'Same goes for con women.' She shifted her focus. 'And you, Mr Hunt, thank you. This is precisely why we decided to hire you, and you've saved us all embarrassment, not to say possible financial reversals.' Now, taking in her fellow members, 'I believe our decision is clear here, is it not? Decline?'

Dodie nodded. 'Decline.'

Deborah sighed. 'Oh, if I must.' She wagged her head sadly. 'Decline.'

Dodie walked Hunt out as far as the foyer. Talking about 'the old battle-ax' in a stage whisper, she kept her hand on Hunt's arm as they walked. 'I particularly liked it when she told me to "quit mushing." I didn't know I was mushing. Did you think I was mushing, whatever that is, Wyatt? Was I bothering you?'

'Not in the least.'

'You're sure?'

'Promise.'

'All right, then. Just so I'm not a nuisance.'

'You'd have to go quite a ways to get to there, Dodie.'

'Well, thank you.' She gave his arm a little squeeze. 'And also, thanks again for the background on Judith. She would have been a cancer here if we'd let her in.'

'I'm glad I could be of help, what little I could do.'

'You did plenty, believe me, and beyond that, you kept it all under the radar, and that's a talent rare as gold. The last thing this club needs is a public scandal.'

For an instant, Dodie stopped and looked up at him. Hunt wondered if she might try to kiss him. When she had interviewed him for the assignment here, her attraction to him had been obvious: She'd hung on his every word. His professional background. His personal story all the way, it seemed, back to his childhood. It had almost been unprofessional enough to make him decide not to take the job.

But now the intensity in her eyes gave way to a smile and she said, 'We will certainly keep you in mind if anything new comes up. Have a nice day.'

In front of the mansion, Hunt was waiting for his car to be delivered to him when he took out his cell phone and powered it back on. Mickey's earlier text message appeared again on the screen, some menu he was working on. Hunt could get back to him later. He pressed 'Close' on Mickey's text, and the next message popped up from an unknown number.

What the . . .?

The message read, *How did your mother die?*

2

Ivan Orloff slouched on the chrome and leather chair in the reception area of the new Hunt Club digs in the Audiffred Building directly above Boulevard restaurant. After a lengthy stint as a San Francisco police officer, he'd finally succumbed to Wyatt's blandishments and eleven months ago had come to work with the firm. Now in his early thirties, slightly heavier than he needed to be, he looked dark and brooding with his low forehead and thick black hair. But his looks were misleading. Upbeat and optimistic, he had a smile for everyone and often a joke to go with it. Although this, of course, was no time for jokes. 'Did you try calling the number back?' he asked Hunt.

'It's the first thing I did. No answer, no voice mail, no nothing.'

Jill Phillips was a forty-two-year-old mother of two teenagers. No-nonsense in demeanor, clueless about fashion, she was four months into what she hoped would be a three-year apprenticeship with the Hunt Club that would give her the six thousand hours of investigative work that she'd need to qualify for her PI license. 'Disposable phone,' she said. 'One of those prepaid things.'

'Probably,' Hunt said.

'Could you text back to it?' Ivan asked.

'I tried. No response.'

Tamara Dade, boosted on her desk, wore a short green skirt with a plain white blouse. She had kicked her shoes off, now was swinging her long legs. 'Maybe it's a prank. Some kids sending texts to random cell numbers.'

'If that's it,' Hunt said, 'they need to get a life.'

'How *did* your mother die, Wyatt?' Jill asked. 'What's that about?'

'I don't know. I never knew her. Neither did the Hunts, my adoptive parents. And I never asked.'

'Well, there's your problem,' Orloff said. 'You've got to ask about these things. You want answers, you gotta ask.'

'Thanks, Ivan,' Hunt said drily. 'I'll try to keep that in mind next time I get adopted. Note to self: Ask new parents about natural mother. I got it now.'

But Orloff pressed. 'You don't remember her at all?'

'Little tiny things, maybe. Snippets, but what I remember might have come from other places, other homes.'

'What about your dad?' Tamara asked. 'Your birth father?'

'I don't know. I mean, I was in the foster system, so both my birth parents were gone. That's all that really mattered.'

'And now,' Jill said, 'somebody's sent you this text message.'

'That's creepy.' Tamara had known Hunt since she'd been in sixth grade, when he'd literally saved her life and that of her younger brother, Mickey. Their mother, dying from a drug overdose, had left them locked inside their apartment. After they'd missed several days of school, Hunt – at the time working for Child Protective Services – had gone to their apartment and talked his way inside, to find them both near death from malnutrition.

Hoping to keep the siblings together and out of the foster-care system, which he'd once known so well, Hunt had helped hook up both kids with their maternal grandfather, Jim Parr, who then raised them both as his own. Tamara was as protective of Hunt as he was of her. 'I think it's creepy,' she repeated.

'Somewhat.' Hunt chuffed out a breath. 'I don't know why they wouldn't just call me.'

'Yes, you do,' Ivan said.

'I do?'

'Sure. There's only one possible answer.'

'That's easy for you to say, since you seem to have all the answers today.'

'Actually,' Mickey said brightly, 'he's got 'em every day.'

'In fact, Wyatt, if Ivan gets any better,' Tamara added, 'we're thinking of electing him boss.'

'I'm not sure it's an elective office,' Hunt said. 'I'd have to check the bylaws.'

'I'm just trying to be helpful,' Ivan said with a trace of defensiveness. 'It just seems obvious to me why they wouldn't have called you.'

Hunt flashed him a smile. 'Enlighten us, O wise one.'

'Because they don't want you to know who they are,' Ivan said. 'You'd recognize the voice.'

Hunt glanced around at the rest of his team. 'I hate it when he makes it look that easy.'

Ivan, smiling, nodded. 'It's a modest gift.'

'But wait,' Jill put in. 'Why does it matter how your mother died? And especially, why does it matter to somebody who doesn't want you to know who they are?'

'All good questions,' Hunt said. 'Unfortunately, I've got no good answers.'

The house in Belmont that Hunt had grown up in looked smaller every time he went down to visit. It was hard now for him to imagine that he'd shared a twelve-by-fourteen-foot bedroom above the garage with his two brothers – first Wyatt alone and then, when his parents had suddenly become fertile after years of trying and failing to conceive, Rich and Ethan sharing the bunk bed. Around the corner at the top of the stairs, Lori and Pam's room wasn't really much more than a closet, maybe eight by ten, with one window. His mother and father's room, the master, such as it was, was on the ground floor down a short hallway behind the kitchen/dining room. Seven people in fourteen hundred feet. Six to eighteen, the happiest years of Wyatt's life.

Now in mid-October the sun was just kissing the tops of the hills to the west outside the large picture window. Wyatt's dad, Bob Hunt, sat in his recliner with a glass of red wine. Bald, trim, soft-spoken with an all-white goatee, Bob Hunt came across as mostly cerebral to anyone who hadn't competed against him in any activity on the planet, from poker to pool to basketball to chess to golf. To those people, including his children, he was relentless, kind, and unbeatable.

'Sure,' his dad was saying, 'you can ask me anything. You know that.'

'It's about my birth parents.'

His father's eyebrows went up a fraction of an inch. His eyes glinted with interest. As a clinical psychologist, Bob had often wondered about his adopted son's refusal to acknowledge his natural roots. But it wasn't Bob's nature to pry. Wyatt had his reasons and Bob had always respected them.

'Well,' Bob said, 'not that I'll be much help. Your mother and I never knew them and you didn't seem too curious.'

'More than not too curious,' Hunt said. 'More like actively hostile.'

'So what's changed?'

Wyatt told him about the text message, trying to figure out where it had originated, then went on, '. . . and then I saw there were really two sides to this equation. One was this mystery text and who sent it, but the other was the message itself, the whole question of my birth mother, my birth parents. And suddenly I realized that I wasn't mad about any of that anymore. Which, you know, after the way I was . . .'

'You were fine, Wyatt,' Bob said. 'You thought it would hurt our feelings, especially your mother's, if you got all emotional and needy about your birth parents. So you didn't. We understood that. Even admired it.'

'I consider you guys my parents.'

Bob cracked a smile. 'Good thing, since we consider you our son.'

'Yeah, but I don't want you and Mom to think—'

Bob cut him off. ' – that we're getting demoted somehow. No chance of that. I'm afraid you're stuck with us. It's just that now, suddenly, something's come up and you've got a reason to look into things.'

'Maybe a bogus reason. Maybe just a prank of some kind.'

'But maybe not.' Bob sipped his wine. 'So what do you need to know?'

Wyatt spread his hands. 'A name would be good. I could start with that.'

His father nodded. 'And it would be a good thing to start with, I admit. But I don't have it.' He held up a hand. 'I know. It's ridiculous, but this was in – what? – '74. Char!' he called out. Then, to Wyatt, 'Your mother will know more about all of this than me. Always.'

Wyatt's mom, Charlene, in the kitchen with the spaghetti sauce that was perfuming the entire downstairs, now came and stood in the doorway with a straw-covered bottle of Chianti in her hand. Tall, rangy, still handsome pushing seventy, she wore her thick gray hair proud and long. She could have been a prairie wife from two hundred years ago. 'And at his beck and call,' she announced, 'your servant arrives bearing wine.'

'And how could it hurt?' Bob asked. 'But that's not what I called you for. Wyatt's got some questions about his birth.'

A shadow crossed her face and tightened her lips, then vanished. 'I've got a few of those myself, to tell you the truth. Your father probably already told you we don't know much.'

'Not even a name?'

She pulled a dining room chair around and sat on it. 'It was a different era. Everything about adoption was so much more hush-hush than it is now. Back then, everybody was so protective.'

'Of what?'

'Of everything, really. First, just the stigma of being adopted. Which right off the bat meant somehow you weren't "normal," whatever that means. You don't remember kids teasing you at school?'

Wyatt nodded. 'Vaguely, maybe. Not really.'

'Ah, repression,' Bob said.

'It was just one more thing to fight about back then, Dad. I don't specifically remember the adopted thing being what it was about.'

'Good. Then your mother and I did our job.'

'Plus,' his mother said, 'you were six when we got you. There wasn't any point in trying to deny you were adopted. That was always part of the package with you. The other kids picking on you used to make me nuts.'

'It seems like a weird thing to tease somebody about,' Wyatt said.

'Some kids,' his mother said, 'anything will do.'

'Well, remember,' his father put in, 'back then, if you were adopted, especially through Catholic Charities, which you were, then you were probably illegitimate, so the fourteen-year-old birth mother just wanted to get back to her real life and pretend you never happened.'

'And then the adoptive parents like us,' Charlene added, 'were terrified that the birth mothers were going to come back and claim their babies and take them away when they got older. So there was this whole legal apparatus keeping the birth parents and the adoptive parents separate, and then of course keeping the kids from being able to go back and find their birth mother, either, and disrupting her whole adult life and family.'

'So my birth mother and father might still be alive?'

'That's not impossible, I suppose,' Charlene said. 'They could be midfifties, sixty. If they were young when they had you, they could be younger than us.'

'Except,' Bob said, 'that your texter knows something.'

'What texter?' Charlene asked.

Wyatt ran down the situation for her. 'So whoever this person is,' he concluded, 'thinks they know who my mother was, somehow connected her to me, and that she is now, probably, dead.'

'How could anybody know that? And why would they care?'

Wyatt shook his head. 'You got me.' He drank off half his wine. 'How about my birth certificate? Didn't I need that to get into the army? I think I did. Don't we still have that here?'

'I'm sure we do,' his mother said, 'but it's not going to help you identify your mother since you're named in it as Wyatt Hunt.'

'How can that be,' Hunt asked, 'if I was six when you guys got me . . .?'

'You were six when we got you out of that last home,' Bob said.

'Okay, but I must have been Wyatt somebody else when I was born, right?'

'Correct,' his father said. 'And Catholic Charities has that name, I'm sure, on your original birth certificate. But you'll have to petition them to get a look at that, and then if they've got a countervailing order from your birth mother or birth father, you're still going to be out of luck.'

Hunt sat back on the couch. 'So when you got me, I was who?'

'To protect your identity, you were Wyatt Doe,' his mom said quietly. 'By the time we made it official, you wanted to be Wyatt Hunt.'

'Still do,' he said. 'So where does that leave me?'

'Maybe,' Bob offered, 'this texter will write you again and tell you something you don't know.'

Charlene twirled her glass on the table. 'You could go to Catholic Charities.'

'I'm definitely going to do that,' Wyatt said. 'But here's another question: Do you know how long I kicked around foster homes or other people's prospective adoptive houses before you got me? I mean, I remember at least three, maybe four of them. I must have been slightly challenging, huh?'

'You could say that, for those people,' Charlene said. 'You were acting out some, dealing with abandonment. Those other people didn't know how to connect with you, that's all. They weren't good fits like we all were.'

'I think it was about three years,' his father said.

'So I was with my birth mother and father until I was about three?'

'That would be the math,' Charlene said.

'So, 1971? That's when I went into the system?'

His dad nodded. 'Pretty close, I'd say.'

'That's when whatever happened, happened,' Wyatt said. 'I wonder what the hell it was.'

Hunt lived in a former flower warehouse on Brannan Street. He'd bought the dilapidated shell in a down market fifteen years before when the neighborhood around the Hall of Justice seemed a step away from outright condemnation. He had renovated it, mostly by himself, into something unique and impressive.

There were two possible entrances on the Brannan side, a

solid-steel door and a garage door next to it. Both were cherry red because Hunt thought the accents went nicely with the purple of the rest of the outside wall. The space inside featured a twenty-foot ceiling, natural light coming through windows all around and way up high. The centerpiece was the hardwood basketball court and professional basket – hung from the roof – that Hunt had scored a decade ago from the Warriors when they'd upgraded. Along the white drywall beyond that, a cluster of guitars and amps filled one corner, while a bank of three computers sat on a couple of old library tables. In the other corner lurked Hunt's surfboards and sails and a new Kawasaki motorcycle.

A nearly invisible door led to the residential side, a nicely designed, functional, well-lit modern apartment – Hunt's bedroom down a wide hall to the left, then a living room/den with books and his TV and stereo stuff, and finally a well-equipped kitchen and eating area – Sub-Zero refrigerator and Viking four-burner stove and six solid but mismatched chairs around a distressed farm table. A back door – like the front entrance, also steel – led out of the kitchen to the alley behind.

Now Hunt sat at his kitchen table, nursing his frustration along with a Heineken. His cell phone was on the table in front of him. He could not understand how a random person could have come to know anything at all about his mother and then, even more impossibly, had connected her to him. Therefore, he thought, the texter was not and could not be a random person. The only solution that came to him was that he or she must be with the Catholic Charities. If Hunt and his birth mother were at either end of a chain, he reasoned, the adoption service was the single link that connected them.

He had to start there.

Reaching over and picking up his phone, he returned to the

original text message, got back into 'Send' mode, and typed, *Write me back. What is this about?*

He sat holding the phone for another minute or two, his knuckles going white around its slim rectangularity. Then he pushed and held the on/off button, swiped the bar to power off, and got up from the table on his way to bed.

3

The Catholic Charities main office was on Howard near Main, easy walking distance from Hunt's home. The clerk there, a kind-looking elderly woman named Melissa Wagner, told him that they had stopped handling adoptions two years before, and now the files and paperwork had been taken over by the California State Department of Social Services, Adoption Support Unit, and shipped to a storage facility in Sacramento.

'You are kidding me.'

Ms Wagner smiled under her bifocals. 'Nothing's easy, you know. That's one of the rules.'

'I've heard about it. But I wasn't planning to drive up to Sacramento today.'

'Oh, there'd be no sense in doing that anyway. You can't just walk in and ask for your birth records.'

'Of course you can't. I knew that. That would be too easy.'

'Exactly.'

'So what do I do?'

'You send them a notarized letter telling them your birthday and your adoptive parents' names, and then request the information you want about your birth mother and father. Then, if one of your parents signed a Consent to Contact form, they can put you in touch with them.'

'What if they didn't? Sign the form, I mean.'

'Well,' Ms Wagner sighed, 'then it becomes more complicated.'

'Why am I not surprised? So what are the complications?'

'Well, you can mitigate some of them, maybe, if you include in your original letter some questions that they're allowed to answer.'

'Such as?'

'Such as your parents' race and general physical description, or how old they were when they put you up for adoption, medical information. Are you looking for something related to a medical condition?'

'No.'

'Are you part American Indian?'

'I don't think so. Why?'

'Because if you were American Indian, you could petition the superior court and they could release those records so you could get any benefits that might accrue from belonging to your tribe.'

'Well, I think that's a long shot.'

'And actually, you don't look very Native American to me,' she said.

'Not so much,' Hunt agreed. 'So I have to send this notarized letter and then if there's no consent form, that's the end of the search?'

'You could petition the superior court, as I said, even if you're not Native American. But you'd need a pretty compelling reason for them to agree, usually medical. Otherwise, I'm afraid if your parents didn't want you to find them, there's essentially no way for you to do it.'

At his desk in his office, Hunt was putting the finishing touches on the letter to Sacramento. Tamara came in with coffee and now sat in one of the armchairs across from him. 'What if it wasn't Catholic Charities?' she asked him.

'But it was. My dad knew that one.'

'No. You said he'd adopted you through them.'

'Right. Didn't I just say that?'

'Yeah, but what if they got ahold of you after you were already in the system? When Mick and I . . . when Mom died, we went directly to CPS, as you know. So even if Catholic Charities eventually got you, you probably spent time at CPS while they sorted through the admin stuff getting you over to them. They're the dumping grounds, wherever you wind up.'

Hunt nodded thoughtfully. 'That's worth a look, except . . .'

'I'm ahead of you.' She held up a finger. 'Fortunately, your first name is not exactly common, is it? What year are you talking about?'

'Nineteen seventy, seventy-one.'

'Okay, so you look through the files and find a Wyatt. How many could there be? The real challenge might be getting them to let you look at their files.'

Now Hunt was on his feet. 'That,' he said, 'should not be an issue.'

When Hunt had been a field-worker at CPS, Bettina Keck had been his partner. A black woman from the projects, she had been funny, smart, tough, and fearless. Unfortunately, the stress of the job – taking children away from their abusive parents – had taken its toll and she'd eventually become addicted to OxyContin and alcohol and was fired, then spent seven years in and out of rehab. Finally clean and sober, she'd gone back and somehow gotten herself rehired at CPS and now, ten years after that, was deputy director. Not only had Hunt never lost touch with her through all the rehabs, but also he had been, along with her husband, one of her mentors during her last rehab stint, the one that had finally worked.

Now with that history between them, they sat in her cubicle at her cluttered office on Otis Street. 'Of course it's an issue, Wyatt,' Bettina said. She wanted to help, she really did, and her frown reflected her disappointment that she wouldn't be able to. 'You know this. The files are private. Even if they still exist, you can't look at them without a court order.'

'I won't really look. I'll just peek.'

'Peeking counts.'

'And what do you mean, if they still exist? Why wouldn't they exist?'

'Well, we're talking thirty, maybe forty years ago. Records from back then should have been purged.'

Hunt straightened up in his folding chair. 'Okay,' he said, 'how about this? First, we go across the street and find out if the records still exist. If they don't, okay, I lose. But if they do . . .'

'No, listen.' Keck was shaking her head. 'The problem is that you're not looking for one particular record. If that was it, I could just go over there and have somebody pull it out. Wyatt Smith, or Wyatt Jones. Probably not technically legal, but I'd do that for you. But for what you want, you're going to have to look through all of the records, and you admit that you might not even have come through CPS in the first place. I can't ask somebody to go back into all those files and look for that.'

Hunt broke a grin. 'Sure you can. It'd be fun!'

'It might take a couple of days.'

'Bettina, everybody's bored to death over there anyway. This could be your chance to brighten up lives. They'll love you for it. Really. You could make it a contest. Find the Wyatt. Give out prizes. I'll supply them. Maybe a bottle of wine or some Giants tickets, or even cash, say a hundred bucks.'

'Going for bribery now.' Keck brought both hands up to her face and pulled down on her cheeks. 'You can wear a girl down, Wyatt.' But she raised herself out of her chair. 'Let's see what's left to begin with, then take things from there.'

Hunt's phone emitted a two-toned chirp when he got text

messages and now, just as he was getting out of his chair, it sounded. He pulled his phone from its holster.

The message said, *'Progress?'*

Hunt's thumbs flew. *Who are you? Call me. We can talk.*

He touched 'Send.'

'What's that all about?' Keck was hovering over him.

'It's what started all this. Somebody's stalking me by text.'

'So change your phone. Get a new number.'

'I don't want to do that. Whoever it is knows something and wants me to discover whatever it is. Why they're doing it this way I don't know, but I'm going to need to find out.'

'What, though, exactly?'

'Who they are and what they want.'

Can't talk. Text.

Why?

Progress?

No.

Later then.

Wait. Records?

Hunt stood glued to his screen, finally looked up at Keck. 'Gone,' he said.

'That was weird.' Keck crossed her arms. 'I don't suppose it's occurred to you that this person has a reason for not wanting you to know who he or she is.'

'Sure.'

'So maybe they won't appreciate it much if you expose them.'

Hunt shrugged. 'They should have thought of that before they started.'

After all the back and forth, the reality turned out to be anti-climactic.

At the records office across the street, Keck and Hunt learned that, yes, the files should have been purged – destroyed – long ago. But, in fact, that bit of bureaucratic housekeeping had possibly not been completed. The head clerk of records management had held the same job during Hunt's tenure there and he told them without much apology that you had to expect these kind of delays on nonessentials in an office like theirs where everything tended to be an emergency.

Hunt looked around and realized that his theory about the clerks being bored to death wasn't holding up. Everybody was working – on their phones, at their desks and computers, in the interview rooms. It brought back to him his own experiences here, when they were always behind. Too much work; too many incompetent, irresponsible, stupid, addicted parents; and too many children who needed to be rescued, interviewed, evaluated, placed. Why did people have kids anyway, Hunt thought for the thousandth time, if they weren't going to take care of them?

But that wasn't his mission here today. 'If these files still existed,' he asked the records boss, 'where would they be?'

'Down the basement.'

Hunt made the request sound casual. 'You mind if we go down? We don't want to get anybody in trouble and Bettina here was worried about confidentiality issues.'

The man didn't really have to think about his answer. 'Anything down there,' he said, 'the statutes got to have run on ninety-nine percent of it, whatever it might be. Really, who's gonna squabble? Y'all go knock yourselves out.'

Five minutes later Keck and Hunt found themselves in the semi-finished, low-ceilinged basement – bare bulbs and concrete floors and a footprint the size of the building above them, maybe twelve thousand square feet. They'd packed the files in moving boxes and stacked them in aisles five tall and two deep by year, the latest being 1992, when CPS had gone to computers.

Hunt stood with his hands on his hips in front of the rows and said, 'I can do this, Bett. Thanks for getting me down here.'

But Keck shook her head, pointed at the boxes. 'Let me have one of those suckers. If this is all there is, shouldn't take us an hour.'

It didn't even take twenty minutes. Going through the 1970 files, near the end of his third box, Hunt came upon the name Wyatt Carson. He pulled out the manila folder and opened it. He must have made some noise, because Keck was suddenly standing over him. 'You got something? Wyatt, are you all right?'

Hunt's neck was flushed and his hands had gone cold and were shaking. Keck touched his shoulder. Hunt, his voice sounding raw, read from the file: 'The subject child's father, Kevin Carson, is in custody awaiting trial for the murder of his wife, the child's mother, Margaret.'

Keck went down to a knee next to Hunt and put an arm around his shoulders. 'It's all right,' she said. 'It's all right.'

'No,' he said. 'No. It really isn't.'

4

'Jesus, Mary, and Joseph. God in His mercy be praised.' The man, in cassock and collar, made the sign of the cross and then held his hands together in front of his chest as though he was in a state of rapture.

And perhaps he was.

In his mid to late seventies, ruddy cheeked, white-haired, and well fed, the priest stood in the door to the Star of the Sea rectory's waiting room, beaming at Hunt, now coming forward with his hand extended, his eyes glassy with emotion. 'Welcome, welcome.' He gripped Hunt's hand. 'Don Bernard,' he said. 'I can't tell you how long I've waited for this day.'

Hunt shook. 'What day is that, Father?'

'When I'd see you again. If I'd see you again.' He backed away a half step and looked into Hunt's face. 'I don't know if I'd have picked you out in a crowd, but looking at you now, I can see your mother like she's here in the room with us. You've got her eyes exactly.' With an effort he stopped staring at Hunt's face. 'How did you finally come to find me?'

Hunt explained how Bernard's name had been in the CPS report as the primary contact in case of emergency. Hunt had then called the archdiocesan office and found out Fr. Bernard was still alive and where he lived. 'And they sent me here.'

'All this happened when?'

'Since this morning. Someone put me on the trail to find my mother and suddenly it became important.'

'You hadn't sought her out before then? Before now?'

'No. I have my parents – Bob and Charlene Hunt – and they've been fine for me. Better than fine.'

'I can see that. At a glance. They've done a good job.'

'Yes, they have.' Hunt shifted on his feet. 'I don't want you to take offense, Father, but have you been texting me?'

The priest's face clouded. 'Have I been what?'

'Texting me. Leaving me text messages on my cell phone.'

The cloud gave way to a sunny laugh. 'I don't even own a cell phone. All this modern technology is too much for me. You send messages now by telephone? Why would you do that if you could just call and talk in person?'

'That's a question for another day, Father, but some people seem to prefer it.'

'So someone has been sending you these messages about your mother?'

'Asking how she died. If I knew how she died. That's what got me going.'

'Since yesterday? It certainly didn't take you very much time.'

'No.' Hunt explained. 'I'm a private investigator by trade. I can generally find people if I'm looking for them.'

'A private investigator,' Bernard said. 'What an amazing world. But you still don't know who contacted you to start you looking?'

'No.'

'Or why?'

'That, too. I was hoping you might be able to help.'

'Maybe not with that,' the priest said, 'but I can tell you about your parents.'

Hunt paused, then asked, 'Did my father kill her?'

'No, your father did not kill her. They never proved that, and they tried twice.'

'Who?'

'The courts. The law. He was tried twice for her murder and they couldn't convict. Because he was innocent. He simply didn't do it.'

'So who did?'

The priest let out a breath. 'No one knows. No one's ever found out.'

'So what happened to my father?'

Bernard sighed again. 'If you've got the time, why don't you take a seat and wait here? I want to get a few things. I can be back in a couple of minutes.'

In the rectory's small sitting room, Hunt held photographs of himself as an infant and a toddler, pictures of the family into which, apparently, he had been born. In every shot, the couple looked impossibly young, innocent, happy. Here was Wyatt, a three-year-old on the merry-go-round in Golden Gate Park. The image brought to his consciousness a memory that raised the hairs on the back of his neck. For a moment, the mnemonic pull of the photograph made him blink.

He turned the picture so that the priest could see it. 'An hour ago, I would have told you I had no memories of my parents. But I remember this, the day. It was warm and smelled like popcorn. I feel a little whacked upside the head.'

'That's understandable.'

Hunt flipped his way through the stack. 'Not her, though. I don't remember her.' He stared at his mother, Margaret Carson, holding him when he'd been a small baby. He wasn't sure he saw what Fr. Bernard had recognized in her eyes as the template of his own, but then, without anything changing in terms of what he recognized as his conscious memory, something turned over inside him and the muscles in his face went tight.

He tucked the picture behind the small pile.

'Or him, either.' His father, Kevin Carson, had Wyatt on his shoulders, holding on to his shoulder-length hair. The man was grinning with swagger under his mustache, wearing a white T-shirt, his arms crossed over his chest. He was leaning up against what Hunt knew – recognized? – as a brown Ford Fairlane 500, one leg braced against the back bumper.

'You said my father was tried twice for my mother's murder?' he asked. 'How did that happen? What about double jeopardy?'

'The jury hung both times,' Bernard said. 'The DA elected not to go for three.'

'So where was I all this time?'

'When your father was arrested, I was his phone call. The Child Protective Services had already taken you in by that time, and since your parents didn't have any other family, I . . .'

'Wait a minute. They didn't have any family, either? How did that happen?'

'They were just . . . well, as you can see, they were just a couple of kids on their own. When your mom was maybe fifteen or so, she ran away from her home, I think it was in Indiana, where she'd been in some kind of abusive situation she didn't like to talk about. No, not *didn't like* to talk about, *wouldn't* talk about. Whatever it was, she was done with it. It was behind her and never coming back.

'Your dad lost both his parents in a car wreck a few months before he met your mother. So it was just the two of them, alone together against the world. Or at least, that's how they felt, and you couldn't really blame them.'

Hunt sat back on the couch, the pictures in his lap. 'How'd you meet them?'

A wistful smile. 'I married them. Smallest wedding in history, I believe. Just the two of them and their two witnesses. They came in and had the nuptials in the middle of six-thirty mass. She was carrying you at the time, maybe four months along.'

'And then, suddenly, three years later, out of nowhere my dad calls you when he gets arrested?'

'Well, not exactly out of nowhere. I'd come to know them fairly well by then.' He hesitated. 'It wasn't always a picnic. They had some problems.' Another pause. 'The truth is they were starting to fight. Money was tight, they weren't having much fun. Your mother was staying home with you, and your father . . .'

Hunt prompted him. 'My father . . .?'

'Well, your father, he didn't make much at the garage. He felt that they needed more, so he got into some behaviors – and Margie thought maybe between the two of us, me and her, we'd be able to talk some sense into him.'

'What behaviors?' Hunt asked.

Bernard finally came out with it. 'He sold some marijuana, stole a couple cars, got caught driving drunk. All petty stuff, really, but it's a slippery slope. They had a few loud fights; the cops got called.'

'I know. I read about the fights in my own file since there had to be a CPS follow-up on those, to see if the house was safe. Plus, there was the one child endangerment – that was my mom, not my dad – where they let her off with a warning, no charge. And then the three DVs.' Domestic violence.

Bernard nodded. 'Yes, sadly, all of the above. Both of them struggled.' He sighed. 'Anyway, long story short, I became their counselor. I helped get Kevin a second job on the weekends, landscaping with one of the parishioners here at the church. And Margie was babysitting and starting to take in alterations. . . . She was quite a talented seamstress.' Bernard's pale blue eyes glazed over. 'They were going to get through it. They were good people at heart, just young and poor and inexperienced. They were in love. I knew that. You couldn't help but see that. Somehow, it was all going to work out. And then

Kevin called me from jail . . .' Bernard ran his hand down his cheek.

'And you moved me out of CPS and into Catholic Charities.'

'I did. In those days, the networks in the Catholic community were very strong. I thought it would be the best for you.'

'But why didn't my father . . .? Why didn't he put me in some kind of holding pattern, some foster home or something, while he was at trial? What was he going to do about me when he got out?'

'Well, yes,' Bernard said. 'All of that.' He pulled himself forward to the edge of his chair, rested his elbows on his knees. 'First, he wasn't sure that he was ever going to get out, to beat the charge. Second, even if he didn't get convicted, he knew the trial would take at least a year. And as it turned out, the two trials took the better part of four years. But I think the main thing, and we argued about this, was that he felt he couldn't be a good father to you, the father you deserved. He was in jail, he might never get out, he didn't want you growing up with all those strikes against you. He wanted you to have a fresh start with a good family. He wanted what was best for you.'

'And he'd get that by abandoning me?'

'I know. I think he was wrong. But that wasn't how he saw it. He saw it as his sacrifice for your good.'

Hunt let out a breath. 'Okay, let me ask you this, Father: How did *you* lose track of me?'

'Oh, there was never any question about that. Once you were placed, wherever it might have been, I was out of the loop from that time on.'

'Why was that?'

'That's just the way they did it then. Back when you were in the system, great pains were taken to keep the child and the birth parents separated forever.'

'That's what my mom and dad said last night.'

'Well, it's true.' The priest spread his hands. 'I realize that nowadays it's not uncommon for birth mothers to be told who is adopting their child, or for the adoptive parents to have a way to contact the birth parents. But back then, that just wasn't done. It was thought to be better all around if the break was clean and final.'

Hunt looked up at the crucifix that hung on the wall over Bernard's chair. 'So after the trials,' he asked, 'after they were over, then what?'

Bernard made a small kissing noise of regret, his eyes baleful. 'Then he disappeared. He came by here and told me he was getting out of the state before they decided to arrest him and try him again. I tried to talk him out of it. I thought I could help set him up with some kind of job, maybe even get him into college, but he wasn't having it. He wasn't going to talk about it. He'd only come by to say good-bye' – Bernard indicated the ancient brown oversize envelope from which he'd extracted the photographs, lying there on the coffee table between them – 'and to leave this package in case you . . . in case I ever saw you again.' He picked it up and shook it and another, smaller envelope fell out into his hand. It had the name *Wyatt* in pencil faded to near invisibility in block letters on the front but otherwise was unaddressed and sealed. 'That's for you, too.'

Hunt reached out, picked it up, held it in both hands. He put a finger under the flap and ripped it open. Inside was one sheet of lined notebook paper, folded over into thirds. The words were again printed, in pencil. There was no date.

'Wyatt,' it began.

If you are reading this, then you've met Father Bernard and you know the cops and everybody thinks I killed your mother, but I swear to you that I did not. When they let me go, I started looking to find out who did, but it had been four years and whatever trail there might have been was totally cold. Meanwhile, some nice people who felt sorry for me after the trials offered me some traveling money and a job down in Texas, and I've decided it's probably the best offer I'm going to get so I'm going to take it. Maybe I should stay but I don't see how it would do me any good. Even if I found whoever was responsible for your mother's death, the cops would never believe me.

Just leaving and starting over is the best thing I can do. I'm sorry I'm such a lousy father. But I did want you to know the truth about your mother and me.

I didn't kill her.

Love, your dad

He had signed his full name formally in longhand. 'Kevin M. Carson.'

5

Devin Juhle's least favorite part of his job was correcting the typed transcripts against the tapes of witness interviews. He'd been doing this at his desk since just after noon and so wasn't in the world's best mood to begin with. This showed on his face as he looked up and noticed Wyatt Hunt picking his way across the homicide detail toward him.

When Hunt got close and said what he'd come to say, Juhle started right back in at him. 'So just yesterday I believe it was,' he began, 'I told you with sincere regret that I wouldn't be able to work for you, and then the next thing I know, you're here standing in front of me at my desk in the midafternoon where, when I'm not out on the street risking life and limb for the citizens of this great city, I do my real job for which I get paid as a homicide inspector, and you're asking me if I could just look up a little something for you in my free time and for no compensation whatsoever?'

'There would be the compensation of performing a small but meaningful service for your best friend in the world.'

'I don't think that's going to be enough.'

'It will be, especially when you hear what it is.'

'I don't want to hear what it is, Wyatt. I've got other work I'm supposed to be doing, as I believe I've mentioned already now a time or two. And after I'm done here, I've got three witness interviews starting' – Juhle checked his watch – 'in exactly forty-two minutes and they will take me through the rest of the afternoon and possibly even into the night and that in turn will make me late for dinner, which Connie hates and I can't say I blame her because I hate it, too.'

'You are in rare eloquence today,' Hunt said.

In his chair behind his desk, Juhle gave Hunt a patient look and lowered his voice. 'That's because, Wyatt, I'm trying to convey to you in the clearest terms imaginable that I can't just stop what I'm doing and take on a freelance gig for you, however small or inconsequential it may be.'

'It's small but it's not inconsequential, Devin. It's a still-unsolved murder, which makes it an active case, and the victim was my mother.'

Juhle was halfway to what would probably have been another snappy comeback when he stopped in midbreath. 'What?'

Hunt nodded. 'My birth mother, Margie Carson.'

Now Juhle shook his head. 'I'm going to wind up doing this for you, aren't I? Whatever it is. It's really about your mother? Who was really murdered? You're not making this up as we go along to get me on board?'

'Scout's honor. It really happened. It really hasn't been solved.'

'And you just found this out?'

'Not an hour ago.'

'That sounds like a story all by itself.'

'It is, but the main event is the trial.'

'They had a trial? I thought you said it was unsolved.'

'It is. The man charged with killing her got off twice on hung juries.'

'Yeah, well, welcome to San Francisco.'

'He was also my father.'

Again, Juhle went all but still, then was shaking his head, chortling. 'Okay, congratulations. You actually had me going there for a minute, Wyatt. That was good.' He checked his watch, pushed back his chair, started to stand. 'And don't think I haven't enjoyed our little interaction here, but I've really got to get going.'

'It's true,' Hunt said.

'I just don't think so.'

'It's easily checked. It'll be out in the warehouse in the Bayview. That's all I'm asking. If you'd just go out there and take a look. I'd go myself, but they wouldn't let me in. You have to be a cop.'

'Really? When did that start?' Juhle collapsed back into his chair. 'What was her name again, your mother?'

'Margie Carson. The first trial was in '71.'

Wearily, Juhle came forward and wrote on a Post-it. He looked up. '*If* I get done with these witnesses, *and* I'm not yet late for dinner, *and* I happen to get back to this building sometime today, none of which are very likely, I *might* try to go out and take a look. No promises, though.'

'You'll do it. I know you will.' Hunt smiled, pointed at him. 'You're my man, Devin.'

'I am most assuredly not your man, Wyatt. I'm just a poor working cop trying to do my real job.'

'Well, then, I'd best be on my way and let you get to it.'

Parking always being what it was, expensive or impossible, Hunt had driven back to his warehouse from Star of the Sea, parked his Cooper inside, closed the double-wide garage door behind him, and walked over to the Hall of Justice to see Juhle and make his request for the case file.

Now, walking back in bright sunshine and rare warmth – October is midsummer in San Francisco – he got to his alley door and lowered himself into the shade that covered the concrete stoop.

He sat straight up, his head back against the door, surprised to find that he was fighting to control his breathing.

Aside from his various sports and exercises, Hunt kept himself in shape by running several miles most mornings, out to the Embarcadero and then around to Crissy Field – sometimes all the way to the Golden Gate Bridge – and back, so it was unusual for him to feel physically weak, and practically unheard of that he would give in to it. Now, though, without warning, he was hyperaware that he'd broken into a cold sweat, he was breathing hard, his head had gone light to the point of dizziness.

He pressed at his temples, then slowly brought his whole self over and down until his elbows came to rest on his knees, all the weight of his head on his two hands.

He didn't know exactly if he'd call it a memory. There wasn't anything substantive to it. All at once there simply seemed to be a new *place* somewhere inside of him. Maybe it had been there all along, and it had just been carefully, methodically, completely covered up and hidden over, but now it felt like nothing more than a yawning, open pit in the middle of his gut.

He kept gulping at the air to see if it would fill that pit up, but it wasn't doing him any good.

Wafting on the light breeze, a whiff of popcorn from somewhere brought the world up into his face and suddenly he knew that he was going to be sick.

Unlocking the back door as fast as he could, he ran through his kitchen and made it to the bathroom in time, but just. Then, afterward, on the cold tile, Hunt sat with his arms crossed over his chest, hugging himself to fight off a chill. Finally, some minutes later, he got to his feet and looked at himself in the mirror. His face was sallow, his eyes bright, nearly glistening. Turning on the cold water, he splashed his face, dried off, went and sat on the couch in his den.

Gina Roake had bought him a quilt about a year ago that he

kept folded over the back of the couch. Now he pulled it close and arranged it over himself and sat back. After a while, he pulled out his phone. Though he'd heard no signal, he checked for a new message, then brought up the day's earlier exchange: *Progress?* And his reply: *Who are you? Call me. We can talk.*

But there was no new message waiting on his screen, no reply. His fingers tapped out another text: *My mother was murdered.*

Send.

Hunt's phone company connection, Callie Lucente, had punched at his phone a few times and now was shaking her head. 'Nothing we can use here, Wyatt. Whoever it was probably just used it once, then tossed it.'

They were alone in the back office of one of the AT&T stores on Market Street – a sparse desk, wall cabinets, bookshelves groaning with inventory. Callie worked out of a different physical shop location every day to keep employees on their toes. Any day she might show up anywhere. She was a lead analyst in the Asset Protection department, and her real daily job was figuring out and thwarting the new and clever ways that AT&T employees could steal from the company. But as a long-term employee and a techno-nerd of the first order, she also knew everything there was to know about cell phones. And now she was telling Hunt that they were pretty much out of luck in terms of identifying his texter.

'What about the phone numbers themselves?' Hunt asked. 'We know the area codes, at least, both local. Doesn't that narrow it down at all?'

Lucente had a tasteful silver stud in each eyebrow and now she raised both of them, surprised at Hunt's ignorance. 'The area code's the whole city, Wyatt, if you want to call that narrowing down the search. But these area codes don't mean anything anyway. When they sold the phones, they picked some random numbers and area codes. Didn't even have to be from where they were buying them.'

'So there's no record of who bought the phone? I know when I bought my phone, I set up an account, didn't I? Signed about half my life away if I remember.'

'Yeah, you did, but you didn't buy a go-phone.' She held up Hunt's instrument. 'This is a righteous AT&T product, connected to a company account. Your texter, on the other hand, bought a number of minutes for this thing at Best Buy or someplace.'

'So wouldn't they have a record of that sale?'

'Not if it was cash, which I'm betting it was. You know the people who buy these, Wyatt, are not always your most upright citizens. These things are how drugs get run, you might have heard; it's maybe their main use. Plus, the clerks selling 'em, it's not like they get commissions. So yes, in theory they're supposed to connect a name with every phone when they sell it, but they can afford to be lazy, and P.S., nobody's checking. You know the name on your texter's phone? Take a guess.'

'Mickey Mouse.'

'Close. "Prepaid Phone."' She held up his phone and showed him the information she'd pulled up from his mystery texter. She tapped Hunt's cell phone screen a few times. 'And on the first text, "Any Customer." And this address? How much you want to bet it's the store's?'

Hunt bucked up. 'So at least then we know where it was bought.'

She shrugged. 'That might be someplace to look, *if* it's actually the store address and not just made up like Prepaid Phone. Be my guest. Check it out. But they're going to have sold a lot of these, I guarantee it. How are you going to identify any one buyer?'

'The one that bought multiple phones?'

'Except if they bought them in two or nine different stores.' She handed him back his phone.

He boosted himself off the desk and slipped the phone into its holster. 'So we just completely strike out?'

She nodded sympathetically. 'On these two texts, I think so. Those phones are long gone, Wyatt, smashed and run over and dumped. They're not going to lead you to anybody. You know the average life span of these things, don't you? Fifteen minutes, an hour. One or two uses. That's what they're for, and then they're discarded because they're evidence.'

'Callie,' Hunt said. 'You got any other ideas? I've got to find this person.'

'I can appreciate that,' she said. She was sitting on the desk, pulling at strands of her short, curly dark hair, thinking. 'The last text, they just asked if you'd made any progress, but you didn't have anything to report. True?'

Hunt nodded.

'And now you do, right?'

'Quite a bit, actually.'

'Okay, then, next time you get a text, the odds are pretty good I can pinpoint where they're calling from, especially if the call's made in the city. In fact, you and I can be talking at the same time as you're texting, so I can get you a location on your texter in real time.'

'Really?'

'Really, Wyatt. That's not even hard. I can show you in thirty seconds. Once I get the number, I can track 'em. But first they've got to call you.'

'All right,' Hunt said. 'When they do, if they do, you'll be the first to know.'

'Are you okay, Wyatt?' Tamara sat across from him, her legs crossed, the appointments book that they'd been going over for the past twenty minutes now closed on her lap. 'You seem a little . . . subdued.'

Hunt cocked his head at her over the expanse of his desk. He tried a smile, but it broke off like the brittle thing it was. 'I'm all right.'

'He's all right, he exclaims in a burst of wild enthusiasm.'

'Not fooling you much?'

'Maybe it was your losing track of three of our clients there for a minute.'

'I would have found them again someday.' Then, seriously, 'Everybody's got work for tomorrow, right?'

'It's more the opposite, Wyatt. We've got too much work and we're light on staff, especially if you're not putting in your own time.' She held up a hand. 'That's not a criticism, just a fact.'

'Noted.' Hunt templed his hands in front of his mouth. 'This text thing's got under my skin. And my mother . . .' He paused for a moment, then spread his palms out in front of him on his desk. 'I don't know what to make of all that. The fact that she was killed, my father's disappearance for all this time. And how could I not remember this? Any part of it. I mean, before today.'

'Maybe because it hurt too much?'

'But not consciously, Tam. That's the thing. You know me. I haven't been walking around in anguish over my early life. I'm a happy-go-lucky guy.'

'Hah!' Tamara let a laugh run for a moment before she corralled it. 'I mean, right. That's you, Wyatt. Easygoing, happy-go-lucky. People constantly remark on it.'

Hunt appeared to be truly surprised. 'They do? I'm not?'

'No. You are. Honestly. Fun and carefree.' She came forward. 'Wyatt, please. Know thyself at least a little bit here, would you? You don't have a laid-back bone in your body. Why do you think you always need to be in such great physical shape? Why do you have to run your own business? Why are you so good at everything you get involved in, not to even mention the winning at sports thing?'

'Those are not necessarily character flaws, Tam.'

'No. But neither are they the signs of a mellow free spirit who doesn't let anything bother him, like for example suddenly having to confront all of this early-childhood stuff you've been repressing for only about all of your life.' She lowered her voice. 'It's okay. You're allowed to have a reaction to all this. In fact, I'd be worried if this didn't hit you on some kind of a deep, real level. If it were me, I'd be lying in a ball in the corner, wondering where the next onslaught was coming from.'

'Probably not,' Hunt said. 'You'd probably be doing exactly what I'm doing, which is figuring out who's doing this and why on the one hand, and trying to solve the murder of my mother on the other. Once I got used to the idea of having a mother to begin with, that is, and her being murdered. And a father . . . who might still be alive. Can you imagine that, what that would be like?'

'I think I can, Wyatt,' she said evenly. 'Mick and I have the same situation, you might remember.'

Her words hit him like a slap, and Hunt blinked at the force of them, then met her eyes. 'Of course you do, Tam. I'm sorry. Of course you do.'

She shrugged. 'The difference is that I've never presumed that our dad was dead, Wyatt. He's probably alive out there somewhere, and he doesn't care about us, that's for sure. Whereas you've got the possibility of this guy coming back from the dead now after forty years. Leaving you this letter . . .'

'Okay, but here's the thing. Is there any way our texter could have known about that letter? Or Father Bernard, or any of this?'

Tamara chewed on her lip. 'I can't see how, unless this Father Bernard . . .'

Hunt was shaking his head no. 'No. I've got to believe what I believe, and there is no possibility that Father Bernard either knew who I was or that I'd be showing up at his rectory, today or ever. And he didn't lie about not knowing how to use cell phones, either. So he's not behind the texts, unless he just completely snowed me, which I don't think is possible.'

'But whoever it is must at least have known about your mother, right?'

'Or at least had a hunch. Maybe they weren't sure. Maybe that's why the first text asked me how my mother died. If I write back and say spinal meningitis or something, they'd just drop it. But if I'm the long-lost son of this woman who was murdered, and they knew something about that, about the murder . . .'

'Then why wouldn't they go to the police? Why come to you?'

'I don't know. Maybe they're trying to hide something, or keep what they know private. On the other hand, if I am the son, and I text back that my mother was killed, now I'm motivated to investigate, and investigating is what I do.' Hunt was sitting forward now, elbows on his desk, feeling that he was at least on some kind of track. 'And they know who I am, don't they? If they got my cell number, which means I gave it to them or called them, they know what I do.'

'Somebody who knew your parents.'

'No, not necessarily. Maybe somebody who found out something about them later. They don't want any official involvement. They don't want to get in trouble, upset their regular life. But if they know who killed my mother, or think they do, and that person is still out there . . .'

'Then they'd better be a little careful,' Tamara said.

'More than a little, Tam. A lot more than a little.'

6

THE NEXT TEXT came in at a little after six as Hunt was finishing a workout on the gym side of his warehouse – crunches and push-ups in his sweats. The two-tone text ring sounded, and Hunt, in the middle of his forty-third push-up, sprang to his feet and grabbed the cell phone. The message on it was the same as the last one: *Progress?*

Yes.

Short, sweet, and fast. He had to phone Callie Lucente and get her moving on tracking the call. Trying to recall her laughably simple instructions – suddenly in the moment much more complex – he put the phone into call mode, hit Callie's contact information, flipped back to his text screen and typed, *My mother was killed.*

Hearing Callie's phone start to ring. Once, twice. 'Come on, come on, pick up,' he said, and then her voice, no prologue.

'Are we live?'

'Just started.' Wyatt stared down at the screen.

Her killer is still alive. You need to find him and take him down.

Hunt tapped at his screen. *You know who he is?*

Yes.

'Okay,' Callie said. 'Closing in. It's in the Marina.'

Hunt, now, barely registering Callie's information. *Who is he? My father?*

No.

Why can't you tell me?

Not can't. Won't. Can't be involved.

Why not? You're involved now.

'Whoever it is,' Callie said, 'is parked at the Marina Safeway parking lot. Can you keep him on? Call some of your people and send them out there?'

'I've already got two lines going, Callie.'

'It's the same process, dude.'

And in the meanwhile, on the screen. *Not true. He would kill me, too.*

Who are you? I'll meet you.

Find him. Get him arrested.

How?

'I don't want to lose the screen,' Wyatt said.

'You won't. Just go back like when you called me. I'll hang here. Oops.'

'What?'

'The signal's gone.'

Tamara, Mickey, and their grandfather, Jim Parr, lived in a one-and-a-half-bedroom top-floor unit in an eighty-year-old building on Irving Street. The total cluttered floor space was less than seven hundred square feet, and they were rent controlled since the midnineties at six hundred thirty-five dollars. The next best thing about the place, after the price, was the roof, not usable about ninety percent of the time because of the fog and the wind but sometimes spectacular with red and purple sunset views, a glimpse of the treetops in Golden Gate Park.

The meal Mickey had been texting about the day before turned out to be barbecued alligator, which he'd picked up at the Bi-Rite out in the Mission. Dirty rice, grilled fennel, arugula, and avocado salad. The four of them were drinking variants on the tequila theme in juice glasses, sitting at the card table they'd brought up, draped with a red-and-white checkered tablecloth. The dusk was still and warm, the sun putting on a kaleidoscope of a light show out over the ocean in its last moments. The alligator steaks perfumed it all with a kind of generic 'smoking meat' smell.

'This person knows who killed your mother?' Mickey asked.

'That's the message.' Hunt sipped his drink. 'You can read it for yourself.' He passed his phone over.

Mickey scanned down the screen. 'They want you to get him arrested? How are you supposed to do that?'

'Dig up evidence, somehow. Forward it along to the police.'

'But if this person knows,' Tamara put in, 'then they've already got some kind of evidence, wouldn't you think? They'd have to.'

'Not necessarily.' Jim Parr was old but far from feeble or slow. 'They could have heard something, or a bunch of somethings, put them together, don't want to get in the guy's face. Maybe they're afraid of him.'

'Maybe they should be,' Tamara said. 'If it's a "him."'

'Yeah, well, either way,' Hunt said, 'this would be easier if we could talk with whoever's sending these things.'

'Well, you're halfway there,' Mickey said. 'You got 'em at the Marina Safeway, so they're local anyway. Keep them on the phone longer; before they trash the phone, we could posse up.'

Hunt shook his head. 'We're talking two, three minutes at the most. They'd have to be calling from my bathroom.'

'You can't keep 'em on longer?' Tamara asked.

'That *was* longer. And I'm thinking that might be the last text.'

'Why's that?' Mickey asked.

Hunt shrugged. 'Well, now I've got my marching orders, right? So the next order of business is to march.'

'Maybe not,' Jim said. 'You want to catch this person, let's assume they're watching you, or they're at least aware of your movements.'

'Not so much, Jim. They didn't know I'd made any progress until I told them. That argues they're not watching me.'

'Okay,' Tamara said, 'they're not watching you, which means you'll get more texts. Bottom line is they want to know your progress. That's what the last text was about. They're going to want to keep up, maybe even for their own protection. So the trick is we've got to be ready to roll as soon as you hook up.'

'To the Marina Safeway?' Hunt asked.

Tamara liked the idea. 'Wherever they might be. It's a small town. We might get lucky. Can you call us when you're on the phone with Callie and your texter both?'

'In theory. Callie showed me, and it's easy. A child could do it, and apparently many do. But in the heat of the moment, I could not.'

'You will next time,' Mickey said.

Wyatt shrugged. 'If there is a next time.'

'You wait,' Tamara said. 'There'll be a next time.'

When Mickey cooked, which was almost always, Tamara did the dishes. Jim got a pass on that chore out of general respect for his age and seniority and also because he tended to drink too much and pass out early.

Now it was full dark, and Mickey was off to his girlfriend Alicia's studio, where he'd probably spend the night without having to worry if they'd made too much noise and woken up Jim and Tamara.

So Jim's snoring, regular and sonorous, echoed out through the door to his bedroom and on into the kitchen, where Wyatt held a dish towel and was taking plates from Tamara after she rinsed them.

'I keep going back and forth,' he was saying. 'One minute all I want to do is find who this texter is, and the next I ask myself why that matters. The main thing is my mom's murder. I'm still trying to get my arms around the idea of somebody killing her, and it's just not fitting anywhere.' He paused and let out a sigh. 'I'm trying to fit her in, too. Just the fact of her. It's kind of hollowed me out a little.'

Tamara let the water go another minute, then shut it off and turned toward him. 'Kind of a little, huh?'

'Maybe more than that.'

'And there's something wrong with that?'

'No. I don't know.' It was a tiny kitchen and he leaned back against the counter at a right angle to the sink. 'I didn't tell you about the pictures, did I?'

'What? Of her murder?'

'No. The priest had some snapshots of my mom and dad when I was a baby, a toddler, say two or three. The thing is . . . I . . .'

'Wyatt.'

'I'm all right.' He took a breath. 'There's this one of me on the merry-go-round over in the park. I mean, I *remember* that day, Tam. I remember the smell of it, and the feel of it, and it's *right there*. I can put out my hand and touch it, it's so real. I close my eyes and it jumps back out at me, this real thing that actually happened, like some kind of ghost. And you know what the unbelievable thing is in all of this?'

'Tell me.'

'Where was it, that memory? Where did it go all these years?'

'Maybe into that place that now feels hollow because it used to be full of the stuff you wouldn't look at.'

'It wasn't *wouldn't*, Tam. I didn't even know it was there.'

'All right. Either way. Now you do.'

Hunt went on in a flat voice. 'There's another one of me on my dad's shoulders. You should see it, we're both incredibly . . . happy. I'm holding on to his hair and we are both just completely radiant. And Mom, so young, and obviously just really blissful, too, with me at the merry-go-round. I mean, you look at these pictures, there's no way these people chose to leave me.'

'Well, now you know they didn't.'

'Something happened. Something ruined their lives. Somebody.'

'And yours.'

'Well, I'm a big boy. I handled it all right.'

'Maybe so did your dad. You don't think it's him, do you? Sending the texts? He learns about you, maybe sees your name in the paper, your job, somehow gets your cell number, maybe you can find something that clears his name.'

Hunt nodded. 'But it is cleared. They never convicted him.' Picking up the dish towel, he continued, 'But you're right. That's the first question next time. If it's him, he should come in.'

'If it's him.'

'If it's him,' Wyatt repeated. 'You want to get back to these dishes?'

'Oh yeah,' she said. 'They're way more fascinating than you and what happened to your family.' She poked his arm. 'You're allowed to talk about this, Wyatt. You *should* talk about it, if not to me, then to Gina or your dad or somebody. This is real stuff, the way you feel.'

'I thought I was talking about this, to you,' Wyatt said. 'And not to change the subject, but I'm guessing I haven't mentioned about me and Gina breaking up.'

Tamara's eyes went wide. She backed away a half step and then narrowed them. 'I didn't get that memo, no. What happened?'

He shrugged. 'Nothing specific. Just general attrition. We ran out the warranty period. She's been gone a lot. I've been working a lot.'

'So how do you feel about that?'

'More feelings, huh?'

'It's cool how you pretend not to have them. Very macho.'

'Well, thanks. I work on it.' He picked up a plate and ran his dish towel around over it.

'You already dried that one,' she said.

'Not enough. Obviously not enough. Finally, at last, it's really dry to my exacting standards.' He put the plate back in the rack. 'Now. How do I feel about me and Gina?' He took a beat. 'It was the right thing to do. Hard, but right. We'd kind of stopped going in the same direction. She started talking about us maybe moving in together and I got to feeling a little pushed around about my space. That, plus the one time I wanted to get married didn't feel the same as what Gina and I had.'

'How can I not know this? You wanted to get married? When? To who?'

'It was a long time ago, Tam. Sophie. Her name was Sophie.'

'What happened?'

'She died. Cerebral hemorrhage.'

'I'm so sorry, Wyatt.'

He shrugged. 'Yeah, well, it happened. Anyway, after that . . . talk about feeling hollowed out. I wasn't going to set myself up for any more pain like that. I mean, if some kind of blazing passion came and took me over, maybe. And Gina's great, but she wasn't that.'

Tamara took the dish towel from Wyatt, turned half away and dabbed at the corners of her eyes. Her shoulders rose and fell with a deep breath and she came back around to face him. 'So let's go back to this parent thing,' she said.

'What part of it?'

She boosted herself up onto the counter. 'How about the part you don't want to talk about?'

Hunt tried a quick grin, then slumped a little, shook his head. 'I'm not trying to be evasive, Tam. I don't know what to do with it. Part of me wants to know everything I can about this, but something's also telling me I might want to just let it be, because I'm not going to like what I find. I mean, I've been doing fine without knowing all this time.'

'But now you've got a big old hollow space you need to fill.'

'Maybe I don't need to fill it.'

'Of course not. Maybe you don't.'

'I like that little eye-roll thing you do. It's fetching.' He broke a small but real smile. 'But just to refresh my memory, why do I need to fill that space up?'

'I already said you don't.'

'Yes, you did. But you weren't being sincere. I could tell.'

'I think you know the answer.'

'I don't, Tam. Or it's not clear.' His face went serious. 'This is just you and me talking now, and I'm not kidding you. Something about this scares the crap out of me. Not just the part about somebody killing my mother. There's this other thing, a personal terror or something.'

She reached her hand out and touched his face. 'You guys,' she said gently. 'You dumb guys.'

'What?'

'This isn't rocket science, Wyatt. You've lived your whole life with all of these early memories tucked away, hidden and inaccessible. Everything you've ever done or remember has been in that context. Or with that handicap, if you want to call it that. Talk about not showing your feelings. Talk about having to be tough at all times. Where nothing bothers you. That's your survival mechanism. It's who you are. So now suddenly, whammo, that wall's been breached. There's stuff you haven't let yourself look at in almost forty years. You think that could be just a little scary? You think that might be a reasonable reaction?'

'Okay, but maybe I just don't want the pain. All this stuff made me feel sick today. I mean literally sick. So if I go down this path, there's going to be more pain.'

'Well, it's the classic old problem, isn't it? You want knowledge with pain, or blissful ignorance?'

'Can I pick door number three? Knowledge with no pain?'

'Adam and Eve couldn't,' she said. 'Why would you be so special?'

'I googled Kevin Carson from work. My father's name. You know how many hits I got? One million and eighty.'

'That's roughly a lot,' Juhle said. 'How many of 'em were alive?'

'I couldn't tell.'

'See? That's the problem with Google. All that information, but where's the stuff you really need?'

'Maybe I could modify my search.' Hunt was sitting at Juhle's desk in the homicide room. Juhle sat on the desk itself. It was a few minutes after ten o'clock. 'You mind?' Hunt's hands on Juhle's keyboard.

'Knock yourself out.'

Hunt typed in *Kevin Carson Alive*.

'Aha!' he said. 'Eighty-eight thousand hits. We're getting close.'

'Yeah, but to what? Type in "Kevin Carson Dead,"' Juhle said.

A couple of seconds later, Hunt said, 'A hundred and ninety-six thousand.'

'You see the flaw here,' Juhle said. 'That leaves about seven hundred thousand Kevin Carsons who aren't either dead or alive.'

'Logic would argue against that, wouldn't it?'

'Unless if by pure chance we've just happened upon a new state of being, neither dead nor alive, which I'm going with is unlikely.'

'At least.'

'So you want to see what I got?'

'I thought you'd never ask. But in all seriousness, thank you. You probably could have waited until tomorrow.'

'I could have, but it would have been wrong. I was done with my stuff anyway and it was either read transcripts or find your case. And you're right,' he said. 'Technically it's still open.'

'So you can work on it with me?'

Juhle shook his head. 'Don't get your hopes up, Wyatt. I don't see this becoming a priority for Glitsky.' Referring to the chief of homicide, Juhle's boss, Abe Glitsky. 'It's got nothing to do with this year's numbers, so it might as well not exist. But best case, he might not call me off a few hours on my own time. If you get something real and I can sell it to him.'

'So where is it? The case file.'

Juhle's mouth turned up in amusement. 'You passed it coming in.' Sliding off the desk, he said, 'Back out here.'

Hunt followed him out through the door that demarcated the homicide detail, into the large adjoining room – lockers against one wall and four old wooden tables in the center, the last one completely filled with cardboard boxes, in some places two deep.

When Juhle stopped in front of the pile, resting his hand possessively on one of the boxes, Hunt said, 'You've got to be shitting me.'

'You asked for it.' Juhle patted the pile. 'Seven zero zero nine six three two one nine. It took me three trips to get it up here from my car. Police reports, transcripts of witness statements, lab work, notes, pictures, toxicology, tapes, motions, index of evidence, even a transcript of the first trial. Everything your little heart desires, and it's all yours.'

'Lord.'

'I hear you. It might take a few minutes to get to it all.'

'Minutes? We're talking days here, Dev, maybe weeks.'

'True, but the good news is we found it, and it looks reasonably complete. And I think I can probably get Glitsky to okay you being up here hanging out so long as you don't take anything and share whatever you find.'

His arms crossed, Hunt took in the mountain of material. 'Where would you start on all this?'

7

From the ocean beach space where Hunt parked his Kawasaki, he could see the familiar bank of nimbostratus cloud beginning to reclaim its customary place several hundred yards off the coast. Any day now, the cloud would roll in low over the water, kiss the world's surface as fog, and pushed along by westerly gusts of wind, launch its assault again upon the land, and the balmy stretch the city had enjoyed for the last couple of days would fade into memory.

But for the moment, they still had the sun, and Hunt wasn't going to let it get away from him before he could get his maximum enjoyment from it. So, in his hiking shorts and a tank top, he took his motorcycle and headed out for the beach.

Last night he'd stayed up with the cardboard boxes that made up the case file, though it seemed something of a misnomer to call the enormous mass of data a mere file. Trying to get his bearings while Juhle finished up some business at his desk before he had to go home, Hunt had had time to glance at some of the police reports and skim the transcript for the first trial. He learned a few things: that the prosecuting attorney was named Ferrill E. Moore, the public defender Steven Giles; that Hunt's mother had died of blunt-force trauma, several blows to the head from one of a collection of large river stones they used for decorations around the apartment; that his father's story was that he had come home from a long walk he'd taken with a six-pack after he and Margie had fought earlier that afternoon; that Kevin's blood-alcohol level when the police had arrived after he'd dialed 911 was .13; that Wyatt had, apparently, been home when the murder occurred.

Now Wyatt was walking across the sand below the Cliff House toward a lone fisherman. The usual angler out here on the dunes would plant his rod in a holder in the sand and sit behind it, waiting for a strike, but this man was standing on the hard sand at the edge of the freezing water, barefoot with his pants rolled up just below his knees, rod and reel in hand, working his bait methodically.

Hunt got up within ten feet on the side of him, stood still there a minute, then gave him a nod. 'Any luck?'

'Nothing yet.' The man, somewhere north of seventy, was an inch or two taller than Hunt's six-two, thin and clean-shaven with a head of thick white hair. 'Got a nice striper last week, though. Fourteen pounds.'

'Sweet,' Hunt said. 'Are you Ferrill Moore?'

The man's head jerked at Hunt. 'Guilty,' he said. 'Who are you?'

Hunt moved over a couple of steps and introduced himself. 'I called your house this morning and your wife said I'd probably find you out here.'

'And she was right, as usual. Why'd you want to talk to me?'

Moore had the metal rod holder after all, and after he'd planted it and rested his fishing pole in it, he walked with Hunt back to the softer, warmer sand, where the two men sat.

'Of course I remember it,' Moore said. 'I remember them all, but especially the ones I tried twice. You say Kevin Carson was your father?'

'I just recently found out.'

'Well, I'm sorry to have to tell you, but he was guilty as hell.'

'But a jury didn't think so. Two juries, in fact.'

Moore gave him a sidelong look. 'Two people on one jury, one on the other, and one's all you need to hang. Leaving twenty-one out of twenty-four voting for guilt. Any other jurisdiction in the country – hell, in the world – he goes down. Again, apologies. But the plain fact is that our jury panels resemble nothing so much as the bar scene in *Star Wars*.'

'No need to apologize about my father. I don't know him. I never knew him.'

'So what do you want to know? And why, for that matter?'

'Good questions. I guess I'd like to know if there were other suspects, anybody else the police were interested in. Why they centered on my father.'

'Because he was the obvious and only choice. Neighbors had heard them fighting, and not just that day, either. Then on the day of the murder, he couldn't really give any kind of reasonable account for his whereabouts. His defense attorneys never found anybody who'd testify they'd seen him on his purported walk.'

'So . . . but there must have been an element of doubt. For the three holdouts?'

'Nobody saw him actually do it, if you want to call that reasonable doubt, which I don't. He was there at home with your mother, the two of them had a fight, he went insane for a few seconds, then got himself drunk in remorse while he figured out what he'd tell the police after he called them. I mean, there was very little question. None, really. And I'm still not clear on why you care if you didn't know him.'

'Well, he was my father, after all. And he wrote me a letter saying – no, swearing – that he didn't do it, which I only saw for the first time yesterday.'

Moore's thin lips went tight. 'You deny something long enough, you come to believe it. The prisons are full of people who swear to this day that they didn't do it, maybe even really in their hearts believe that they didn't do it. And you know what? They did. So how'd this letter come about?'

'He left it with a priest to give to me if I ever showed up.'

'Bernard,' Moore said.

'You know him?'

'I knew him then. He was going to be a character witness for your father if it ever came up, which it didn't.'

'Why not?'

'Because the defense decided not to introduce character, probably because if they had, I could have rebutted with evidence of bad character. And character was probably a winner for us.' Moore picked up some sand and ran it through his fingers. 'Your father was, to put it kindly, underemployed. He'd also had a marijuana-dealing charge knocked down to misdemeanor possession of over an ounce and then several domestic violence calls. In those days, you didn't get the DVs automatically and the judge kept 'em out because they never got charged. So the defense decided to forget about character and leave well enough alone.'

'Several DVs?'

A shrug. 'Three, four, I don't remember exactly. So the jury never heard the good Father Bernard try to paint your father as a good guy – doting husband, caring father, hard-luck young man now looking at raising his young son all by himself.'

'Well, he didn't do that.' Hunt paused. 'He put me up for adoption.'

'But now you want to go back and somehow clear this guy's name? This loser who killed your mother and abandoned you while he was at it?'

'No. I want to find out who killed my mother, if in fact my father didn't.'

'But in fact,' Moore said, 'your father did.'

'I'm not ruling it out,' Hunt said. 'And I hear what you're saying about everybody who's guilty sings the same old song that they didn't do it. But what I don't really get is why a father writes to his three-year-old boy he may never see again to tell him he didn't kill his mother. I mean, why not just go away and leave it at that?'

'How about he's a congenital liar?'

'That's one possibility,' Hunt said. 'But there might be others.'

'Well, you want my advice, I wouldn't lose any sleep over them.'

'It's already too late for that,' Hunt said. 'Thanks for your time.'

'Hey,' Hunt said.

Hunt hadn't laid eyes on Gina Roake since they'd officially broken up five weeks before. On a hunch she'd be there, he swung by her Pleasant Street town house and rang her doorbell, and here she was, dressed almost identically to him – hiking shoes, hiking shorts, and an orange tank top that looked a hell of a lot sexier on her than his did on him. 'Hey, yourself,' she said. 'This is a nice surprise. How've you been?'

'Good. Busy. You?'

'Pretty much the same. What's up? I was just going out for a walk. You want to join me?' Gina looked him over, then glanced down at herself and chuckled. 'Color coordination, the key to adult happiness.'

'We got it,' he said. 'Where're we goin'?'

'Up,' she said, pulling the door closed behind her and starting off uphill.

Pleasant Street was on Nob Hill, and as they walked first past Grace Cathedral and then over toward the Fairmont and Top of the Mark hotels, Hunt filled her in on what had happened. When he finished, they were on the way down California Street.

She asked him, 'So you have no idea about this texter? Who it is.'

'None.' He hesitated. 'Actually, I haven't ruled out the possibility that it might be you.'

This stopped her in her tracks on the corner of Grant Avenue, now in the heart of Chinatown, tourists milling by, flowing around them in the still-beautiful noon hour. 'Me?' Gina's confusion evident in her face. 'Why would I do that?'

'I don't know. Probably you wouldn't. But you always said it would be good if I knew more about my birth parents, to have those missing pieces fit in. This would be a way to get me to check them out.'

'Yes, Wyatt, but . . . no. I would never do anything like that. You should know that. I'd just come out and tell you to go look into it if I thought it was that important. I'd talk to you, the way we're talking now. I'd never just text you and hide behind that.'

'Okay. I had to ask.'

'Is that it? Is that why you came by? If it is, I must tell you I'm a little hurt.'

'The last thing I want to do, Gina, is hurt you. It was a dumb question. I'm sorry. I'd withdraw it if I could. But I just feel like I have to find this person.'

'Why? It seems to me that the important thing is to find out who killed your mother. This text person is just the gateway to that.'

'But they must know something.'

'I'm sure they do. And they want you to find out what they know. So do that.'

'I'm trying. In fact, that's why I came by today. I wanted to get your gut feeling about part of this.'

'Well, that's a little better. What do you want to know?'

In the next block, he told her about his father's letter, the reference to the other people who'd offered him money and a job, Kevin Carson's decision to forget about finding his wife's killer, the protestation of innocence to his three-year-old son.

'Anyway,' he concluded, 'I talked to the prosecutor who did the trials this morning and I thought I'd get a defense attorney's perspective as well.'

'Who was the prosecutor?' Gina asked.

'Ferrill Moore. You know him?'

'Yeah, sure. Retired now, I think. A pretty good guy, but, you know, a prosecutor, so everybody's guilty.'

Hunt nodded. 'That's him all right. He said people like my father always just keep repeating that they're not guilty to anybody who'll listen. They come to believe it themselves.'

'Well, sure, that happens,' Gina admitted. 'But once in a while people keep insisting that they're innocent because they are, in fact, innocent.'

Hunt stopped now at the bottom of the hill and Gina pulled up beside him. 'So that's what I wanted to get your take on,' he said. 'Listen, Kevin Carson thinks he's probably never going to see me again. By the time he writes this letter, I'm maybe six years old, now living with the Hunts. I've got no way to reach him and vice versa, then or ever. So whether or not I believe he's guilty, what could it matter at all? And yet he sits down and goes out of his way to set the record straight that he didn't kill Margie. I mean, why would he do that? To me, it almost has the feel of a deathbed confession, in a way, except the opposite. Why would he lie? Psychologically, it just doesn't make much sense, does it?'

Gina chewed at the inside of her cheek. 'If you want my gut,' she said, 'for what it's worth, it's the same as yours. It feels to me like a blind shot into an empty and indifferent universe, just putting the truth out there.'

Hunt exhaled. 'That's what it feels like to me, too. I don't think he killed her.'

'Of course I might be wrong,' Gina said, 'and I've got that horrible defense bias where sometimes people have some goodness in them, but I agree with you. And you know what that means?'

'Tell me.'

'It means somebody else killed her.'

Hunt had gone back home and changed into slacks and a dress shirt. Now, waiting for Juhle to get back to the Hall of Justice, enduring the strained forbearance or sometimes the barely contained hostility of the rest of the homicide inspectors, he sat amid his cardboard boxes just outside the detail.

Head of homicide Abe Glitsky had looked in on him twice, wanting first to make sure that Juhle had set up this meeting and that he was in fact on his way back to the hall to supervise Hunt's endeavors, and second that Wyatt wasn't removing any of the material contained in the file.

Satisfying the lieutenant on both fronts, Hunt had spent fifteen minutes or so turning pages in the first thick binder of the trial transcript when his cell phone chirped. More wound up and attuned to the sound than he'd realized, his whole body jerked with his reaction.

Progress?

Yes. But are you my father?

No. Is that all?

After several tries practicing the few key taps he needed to keep his texter on the screen while talking to Callie Lucente, this time Wyatt picked up a touch of impatience and annoyance in her voice. 'Is this another test, Wyatt?' Callie asked him.

'No. I've got them on. They just connected.'

'Okay. I'll get looking.'

My father, Hunt tapped. *Who were the friends who gave him the job?*

Not his friends.

???

They needed to get him out of the way.

Why?

Too close. Lucky they didn't kill him.

'Got 'em,' Callie exclaimed in speaker mode. 'Just west of Santa Rosa.'

This was most of an hour north of San Francisco, and Hunt grimaced and swore at the news. He couldn't be sending any of his staff up there to try to pinpoint where this call had originated. 'Can you narrow it down any more?' he asked.

He heard an exasperated sigh over his speaker. 'Keep 'em on,' Callie said.

'I'm trying,' he whispered.

Still there? he tapped.

Yes.

Trial transcripts.

??

Reading them now. Worthwhile?

Don't know. Police must have seen.

Maybe missed something.

'Okay!' Callie said. 'They're at a place called Zazu. I can get the number!'

'Get it!'

Any suggestions? he tapped.

Can't.

Why not?

Too dangerous.

'Here it is,' Callie said. 'Take it down.'

'Got it,' Hunt said.

Callie: 'Open another line. Or, better, I can patch you.'

'Do it.'

The texter wrote: *If he finds out, he'll kill me.*

So, it's a man, then?

'Fongaloo!' Hunt heard, apparently one of Callie's swear words. 'Zazu's busy.'

One person? he tapped. *My father wrote they.*

'I'm on auto redial,' Callie said.

Yes. One person.

You? Hunt wrote. *Male or female?*

Stop asking. Find him. Good-bye.

Hunt all but collapsed into his chair.

Four minutes later, Hunt finally got through.

'Thank you for calling Zazu Restaurant and Farm. This is Brittany. How can I help you?'

'Hi, Brittany. My name is Wyatt Hunt and I'm an investigator in San Francisco working on a murder case.' Hunt neglected to say *private* before the word *investigator*. It was often a useful omission.

'Are you kidding me?'

'No. I'm completely serious. We have just identified that a person of interest in my investigation is in your restaurant and has been using a cell phone sometime in the past couple of minutes, texting.'

'Oh my God. This isn't a joke?'

'No. No joke. Don't panic, okay, please. This is just a witness, not a suspect. Nobody's in any danger. But I'd like to identify who it was. Do you remember anybody obviously texting, maybe sitting alone, over the past few minutes?'

'A man or a woman?'

'I don't know.'

'But you know they were here? How did you know that?'

'Cell phone magic, where luckily the magicians are on our side. So can you remember anybody? Or are there only a couple of people sitting alone?'

'No. Not that I was looking. I've been on the phone most of

the past half hour. And we've got . . . we're really crowded, so eight, nine, no, maybe ten people alone at their tables.'

'How about people on cell phones now?'

'Just a second.' She sighed into the line. 'Two people are using their cell phones right now, but neither of them is alone. We're talking about asking clients not to use them while they're eating, but it's kind of a losing fight, you know? And texting, you almost really can't tell at all.'

8

In the case file room outside the homicide detail, Juhle was enjoying his late bag lunch at the table as Hunt finished and closed the first binder's worth of trial transcript and reached for the next.

'You finding anything good in there?'

Hunt looked up. 'They haven't even gotten to any witnesses yet, or even what the crime's about. Half of this thing' – he motioned to the binder – 'is early motions and about the admissibility of different kinds of evidence that the judge is supposed to rule on. But I'm afraid to skip anything because you know that's exactly where it will be, whatever it is I'm looking for.'

'Do you even know what it is?'

Hunt shook his head. 'I'm hoping I recognize it when I see it.'

Juhle finished chewing, drank some Diet Coke, and swallowed. 'Might I make a suggestion about how your time could be better utilized?'

'Of course.'

'Read the police reports. There's only about a hundred pages of them. Go over in the corner there and copy them. That's where the action is. With the added bonus that if they're copies, you can take them, and with a forty-year-old case, nobody's going to care.'

By 6:30, back in his office, Hunt looked up at Tamara and said, 'I appreciate your help in all this, but you might as well go on home. I don't think it's going to be here, whatever it turns out to be.' He sat back in his office chair and stretched. 'We almost got our texter today. That's where we're more likely to catch a break.'

'Yeah, but that all depends on getting the next call, which we've got no control over, and in fact, might not even happen again.'

'It'll happen,' Hunt said.

Tamara made a face. 'Maybe not, though. Whoever it is knows that you're on the road, you've made some discoveries. If they're truly worried about actually getting killed if they're caught texting you . . .'

'They are.'

'Well, then they might think they've done enough. It's not worth the risk.'

'Let's hope that's not it,' Hunt said. He flicked at the pages in front of him. 'Because there's nothing here. Sixteen prosecution witnesses, basically none for the defense, no hint of somebody else who might have done it.' Hunt chuffed out a breath. 'I can't believe they let him off, you want to know the truth.'

'Twice. So there must have been something.'

'Not necessarily. Moore seemed to think it's the city's water supply, makes people feebleminded and fuzzy-headed.'

Tamara frowned.

'His words, not mine.' Sighing, he shook his head wearily. 'I ought to let it go for today. Get a fresh start tomorrow. You want to go get a drink? On me?'

Tamara paused, came forward in her chair, sat back again.

'She thinks,' Hunt said. Another few seconds. 'She thinks some more. Tam?'

'I'm thinking some more.'

'It's not that hard a question. To drink or not to drink.'

'That's not the question.'

'No? I thought that was the question.'

Tamara shook her head. 'Not really. The hard question is, Do you think we're spending too much time together?'

Hunt hesitated, then asked, 'For what?'

'You know. For an employer and his employee.'

'We're a little more than that, Tam. But I think we can share a preprandial cocktail without risk of scandal.'

'I'm not worried about scandal, Wyatt.'

Hunt's head canted to one side. The tone in his voice went softer. 'But you are worried about something?'

Tamara didn't answer for a few seconds. Then, 'I'm worried about you and me starting to spend a lot of time together more or less out of work or routine or habit, and then just letting something between us start to change without anybody really *deciding* to change anything. I know you know what I'm talking about. And I wouldn't be into that.'

'Into what, exactly?'

'Something casual and undefined, like you and Gina were. That's not who I am. I think you know that, but I just wanted to be completely straight about it.'

'I got it,' Hunt said. 'Message delivered. I'll keep it in the front of my mind.'

'It's too important to mess with,' she said.

'I agree. I won't mess with it. Promise.' He stood up behind his desk. 'That still leaves the field clear, though, to go and have a drink together, wouldn't you think?'

Boulevard on this Thursday night throbbed with the manic energy of glamour and effortless success that San Francisco often promised but did not so reliably deliver. This place did. Well-dressed and fashionable patrons were three deep at the bar, all the dining tables were full, a small crowd clustered near the waitress station by the front door, waiting to be seated.

As upstairs tenants, Hunt and Tamara were both known to Theodore, the bartender, and within five minutes of their arrival he had somehow magically procured two 'reserved' seats for them next to one another at the far end of the bar.

Now they clinked glasses – Tamara's Cosmo and Hunt's Oban – and she sipped and said, 'I know we're supposed to be taking a break from all this, but I've been thinking about your texter and your mother's killer, and I've got a couple of ideas if you've got the patience for them.'

'I'll stop you when I get bored,' he said.

'Well, first, this may be obvious, but I hadn't thought of it until just now. Your killer now is an old man, at least sixty and maybe way more. Though he's still dangerous. At least he scares your texter. So what does that tell us?'

'He's really ugly?' Hunt said. 'Scary ugly?'

Tamara put down her glass on the bar. 'All right, if you don't want to do this . . .'

'No, actually, I really do. I hadn't thought about his age much, either, but you've got to be right. Okay, he's old and scary, and this means . . .?'

'I think it means your texter is a woman, maybe a woman who is living with your killer, maybe married to him.'

But Hunt shook his head. 'I don't think so. She'd just leave him.'

'Not necessarily. Maybe he's told her if she tries to leave him, he'll kill her. And she knows – maybe because he's told her – that he's killed before. So what she really needs is to get him arrested for this other murder. That gets her out from under him, but she's no part of it.'

Hunt sipped Scotch. 'That's a good theory, but how do we know it's a her?'

'We don't. Not for sure. They could be gay, I suppose, both of them, and that would be the same dynamic. But either way it's got to be somebody close to the killer on a more or less day-to-day basis, don't you think? Otherwise, there'd be no danger of getting caught sending these texts.'

'That is, in fact, an excellent point.' Hunt twirled his glass on the bar. 'In my father's letter, though, he talks about the money he's being offered, and talks about "they" or "them." Which makes me think there was more than one person involved. Even though our texter said there's only one.'

'That could be,' Tamara said, 'but that doesn't change much, even if it's true. It still leaves one of the killers living with somebody who found out. Everything works the same. And another thing . . .'

'I'm listening.'

'He's rich. He was rich then, and he's richer now.'

'How do you get that?'

'Well, he, or they, offered your father money to leave. Actually gave him money to get out of town, right?'

'Apparently.'

'Okay, he had money then. So now let's just say we've got this very rich guy, which is another reason his wife doesn't want to leave him, other than she's afraid of him. If she leaves him, or even if she just pisses him off and he divorces her, she loses at least half of her money. Whereas if he's arrested . . . well, you see where I'm going.'

'I do, but the last part's mostly a guess.'

'Actually, the whole thing's a guess, except it's probably a guy and we know he's over sixty. Those are real.'

'And I buy that he might live with our texter. Or at least sees her regularly.'

With a victorious smile, Tamara pointed at Hunt. 'You just said "her."'

'I did.' He nodded. 'That must mean I pretty much buy that, too. It feels right, anyway.' He tipped up his drink. 'Which means if we can identify her, we've got him, or at least we're damn close.'

Tamara's face fell. 'Well, yes. But even with a positive ID, we still don't have a case, do we? We don't have any evidence. We don't have any facts.'

At this stark and true assessment, Hunt slumped a bit on his stool. 'It's got to be in that stuff upstairs, don't you think?'

'Either that,' Tamara replied, 'or it doesn't exist.'

Tamara called a cab and left him with a chaste kiss on the cheek. Hunt stayed at the bar. He had every intention of finishing his Scotch and then going upstairs for another run at the police reports, but then Theodore asked him if he'd like a refill, and without thinking about it too much he said, sure, why not? The second drink was again one of Theodore's trademark heavy pours, and by the time the glass was empty again, Hunt realized he wasn't going to get much technical or any other kind of work done tonight.

And since that was the case anyway, he ordered one more.

The merry-go-round was spinning too fast. Hunt was holding a cherry snow cone and it was making his hands cold, but he couldn't let go of it, or it would get all over his clothes and even maybe the other horses. But holding on to the snow cone, he couldn't control the spin or the speed of the horses, and it felt as though he was going to tip over and fall, but then suddenly, just as he was about to come off the horse, there was his mother standing next to him, holding him straight, then taking the snow cone and putting his hands down on the pommel so he could hold on.

But the horses continued to pick up speed and he saw his mother begin to fall behind where he was and then she was gone out of his sight completely and he heard a kind of a strangled cry as she must have been thrown off the merry-go-round behind him, bumping as though she were falling down stairs. And he was still turning and turning, but couldn't turn around to look and see where his mom had gone.

He called out. 'Mom! Mommy!' She didn't answer.

So now, in a panic, he decided he had to dismount and look for her, but somehow now his clothes were different, more like blankets, and he was all tangled up in them. He struggled as they seemed to take on a will of their own, holding him down so that he couldn't get free of them, so then he just leaned out from his perch on the saddle and slipped off and now he was still wrapped in the blankets, but on a rug in a hallway where the spinning had stopped, but his mother was still somewhere off behind him.

Turning around, he could see a bright light through the bottom crack of a door at the end of the dark hallway, and he wrestled himself out of his blankets and fell down because he was dizzy from the horses. But then he got on his feet again and saw the red cherry juice coming out toward him from under the door where his mom had dropped the snow cone and he reached down and touched it and the juice was thick and sticky and warm and he opened the door and his mom was lying on her side on the ground, facing him with her eyes open and he called out to her and her mouth gaped and he . . .

Hunt jerked up in his bed and yelled out, 'Mom!'

His breathing came in gulps as he brought both his hands up to his face.

He was in pitch darkness and he reached out blind and found the light next to his bed and turned it on, trying to get his bearings. He recognized his own home, of course, though he had no immediate recollection of how he had gotten there. Gina's comforter was bunched up around him. He was still dressed except for his shoes. The digital clock by his bed read 3:12 a.m. Sucking in several more deep breaths, his eyes scanned around the room until it finally began to feel familiar, unthreatening.

'Jesus,' he whispered.

Closing his eyes, steeling himself, he tried to visualize the scenes from his dream again – he'd come out of a hallway into a brighter room with windows on his left. But the main thing was his mother on the floor, unmoving, blood pooling under her head.

In his gut, he knew that part wasn't a dream. It was a memory.

Hunt untangled the comforter, shifted to the side, and swung his feet down to the floor. He needed some water, and there was a bottle of aspirin in the bathroom. He started to get to his feet, but halfway up, a realization struck him with enough force that it knocked him back down on the mattress.

He had discovered his mother's body.

9

Tamara knocked on his office door and opened it. 'I might have something.'

At his desk, Hunt sat with his head cradled in both hands, hovering over the pages of the file spread out in front of him. 'Something would be good.' Turning a page over, he lifted his head and fixed her with red-rimmed eyes. 'Hit me.'

Moving up to the desk, she placed one of his copied pages down in front of him. 'It's not exactly a smoking gun,' she said, 'but you'd have already seen it if it was.'

A faint smile. 'I'm not so sure about that. But what've you got?'

She pushed the paper toward him. 'This is that apparently unrelated child-endangerment police report from before your mother was killed.'

Hunt brought it closer. 'Sure. I've seen it,' he said. 'I've read it over twice, as I have most of the rest of this stuff. That one can't have anything to do with the murder, though. It's five months too soon.'

'Right. I know. But as requested, and because I'm a total stone pro, I looked at it again, too. And went right by it, as you did, and then came back because something nagged at me.' She reached out and turned the page over. 'Check out the last line.'

Hunt read aloud from the nearly illegible scrawl. '"Copy to CPS for follow up."' He looked back up at her. 'They always do that when they get a complaint and there are kids involved.

They go back a couple of weeks later and make sure everything's still going along fine.'

'I know.' She straightened up and crossed her arms over her chest. 'You're a smart guy. You tell me, Wyatt.'

His eyes went from her back down to the piece of paper. 'I've already been down to CPS for my file when I was checking out my adoption status. That report was in it. I saw it the first day.'

'Right. That's my point. And we know why it was with your CPS file. It was about you as a baby being left with some six- and eight-year-old babysitters. My question is, Why is it also in the case file we're looking at now? As you say, it doesn't have anything to do with the trial. It shouldn't be here.'

Hunt, suddenly beginning to feel galvanized, straightened up in his chair. 'Another witness,' he said. 'Somebody on the prosecution team found this report or somehow got wind of it and thought the guy who'd called in the complaint – ' Hunt moved the police report over to get better light. 'Ernest Talbott, their neighbor. Or the mother of the other kids, Evie Secrist, might give them something they could use at the trial.'

'Except they never called either of them at the trial, did they?'

'Evidently not.'

Tamara cocked her head. 'Your mom really left you alone with this other woman's two little kids to babysit you?'

'It doesn't literally say that. The case worker let it go with a warning. And then actually did the job and wrote it up. What it sounds like to me, seeing this, is my mother and her friend Evie were back in the apartment by the time CPS arrived. But Talbott's testimony is that they'd both been gone a couple of hours, leaving us kids alone.'

'Gee,' Tamara said gently, 'I wonder why you have abandonment issues.'

'Let's not go there right now,' Hunt said, then added, 'and for the record, Tam, I'm not being evasive. As you may have noticed, I'm working on a bit of a case.'

'You think this guy Talbott is worth trying to find? Or Evie Secrist?'

Hunt did the voice perfectly. 'Can Geico really save you fifteen percent or more on car insurance?'

'Mr Ernest Talbott?'

'Yes.'

'My name is Wyatt Hunt and I'm a private investigator.'

'Good for you. I'm a retired Muni driver. What can I do for you?'

'Well, this may seem a little out of the blue, but I'm calling about an event that happened forty years ago. You called Child Protective Services about some problem in your apartment building.'

'Sure. I remember. Couple of idiot hippie chicks left their kids together with nobody watching them. It was a miracle none of them got hurt. 'Course, later, one of them got herself killed, didn't she? The husband, as I recall.'

'Yes, sir. But maybe not the husband after all. That's what I'm looking into after all this time. The woman was my mother. I was one of those kids that got left alone. I wonder if you'd mind if I came by and picked your brain for a few minutes.'

'What's left of it. Sure. I don't see why not, though I can't promise you I remember much more than we've already talked about. You found my phone number, so do I assume you've already got my address?'

Cresting the rise on Geary just after crossing Van Ness Avenue at a few minutes after noon, Hunt ran into fog that may as well have been a solid wall – visibility dropped within a block to no more than thirty feet. He slammed on his brakes, switched on the Cooper's lights, rolled up the driver's-side window, and slowed to twenty. As he squinted ahead into the whiteness, his hangover kicked back in big-time and he drove along pressing a couple of fingers against the right side of his head just over his temple.

Normally not a heavy drinker, Hunt didn't remember the last true hangover he'd had. And while he knew why he had one now – six of Theodore's double Scotches could do that – he wasn't nearly as certain about why he'd decided to keep drinking in the first place, other than the fact that this nugget of factual information had gotten inside him and continued kicking around in his guts like an emotional pinball.

After he'd pulled over and parked, he sat in his car for the better part of ten minutes, atypically wondering what this next interview was going to tell him, and whether he really wanted to hear it.

But this, he knew, was the devil. You had to simply push through these doubts, get to the core of them, kick their ass if you needed to, and move on. Nothing wrong with that, regardless of Tamara's reservations. That's just what a man did.

Eventually, he opened the door and stepped out into the fog. The wind was whipping, too, out here, the temperature in the midforties. It cut through his sports coat and down into his bones in the one block he walked to get to Talbott's, hands in his pockets and head pounding.

Talbott lived in a back second-story apartment of a six-unit building on Fulton, across from the northern border of Golden Gate Park. Wyatt pushed the button by the metal gate in front of the entryway. A concrete path created a corridor along the side of the building, at the end of which an iron stairway rose off to the left.

Hunt climbed and suddenly faced a black man who could have been an NFL tackle in the doorway to number 4, blocking it just about completely. He wore a gray sweat suit with no logo and white tennis shoes. His hair was short and gray, with a mustache that matched it over a generous mouth.

'Mr Hunt?'

'That's me.'

'Just making sure. Come on in.'

They walked down a short hallway, on their left a small kitchen and then a living room, pin neat and spartan with its Barcalounger, a low leather couch with a modern lamp next to it, chrome and glass coffee table, and a wall-mounted flat-screen television.

Motioning Hunt to take the couch, Talbott lowered himself into the lounger. 'I've been thinking about it since you called,' he began right away, 'and I can't say I have much specific that I remember about this case you're talking about. I mean, of course, I remember that there was a trial. At first, they thought I'd be some kind of witness. It's the only murder that was ever even a small part of my life, thank God, but I was working the day your mother was killed and couldn't be any help to anybody. I mean prosecution or defense.'

'Did you know my mother well? Or my father?'

He considered a moment. 'Not really. We didn't socialize, if that's what you mean. We said hi in the hallway, that kind of thing. They had a kid – you, I suppose that would have been – and I was young and single and, of course, black.'

'Was that a problem?'

Talbott chuckled. 'Was being black a problem? Not as much as some places, I guess, but if you paid real close attention, you might have noticed.' He waved that off. 'But with your parents, no. Nothing special. They were polite, I was polite. Then that day I called Child Protection, we didn't talk much after that.'

Hunt was sitting forward on the edge of the couch, relaxed,

his elbows on his knees. 'How about the other woman, the one with the older children they left me with? Evie Secrist.'

'They weren't all that much older.'

'Six, I believe, and eight.'

'That's my point. It was insane.'

'I won't argue with you. It sure wasn't smart.'

'You were all crying and screaming bloody murder. I thought somebody was bein' killed in there. That's why I called the police in the first place.'

'You called the police? Not CPS?'

'Right. But they both came eventually. Except the women, the two mothers, they got back here first. All pissed off at me for getting the law involved. You tell me, what was I supposed to do?'

'I think you did the right thing.'

'I never beat myself up over it, I'll tell you that.'

'So this other woman, Evie. Did you know her?'

'No, not really.' Talbott's moment of pique passed and he chuckled. 'Seems like you found me easy enough. You know her name and you can't find her?'

Hunt acknowledged the point with a small grin. 'You're in the phone book, not exactly hiding out.'

'You think she's hiding out?'

'We don't know what she's doing. I don't even know if she's still alive. She's not listed if she's got a phone. And I Googled the name and got four thousand hits, none of them local. You were easier. And, by the way, thanks for all this cooperation.'

'Are you kidding me? You're making my day here. You're the first person's been in my apartment since the TV guy came to set me up with the dish. Makes me think I ought to get out more.' Talbott's trademark chuckle rumbled again.

Hunt thought he could become friends with this guy. Talbott was making him forget his hangover. 'Good idea,' he said, 'but

I'd wait till the fog lifts.' Then, 'You said you didn't really know this Secrist woman. Does that mean you knew her a little?'

'I knew her enough to know I didn't want to know her.'

'Why not?'

Talbott thought a minute. 'Best way to say it is she gave me the creeps. I only saw her with your mother maybe ten times, a dozen, but that was enough.'

'What was creepy about her?'

'Everything. Mostly, though, it was like she was spaced out. Tripping.'

'Using drugs?'

He nodded. 'Acid, probably. Or maybe had used a lot in the past and it fried her brain, which was like an epidemic back then here in the city. You could just tell this woman wasn't right. But beyond that was the whole Jesus freak thing. You nod hello to her and she lights up and says "Praise the Lord."'

'Was my mom like that?'

'I don't think so. I never saw it if she was.'

'So why'd she hang out with this Evie?'

'I don't know. They both had young kids. Maybe she needed the company.' He paused. 'You mind if I ask you something?'

'Sure. Go ahead.'

'Why do you think your father didn't kill your mother?'

'You're going to laugh, but he left me a note and that's what it said.'

'I'm not laughing.'

Hunt sighed. 'He said I had to believe him. That was the whole message. He didn't do it. Why? Do you have some reason to think he did?'

Talbott shook his head. 'I didn't think so at the time. I didn't know what happened that day, of course, but your father wasn't mean or violent. I'd hear him and your mom yelling sometimes next door, but nothing physical, no sounds like that. Just struggling and frustrated and angry. They acted mostly like they loved each other from what I could see. Day to day, I mean.'

'Except when he beat her up and the cops would come.'

'Okay, but as far as I know, your father never put a hand on your mother. Those walls were paper-thin, and when they got loud, some neighbors called the cops and said they were fighting. That's all that was. That's why he never got charged, or even arrested, you ask me.'

'That's good to hear.' Hunt swallowed. 'Do you think this woman Evie might have been violent?'

Talbott shook his head. 'You're trying to get a handle on somebody else who might have done it.'

'Yep.'

'I gotta believe the cops looked at all their friends, wouldn't you think?'

'I don't know. Maybe they saw the husband and he looked good enough for it and they stopped looking after that.'

'No. I can't believe they'd ever do that,' Talbott said with thick sarcasm. 'And you think you're going get a new trail to follow after all this time?'

'I can't say I actually think it. I'm hoping something pops up.'

'Like Evie Secrist?'

'Maybe. Maybe she's step one.'

'If you find her.'

Hunt nodded. 'If I find her.'

Hunt got back to his car, started it up, and turned on the heat. Taking out his cell phone, he went to his message queue, hit his text icon and started tapping the screen.

We need to meet. I will protect your identity. I am looking for my mother's companion, Evie Secrist. Do you know that name? Anything about her? I need to know who you are. I know some cops. We could arrange witness protection. Please respond.

Send.

Hunt sat in the warming car pondering his next move, and suddenly his cell phone went off in its regular tone. A call, not a text message!

'Hello.'

'Hello, who is this?' A woman's voice, and Hunt pumped a fist in exultation. He'd flushed her!

'This is Wyatt Hunt. Who am I talking to?'

'This is Brittany. From Zazu?'

Hunt's euphoria evaporated. 'Brittany?'

'Are you the officer who called yesterday? You were working on a murder case?'

'That's me. Wyatt Hunt. How did you get my number?'

'Well, that's the thing. Somebody left a cell phone under a table and we picked it up last night and it was here by the reception phone and about a minute ago it just beeped and came up with your message. So I hit reply and it connected us.'

Hunt gripped the phone.

'Mr Hunt?'

'I'm still here. Listen, Brittany, do you have any idea of who was sitting at the table you found the phone under?'

'Last night, you mean?'

'No, I mean lunchtime yesterday.'

'No. I'm sorry. I mean, it could have been anyone. I don't even know who found the phone last night, which waiter, I mean, or where. It was just a lost phone above the reception stand when I got in here. We get a couple a week, you know, and then usually somebody calls or texts, like you did, and we hold it for them until they can get back and pick it up.'

'Brittany, would you do me a favor? As I told you yesterday, this is a murder investigation. If somebody comes in looking for that phone today, would you try to find out who they are, or at least get a description or a license number on their car?'

Real fear thrummed in her voice. 'I thought you said the person wasn't dangerous.'

'I did. They're not. But we would very much like to talk to whoever it is. Meanwhile, I'd going to send one of my associates up there to pick up the phone, if you wouldn't mind holding it for him. His name is Mickey Dade. He could probably be there within an hour, two at the most.'

'But what if the person comes and claims the phone first?'

'That probably won't happen. If it does, then just give it to them. But get some kind of ID if you can. In fact, tell them you need to see an ID before you can give them the phone. That might work. Otherwise, if that worries you, as I said, get their license number or something. But it's extremely unlikely the person's going to come claim the phone. I think whoever it was ditched it at your restaurant on purpose.'

'This is all pretty scary, you know that? I should tell my manager what's going on. Maybe he'll want to do something.'

'That's fine. Have your manager call me if you want. But the main thing is, hold on to that cell phone if you can. If you could put it in a baggie or something, that would be helpful, too. We're going to want to check it for fingerprints and DNA and the SIM card for previous use, okay? Until Mickey Dade comes to pick it up. Mickey Dade.'

'I've got it. Is he a policeman, too?'

'No, but he'll have ID.'

'Okay, then. In an hour or two?'

'Maybe a little more, depending on traffic. But he'll be there.'

As soon as Hunt hung up with Brittany, he called Mickey, gave him his instructions, and told him to fly. Then he left a message with Devin Juhle saying that Mickey would be dropping by with one of the mystery texter's cell phones and that he should feel free to run any forensics tests he wanted to try to identify who'd used the damn thing.

Sometime in the course of these two phone calls, Hunt realized that he'd come to an unconscious decision that made as much sense as anything else. He was more than halfway out to Star of the Sea anyway, and if Evie Secrist had been a religious fanatic of some kind, and a close friend of his mother, maybe Father Bernard had known her.

'Yes, I remember her, that poor girl.' They were back in the small rectory visitor's room with its cold faded yellow vinyl furniture, its green walls, and its crucifix. The housekeeper had offered coffee and it was balm to Hunt's hungover soul, just now starting to mend. 'But it wasn't Secrist,' Bernard went on. 'They must have got that wrong in your report when they wrote it up. She called herself See Christ. Evie See Christ. I'm afraid she fell victim to too many drugs.'

'That's what one of the neighbors said, too.'

'You haven't been letting much grass grow under your feet, have you, Wyatt?'

'Well, I'm trying to see where all of this might lead, Father. I've got at least one other person now, besides you and me and my texter, who doesn't believe my father could have been a murderer. Which if we're right, of course, means somebody else was. I'd like to find him if I can.'

'And how does Evie fit in?'

'I don't know. She hung out with my mother. She was around drugs. Maybe there's something there.' He shrugged. 'It's the only thing resembling a lead that I have. Have you heard from her? Do you know what happened to her?'

'No. I only saw her with your mother once or twice. She wasn't a parishioner here, or anywhere, I don't think.'

'And yet you remember her?'

Bernard let out a small sigh. 'To tell you the truth, I don't really have much memory of her, the person. The main reason she stays with me is because she was one of the major sources of conflict between your mother and father.'

'Why was that?'

Bernard looked up at the ceiling. 'God forgive me, but from what I knew of her, she was a fundamentalist, cult-following religious nutcase. You know how many people back then moved right on through from LSD directly to Jesus, blessed be His holy name?'

'So what did my mother see in her?'

'I don't know. They must have had some kind of history, and your mother felt she couldn't desert her. Or maybe even that it was up to her to save her. In any event, your father hated Evie, hated your mother's relationship with her, worried about her influence on you. It was a big problem.' The priest put his hands together. 'That's why I remember who she was much more than I remember knowing her. Every time I went to counsel your parents, her name came up.'

'And you have no idea where she is now?'

'None. I'm sorry, but none.'

Hunt let out a breath. He reached for his coffee and drained the cup.

'You know, Wyatt,' the priest said, 'young women with young children sometimes form very strong bonds with one another. They might not otherwise be particularly well suited. They might not become friends at any other time of their lives, but while they're both in this strained and trying situation with toddlers and other young children, often without their men around during the day, they connect.'

'So was my mother . . . Did she lean toward being nuts around religion?'

'Not that I saw. Maybe she was a little more devout than most people nowadays, but she struck me back then as relatively normal.'

Hunt huffed out another frustrated breath. 'Do we have any idea of Evie's real name? Was she married? And would her real name have been her married name or her maiden name?'

Bernard spread his palms, shook his head in ignorance and defeat. 'I wish I could help you, Wyatt,' he said, 'but I don't know. I don't know where you could find any of that.'

10

At ten minutes to five on that Friday afternoon, Abe Glitsky, head of San Francisco homicide, stopped by to have a word with Devin Juhle, who sat at the table that was laden with the case file of the long-ago trials of Kevin Carson.

Glitsky's demeanor tended to be off-putting. His brow perennially jutted over anomalous, soulful blue eyes, made more startling in contrast to his dark skin. A prominent hooked nose seemed to gain definition from a slash of an ancient scar that ran through both lips. His colleagues had been known to place bets on whether he would break even the smallest semblance of a smile on any given day.

'How's all this coming along?' he asked.

Juhle, engrossed in witness testimony, started in surprise, looking up. He jerked his feet off the table and back onto the floor.

'And by coming along,' Glitsky added, 'I mean going away.'

'Pretty soon, I'd guess.' He gestured toward the pile of boxes. 'This bothering anybody?'

'Not that I've heard of, though it's wreaking havoc with the feng shui, you must admit. You discovering anything?'

'Not so much.'

'Are you looking for anything specific? That you're spending all this time on?'

Juhle hesitated for a lengthy beat before putting the folder down onto his lap. 'Somebody complaining?'

Glitsky hefted a haunch on the adjacent table. 'I just got a call from Vi Lapeer' – the chief of police – 'who in turn just heard from a retired ADA named Ferrill Moore, who tried your case twice back before the Civil War and who apparently talked to your pal Wyatt Hunt yesterday morning. And stewed about that conversation all day today and seemed to be under the impression that we've reopened the case.'

Juhle took a breath. 'Not to get technical, Abe, but the case has never been closed, so it can't be reopened. They never got a conviction. It sounds to me like Mr Moore might just be an old geezer with too much time on his hands.'

Glitsky was all agreement. 'There might be some truth in that, Devin, but he seems to have the connections and ability to make a political stink somewhere up the food chain. So much so that the chief asked me how much department time I was devoting to this thing in these times of budgetary constraints. And if any, why? And I didn't have a really good answer.'

'Two hours,' Juhle said. 'Maybe three.'

'Plus the lab time to check out this cell phone somebody brought in to you.'

Juhle held up a finger. 'Come on, Abe. Two hours max, also approved by you.'

Glitsky's lips went tight. 'I realize that. But it still leaves the chief's question: Why are you devoting any time to this at all? We've already got people, as you know, who do cold cases. And you're not them.'

'Because maybe I'll find something they missed last time.'

'Last two times. And I think the consensus is that they didn't miss anything. The jury just didn't do its job. Sound familiar?'

Juhle met Glitsky's glance. 'You want me to quit?'

'I'd like to avoid the impression that we are using the people's money to do the personal work of a private investigator.'

'It's an open case, Abe. You okayed a few hours.'

Glitsky nodded. 'I did. And you've worked a few hours, have you not?' He raised a hand. 'Look, Dev, I'm not busting your chops. The weekend is coming up. You'll find out whatever you find out from the lab about this cell phone. Mr Hunt can peruse this stuff to his heart's content. You can even be here and help him out, although do me a favor and keep a low profile. But it would be a nice surprise if all this stuff was back over in the warehouse come Monday morning. How's that sound?'

Juhle worked his mouth, then exhaled audibly. 'Sounds like an order.'

'Communication.' Glitsky nodded. 'It's a beautiful thing.' Then, after a pause, he added thoughtfully, 'Though I've got to admit I agree with you. It's pretty bizarre the chief considers this important enough to call me personally to shut you down.'

'The other thing it sounds like . . . I hate it when stuff like this happens . . . I can't even say it.'

'Sure you can.' Juhle's wife, Connie, sat next to him, both of them wrapped in a blanket on the hard cold bench, peering through the fog for the occasional glimpse of their son, Eric, who played tight end on the junior varsity for the Riordan Crusaders. The game was still in the first half and the stands wouldn't be full for another hour at least, and they had lots of room around them for privacy. 'Come on, Dev. What?'

Juhle looked in both directions, even turned his head to check behind him. 'I don't think any part of this is Glitsky, you understand. He got a perfectly reasonable call from the chief, who herself got an earful from an ex-DA, and you know how they are.'

'Okay, but again, what?'

'But you know what I just can't help thinking when there's an open case – even just a technically open case that was probably a jury malfunction – and not just some bean counter, but the honest-to-God, no-bullshit, actual chief of police calls off an investigating inspector? You know what that makes me think about?'

'You really can't say it, can you?'

'I can hardly think it.'

Connie leaned over and put her mouth right next to his ear. 'Cover-up,' she whispered. 'Maybe even conspiracy.'

Juhle's mouth turned down. 'Just hearing it said out loud makes me cringe. I don't believe in that stuff. I don't even believe it when I see it in the movies.' He hung his head, frustration weighing on him like a yoke. 'But the thing is, there's no reason on God's green earth to call me off of this thing. I don't care how tight the budget is, we're talking three or four hours of my time, an hour or two of lab time. Tops! To say anything about that impacting the budget is just absurd.'

'Or maybe it's just the usual lab personnel whining about their workload.'

'So the chief of police gets involved?'

'I know, I know.' He squeezed her hand under the blanket. 'I'm sure I'm just overreacting.'

'But you're not really sure.'

'Well, I'm sure of one thing. I'm damn sure now that I'm looking for something, that something is in those files, where before I was just helping Wyatt to feel better about his father. Now, for no apparent reason, Glitsky tells me to wrap it up in a day or two and don't give it another thought. Which of course makes me give it a whole lot of other thought.'

Connie glanced toward the field and followed the play until it ended. 'I can't even see who had the ball on that play. I can't even tell which *team* has got the ball.'

'Our ball,' Juhle said. 'But Eric isn't in.'

'How can you tell? And why don't they play when it's warm?'

'Football's a cold-weather game. It's supposed to be like this.'

Connie blew out a trail of vapor. 'Nothing is supposed to be like this.' Then, 'Okay, thinking about it. Did either of Wyatt's parents have anything to do with the police? I mean, other than his father being arrested by them. Or politics? Or money? Or anything? Didn't you say they were just two poor kids trying to get by?'

'That's who they were. But that was forty years ago. Somebody they knew back then might have turned into somebody important by now. Might have been on the way to being somebody back then.'

'And he killed Wyatt's mother? Why?'

Juhle shrugged. 'Don't know. Can't say. Jealousy? Some kind of love triangle? But I'll tell you one thing: This makes me realize how weak the case was against Wyatt's dad. Which, of course, nobody is mentioning. Maybe I should go talk to this guy Moore, the prosecutor. See if I can drag more out of him than Wyatt did.'

'Not a good idea. Maybe you should just do what Abe says and leave this alone.'

'I want to. I would have. No, honest.'

'You just don't like being told you can't do something.'

'That, too.'

'So you're going to find a way to keep at this, aren't you?'

'I'm not sure. I have to think about it some more.'

She turned to look into his face. 'You are such a liar,' she said.

Tamara's life outside of her job, her brother, and her grandfather was essentially that of a widow. For several years, starting in her early twenties, she had been involved with one of Wyatt's other employees, Craig Chiurco. Like Jill Phillips – amassing investigative hours on the way to her PI license – Craig had been an everyday feature of the job, and Tamara's social life revolved around him and their small circle of friends. The problem was that Craig wasn't 'into' settling down. He was also a serious stoner with a very dangerous hidden side to his life. Three years ago, Tamara had broken it off with him after a fight over his drug use. Shortly after that, one of Craig's terrible secrets caught up with him and he was gunned down in a San Francisco courtroom.

In response, Tamara quit coming to work and stopped eating. Her breakup with Craig had been a tentative thing; they might have gotten back together if he hadn't been killed. But more than that, she had lost confidence in her instincts, in who she was. If she went out, she went alone. She'd see a movie and come home and go to sleep. Mostly, she stayed in the tiny living room of their one-and-a-half-bedroom apartment, reading or watching television. Finally, a little over a year ago, Hunt and her brother, Mickey, had persuaded her to come back to work. Gradually, she'd put back on most of the twenty pounds she'd lost.

Now, after an exciting dinner of Kraft macaroni and cheese, with her grandfather already asleep by nine and Mickey gone to meet his girlfriend, the rest of an empty Friday night yawned before her. She had *The Girl Who Kicked the Hornet's Nest* sitting on the small end table next to her reading chair, but suddenly she'd had enough for the moment of Mr Larsson's men and their misogyny.

She briefly considered calling Wyatt and then realized that he had a telephone, too, and if he wanted to see her, he could make the call. Something seemed to be changing with them over the past few days, the banter veering over into unexpected substance. And, of course, Wyatt and Gina had broken up. But though she liked Wyatt, maybe even sometimes thought she might love him, Tamara wasn't going to let herself inadvertently slip into a romantic entanglement with her boss – she'd addressed that issue head-on with him and they seemed to be on the same page. He wasn't going to do anything unless it was unambiguous and he meant it, and that was fine with her. If and when that time came, she'd listen to her heart.

But until then, she was dying here. She had to get herself a life.

Checking her face in the mirror over the dresser in Mickey's room, she couldn't deny that she looked pretty decent, even hot – good bone structure, clear green eyes, luminous skin, shining dark hair. Still, she had enough experience in the city to know that you didn't want to get too caught up in expecting to meet an unmarried straight man. Her basic intention was simply to get out into the night, maybe do something that could be construed as fun.

At the mirror, she applied a touch of bright red lipstick, then went to the hall closet and pulled out a heavy leather coat.

The Little Shamrock was about four blocks west of Tamara's apartment, on Lincoln Way near Ninth Avenue. It had been around since late in the nineteenth century, pouring honest drinks, anchoring the neighborhood. Like most Irish bars, it had seen its share of fights, but mostly it was a friendly place, filled with working locals as opposed to the yuppies in the downtown establishments. People played serious darts in a low, dark room down a short hallway in the back; other patrons sat on low, dilapidated chairs and couches by the bathrooms. Up front, where the room narrowed to about twelve feet, the crowd filled all the space here at prime time on a Friday night.

Tamara managed to get up to the actual bar and snag a stool and was waiting for her Cosmo to arrive when she heard the guy next to her say to the guy next to him, 'So here I am in my car with this line behind me at the ATM machine and suddenly I'm totally blanking on my PIN number.'

She reached over and gently touched his forearm. 'Excuse me,' she said.

He turned and, seeing her, smiled and said, 'Just this one time, I believe I will.'

'Will what?'

'Excuse you. Which is what I believe you asked.' He reached across himself with his right hand. 'I'm Will. This is the derelict I live with, Robin, which is really a girl's name.'

'Robin Hood was a girl?' Robin asked. 'I don't think so. Robin Roberts, ace pitcher. Batman and – please note, not a girl – Robin.' He leaned over and shook Tamara's hand as well. 'Robin,' he said, 'with an *i*.'

Tamara surprised herself with a small but genuine laugh. 'With an *i*? As opposed to what?'

'Robyn with a *y*,' he said. 'Which is the girl's spelling.'

'But we digress,' Will put in. 'You said "excuse me" as though you wanted to tell me something.'

'I did. If I can just remember . . . ah, I've got it. I overheard part of your ATM story and I just couldn't let it go by. Do you know what *ATM* stands for?'

'Of course. Automated teller machine.'

'He went to college,' Robin said.

'Okay, how about *PIN*?'

'You mean as in PIN number?'

'Aha!' she exclaimed again. 'Now do you see it?' The bartender brought her drink and she took a careful sip, then came back to them. 'You said you were at the ATM machine and forgot your PIN number. The automated teller machine *machine* and the personal information number *number*. Redundancies everywhere you look.'

'Is my face red?' Will asked. 'I am so embarrassed. Is my face the color of your Cosmo? That's what it feels like.'

'Only a little,' she said, and held out her hand again. 'I'm Tamara.'

Hunt's brother Rich was the only one of his siblings who'd settled in the Bay Area. A vice president and certified financial planner with Schwab, he lived in San Anselmo in Marin County with his wife, Emma, and their four-year-old, Kaitlin. Tonight they'd finished their dinner, and then Rich had barely eked out a two-games-to-one table hockey victory in the night's tournament with Wyatt before they'd all piled into Rich's car and driven, cold or no, to the local Marble Slab ice cream parlor to slap on another thousand or so calories.

Now they all sat together at their cast-iron and marble-slab table. 'I like it when Uncle Wyatt comes over,' Kaitlin said to the group at large.

'I like it, too.' Hunt was sitting across from her and leaned over closer. 'But are you sure it's not just because we always come down here and get ice cream?'

One of her eyebrows shot up in surprise, perhaps that Hunt had caught her out with a deeper truth than she'd been aware of. 'No,' she said, recovering with a calm certainty, 'that's just a bonus.'

'Good answer, sweetie,' Emma said.

'And a great bonus it is,' her father added, 'even if it means your mother and I get to run an extra three miles tomorrow. But hey, we love running, don't we, Em?'

'It's our favorite,' she said. 'Better than ice cream.'

'Now you're teasing,' Kaitlin said. 'You don't like running more than ice cream. Not even close. And I don't like anything more than ice cream . . .' She paused for the effect and broke a beautiful smile. 'Except Uncle Wyatt coming over.'

Wyatt pointed at her with an approving nod and said to her parents, 'This is a wonderful child.'

Wyatt and Rich were in the living room with coffee, talking about the Giants, who were in second place, three games out with three weeks to play. Even though they'd won the World Series last year, the Giants had broken the hearts of both of the brothers enough times in the past that neither believed another miracle was possible.

Although Hunt was closer. 'You gotta believe,' he said. 'It's only three games. The team needs you to believe.'

Rich was shaking his head. 'I can't do it again, Wyatt. They had the right word for it, you know. Last year was torture, even if they eventually won. That wasn't just a slogan, you know. It was a profound reflection of reality. Rooting for those guys could kill you. I damn near had a heart attack in the play-offs. I mean, literally a heart attack. So now, at last, they're the world champions, at least for a few more days. I've seen it once. I don't need to see it again. I can die happy.'

'If you give up now and they lose this year, it'll be your fault.'

'Don't pull that bullshit. What I do or don't do does not affect baseball standings.'

'Okay, if you believe that. I'm just saying, why take the risk?'

Emma was no dummy. She'd graduated from the Wharton School of Business and currently did financial analysis from her home for a small private equity firm in Mill Valley. Having gotten Kaitlin down to sleep, now she was standing in the doorway, a glass of white wine in her hand, listening to these men and their sports.

Clearing her throat, she stepped into the room and said, 'He can't help it, Wyatt. You don't have to worry. He'll be there till they clinch it.'

'Or not.'

'All right. Or not.' She sat down on the other end of the couch from her husband. 'But you know, I was under the impression that Wyatt had a few things going on in his life right now that might be more important than the Giants, and I was just wondering what it would take for you guys to get around to talking about them.' She sipped her wine to silence, then smiled and said, 'Okay, I'll start. You and Gina broke up?'

'So the trail stops with this Evie See Christ?' Emma said.

'So far. The priest, Bernard, had no idea what became of her, and didn't know much to begin with.'

'What are the odds,' Rich asked, 'that she's your texter?'

'I don't know,' Wyatt said. 'Slim, I'd imagine, but I couldn't rule it out.' He paused. 'I'm going on the assumption that somewhere I must have met this person, and I don't remember ever meeting an Evie.'

Rich nodded. 'If she kept her first name, and she did change her last.'

'Right. I know. But changing a first name is different. I mean, it's what you answer to.'

'And why do you think you must have met her?' Emma asked.

'Well, she's got my personal cell number, which I don't give out except to people I know.'

'Maybe somebody else gave it to her,' Emma continued. 'One of your people. Maybe thinking she was a potential client.'

'Possibly, though that would be unusual.'

'So what's your next step?' Rich asked.

'I'm a little stuck on that,' Wyatt said. 'At first I thought the killer must have been one of the witnesses, but there's no hint of any suspicion, and I mean none, in any of the police reports. A few neighbors, some cops, but no personal connections at all to either Margie or Kevin.'

'Your birth parents,' Emma said. 'How hard is that for you?'

Hunt took a beat, his head down and then back up. 'Not the easiest thing I've had to deal with, honestly. Especially considering I kind of consciously kept it locked up all this time. Or unconsciously, since it seems to be coming out in dreams and in my guts. I mean, it's one thing to have come to grips a long time ago with the fact that you were abandoned. Okay, so move on. Don't dwell on it. And then you find out you weren't.' Hunt let out a breath. 'It just whacks you unexpectedly. I don't think I'm done with the reactions.'

'I'd be surprised if you were,' Emma said.

'But your dad. Kevin.' Rich wrestled with how to say it. 'It feels weird to call him your dad. He did abandon you, didn't he?'

'Yeah, I suppose so. Technically. But he got driven to it. It's not like he just woke up one day and didn't want a kid and left me on some doorstep. He thought he'd be in jail and I'd be better off with another family. I know that might not be a real distinction, but it feels different.'

'It does to me, too,' Emma said.

'Yeah,' Rich countered, 'but you don't leave your kid.'

'Maybe some cases you think you have to. I'm not really defending him, Rich. I'm saying the way it feels to me. Now. And it feels, somehow . . .' Hunt sat back in his chair, put a hand over his stomach. 'It seems like it's all in here, sorting itself out.'

'Well, we'll let it, then,' Emma said. 'But if you need to talk about any of this stuff anytime, we're here. You know that.'

'I do. And I thank you. But in the meanwhile, unless I can find a way to Evie See Christ, or whatever the hell her name was or is, I'm not getting any closer to finding out what really happened. And something tells me I'm going to need that if I want to get all this unconscious stuff worked out.'

'She wasn't in any of the police reports?' Rich asked. 'She wasn't one of the witnesses?'

'How odd is that?' Emma drank some of her wine. 'If she was Margie's best friend?'

'If she wasn't around,' Wyatt said, 'what was she going to be a witness to? But it's worth asking. Maybe I'll go back to Moore. He was the prosecutor. If Evie hated Kevin, or Kevin hated her, he might have known something about her, even if she didn't make it to the trial.'

'Or Kevin's defense attorney,' Rich added. 'Same thing.'

Wyatt started to get up. 'That's a good call. Worth a try, anyway. If I don't get to Evie somehow, I don't know where else to look. She knew Margie, my mother. They were friends. If I find her, she can give me some context. That's what's missing here, and without that I'm kind of lost.'

'I might have an idea,' Emma said. 'Didn't you say that Evie was in this CPS report about your mother leaving you with her children?'

Hunt nodded. 'Right. That's where I got her name.'

'Well, wouldn't there be a report on her there, too? I mean, a separate one. Her two kids were underage and at risk, weren't they? Wouldn't they have had a file on them, too?'

Wyatt, on the front inch of his chair, went dead still, staring at his sister-in-law. 'You, my dear,' he said, 'may have just won the grand prize.'

11

HUNT AND JUHLE were standing around at the case-laden table outside homicide.

'It would be great,' Hunt said, 'except Bettina's not answering her phone. I've left two messages already.'

Juhle checked his watch. 'Wyatt, it's ten o'clock on a Saturday morning. Could it be she wants to sleep in? Maybe she unplugged her phone.'

'I should drive by her house. Bang on her door.'

'Yeah, she'd love that. Maybe, really, you should give her time to wake up and call you back. Besides, it's not going to be about Evie whatever-her-name-is anyway.' He motioned toward the stack of boxes. 'I had a little discussion with Glitsky last night.'

'What about?'

By the time Juhle finished telling it, Hunt had drifted down into one of the chairs. He took his time before he spoke. 'Dev, this was a young woman who didn't know anybody. She's not going to be in the middle of some grand conspiracy.'

'It doesn't have to be grand. I'm just saying that if it really wasn't your father, if it wasn't the jury screwing up . . .'

'You're saying Glitsky and Moore are in on this?'

'No. If Glitsky knew anything, he would never have let us start with this stuff. But Moore? I don't know Moore. Was he political? What about the inspectors? Jerome Armanino and, you'll like this, Dan Rigby.'

Hunt's eyebrows went up. Rigby was a former chief of police. 'You've been thinking about this.'

Juhle nodded. 'Up about half the night with the basic idea.' He sat down across from Hunt. 'I didn't even think about the inspectors doing the case until this morning, and then I came in and saw it right away. And it gets better.'

'Hit me.'

'The officers who got called in on the child endangerment with your mystery woman Evie? When all you kids were left alone? You want to guess who they were?'

'You're saying Rigby?'

'One of 'em, yep.'

'Why would a homicide inspector go out on a call like that?'

Juhle broke a smile. 'He wasn't yet in homicide. He got promoted in the intervening five months before the murder. I looked it up this morning.'

'I knew you'd be great working for me.' Hunt thought a moment. 'So who was the other guy on the call?'

'Jim Burg, who, you'll love this, was also the R.O.' – the reporting officer – 'on the murder. He's the one who actually put the cuffs on your dad at the scene.' Juhle sat back. 'Which, unfortunately, is actually not as weird as it sounds.'

'Why not?'

'Your parents' address was on Burg's beat. So you'd expect he'd be a responder if there's a call. But you must admit, the stuff with Rigby, it's something to think about.'

Hunt wasn't so sure. But if this is what it took to maintain Juhle's enthusiasm for the investigation, he'd take it. 'So what's your theory, exactly?'

'That's the problem. Everything stops before it goes anyplace. But at least we've got some moving pieces to play with. I'd love it if there was some sign your mom hooked up with one of these guys.'

Hunt sat, his arm slung back over his chair, his brow creased, frowning. 'My mother wasn't having an affair, Dev. Bernard would have known about it.' After a minute, Hunt added, 'I think I would have had a feeling about it, too.'

'You? I thought you didn't remember anything about that time.'

Hunt hesitated. 'I've been having dreams,' he said.

Bettina Keck still hadn't called Hunt back, so Juhle drove him out to Telegraph Hill to talk with Steven Giles, who'd been Kevin Carson's public defender in both trials. As they crossed Market under glowering skies, Juhle glanced over from the driver's seat.

'So how much of this is coming back?'

'Coming back isn't how it feels. It's not like an actual memory, or most of it isn't anyway. It's mostly dreams. I wake up. I'm in a sweat and don't know where I am and I'm really, really, really scared.'

Juhle had been friends with Hunt in high school, and for close to ten years as an adult. He said, 'You don't get scared.'

'Yeah, well, that's what's so scary. I keep finding my mother's body. I'm alone and it's the middle of the afternoon . . .' Hunt blew out hard. 'And there's my dad, in a different scene. And I'm always riding around on his shoulders and I keep looking down and trying to see his face, but I can't.'

'Maybe it's not your dad.'

'No. It's definitely him. I just can't see him. And there's no other guy, somebody Mom could be having an affair with. I think I would have seen him, or felt him, or something. Some kind of ominous presence, wouldn't you think?'

'I don't know.'

'The only other guy is in a black robe. You want to talk scary as far as images go. But I figure that's just Bernard and the cassock. He ought to be around somewhere if he was counseling them, which he was. Harmless enough.'

Juhle shot Hunt a glance. 'Well,' he said, 'maybe this guy Giles can tell us something.'

Draped in a down comforter, Steven Giles greeted them in his sitting room in a wheelchair. The view, even through the clouds, seemed to encompass about half the Bay. Giles was hooked up to an oxygen supply with two clear plastic lines and nose inserts. His wife, Dorothy, after bringing everyone coffee in large orange Princeton mugs, sat down next to him on a rocking chair and rested her right hand on his left arm, from which it would never move in the course of the interview.

'We appreciate you taking the time to see us,' Juhle began.

'You two are working together?' Giles asked in a surprisingly robust voice. 'I don't remember too many instances of cooperation between cops and PIs.'

Juhle could be smooth when he needed to be. 'We have overlapping interests. The case I'm working on involves Mr Hunt's mother, who was killed back in 1970.'

A small chortle. 'Not exactly yesterday.' Then, more seriously, to Hunt, 'I'm sorry for your loss, son, even if it was so long ago. What was your mother's name?'

'Margie Carson.'

Giles's back straightened, his eyes sharpened. 'Kevin Carson.'

Dorothy piped in. 'Steve never forgets anything, you know. I should warn you.'

'That's good to hear,' Juhle said. 'We've been kind of hampered by the police reports and witness and trial transcript, which are fine as far as they go but don't shed much light on some of the background stuff.'

'Such as?' Giles asked.

'Well,' Juhle replied, 'that's kind of why we're here. To find out what, if anything, there might have been.'

Hunt spoke. 'Evie Secrist, or See Christ, for example. Does that name ring any kind of a bell?'

Giles took a moment considering. 'I can't say that it does.' He squinted into the middle distance. 'Does she appear in the record?'

'No,' Juhle said.

Hunt picked it up. 'But she was a friend, maybe a best friend, to my mother. She had a couple of young kids a little older than me, and apparently they hung out together.'

'And how,' Giles asked, 'would she have been involved in your mother's death? Theoretically.'

'We don't know,' Hunt said. 'We've heard that Kevin, my father, hated her. Maybe he would have mentioned her to you.'

'In what context?'

'Apparently, she introduced elements into my parents' marriage that caused problems between them. She was Bible-thumping religious and my father didn't like it. He thought she was trying to convert my mother and they fought about it.'

'And who is your source on that?'

'Don Bernard. He's a priest who . . .'

'Yes.' Giles cut him off. 'I remember him. He believed in your father's innocence. One of the few. So he is still alive?'

'Very much so. Out at Star of the Sea.'

'And Father Bernard thought that this Evie might have had something to do with your mother's death?'

'Only in the sense,' Hunt said, 'that she might have been one of the things they were fighting about.'

'If it was,' Giles said, 'I never heard about it. And I would have, because the weakness in the prosecution's case was motive. There just didn't seem to be any reason strong enough to make your father feel like he had to kill your mother. Of course, motive gets trumped by means and opportunity every time, and Mr

Moore knew that, so he didn't worry about it too much. But I think in the end it's why they couldn't convict. This was before DV was the flavor of the month here in the city. Nowadays, of course, the jury doesn't need much more than an accusation to vote guilty.

'So there just wasn't a reason, beyond them arguing and, you know, juries like a reason, even a bad one. It's one of those things.' Giles seemed to realize that he'd been making a little speech, and he smiled with a bit of sheepishness. 'My point is that if there was any specific motive, almost anything, I would have heard about it. Moore would have brought it up just to hang his hat on it. And he didn't.' He spread his palms. 'Anything else?'

Hunt looked the question over to Juhle. 'We were wondering,' he said, 'if you gave any thought to an alternative theory of the case. You know, if Kevin Carson didn't do it, then who did?'

Giles brought a hand up and squeezed at the sides of his mouth. 'No. I can't say that I did.'

'And why was that?' Hunt asked.

The answer clearly pained him, but Giles came right out with it. 'Because I thought that Kevin did do it. Factually. I'm sorry. Do you have any substantive reason to believe he didn't?'

'Nothing as strong as proof,' Hunt said. 'But something.'

He took his father's letter out of his jacket's inner pocket and gave it to Giles, who read it quickly – almost at a glance – and then handed it over to his wife.

'When did you get that?' Giles asked while she read.

'Bernard gave it to me a couple of days ago.'

'He'd been holding it for you all this time? Not knowing if you'd ever come for it? How did you find him?'

'I was an adopted kid and finally got interested in finding out some of the details about my birth parents. I'd lost track of who they'd been, and Bernard's name came up through Catholic Charities, so I hunted him down through the archdiocese.'

'So you've only recently found out that your mother had been murdered?'

Hunt nodded. 'A couple of days ago.'

'Oh.' Dorothy's hand went to her own mouth. 'What a terrible shock.'

'Yes, ma'am,' Hunt said, 'about equal to learning that my father had been tried for killing her. Twice. So now I'm trying, with Inspector Juhle here, to find out what really happened.'

Dorothy handed the letter back to Hunt.

'And you think *that*,' Giles said, pointing to the letter, 'casts some doubt on whether he did it?'

'I don't see why he'd have written it if it wasn't the truth.'

The implied question was not a hard one, and to the old attorney, the answer was clear. Giles shook his head, answered in an avuncular tone. 'Because if it ever came up, and maybe it never would, he wanted his son to believe that he was innocent.'

'Even if it wasn't true?'

'Especially if it wasn't true.' Giles spread his palms again. 'It costs him nothing. If it ever comes up, it makes you feel good about him. Why not? I'm sorry, but that's how I read it.'

'How about the other people he refers to?' Hunt asked. 'Offering him a job?'

Giles scratched at his cheek, perhaps embarrassed by Hunt's obvious need to believe in his father's innocence.

Juhle cleared his throat and stepped in. 'We were just wondering if there was some drama in the background that you might have been aware of that didn't make the trial. Maybe a jealousy angle, maybe Margie having an affair? Or Kevin?'

Giles slowly wagged his head from side to side. 'If there'd have been anything like that, don't you think I would have brought it up? Now, as it turned out, I didn't need it, but if I had anything like another even remotely viable suspect to point to, don't you think I would have been all over him, or even her? I assure you, I would have. There simply wasn't any such person, neither then nor, I believe, now. Certainly your father couldn't give me anybody, and we talked about that a lot.'

'Well, that was splendid,' Juhle said when they were back in his car, rolling again down Telegraph Hill. 'Broke a lot of new ground.'

Hunt's jaw muscle worked.

'And showing him your dad's letter,' Juhle went on, 'that really pried him open.'

'I believe that letter,' Hunt said. 'I don't care what Giles says, or anybody else.'

'Atta boy. That's the spirit.'

'There's no spirit involved, Dev. There was somebody else involved in this thing, and my father knew who it was.'

'Not to say there wasn't, Wyatt, but why didn't he bring it up when it could have done him some good at his trials?'

'He didn't know about it until afterward. My texter says they gave him money to get him out of town. Obviously, he thought it was just friends helping him out. And what was he going to do here in the city if he stayed? Work as a gardener or something for one of Bernard's parishioners?'

Juhle shot him a glance. 'Maybe it's him sending you these texts?'

'It's crossed my mind, of course, but I asked specifically and got told no. Besides, I just don't think it would be.'

'Any reasons?'

'Some. The first being that I think if he were that close to me, if he had my cell number, he'd come out of wherever he's been hiding and say hi. There's no reason to hide from me after all this time. It might be awkward for a few minutes, but why hide out, especially if I could help him?'

'Maybe he's afraid he'll wind up being the prime suspect again.'

'And what? I'm going to turn him in? I don't think so.'

By four o'clock, Juhle had gone home. Hunt, back at his warehouse, had called Bettina Keck and gotten her machine again. He'd copied more pages from the case file outside the homicide detail and had piled them on one of the library tables that held his computers. He'd been sitting at one of those computers for more than an hour now, reviewing the professional histories of former police chief Dan Rigby and former assistant DA Ferrill Moore – neither had interacted much with the other, had had any apparent influence on the other's career, or had been in any scandal involving women or sexual indiscretions of any kind. If they had spent any time covering up for themselves or for one another, they'd done an impressive job of it.

Now Hunt, still at his computer, was just starting to check out the background on Jerome Armanino, who had been Dan Rigby's partner investigating Hunt's father. He located the man's current address and telephone number and then, firmly believing that it was always better to ask forgiveness than permission, found himself picking up his telephone and punching numbers.

'Hello.'

'Inspector Armanino?'

'Not for a while now, but that's who I used to be. How can I help you?'

Hunt introduced himself and plunged right into his pitch.

'Excuse me,' Armanino said before he'd gotten very far. 'Forty years ago?'

'Give or take. You arrested a man named Kevin Carson for murder.'

'If you say so. What about him? Who'd he kill?'

'He never was convicted. But the victim was his wife, Margie.'

'Why wasn't he convicted?'

'The jury hung. Twice.'

Armanino tsked. 'This crazy town,' he said. 'You wonder why you bother picking up the scumbags if they're just going to let 'em go.'

'Yeah.' Hunt at his most noncommittal. 'So you don't remember the trials?'

'It's not ringing a bell, tell you the truth. Kevin Carson, right? Early seventies? I could look it up. I got a record of who I collared somewhere around here, I'm pretty sure. Filed away. What do you want to know?'

'Well, this is a long shot, but I'm trying to find a woman named Evie Secrist, who sometimes called herself Evie See Christ. She was a friend of the victim.'

'What'd she do? Was she a witness?'

'At the trial? No.'

'So what's her connection?'

Hunt decided he had to stretch things. 'She was possibly involved in drugs, maybe the sale of them, maybe to the victim. The son of both the victim and the suspect, my client, thinks this wasn't explored sufficiently at the trial. He thinks the murderer might not have been his father, might have been somebody in the drug trade, connected to this Evie Secrist. She shows up in the case file, but never made the witness list.'

'Maybe she didn't have anything to say.'

'That's probably it. But it's something my client wants to look into. I thought that you, as one of the inspectors, might have had a memory of her.'

'If I talked to her, I wrote it up,' Armanino said. 'It would be in my files someplace. You know offhand who I was partnered up with on that one?'

'Dan Rigby.'

'If Dan talked to her, he *really* wrote it up.'

'But he didn't, that's the thing. I've gone through all the paper.'

'So how'd she get in the file?'

'That was from a child-endangerment call at the Carson apartment a few months before the murder. Rigby was one of the responding officers on that call. Obviously, before he got to homicide.'

'Well, there you go.'

'What?'

'How this Evie person got in your file. Dan remembers the endangerment call and a few months later there's a homicide at the same address? No way, being the most tight-assed man who ever wore a uniform, no way Rigby doesn't pull up the earlier report and at least throw it in the file, even if he never went back and interviewed anybody.'

'Why wouldn't he, though? Interview her.'

'Well, for example, if the husband looked good enough for it right away. Which he must have. So what's the point of talking to her?'

'So you wouldn't have looked too much for other suspects?'

Suddenly the warmth of Armanino's tone dropped a few degrees. 'Not so much. Why would we? We get the one good one, we tend to stop there. If the husband did it, and he usually does, it narrows the field right on down, now, don't it?'

12

AT 11:15 ON Monday morning, Hunt flung open the door to his office and raised a fisted hand in triumph. 'Success at last.'

Tamara turned from her computer and gave him a tight smile that he might have missed, it came and went so quickly. 'He arrives,' she said. 'Success at what?'

'Evie Secrist. Or, her real name, Spencer. Lived on Arguello around the corner from the Carsons. Bettina at CPS finally got back to me this morning and I went out there and it didn't take us ten minutes. Secrist, see also See Christ and Spencer.' He hesitated, cocked his head. 'Are you all right?'

'Fine.'

'You're sure? How was your weekend?'

'Good.'

'I tried to get you Saturday night. I thought you might want to eat something, maybe go see a movie.'

'I know. I got the message, but I was out. Sorry.' She grabbed a pen and tapped it a couple of times on her desk. 'So Evie Spencer, what does that mean?'

'I don't exactly know, which I realize is kind of ridiculous since I spent most of the weekend trying to find out almost anything about her. True, under the wrong name, but still. But she's the only actual link to my parents so far. If she doesn't lead me someplace, I'm back at square one.'

'Have you gotten any more texts?'

'No, not since Friday.'

'Taking the weekend off.'

'Looks like.'

'Oh, but on that, Devin called and said he'd gotten the lab results on the cell phone Mickey picked up in Santa Rosa.'

'Yeah, I called his cell to tell him about Evie.'

'So he told you about the phone?'

'What there was. No other calls from the phone, in or out. Fingerprints, but none from any criminal database, and no DNA. And also nothing on the SIM card about who owned it. Although he thinks he knows where it was bought. All in all, not much help, but I wasn't expecting much from that quarter anyway.' Hunt crossed over and boosted himself onto Tamara's desk. 'Are you sure you're all right?'

'That's the second time you've asked me that.'

'I know. I've been counting. It seems like something's bothering you.'

'No.' Looked at him. 'Or yes.'

'If you want to talk about it . . .'

'I don't know if I do.'

'Okay, then. If you change your mind, I'm in my office. Or, in a virtuoso display of my legendary flexibility, in a pinch I could come back out here.' He pushed himself off the desk. 'Meanwhile, I'm going on a computer hunt for the ever-elusive Spencers.'

But he never got to it. Before he'd even sat down at his desk, he heard the familiar two-toned beep telling him he was getting a message.

Progress?

By now, Hunt felt like an old pro getting connected to his phone company person, Callie Lucente, while he kept the message line open to his texter. 'I've got 'em again,' he said on speakerphone.

'Keep 'em on.'

'Will do.'

Evie Spencer?

Yes. Be careful. You are close.

Dodie?

Who?

Dodie Spencer.

??? No.

I need to talk to you.

No. Evie.

'I've got it, Wyatt!' Callie's voice on speaker, excited now that the chase was on again. 'The call's from the Ferry Building! You guys are almost on top of each other.'

Hunt moved to the window from which he could see the Ferry Building down the block across the street. Although, naturally, he couldn't make out any individuals talking or texting on their cell phones.

Please. I need more information.

Tapping at his keypad, he crossed the room to his office door and pulled it open. 'Tam! We got a live texter. They're at the Ferry Building.' He stopped moving, tapped some more.

Are cops involved?

???

Tamara, on her feet, was already leading him out, on her way to the main door, holding it for him as he tried to keep the contact alive.

Rumor of cop cover-up.

???

Father Bernard?

???

Tell me something I don't know.

Can't. Can't.

'Callie,' Hunt all but screamed into his cell phone, 'I need an exact location!' Out in the hallway, he and Tamara had gotten to the door to the stairs leading down and outside. They could make it to the Ferry Building within a minute.

'Looks like just outside the Slanted Door, maybe just inside,' Callie yelled. 'Right at the water!'

Hunt looked down at the screen.

You have enough!

I need to meet you! Please!

'Bafongool,' Callie said over the speakerphone. 'It's gone. Lost it. The entire signal.'

Hunt and Tamara stopped on the second-floor landing and shared a look of disgust. 'Want to bet,' Hunt said, 'they dropped the phone into the goddamn bay?'

Beginning with the Slanted Door, the Vietnamese restaurant at the far end of the structure, Hunt and Tamara spent the next hour together and singly combing over every inch of the Ferry Building, with its dozens of food shops and hundreds of customers. It was lunchtime and the place throbbed with humanity. If Hunt's texter was someone he knew, which had been the assumption all along, then that acquaintance had disappeared by the time they had arrived.

Now, since they were there anyway, Hunt suggested they take advantage of the opportunity and have some lunch, so they were sitting at the bar at the Hog Island Oyster Company, chowing down on raw oysters just in from Tomales Bay. 'The worst thing is,' Hunt was saying, 'I get the feeling that might have been the last text.'

'Why?'

He took his phone out, brought up the screen to the beginning of the latest string of messages. 'Well, look. First it tells me I'm close, then says to follow the Evie lead, and then finally says I've got enough. I'm on the right track. Now I'm supposed to run with what I've got.'

'Which would be Evie.'

'Right, and that's pretty much all.'

'Maybe it is enough.'

'Let's hope.'

Tamara sipped from her beer. 'So who is Dodie Spencer?'

Hunt shrugged. 'She's a woman on the hiring committee from the Mission Club. Suddenly, with the name, Spencer, I just thought it might be her. Unlikely, I know. But not impossible. I thought I'd ask.'

Tamara scrolled down through the message. 'And what's this about a cover-up?'

'Devin's idea, which kept us going over the weekend. To no avail, I might add. Everybody involved in the trials, even his own attorney, thinks my father did it.'

'But Devin agrees with you? He doesn't think it, either?'

'Well, let's say he's marginally open to the idea. Which, for a cop, is a pretty big step. He got ordered to stop looking into the case, and that got his back up.'

'He got ordered to stop looking into the case? When did that happen?'

'Friday.'

'I've been out of the loop.'

'Not on purpose. It was the weekend.'

'Who wanted Devin to stop?'

'Glitsky. But the word came down through Vi Lapeer and Ferrill Moore, the prosecutor.'

Tamara whistled her reaction. 'Big guns.'

'Somewhat.' Hunt went on to explain Juhle's conspiracy theory and his conversations with Steven Giles and Jerome Armanino, both of them striking out on the Evie connection. 'I tried to get to Jim Burg, too,' he concluded. 'He was the arresting officer and also one of the cops on the original child-endangerment call on my mother and Evie, but he committed suicide in '75, so that was the last of who might have known Evie or something about my parents that wasn't in the trial record.'

'Except for Rigby, though, right?'

With a resigned nod, Hunt said, 'Well, right. But Devin swore a solemn oath to kill me if I tried to get in touch with Rigby. So that's on hold for the moment, though if I have to, I'll go rattle his cage.'

Tamara picked up her last oyster by the shell and slurped it into her mouth. 'God, how good are these?' She tipped up her beer mug and finished that, too. 'How did Jim Burg kill himself?' she asked.

'The usual for cops. His own service weapon. One shot to the temple.'

Hunt wasn't five minutes back at his desk, his computer booted up, just starting to finally get to some research on Evie Spencer, when Tamara knocked and came in, closing the door behind her. Her color was high. Her eyes shone as though she were close to tears. 'Okay,' she said by way of introduction, 'I think I want to talk about it.'

Pushing his chair back from his desk, Hunt laced his hands over his stomach. 'Good. I'm listening. You want to sit?'

Nodding in assent, she went to one of the comfortable dark brown leather chairs usually reserved for clients and plopped down in it, drew in a deep breath, and let it out in a rush. 'Well, here's the short version,' she said. 'I picked up a guy the other night and I feel like shit about it.'

Hunt went still for a long beat, then let out his own heavy load of air. Getting up, he went around his desk to one of the other chairs and sat facing her. He hesitated a moment, then said, 'You're an adult, Tam. You can do whatever you want.'

She waved it off. 'That's not what I'm talking about.'

'No,' Hunt said, 'I know that. You like him?'

Shaking her head. 'That's not the point, either.' Another sigh. 'The point is that now I feel like I've betrayed . . . I don't know, everybody, somehow. You, me, him. I just flat-out led him along and he called me yesterday and again this morning and wants to go out with me.'

'Is that bad?'

'Yes, it's bad.'

'Why?'

She came forward to the front of her chair and leaned toward him. 'Because you shouldn't be going out with other people when you're in . . . involved with somebody else.' She met his eyes and tried a feeble smile. 'But I don't know if I am.'

'You don't?'

'Not really. I don't want to be forward here. And I know you just broke up with Gina and you probably need some time. But when you told me about that, about you and her breaking up, I thought . . .' She eyed him hopelessly. 'I don't know what I thought.'

'Yes, you do. And you want to guess why Gina and I broke up?'

'You told me. You didn't want to be committed.'

'To her. Committed to her, Tam. It was kind of specific. But that wasn't really it. You know that wasn't really it, because you know what it really is, don't you?'

She nodded. 'I'm a little afraid of it.'

'I don't blame you. I'm a little nervous about it, too. We could start a club.'

'But I don't want uncommitted. Even with you, Wyatt. I'm twenty-eight. I've done uncommitted. I'm not doing it anymore.'

'I'm tired of it, too. But talk about not wanting to be forward. I'm your boss and there are rules about that. I couldn't say anything, you know, without . . . I mean, if I was wrong, you could be gone. And no matter what, bottom line, I didn't want to lose you.'

'You could never lose me.'

Hunt stared across the two feet separating them. 'You won't lose me, either. And I'm not talking as your boss.'

This, finally, brought a small murmur of laughter, a wash of relief. 'This is quite a conversation for two people who've never even kissed each other, isn't it?'

Hunt got up out of his chair. Took her hands in both of his. 'We can fix that.'

The telephone rang on Tamara's desk in the outer office.

'Timing is all,' Hunt said.

'I should get that.'

'You shouldn't even think about getting that.'

'If I don't, my boss will bust me.'

'I'll talk to him and smooth things out.'

'It won't work. He's really mean. Besides, it might be important.'

'All right, go,' he said, releasing her, 'but come back.'

She got to it on the third ring and he followed her over to the doorway and heard her say 'Hi, Devin' and then 'Sure. He's here. I'll tell him. Hold on.' She turned and gave him a 'what can you do' smile. 'He's says it's important.'

'Of course it is.'

Hunt went back to his desk and picked up the phone. 'You talked to Rigby and he confessed,' he said.

'Not even close. Evie Spencer.'

'What about her?'

'You really haven't got it yet? How long have you been in at work?'

'Since twenty minutes after I called you and left the message about her real name. Got what?'

'What happened to her. You really haven't Googled her yet?'

'I've been busy.'

'Do it. Now.'

Obediently, Hunt pulled his keyboard around, typed in the name *Evie Spencer*, and hit 'Enter.' The screen filled up with its results, one hundred and forty thousand hits, several under that name on the very first page. When he clicked on one of them, a picture of a pixie-ish, somewhat spaced-out young woman came up centered over what looked like some kind of official document. Scanning down the left side, past Last Name, First Name, a.k.a., Date of Birth (4/19/1948), Age at Death (30), Residence, Race, Religion, Gender, Hunt paused briefly on Information on Source of Death to read 'Home Foreign Affairs Committee Report' followed by an FBI document number.

Further down, another line popped: 'Occupation Outside People's Temple,' then 'Entry in Guyana, 7/23/77.'

'You got it?' Juhle's voice rasped with tension.

'I'm looking now. Is this what I think it is?'

'It couldn't be anything else, Wyatt. Evie Spencer and her kids, they all died with Jim Jones at Jonestown.'

13

For the remainder of the day, Tamara and Wyatt never got another minute alone. Ivan Orloff came back to the office and needed to be at the LexisNexis portal in an open cubicle in the main reception area, just across from Tamara's desk. Jill Phillips also returned to the office needing Hunt's input and instruction on some work she was doing with a jury-selection expert who'd been hired by one of the firms they worked for. Hunt then had to run out himself to interview a witness they'd just located who'd been a former employee of the nursing home where their client's grandfather had died. Monday also was the night Tamara's brother put on multicourse dinner parties at private homes, where she helped him serve the food and clean up after.

Hunt jerked awake calling out in the middle of the night.

A faint glow through the upper windows from the streetlight in the alley behind his home kept his bedroom from total darkness, but only just. While his panic subsided, he looked around to get his bearings. The memory of his scream still seemed to hang in the air, somewhere. Reluctant to lie back down – fearful if he did that the dream would return – he swung his feet to the floor. The digital next to his bed read 3:11.

Padding down the hall in the sweats he'd been sleeping in, he turned on every light he passed and then opened the refrigerator and poured himself a glass of milk, sitting down with it at the kitchen table. By the time he'd finished, his hands had stopped shaking, so he brought the glass over to the sink, then retraced his steps halfway down the hallway to the door that led out to the wide open side of his warehouse.

Out here, having turned on all the lights as well, it was significantly cooler than the residence side of his building. He was barefoot, but the wooden floor of the basketball court was okay, much better than the concrete. Standing at the free throw line, he pumped in shot after shot, six in a row, then a miss, then four, miss, miss, eight, miss, following up each shot with a jog to retrieve the ball, dribble back to the line, the place echoing like a high school gym.

After about twenty minutes, he bounced the ball at the line one last time and then stopped without taking the shot. His breathing had slowed, though sweat dripped down his body.

Now he crossed over to his computers, pulled up his ergonomic chair, and booted up one of them. For the tenth or twentieth time that day, he typed up Evie Spencer and followed her to Jonestown and then took off on the various links to that tragedy. But, as he'd told himself every time he'd gotten here earlier in the day, what could any of this possibly matter? Evie had died with all the others on November 18, 1978. By that time, Margie was long dead. Kevin Carson had hung his second jury and disappeared four years before. And Wyatt was already living with the Hunts, now forging his own new and better life.

Evie Spencer's connection to his birth mother, tenuous at best when they'd briefly been possibly good friends in 1970, was by 1978 so remote in time and memory as to be wholly irrelevant. And still Hunt kept returning to Google to see what he could find, to get any kind of spark.

Because he didn't kid himself. If something didn't turn up around Evie, the trail he'd been following for the past few days was at an end. His texter had told him that he had enough; he believed that the prodding texts were now going to stop.

Devin Juhle had called again before Wyatt had gone home this evening to tell him that he had finally worked up the guts to talk to ex-police chief Dan Rigby and had discovered nothing even marginally suspicious about Rigby's connection both to the original child-endangerment call or to the arrest of Kevin Carson. Rigby had not remembered Margie Carson except, barely, as a name on a file – he hadn't gotten defensive getting asked about his relationship to the case, either. If the case was still technically open, he welcomed Juhle's efforts to solve it at last and would do anything he could to help him.

There remained no other obvious unexplored area he could think of to look into. If the solution wasn't somehow tied to Evie Spencer, Hunt was stuck.

Of the dozens of ways to approach the Jonestown research, Hunt had started with one of the most obscure – the death of one of the cult's members, and not a leading member at that. This time, spreading out and riding the information wave on Google, he found himself reading over again some of the facts about Jonestown and the People's Temple.

The story of Jim Jones and the Jonestown massacre had dominated the news in November of 1978, but of course Hunt had still been a young child at that time, and he had no firsthand memory of it. He'd already familiarized himself with the colony's last days, the visit of U.S. Representative Leo Ryan and his party, which was the proximate cause of Jones's decision to order the mass murder, or 'revolutionary suicide,' of his followers. In all, 914 people died there that day, including Ryan and Jones himself. Hunt found himself staggered by that number. He'd known somewhere in his memory that there had been a significant disaster with many deaths down in Guyana featuring Jones and his cult of followers, but now for the first time, he let his mind wrap itself around the enormity of the number of dead – *nine hundred and fourteen people*! Including a U.S. congressman and some of his staff. Hundreds of children drinking cyanide-laced Kool-Aid administered by their own parents, who drank the stuff themselves, then lay down like cordwood to die in mostly neat rows. The pictures of the dead, even at a remove of more than thirty years, remained heartrending.

There were other almost unfathomable numbers. The colony had leased 3,842 acres of jungle from the Guyana government, which, like Jones himself, was Marxist. So this wasn't some small agrarian community that had gone down there to do a little farming. In fact, it was a full-size settlement of what was to be a new 'Promised Land.' The makeup of the settlers, too, was unusual: Seventy-five percent of them were black, sixty-six percent were female, and a third were under eighteen.

By the time the settlement was three years old, rumors of the systematic mistreatment of its citizens – including physical punishments, bad food, horrible working conditions, tranquilizers and armed guards, nightly hours-long diatribes by Jones over loudspeakers, censored mail and phones – were filtering back to the United States, until eventually Congressman Leo Ryan had gone down with an entourage to investigate what was really going on. And it was this visit, and the fact that some of the settlers wanted to leave the colony, that had pushed Jim Jones over the edge.

Ryan chartered two airplanes – an Otter and a smaller Cessna – to transport the would-be defectors, but Jones blocked the runway with a tractor pulling a flatbed trailer. Inside the Cessna, a false defector opened fire, and this was the signal for the men on the trailer to fire on Ryan and the others waiting to board the Otter.

Knowing what was going on at the airfield, Jones gathered his followers, had them surrounded by armed guards, and directed them to use syringes to squirt the poisoned punch into their children's mouths and then to drink the rest on their own.

Astoundingly, Hunt thought, the armed guards apparently weren't needed. Most of the murder/suicides simply complied.

Finally, Hunt was also stunned to learn that something on the order of fifty million dollars in cash and assets – perhaps much more – was part of the story, although a strict accounting of all the money seemed difficult to come by, particularly the cash part. A few people had evidently made it out of Jonestown with a lot of cash; one story had it that Jones had left his estate to the Communist Party and asked some of his followers to go to the Russian embassy and deliver it.

But now Wyatt decided to click on the background and personal history of Jim Jones himself. He didn't get beyond the very first line of the Jones biography before he came across something that straightened him up in his chair, then brought him forward again, closer to the computer screen, with a fresh jolt of adrenaline.

The fog had retreated back to the coast and the sun had not yet cleared the Oakland hills when Tamara knocked and poked her head into Hunt's office. 'You're here early.'

He cracked a weary smile. 'You, too.'

'I woke up and couldn't get back to sleep, so I thought I'd come in.'

'Same with me.'

She shifted from one foot to the other. 'Can I get you some coffee?'

He touched the mug on his desk. 'No, I'm good. You go ahead, though.'

She didn't move.

'Are you all right, Tam?'

'I'm not sure. How I am kind of depends on how you are. If you're not embarrassed or anything by our talk yesterday, or wish that nothing had happened between us.'

'None of the above.' Hunt got out of his chair and came around his desk. 'In fact, I wish more had happened.'

'I was awake half the night worrying about us.'

'What about us?'

'Only everything.'

'You don't have to worry. Nothing's changed since yesterday.'

'No,' she said. 'Really, Wyatt. Everything's changed since yesterday.'

'Would a hug help?'

Nodding, she stepped into his embrace. They stood entwined for a long moment before Hunt brushed her hair away from the side of her face and kissed her cheek. 'This has the potential to wreak havoc on intraoffice discipline around here, you know that?'

Still with her arms around him, she nodded. 'We'd better be vigilant.'

They sat together in the love seat in Hunt's inner office, still a good half hour before they expected anyone else to arrive.

'More dreams?' she asked.

'Some.' He paused, then shrugged. 'One, actually. It was pretty impressive, though. Where I'm coming up from under water to my board and there's, like, six people already squeezed on it and I'm reaching up to get a hold and somebody is trying to keep me off it and pushing me back down so I'd drown.'

'Not about your parents?'

'Not that I noticed. I didn't see them on the board.'

'Did you recognize anybody?'

'No. It was just a clustered mass of people.'

'Kicking you out, keeping you out of your home?'

'It wasn't my home. It was a surfboard.'

'Oh. Okay. Huge difference.'

Hunt turned his face to her. 'I didn't try to analyze it. I just wanted to get away from the dream.'

'So before you got with the Hunts, how many foster homes kicked you out?'

He shook his head. 'I don't know for sure. It was over a three-year period. I think I might have heard five or six.'

'And this is the first time you've dreamed about it?'

'That I know of. If you accept your interpretation.'

'Do you have a better one?'

Hunt shook his head no. 'This stuff's really messing with me, isn't it? All this birth parent stuff, the early years.'

'Getting dumped by your birth father, and then dumped again . . . what? Six times? So that every time you start to get close to somebody, they dump you? Where the world is a place where you get abandoned?'

'I don't think that. I don't want to think that.'

'It's not like you get to choose, Wyatt. That's the hand you've been dealt, in case you're wondering why commitment seems to be a recurring theme in your life.'

Wyatt had his arm around her and tightened his hand on her shoulder. 'I want it to end. I need it to end, Tam. I've got to fix it. To get to the bottom of all this stuff.'

'Closure,' she said.

'Whatever you want to call it.'

'Jim Jones was born and grew up in Indiana. His first church was there.'

'Okay,' Tamara said. 'And this is important because . . .?'

'Because my mother was from there, too. Father Bernard told me she ran away from a bad situation in Indiana when she was fifteen.'

'A bad situation?'

'Some kind of abuse.'

'Well, that narrows it down.' She gently touched his face. 'I don't mean to dampen your enthusiasm, Wyatt, but isn't Indiana kind of big? Lots of people, too, if I'm not mistaken. The odds of your mother having some connection to one other guy in the entire state of Indiana are pretty steep against, don't you think?'

'Very. But on the other hand, it's the only place left to look.'

'Maybe you'll get another text.'

'No. I don't think so. Those are done. I don't need any more texts. They don't want to risk getting caught by my mother's killer, sending any more of them. And they said I was close.'

'Well, there you go. Indiana isn't close.'

'No, not physically close. Close to the answer. As soon as I mentioned Evie Spencer, I was suddenly right on top of it. The exact quote was "Be careful, you are close." It couldn't mean anything else.'

'Okay, it means your texter thinks that Evie was involved somehow in your mother's death. But how many years after that was Jonestown?'

'Eight. And I know what you're saying. How could they possibly be related? But guess what? Jones was out in California starting in '65 and straight through until he moved to Guyana.' At her skeptical glance, he asked, 'What?'

'I was just going to say that California is even bigger than Indiana, but I believe you already know that. More people, too. Was Jones anywhere near here, in the city?'

'He moved here in '72.'

Tamara cast a glance toward the ceiling. 'A mere two years after your mother's death. Where was he before that?'

'A place called Redwood Valley, about a hundred miles north of here.'

'Practically in your mother's lap.'

'Sarcasm ill becomes you.' Wyatt sat back. 'I'm not convincing you.'

'Not really, no.'

Ferrill Moore didn't hide his displeasure when he opened his door and saw Wyatt Hunt standing there at nine o'clock on this Tuesday morning. His mouth turned down sharply as if he'd encountered a sour taste, but then he dredged a thin smile, although stopped short of extending his hand. 'Mr Hunt, again, isn't it?'

'You've got a good memory.'

'Yes, I do. Indispensable tool of the trade, I'm afraid. Better not become a lawyer if you have trouble remembering things. You're still on the Carson case, I presume.'

Hunt nodded. 'Taking a little bit of a different tack. I wonder if you could spare me some time?'

The smile got thinner. 'I thought I was doing just that.'

This was as close to outright rude as it could get and Hunt had to fight back the temptation to respond in kind. 'As of course you are,' he said, 'but I was hoping to have more of an extensive chat.' He broke what he hoped was a conciliatory smile. 'I'm not trying to undermine the work you did in that case.'

'Well, as a matter of fact, yes, you are if you're questioning your father's guilt.'

'That's not really my main interest, to tell you the truth. I'm not even so sure it was last time we talked. I just got caught up in the emotion of it. Bastard, killer, son of a bitch, whatever he might have been, Kevin Carson was my father, after all. I was still just getting used to that idea.'

Moore cocked his head. 'So what's your focus now?'

Hunt shifted his feet, thrust his hands deeper into his jacket pockets against the cold. 'I've been looking a little into the background of my mother's life and I've run across something that we think is kind of provocative. Do you remember ever running across the name Evie Spencer, also known as Secrist, or See Christ?'

For the first time in any of his interviews, Hunt thought he detected a spark of recognition in Moore's eyes. 'I don't believe she made it to the trial.'

'No, sir. She didn't. She wasn't even on a witness list. But did you talk to her?'

Moore appeared to be concentrating, his face gathered on itself. 'I don't believe that I did. As I said, I'd remember. But I recall the name. See Christ is the one that rings a bell, which is probably why I remember it. Not the other two. How does she fit in?'

'That's what I was hoping to get from you.'

The man's eyes squinted down. 'You get any statements from her in any of the police reports?'

'No. Which means none of the cops talked to her. I got that right?'

A curt nod. 'That's the theory.'

'Is that what happened in this case?'

'If it did, I don't know anything about it.'

'But her name came up in some context, didn't it? Such that you remember it here forty years later?'

From back in the house, a woman's voice carried. 'Ferrill! What are you doing in that open door so long? Close it up, for God's sake, it's damn near freezing in here!'

Moore called back over his shoulder. 'I'm talking to somebody.'

'Well, shoo 'em off or ask 'em inside, then, would you?'

But instead, the old prosecutor moved forward onto the stoop, closing the door behind him, folding his arms over his chest. With another cold smile, he said, 'Compromise.' Then, 'I don't recall the context. It's a name I know I've heard, Mr Hunt, but I can't tell you where I've heard it. Or whether it was specifically with the Carson case. Does the woman have a sheet? Do you know where she is now?'

'She's dead,' Hunt said. 'She died at Jonestown.'

'Indeed?' His head bobbed up and down. 'Well, that's interesting.'

'In what way?'

'All by itself,' Moore said. 'It's something we don't hear very much about anymore. You're thinking maybe that Margie Carson was perhaps in a cult of some kind. Not with Jim Jones yet, but something similar? And this Evie might have put her in touch with someone who could do her harm? Or maybe harmed her herself?' He flexed his arms against the cold. 'But let me assure you that there was no sign of that, of any kind of cult involvement. What happened with your mother was a marital fight that got out of hand, and that's all that happened.'

'If that's the case, then maybe you can tell me why you're so sensitive to anybody revisiting it?'

'What are you talking about?'

'I'm talking about you calling the chief of police after we talked last time and requesting that no more police resources be spent on the case.'

'I did no such thing,' Moore frankly blustered. 'I simply called to ask if new facts had come to light. It was my case and I was interested.'

Hunt decided to jack him up a little to see what would happen. 'That may be so,' he said, 'but you gave the impression that there would be unstated repercussions down the line if we didn't stop looking into it.'

'Someone misinterpreted my intentions,' Moore said. 'Besides which, no matter what you've heard, I don't have any power to make repercussions happen to anybody. I'm an old man, and P.S., I'm retired.'

Hunt met Moore's eyes and was tempted to believe him. He pulled out his wallet and a business card and held it out. 'If your memory kicks in on Evie, would you give me a call?'

Jill Phillips walked into Hunt's office, looked at him slumped back in his chair leafing through copies of police reports from the stacks of paper piled on the table over by the window, and stopped in her tracks. 'When's the last time you slept?'

'Recently.'

'Really? As recently as last night?'

'Yes.'

'And how long did you stay asleep?'

'Hours.'

'How many hours? Please be specific.'

Hunt sighed, put down his current reading. 'What can I do for you, Jill?'

'I was going to ask you about this idiot jury-selection expert I'm supposed to be helping, but I see you exhausted like this, and the mother in me comes out of hiding and gets all protective and weird.'

'And I appreciate it, but I'm fine.'

Jill didn't believe him. 'You might consider sharing some of this with us, whatever it is, and I assume it's this case involving your parents. We are your team, you know. We could be helpful. You could use our talents, meager though they might be.'

'They're not meager.' Hunt motioned toward the door. 'Who's out there?'

'Everybody. Even Mick.'

Hunt closed his eyes, nodded to himself, then boosted himself to upright. 'All right,' he said. 'Let's have a meeting.'

Now, with a semicircle of troops arranged on chairs in the

reception area, he started at the beginning and brought them along through the texted messages, Father Bernard, the discovery of his mother's murder and his father's trials, Juhle's conspiracy theory, Evie Spencer, and finally Jonestown.

The whole recounting and analysis took less than a half hour, at the end of which Ivan said, 'Now I know why I stopped being a cop. Eight years on the street and nothing remotely as interesting as this.'

'Maybe you can pass the word along to Devin,' Tamara said. 'Wyatt's been trying to poach him for a while now and he's not biting.'

'My eventual goal,' Hunt said, 'is to decimate the whole PD, get 'em working with us here, and then take over the city as a benign dictator.'

'I like it,' Mickey said.

Orloff ran with it, too. 'If you're benign, though, why would you need so many cops?'

'That's a good point,' Hunt responded. 'In case some people didn't get it. I'd need an enforcement arm. For my benignity, I mean. If that's a word.'

'It should be,' Tamara said. 'And of course you'd need a title.'

'Gotta be emperor.' Ivan had no hesitation. 'The city hasn't had an emperor since Emperor Norton.'

'Well, there you go,' Mickey put in. 'The precedent's established already. Emperor Hunt. And his merry men.'

'And women,' Tamara added.

'I don't know,' Ivan said. 'As titles go, merry men might get a little squirrelly in this town. Especially for a bunch of ex-cops.'

'True.' Hunt nodded sagely. 'But can we keep *emperor*? I've always wanted to be an emperor, now that I'm thinking about it.'

'But maybe,' Jill finally spoke, 'we can back-burner the whole emperor thing for a while and get back to what we were talking about. Which is Wyatt's real problem. How 'bout that?'

Two minutes later, any vestige of humor was gone and Hunt was wrapping up again. 'I've tried to be as complete as I can here,' he said. 'If there's anything that sticks out for any of you as a lead worth pursuing, or that I didn't take far enough, feel free to speak up. I'm about tapped out.'

Mickey had the first question. 'What about your texter? You got the one phone, which was a burner. Devin knows where it was bought, and probably your texter bought more than the one, right?'

Hunt nodded. 'Likely.'

'Well, if the clerk sold a bunch to one person, he might remember.'

'Worth checking,' Hunt said without much enthusiasm.

Jill cleared her throat and spoke up. 'I don't really get this Jonestown thing. Why does that matter?'

'I'm not sure it does. Other than Evie Spencer died there.'

'But your mom wasn't involved?'

'Right, or at least not directly, since it happened eight years after she was killed.'

'And why, again,' Ivan asked, 'is Evie important?'

'I don't know if she is,' Hunt replied. 'She was a friend of my mom's and her name shows up in the documentation for no apparent reason. But nobody who worked on the trial seems to remember her except Ferrill Moore, who thought he recognized the name but couldn't remember a context.'

'Was she married?' Ivan asked.

'I'm not sure. She had two children, so she might have been.'

'So maybe the husband's around? And his last name's Spencer?'

Hunt nodded. 'Either that or something else. If Spencer was Evie's maiden name and she kept it, who knows?'

'Maybe nobody. But I could run with that for a while, see what turns up.'

'Go for it,' Hunt said.

'That gives me an idea,' Jill said. 'What about Burg's wife?'

'Burg?' Hunt forced a tolerant smile. 'What about him? Was he even married?'

'Either way, maybe he's got family. Brothers, sisters, wife, somebody.'

'Okay. And?'

'And he's a dead guy who showed up at your parents' place at least twice and maybe more. Maybe he got called in on the domestics, too. There might be something there, is all I'm saying, if we're down to the dregs.'

'Which, apparently, we are,' Hunt said. 'Although, Jill, that's a good call.'

'If we are down to the dregs, information-wise,' Mickey put in, 'what about your birth father?'

'What about him?'

'If he's alive, I can't believe he's not findable.'

'You're welcome to try, but I looked for him first thing when I got his name, Mick. I tried every database we've got access to in the universe. There's like in the high thousands of Kevin Carsons in the country.'

'What about his social?' His social security number.

'What about it?'

'Get him on LexisNexis; you got his address, right?'

'I'm gratified that I've trained you so well, my son, but I've already done that. His last address is Fulton Street, where he lived with Margie.'

'But I thought he was going to work in Texas?'

'That's what he said, but there's no record he actually went.'

'But he went somewhere, Wyatt. You're saying there are no addresses associated with his social since he was in jail?'

'Right.'

'Do you think somebody killed him?'

Hunt nodded somberly. 'I think it's possible, but he could have just changed his social, his name, whatever. He was notorious enough and maybe didn't want to be.'

'You can just change a social?'

Hunt had to laugh. 'You want a social, Mick, go down to the street and you can get yourself a new one in about fifteen minutes. Ask every undocumented worker in the state if you don't believe me.'

Tamara raised her hand, and Wyatt pointed and couldn't suppress a smile. 'You in the back,' he said.

Her mouth turned up a fraction of an inch. 'I'm wondering about the money,' she said. 'The traveling money they paid your father to go to Texas.'

'What about it?'

'Well, it's just laying out there and it's something we haven't talked about at all.'

'I don't know what there is to say about it. We don't know anybody connected with this thing that had money back then.'

'Well, that's what I was thinking,' Tamara said. 'There was somebody.'

'Jim Jones,' Jill piped in.

Tamara nodded. 'And that brings Jonestown and Evie back into it.'

14

There were no other customers when Mickey walked into the cell phone section at the Best Buy on Geary. Behind the counter, a tattooed, megapierced salesgirl of about twenty with chopped henna hair was rearranging the display, her back to the store.

Mickey stood waiting for about a minute that seemed longer before he ventured to knock one time on the counter and say 'Excuse me.'

Nothing.

Knocking louder this time, he raised his voice as well. 'Yo, cell phone person!'

This time, with a theatrical sigh, the young woman turned. Mickey thought he discerned a slight tinkling from the hardware dangling from her ears. Her name tag read 'Den' and she cultivated a look of glazed boredom.

'Hi.' Mickey, swimming against the current, smiled and followed the protocol. He took out a business card and placed it on the counter. 'I'm Mickey Dade, working with Hunt Club private investigators. I wonder if I could ask you a few questions?'

Den shrugged and said, 'Sure.' She met his gaze for a millisecond and then looked over his shoulder with such intensity that Mickey turned around to check out what was there, only to see nothing.

Coming around back to her, he asked, 'Is this where I'd come if I wanted to buy a prepaid phone?'

For a response, with a barely concealed roll of her eyes, she turned her head, perhaps thinking she was indicating the array of cell phones all around her. 'What kind?' she asked in a tone of sublime boredom.

'You know, where there's already a certain number of prepaid minutes and . . .'

She cut him off. 'Brand,' she said. 'What brand? They're all the same.'

'Yes. I mean, I know that. I just wanted to make sure I was talking to someone who could help me.'

After another pause, she said, 'If you want a phone, that would be me.'

'Okay, well, what I'm here about . . .' Mickey pushed on. 'Someone was in here probably in the past week or so and bought a go-phone. In fact, we think he or she might have bought several go-phones at the same time. Offhand, do you remember any customers like that?'

'A lot of people buy more than one phone.'

'This might have been three or four or even more.'

'Okay. That happens. Deals, you know?'

'Did you have a special deal on them recently?'

She shook her head once, slowly. 'No. Not deals here,' she said. 'Not *sales*. Drug deals. They use the phones once, then toss 'em.'

'Ah,' Mickey said. 'Of course. But I don't think our person would have looked like your typical drug dealer.'

'Your typical drug dealer?'

'I mean, it was probably an older person.'

'Older people don't sell drugs?'

'Well, I mean, yeah, sure, but . . . anyway, do any of the people who bought more than one of these phones stand out in your mind?'

'No.'

'For a minute there I thought you were going to say yes and describe who it was in great detail.' Flashing what he knew was his winning smile, trying to break through.

'No.'

'Okay, how about this? You keep records of what you've sold, right?'

'Sure.'

'And maybe who you've sold to?'

She sighed heavily. 'In theory. But nobody signs up.'

'But you've got records of multiple sales, right? Maybe somebody used a credit card and I could tell who it was from that.'

She just looked at him. Finally. 'You'd have to talk to the manager.'

'That's a good idea. Where do I need to go for that?'

Her shoulders raised a centimeter or so. 'Follow the signs,' she said.

'Wyatt's not picking up, sis,' Mickey said.

'That's 'cause he found Mrs Burg and went out to interview her.'

'That was fast.'

'She was still getting a pension check from the city. It was like one call, and bingo. The man's a wizard sometimes. How'd your thing go?'

'About, roughly, the worst ever. We may have even gone backward.'

'How'd you do that?'

'Well, Devin was sure that the go-phone was bought at the Geary Best Buy, right? But the girl I talked to . . . no, scratch that . . . tried to talk to, she has never in her life sold anything to anybody, period. I've had better conversations with succulents, I'm not kidding. She didn't remember anybody buying multiple phones. She didn't volunteer anything. She barely answered direct questions. Why do people like that get a job working with the public?'

'That's one of the great questions, Mick, but we'll take it up another day. Did you get anything at all if Wyatt checks in?'

'All negatives. I finally went to the manager, a human being at least. We checked receipts and they had twelve multiple sales in the past twenty days, which is about our limit out in time. And all of those were cash. Evidently, you buy a go-phone, you pay cash.'

'Yeah, but aren't you supposed to register them somehow where you buy them?'

'Yes. Absolutely. And how many people do? Guess.'

'Approximately none?'

'Exactly none. It's totally unenforced. And salesclerks, they just put anything they want into the phone itself. Name of buyer: "Prepaid." Last name: "Phone." Like that. They don't make commissions on sales. They're not motivated. Basically they are clueless and uninterested, my own girl today being the most perfect example ever.'

'And no videos of purchases? Nothing like that?'

'No. They've got tapes, but they only save 'em for three days. And our texter started long before that. So basically, we're back at zero with the phones, if you want to pass the word along.'

'It's not my favorite message, Mick, but will do.'

A very handsome woman, apparently somewhere near her late sixties, stood in the doorway to the downstairs duplex unit as Hunt came up the sidewalk on Balboa from his parking spot two blocks away, checking addresses as he walked. She stepped out while he was still a few buildings down the block and called out with a prim little wave.

'Mr Hunt? This is the place.' Advancing on him, she held out her hand. 'I'm Elinor Burg and I can't express how glad I am to see you. Ever since your call I've been sitting inside getting more and more excited until I had to get up and wait here by the door so I wouldn't miss you. And you wouldn't miss me, the address.'

She closed her other hand over the one she'd been shaking and held him with both of her hands. 'And now I'm afraid I'm just going to be a babbling old fool. But do you realize that nobody in the past thirty-five years has ever wanted to talk to me about Jim's death? And even before that, right after it happened, nobody really delved into it very far. They all thought it was so obvious, what had happened, I mean. Cops kill themselves all the time. And because of, you know, the gun and all, and the way it looked, nobody seemed to think there was any doubt at all about it. Well, there I go, finally getting to talk and now I'm afraid I'm going to drive you off.'

Hunt brought his other hand up to cover hers. 'You're not going to drive me off. You can just keep talking all day.'

'Well, all right, but maybe we should move inside.' Astoundingly to Hunt, she brought all four of their hands up to her mouth and quickly kissed his.

She cut a trim figure in blue jeans, with a generous bosom under a couple of layers of beige sweaters. She'd tastefully applied a light coral lipstick and a brush of eye shadow and mascara to accent her green eyes. Her gray hair was pulled back rather severely, revealing the facial bone structure and announcing that she had been extraordinarily attractive when she'd been younger. She was attractive still.

She held the door and closed it after them, then led the way into the living room, which fronted the street. Plantation shutters over the picture windows. Light hardwood floors and a Navajo rug, brown leather couch and two matching chairs, with a coffee table, a built-in wall of books, and a fireplace. Pointing out the framed pictures on the mantel, she said, 'Obviously, that's Jim in the uniform. Then Tim, Douglas, and Carol each when they graduated from college. And these others are all my pride and joys, the grandchildren, though I won't bore you with all their names.'

'Good-looking family,' Hunt said.

'That's all Jim,' she said. 'He was great-looking, as you can see.' Her chest rose and fell in an unconscious sigh. 'I can make some coffee in about two minutes if you'd like some. I've got one of those new espresso makers and Peet's French roast, which is the best, you know.'

'I could do that,' Hunt allowed. 'Black and a little sugar?'

'Done.' She told him to have a seat, and Hunt took one of the easy chairs and, while he waited, felt his eyes drawn back to the smiling husband who still had such a presence in this home thirty-five years after his death.

And then she was back, carrying a tray of biscotti, a bowl of sugar, and their two cups. Putting the tray down on the coffee table, she sat catercorner to him in the other easy chair. 'I promised myself in there that I wasn't going to come back in here and start rambling on again. You're the one who called and said you had some questions you wanted to ask me, so maybe I should let you ask them. How's that sound?'

'To tell you the truth, you were hitting some of the notes I thought we might talk about. I gather, for example, that you're not convinced that your husband killed himself.'

She placed a lump of sugar in her coffee and stirred for a long moment. 'I don't want to mislead you,' she said. 'There was no evidence that he didn't. Maybe I was just a foolish young wife who didn't recognize the signs and didn't want to believe he'd leave me, leave us all, like that.'

'What were the signs?'

'Well, that's just it. That's what I'm saying. If there were any signs, I didn't see them. It just was completely out of the blue.

He seemed . . . no, he *was* happy. We were good, the kids were healthy, we had plenty of money . . . I mean, not rich, but okay. Plus, the job was going so well. He'd just been promoted to inspector, and the future, from my point of view anyway, looked really bright.'

Hunt sipped the coffee – it really was remarkable – to give himself time to keep the excitement out of his voice. 'I didn't realize,' he said, 'that he'd been promoted.'

She nodded. 'A couple of months before. Which of course helped a ton with the pension, not that I wouldn't have gladly given it up.' Sighing again, she added, 'But that was just another reason it didn't make any sense. I mean, it's a hurdle, you know. You go through a lot, especially if you've got three kids, to study for the sergeants exam and then you do pass and finally make inspector and suddenly it's a different career than a patrolman's.' She met his eyes. 'You don't make inspector and then kill yourself two months later, Mr Hunt. You just don't.'

'I can see that.'

'It was very hard,' she said. 'And as I say, I might have been wrong. Nobody else seemed to have any doubts.' She took another sip of her coffee, then shook her head. 'I don't know. Has this been any help to you?'

'It might be,' Hunt said. 'It might come into play at some point.'

'Into play with what?'

'The case I'm working on.'

Hunt saw this admission – that he wasn't here primarily to investigate Jim Burg's suicide – take a toll on her. 'When you said you wanted to ask me a few questions about Jim,' she said, 'I thought it would be about this. I thought somebody might be looking back into this for some reason.'

'It might become part of what I'm doing,' he said. 'But what

I'm really investigating is another case where your husband had a very small role. He was the arresting officer on a murder case about three or four years before he died.'

To Hunt's surprise, she nodded. 'That would have been the Carsons.'

'Exactly,' Hunt said. 'If you don't mind my asking, how could you have remembered that?'

She let out a small laugh. 'Well, it's not as though Jim was involved in a lot of murder cases, Mr Hunt. He was a patrolman. He never got to homicide as an inspector. I think . . . was his name Kevin? I think Kevin Carson was the only time he ever arrested a murderer. And actually, that came up a lot between us when he went to trial.'

'What did?'

'That he'd been the first one there and had to put handcuffs on him.'

Hunt turned his coffee cup around in its saucer. 'And so . . . was that significant to him for some reason?'

She nodded again. 'Oh, very.'

'And why was that?'

'Well, because he didn't think Kevin was guilty. But he was the first one to the scene after the call, you know. And if the man's standing there over the victim with blood on his hands and you're a cop, your job is to get him into custody if you can, which is what Jim did.'

'Why didn't he think Kevin was guilty?'

'I think mostly because he knew him.'

When Hunt picked his jaw up, he asked, 'You mean they were friends?'

'No, no, no. But Jim had gone on some calls to their apartment – squabbles and things like that – a couple of times, where a neighbor would complain, and Jim would have to go up and help settle things down. And he'd talk to them and see what the problems were, and he got to know them a little. I know that might sound a little strange, but that's the way Jim was. He didn't judge people. Plus,' she said, 'he kind of identified with them a little. They evidently had a little boy about Douglas's age. They were a young couple just trying to get their feet on the ground and they didn't have much going for them. That was how Jim saw it anyway. He said when he put the handcuffs on Kevin, he apologized and Kevin said it wasn't a big deal because he didn't kill his wife and he was sure they'd figure that out soon enough. Except they didn't.'

'But they didn't convict. You know that, right? And they tried twice.'

'I know. Such a waste of time and energy. Actually, Jim followed it all pretty closely.' She chuckled. 'Me, I had three kids, 'nuff said.'

Perhaps inadvertently, Elinor had opened another window a crack, and Hunt took a second, then decided to push at it. 'So if Jim didn't think Kevin was guilty, did he have another theory as to who might be?'

'I think so, yes.'

'And?'

'And you're going to hate this, but he didn't want to mention any names, even to me, before he had evidence, and he never had time to get any.'

'In four years?'

'No. It wasn't four years. He was only an inspector for two months. And he felt that there wasn't any real point in looking into anything while the trials were still going on. Besides which, being a patrolman . . . that's not something patrolmen do. They don't go looking for killers. Even inspectors not assigned to homicide don't usually go looking for killers. Poaching on homicide detail turf makes you enemies.'

Hunt could relate. He tipped up the last of his coffee, then put the cup on its saucer and sat back. 'Then the second trial ended, and by that time he was an inspector?'

'Close, anyway. Within a few months.'

'So he could look? And question people?'

She hesitated, remembering. 'He thought it would be a feather in his cap if he could come up with something everybody else had missed, but he just never got the time.' She gave Hunt a hopeful smile. 'And you being here tells me he would have found something, doesn't it?'

'I don't know that. I'm not finding much. Just more questions.'

'Yes, but they're not just questions, are they, Mr Hunt? Do you have any idea how much those questions mean to me, even if you don't have any answers for them?' She put down her cup and fixed him in her gaze. 'Those questions give me a reason to believe that Jim didn't kill himself after all. Do you realize that? He found something and confronted somebody and got killed for it. He didn't leave us. Somebody took him. And that's a whole different thing. Completely different.' A tear broke down her cheek. 'I'm sorry.'

Hunt reached out and handed her a napkin from the biscotti tray. She dabbed at her eyes.

'I'm sorry to have upset you.'

She broke a brittle laugh through her tears. 'Oh, but you haven't upset me,' she said. 'This is relief. This is happiness. This is redemption.' She glanced up at the photograph of her husband on the mantel. 'Oh, God. Jim. Why did I ever doubt you?'

Hunt left her to her emotions for a moment. Her newfound explanation for her husband's death, though perhaps far-fetched, was not after all impossible. She could accept it as a comforting truth without having to prove any part of it.

Hunt did not have that luxury – he needed some answers. 'Let me ask you this, Elinor,' he said after she'd regained some composure. 'Did Jim ever mention a woman named Evie See Christ?'

'If he did,' Hunt said, 'she has no memory of it.'

At their spot at the corner of Boulevard's bar, true dusk still an hour away, Tamara took a sip of her Cosmo. 'But we know she was Margie's friend. You and her kids played together, right?'

'I don't know if *played* is the word. We were locked in an apartment together for a few hours at least once and evidently made a lot of noise. That's all I know, except Father Bernard says they were friends and she was around a lot.'

'And Kevin didn't like her. Evie, I mean.'

'Right. But that doesn't mean she had anything at all to do with anything. All this sniffing around Evie, and what do we have to show for it?' Hunt swirled the ice cube in his Scotch with his index finger. 'She's just a trail that goes nowhere.'

'Except Jonestown.'

'Which is pretty much your definition of dead end, isn't it? And speaking of that, you want to hear a scary thought I had driving back here tonight?'

'More than anything.' She put her hand over his. 'No, really.'

'I was thinking about if my mom hadn't been killed when she was and she'd kept hanging out with Evie, there was a pretty good chance she and my dad would have broken up over money or religion or something. Which would have left Evie as her only friend in the world. So Evie hooks into the People's Temple and my mom goes along with her, taking me with them. And guess where we all wind up?'

'Wyatt.' But gently. Tamara squeezed his hand. 'Do you want to count out loud how many *ifs* are in there?'

'I know,' Hunt said.

'But all this is still knocking its way around inside you, isn't it?'

He let out a breath. 'Must be.'

After a minute, Tamara leaned over and kissed his cheek. 'You're not going to want to hear this, but maybe you ought to think about taking a little break.'

He turned to her, his face hard. 'I don't want to do that at all.'

'I believe I just predicted that response.' She leaned in and kissed his cheek again. 'But really.'

Hunt lifted his glass, put it back down. 'Somebody killed my mother, Tam,' he said evenly, 'and got away with it. How can I let that go?'

'You just walk away. Forget about your texter. You don't know what the motivation is there. The texter might even be who you're looking for, you ever think of that? Maybe lure you into some kind of trap that would wind up hurting you. Or worse.'

Hunt shook his head. 'That's not happening.'

'Well, that's the point, isn't it? We don't know what's happening. We haven't gotten anywhere.' She lowered her voice. 'Your mother died forty years ago, Wyatt. Your father's been gone thirty-six or so. Meanwhile, you've built a good business and a great life. And looking into all this the way you are has just been tearing you up.'

'This is unusual stuff, Tam. I'm trying to work it out.'

'I know it is. I know you are.' She rubbed her hand over his arm. 'And I know you said that you needed to solve this for your own peace of mind, too. But look what's happening. You're not sleeping. You're having nightmares and these Jonestown scenarios you're in the middle of. That's not peace of mind. That's torment.'

'Which ends when I get an answer.'

'No guarantee of that. And that's only if that answer doesn't hurt or kill you.'

'Now you're being melodramatic.'

'Not really, Wyatt. Not really. You are trying to find somebody who committed murder forty years ago, and maybe again with Jim Burg, and has gotten clean away with it all this time. And you think when you get close, they're just going to go gently along with you or Devin? I don't think so. I don't think I'm being melodramatic at all.'

Theodore appeared in front of them. 'You kids having a good time?'

Tamara half turned, shamefaced. 'Was I being loud?'

'Enthusiastic,' Theodore said, understanding and avuncular. He pointed to their drinks. 'Get you both another round?'

'Not for me,' Hunt said.

'I'm good, thanks.' Tamara pushed her cocktail glass away from her to the edge of the bar's gutter. Waited while Theodore moved down away from them, then came back to Hunt. 'I didn't mean to get mad.'

'You have a point,' Hunt said. 'I don't know what I'm going to do.' He, too, pushed his drink away, turned to face her. 'Do you want to go someplace quieter?'

'Except that after I get there,' she said, 'it won't be.' Then she put her arm around his neck, came forward, and kissed him on the lips. About ten seconds later, the kiss ended and she pulled away. 'But let's give it a try.'

Connie Juhle walked out of the kitchen and into the small dining room, where her family and a couple of tonight's strays from the neighborhood – the boys' pals Steve and Rasdip – were making an ungodly racket at the table. As far as she could tell, her two boys and Steve were arguing about – what else? – football, and Devin and the other two kids were taking it to the mat about whether *Glee* was better than *Friday Night Lights*, as if – in Connie's opinion – there could even be any discussion about the matter.

It was glorious, she thought, all this noise. There wasn't an ounce of shyness in Devin or in any members of the family they'd made together, and the friends her kids brought home mostly seemed to fit that mold as well. So it was always loud in their house, and she loved it.

Connie had grown up in a family of academics where if NPR got left on so that you could even hear a whisper of it in the next room, someone would be dispatched to go in and please turn the darn thing down. The first time Devin had picked her up at her parents' home, now a million years ago, he'd honked his horn from the street several times, and that had just about done it in terms of winning her heart. When she'd opened the door, he'd howled from the car in excited greeting, and she'd howled back, ignoring her parents' patent disapproval, and that – it had seemed – was that.

Now she carried a large ceramic platter onto which she'd piled his favorite meal, spaghetti in the middle with a circle of her famous homemade meatballs around it. They were already well into the garlic bread. Devin, she noticed, had popped the Two-buck Chuck and already had filled her glass – first things first.

'Anybody want some spaghetti?' she called out as she entered, to a round of applause. Placing the platter in the middle of the table, she pulled out her chair and sat down. Someone had also saved her two pieces of the garlic bread and put them on her plate. 'Salad clockwise,' she said, 'spaghetti counterclockwise.'

When everybody was served, Devin rang his glass and everybody went quiet. 'Ras, you want to do the Tofu Moment tonight?'

Due to the extraordinary diversity of San Francisco, of which the kids' friends made a representative sampling, it had early on become clear in the house that Devin's familiar old Catholic 'Bless us, O Lord' grace wasn't really going to cut it. So Connie had come up with the idea of the Tofu Moment, in which everybody held hands on both sides, and someone offered a nondenominational acknowledgement that they were all eating together and life was good. Different volunteers, guests as well as family, were pressed into service and had to say something – by now it was old hat to the regulars – and at the end, the whole table screamed 'Hey men!' Loud.

Rasdip held Connie's hand on one side and Alexa's up off the table with their fingers intertwined and Connie made a note to keep an eye on the two of them as the young man said, 'It's great to be here with all of you and thank you, Mrs Juhle, for this awesome, awesome food, which tonight is like my total favorite.'

'Wait for it,' Juhle said.

The chorus erupted. 'Hey men.'

And Juhle's cell phone rang.

'Let it go,' Connie said. 'Check it after dinner.'

But Devin already had it unholstered and was looking at the display. He held it up as if Connie could see it. 'It's Sarah,' he said. Sarah Russo was his sometime partner, and if she were calling him at home at dinnertime, it was something he wanted to know about. 'I'll just get it out in the living room.' He pointed around the table. 'If any of you kids touch one of the meatballs on my plate, I will have you arrested.'

Amid the general laughter, Connie with a sinking heart watched him walk through the archway to the other side of the house and wasn't at all surprised when, two minutes later, he reappeared but stopped to lean against the side of the arch, his face drawn.

'We've got a problem downtown,' he said. 'I've got to go.'

Juhle didn't want to tell Connie and the kids where he really had to go, which was the Tenderloin district. Though technically downtown, it was a blighted area that was home to a host of bums, prostitutes, drug dealers and users, pimps, and other assorted lowlifes. Even a policeman like Juhle driving a city car risked losing his ride if he parked it too far from where he had to go.

The sidewalk in front of Original Joe's was already marked off with yellow tape, lit up with kliegs, the concrete shining with the mist that had condensed out of the air. The coroner's van waited at the mouth of the adjacent parking lot, and Juhle pulled in there, too, for a minute, before spotting Sarah down near the end of the block with a team of other cops and paramedics, then flashing his ID to the patrolman guarding the scene by the van.

There were no news vans, though. People dying in the Tenderloin didn't really count as news. Nobody mattered here in this wasteland.

As Juhle walked down, hands stuffed into his jacket pockets, broken glass crunched under his feet. In the bright artificial light, he counted no fewer than six used syringes in the gutter, three empty liquor bottles, and a dead rat. The smell everywhere was rancid with urine and garbage, but near the Dumpster in the street halfway to Sarah, the odor was all but overwhelming. Maybe someone else had died and was stashed in there, too. And who knew? If somebody bothered to check it, they might find out. But Juhle wasn't going to do it.

Glad that he didn't have much in his stomach, he got down to the knot of his colleagues and waited at their periphery until Sarah came over to him from where the body still lay in the gutter.

'Sorry about this,' she said. She was a few years his junior, smart and no-nonsense. 'But I thought you'd want to know.'

'You sure it's him?'

'Well, not a hundred percent, tell you the truth. He got robbed, so there's no ID or cell phone, but he had some business cards in his jacket pocket, and look at how he's dressed.

He's not one of our homeless. I figured if it was him, you'd make him solid.'

With a heavy sigh, Juhle nodded. 'Let's go have a look.'

They crossed over to where the body lay on its side, facing away from them. No one had moved it yet – the crime-scene photographer was still snapping pictures. In the bright, artificial light, it didn't take a skilled investigator to see the hole in the back of the man's head, nor the stream of congealing red-turning-black stuff that had gathered in the gutter under him.

Juhle knew who it was before he'd even gotten around to see the face, but he stepped over the torso and looked down to be sure. There was no doubt. He straightened up, stepped back over the body, got next to Sarah. 'That's Ivan all right,' he said. Then added, 'It's bad enough when you don't know 'em.'

Sarah touched his shoulder. 'I hear you.' The techs were getting ready to move in and start their work in earnest, and Sarah issued a few crisp instructions, then backed away and came back over to Juhle. 'I pulled this solo, and I notice you've been doing the same lately, if you want to be part of it.'

'Absolutely. You got anything at all?'

Sarah snorted a broken laugh. 'Oh, sure. Helpful neighborhood witnesses lining up out by the restaurant.'

'Nobody saw nothing?'

She nodded. 'Actually, you won't believe this, but we have one witness who was coming out of the restaurant behind him, who called nine one one. Other than that, the usual from the locals, though we did get a second nine one one call. Beyond that, nobody heard anything, either, which is slightly harder to believe seeing as that looks like a big hole in Ivan's head. But nobody heard the shot.'

'Funky acoustics down here,' Juhle said. 'Sounds get swallowed up.'

'Yeah, that's it.'

'So who's the witness?'

Sarah checked her notepad. 'Mike Morrisey.' She motioned toward the doorway to Original Joe's, maybe forty feet away, where a saggy, middle-aged man in a business suit and topcoat, hands in his pockets, stood next to a uniformed policeman. 'He's not positive the victim was in the restaurant. He doesn't remember him specifically. But Mike was just coming out the door when he sees our guy walking toward a Yellow Cab as though he had just flagged it, and then suddenly he hears the big bang and the guy goes down and the cab flies off.'

'Wait a minute. Somebody shoots him from inside a cab?'

'That's what Morrisey saw.'

'He get the plate?'

'No.'

'No. Of course not.'

Sighing seemed to be the preferred means of communication for the evening, and Sarah added one more riff. 'So Mike's standing there, just dumbstruck, he says, and before he can move, some other guy, a street guy, Mike says, is suddenly over the body, so Mike figures he's checking on the guy and pulls out his phone and calls nine one one. But in actual fact, the street guy wasn't seeing if the victim was all right. He's taking his wallet. At least, the wallet's gone. So's the cell phone. Gone in ten seconds, and so was the guy.'

'Working with the shooter?'

'Who knows? I'd say unlikely, but what do I know?'

'A *cab*?'

'I know. I did have one thought. If he was on a job for your friend Hunt, maybe that's part of this.'

'That's worth checking.' He paused, then swore under his breath. 'I don't think he was thirty yet, you know that?' He looked back over at the body. 'I should let Wyatt know.'

'And everybody else,' Sarah said, meaning his parents, wife or girlfriend, children if any. It was going to be a very long night.

They had turned the body onto its back. The entry wound high on the forehead looking something like a small clump of black mud leaking into his hairline. Juhle glanced down.

And just as quickly looked away.

15

THE QUIETER SPOT to which Wyatt and Tamara retired turned out to be the intimate Venticello, perhaps the city's most romantic restaurant. They had no reservation, but early on a Tuesday night, luck had been with them. They had apparently reached a mutual and tacit agreement not to talk about Wyatt's continued pursuit of his mother's killer. Instead, they'd both had the petrale and split a bottle of Gavi di Gavi, talking about their history together, the mostly ill-timed ebb and flow of their various eras of attraction to each other – Tamara's crush on Hunt when she was eighteen, and again at twenty-two; Hunt's infatuation with her when she was first working for him but going out with another of his employees; then the current phase that had led to him breaking things off with Gina Roake.

Now the warehouse's large garage door slammed down behind them. Hunt turned off the engine, which also extinguished the Cooper's lights, and they sat in the muted darkness with their fingers intertwined.

'Well?' Tamara said. 'Here we are.'

'Taken us long enough, hasn't it?'

'Just long enough,' she said. 'Just the right amount of time.' She squeezed his hand.

'Should we go in?' he asked.

'I was thinking we might.'

They both opened their doors. 'Shoot some hoops first?' he asked.

She came around the car and reached for his hand again. 'Maybe later.'

As they got to the door that led to the residential part of his building, Hunt's cell phone rang. 'This is not happening,' he said, taking the phone from its holster and muting it. 'Devin,' he said, glancing down at the screen. 'Devin can wait.'

But they hadn't gone five steps down the hall toward Hunt's bedroom when the house phone rang. 'It's a conspiracy,' he said. 'Somebody's got surveillance cameras on us.' When they got to the bedroom door, Hunt gave her a quick kiss and said, 'Let me just run back and unplug the damn thing.'

He turned around, heard his answering message, and then Devin Juhle's voice kick in just as he got to the kitchen. 'Wyatt. Pick up. It's urgent. And it's bad.'

Behind him, framed in the entryway to the kitchen, Tamara stood with her face set in hard stone, arms crossed over her chest. 'You better get it.'

Hunt gave Tamara his key and the Cooper so she could drive herself home while he took the Kawasaki and made it to Joe's in less than five minutes.

Hunt pulled up and flashed his ID to the patrolman guarding the scene. 'Inspector Juhle down there,' he pointed, 'just called me and told me to get down here. The victim is one of my employees.'

The cop nodded and asked Hunt to wait while he went down to the homicide inspectors and cleared the request, but Hunt fell in a couple of steps behind him. The patrolman didn't notice or didn't care, but either way, Hunt tagged along to the small group that included Juhle and Sarah Russo, who all stood on the far side of the sidewalk, away from where Ivan's body still lay on the cold, wet concrete.

Hunt nodded vaguely in the direction of the group. Then,

motioning a question with his head, Hunt got a grim silent assent from Juhle, and the two of them walked across where two people from the coroner's van were just laying out a bag next to the body.

'Can you guys give us a second here?' He put a hand on Hunt's arm. 'You all right?'

'No part of me is all right,' Hunt said. He went down to a squat and reached out to uselessly feel for a pulse in Ivan's neck, then moved his hand and rested it inside the fold of his jacket, on his shirt over his heart. There was still some warmth in the body. Standing up, he took a few deep breaths, then scanned the street both ways. 'What the hell was he doing down here?'

'Eating at Joe's, we think. Probably. We're thinking it might have been something he was working on. Somebody just pulled up in a cab and whacked him.'

'In a cab?'

Juhle nodded. 'We've got a witness. That's what happened. You know what he was working on?'

'Generally, yeah. Five or six things. If he had a witness down here he needed to interview, I don't know who it was.' Hunt stared away into the distance for a long moment before he came back to Juhle. 'You know the first thing that springs to mind? The Spencer connection.' Hunt ran a hand down the side of his face. 'I really don't want to think that's what got him killed.'

'I'm blanking. What's the Spencer connection?'

'Evie Spencer. Evie See Christ.'

'Again?'

Hunt nodded. 'The woman just won't go away.'

His eyes burning – the time was 11:52 – Hunt sat at the LexisNexis monitor in his front office, set up in a cubicle in the northwest corner. Windows flanked it on both walls, one looking out on the now mostly deserted Embarcadero, up past the Ferry Building, and one facing the bay with a slice of the Bay Bridge and Treasure Island off to the right.

Ivan had definitely been working on Spencer when he'd last sat here. He'd pulled up about a hundred of them in San Francisco, and maybe that's where Hunt would start tomorrow, with those first one hundred. He would have printed them out, but each history ran a minimum twenty pages, some many more.

And paper was already eating him up.

Available only by subscription to accredited entities such as police departments, government offices, newspapers, and law firms (and through those law firms, sometimes to private investigators), the basic LexisNexis record begins in the present with an individual's name, date of birth, social security number, and last known or current address. Then it goes back through other addresses, other names associated with those addresses, census data for the geographical region of the address, real property records, businesses and fictitious businesses associated with the individual, previous owners (if any) of those businesses, potential relatives, a.k.a.'s, associated persons, neighbors, employment history, and so on. In all, the service is a tremendously powerful search engine and person-locator tool.

In Hunt's estimation, the only real drawback was that the information in the records tended to be rife with misspellings, so that if you went searching for specific data, quite often the automated aspect of the system wouldn't give you your result. And then you had to go through the records manually anyway. Nevertheless, if you were willing to put in the time, you could almost always get the information you sought.

But Hunt had no stomach to even start printing pages out now, at this time of night. Still, all in all, it had probably been wise to have come right down to the office from the terrible street scene in front of Original Joe's. The history function of LexisNexis cleared itself every midnight. When Hunt had left Juhle, he felt there had been no time to lose, and it was compelling that Ivan had been looking at Spencers.

But in spite of the glut of Spencers, the situation really wasn't all that promising. There were about a million of them, or at least so many that it made no sense to keep checking the name. True, he and his staff could over the next few weeks call every one of the five hundred or so Spencers living in San Francisco, and then branch out to the greater Bay Area for the next few thousand, but ultimately that seemed a futile exercise. He had to come up with something else or a reason to settle on one individual. And that he did not have yet. Not close.

Finally, stretching, sick in his gut, Hunt logged off the machine and got to his feet, then walked by Tamara's desk and his own office and down the hallway to Ivan's small workspace, where he opened the door and turned on the light. The room featured its own window, an IKEA chair and desk with a computer monitor and some framed photographs, and a four-drawer filing cabinet. On the wall, Ivan had pinned up a Giants 'Torture to Rapture' poster.

Hunt pulled out the top filing drawer and stared for a minute at the neatly organized Pendaflex folders with their alphabetized tabs before he reached in and, more or less at random, lifted out the file labeled 'Doyle,' which he vaguely remembered as a *sub-rosa* case from a year ago about Mr Doyle's bad back and his workers'-comp claim. In the folder was a write-up for the insurance company, some field notes, and a CD that Hunt knew contained the pictorial evidence of Mr Doyle's fraud.

Replacing that file's contents, then putting the whole thing back in its place, he closed the drawer and opened the second, then the third one, which contained 'R' to 'Z.' Although there was no actual filed 'Z' entry. There was no Spencer, either.

Hunt let himself down into Ivan's chair, then came forward and picked up a framed picture of the poor guy with a pretty brunette, Lucy, whom Hunt had met once or twice. They were outside on a sunny day, smiling with the ocean in the background. Putting the picture back, he looked at the others – Lucy with a black cat in her arms, an elderly couple somewhere that looked like Las Vegas, Ivan in a group of people his age, maybe his brothers and sisters and their spouses, maybe just some pals.

This was getting him nowhere.

With the weight of his forehead on his hand, he hung in the chair and closed his eyes. Rousing himself, he got up again, turned out the light and left the office, and came back to his own desk. On his cell phone, he went to his Contacts list and touched a number. The phone rang four times, then picked up with Ivan's voice telling him to leave a message and he'd get right back to him.

Except . . . not.

He punched up his Contacts list again and this time sent a text to Callie Lucent, typed in Ivan's cell number, and asked, *Two quick ones: Can you ping this phone and tell me where it is? We can get a warrant if it's necessary, but meanwhile can you get me recent records on calls to or from this same number? He's one of my employees and he's been killed.*

'Mingya' – another of Callie Lucent's private cache of exclamations – 'Wyatt, is this some kind of sick joke?'

'I can't believe you're awake.'

'Damn straight I'm awake. I never sleep. But really, this is one of your guys?'

'Really.'

'And he was killed? Like murdered?'

'Shot in the face, Cal. About as murdered as it gets. So I'm trying to narrow down what he was working on. Maybe his killing had something to do with whatever that was and I'm thinking there might be a clue on his cell, but whoever shot him took it.'

'Well, let me try to ping it right now if he's left it on.'

'I'll wait.'

After his original text to Callie, Hunt had prowled the office in frustration, back and forth, until finally he had stretched out just for a second on the couch in his office. Now he checked his watch and saw that it was 2:04. He switched his cell phone to speaker.

'I'm not getting anything,' Callie said. 'They must have taken out the battery.'

'Or just turned it off.'

'No. That wouldn't do it, Wyatt. Even off, we can get a ping. But not without the battery.'

Swearing to himself, Hunt went back over to his desk. 'How about checking his cell's history? Do you need a warrant for that?'

Callie's laugh echoed in the quiet offices. 'Warrants? Please. Wyatt, I can pull up whatever I want whenever. It just might take a little time, that's all.'

'How long?'

'A day, maybe two.'

'Well, whatever you can do. Yesterday would be good, though.'

'I'm on it even as we speak. Where'd he get killed?'

'In the Tenderloin. Why?'

'Towers. If he calls between your office and the Tenderloin, that narrows down where I'll find the records. And hey, what about your texter? Any news there?'

'Nothing new. The last call was where you got 'em at the

Ferry Building. I'm thinking they stopped. Whoever it is says I'm getting close and they feel threatened.'

'And you think your dead guy . . .'

'Ivan.'

'You think Ivan might have been part of this? Your texts?'

'Not impossible, Cal. I'm actually pretty worried about it.'

'So what are the cops doing? Are you with them?'

'Not exactly with, but not against, either. They'll be investigating, too. And I'll share whatever I get with them. But they've got lots of cases they're working on all at once, whereas me, as of tonight, I've got only one.'

'Okay, I'll get back to you the minute I get something.'

'You know the cops will be looking for these numbers, too.'

'That's all right. They'll go through channels with warrants and all that. They'll never get within a mile of me. We'll kick their ass.'

'Okay, Callie. And thanks. I'm really going to owe you.'

'Are you kidding me? I live for this stuff.'

When he finally got home, he had a message from Tamara asking him to call her whatever time it was. She picked up on the first ring and he had just started to fill her in on what he'd been doing since they'd left one another, when she stopped him.

'He was still, I mean his body, his body was still there when you got there?'

'Yeah.'

'And you saw him? It was really Ivan, then?'

'No question.'

'Oh, Wyatt.'

'I know, Tam. I know.'

'So what are we going to do now?'

'About what?'

'I don't know.' Her voice had a catch in it. 'Everything.'

'Well, first, we're going to find out who did this, if we can.'

'How are we going to do that?'

'We know what he was looking at with his cases. We're hoping he'll have left some clue behind someplace.'

A silence hung on the line. 'You're telling me you think this was related to something he was working on? With us?'

'That's the working assumption. He had an appointment and got ambushed. Maybe, anyway. Nobody knows. But if it's part of one of his cases, it gives us someplace to look.'

'But that means we're working on it, too, doesn't it? The office, I mean.' She went silent for a beat, then said, 'This is getting scary, Wyatt, you know that?' Another pause. 'It would be nice to hear you say something.'

'We don't know absolutely it was one of his cases, Tam. Devin perked up at the work connection to us because it might give him somewhere to look, that's all.'

'That's not all, Wyatt. You said you agreed with him.'

'I do agree with him,' he admitted. 'I can't shake the feeling that Ivan's murder is connected to my mother's case. When you and I left work tonight, he was on Lexis looking at Spencers. That's the last thing we know. It's got to mean something.'

'You know what I think? I think it means he ran into her killer.'

'I think you're right, Tam,' Hunt said. 'I think you're right.'

16

Devastation.

The office was technically still open, but nobody was even pretending to do any work. The phone calls – people reading about it in the paper or seeing the news on television – had started long before Wyatt had gotten in around 8:30, and the ongoing flood kept Tamara marooned at her desk. Blotch faced and teary eyed, Jill holed herself up back in her own office, the door closed. Mickey busied himself drinking coffee and arranging the bouquets that were getting delivered about every fifteen minutes by the law firms and insurance companies with whom they did regular business.

Hunt sat zombielike in the corner LexisNexis cubicle, staring at the monitor in between fielding phone calls, from time to time making a more or less random search among the Spencers as an idea occurred to him.

Juhle had called to check in, and Hunt had learned that Callie's prejudices and skills notwithstanding, formal law enforcement could beat her on a few things, at least. Or maybe she just hadn't gotten around to looking yet. In any case, armed with Ivan's cell phone number, Juhle had learned that Ivan's last and only phone call, back to midafternoon yesterday, had been to his girlfriend.

Hunt suggested, the idea just occurring to him, that Juhle should try to get ahold of the telephone records from the office's landline. Ivan was the last one in the office last night. If there had been an outgoing call after about five o'clock, he would have made it. Juhle said that this was a good idea and he'd follow up. Otherwise, they had made no progress on Ivan's murder.

Hunt had had another dream in his few hours of sleep and had come in relatively pumped up with the idea that he could locate his father, who after all might still be alive.

Why this had assumed a sudden urgency was something he couldn't have explained, even to himself.

He didn't know why he hadn't considered this latest strategy earlier, but he had an address where his father had lived in 1970 and thought that he could find it – as indeed he could, with relative ease. So now he knew who presently lived in his parents' former apartment, but that turned out to be no help. Kevin Carson was in the database, all right, and associated with the property back then. But that information couldn't take Hunt anywhere toward the present. Kevin Carson had lived there, but so what? Where was he now? That was the question. And apparently one for which there was no answer.

Everything had happened so damn long ago.

Tamara opened the door and came into Hunt's darkened inner office, where he lay stretched out on the couch, his eyes closed and his breathing slow and regular. Going down to one knee, she touched his face and whispered his name.

'I'm here,' he said. 'What time is it?'

'Eleven-thirty, as requested.'

'You're a gem.'

'I am,' she said. 'Do you want some coffee?'

Blinking a couple of times, Hunt boosted himself up. 'I can get it.'

Tamara was back on her feet. 'I know you can. I was asking if you'd like me to get it for you.'

'Did I already say you were a gem?'

'You did.' She reached down and again touched the side of his face. 'Let me go get that coffee.'

'I will in a minute.' He nodded toward the door. 'How are things out there?'

'About the same. Awful.'

'I should send everybody home.'

'Probably.' She stopped at the door. 'You want me to get the light?'

'How about on the way back?'

The corners of her mouth turned up. 'I'll try to remember.'

In the dim light, Hunt sat on the couch, still half asleep. Suddenly, cocking his head as though trying to identify a barely audible sound, he then straightened all the way up, crossed over to his desk to get his hands on his folder, and a few seconds later got to his office door going out just as Tamara reached it coming in with his coffee.

'Tie goes to the runner,' she said, holding it out for him.

'Thank you.' He took the mug, sipping without slowing down. 'I'm an idiot,' he said. 'It wasn't my father. It's Spencer.'

Prompted by his dream, he'd come in that morning with his father on his mind, believing – perhaps irrationally – that if he started with his father's address on Fulton Street back in 1970, he might somehow surf the Lexis wave into the present. When that hadn't proved to be true, he'd felt himself to be at yet another dead end.

But in reality, it had just come to him in his latest dozing state that it wasn't his father's address he needed if he wanted to locate somebody in the present, but rather another 1970 address that he did have – Evie's, from the CPS document Bettina had recovered Monday morning. That address might in fact lead him forward in time to what Ivan had possibly already discovered to his fatal misfortune, the identity of her husband.

At the LexisNexis terminal, his folder open on his lap, he sipped coffee as his fingers flew over the keys.

Tamara had followed him over and now hovered. 'What are you looking for?'

'I'm finding it.' Pointing down to his folder, he said, 'Here's the address where Evie lived in 1970, now with its current owners. See this? Now persons associated . . .' He hit another key. The screen scrolled down, and down again, back through the decades. The free-standing house on Arguello – right around the corner from the Fulton Street address where Kevin and Margie had lived – had been sold most recently in 2003. There had been different owners – sales – in 1998, 1991, 1982, 1976, and, finally, the owner Hunt was looking for, who'd bought the place in 1968.

Tamara rested a hand on his shoulder.

Hunt pushed a last key and sat back with a contented exhale. 'Lionel Spencer,' he said, turning to include Tamara. 'Got him.'

Even in her heavy leather coat and wearing gloves, Sarah Russo shivered in the gale-force wind that whistled past them. On the sidewalk, she rang the doorbell to the mansion that loomed in front of them behind the rock wall with its heavy iron gate. She and Juhle were at the peak of Russian Hill on Larkin Street, where the cable car line seemed to fall straight off the face of the earth at the nearby intersection. 'If I had enough money to own a house here, much less this monster,' she said, 'I'd live somewhere else.'

'But then you wouldn't have the view.'

Russo briefly glanced over to her left. Below them spread

a stunning panorama, albeit familiar to both of them. A couple of container ships and upwards of fifty sailboats were beating through the whitecaps below. Alcatraz, the Marin shoreline, Angel Island, and the Richmond Bridge all supplied slightly different flavors of eye candy over the gunmetal water. Closer in, the orderly, almost sculpted-looking neighborhood behind the piers and churches of North Beach shone in the nacreous light of late afternoon. 'It's pretty in Antarctica, too, I hear,' Russo said. 'As you may know, my motto is, If it's too cold to play baseball, you don't want to live there.'

'Last time I checked we had baseball here.'

She threw him a look of scorn. 'Just 'cause we've got a team doesn't mean it's not too cold to play.' Shifting her attention back to the gate, she gave it a little kick. 'Come on, come on, open up. It's not like we weren't invited.'

'Well, not exactly.'

'Hey, we're cops. Close enough.'

Lionel Spencer buzzed the gate and they took a winding footpath through a small grove of cypress and juniper about forty feet back from the sidewalk, then up four steps into a covered, circular stoop. He was waiting for them in the open front door, dressed in what appeared to be black silk pajamas under a monogrammed velour bathrobe and matching slippers. 'Sorry if I kept you waiting,' he said. 'Sometimes I don't hear the gate bell the first time. I miss deliveries and they've got to come back twice. I really ought to get it changed into something louder. You want to come inside?'

'That would be nice, thank you,' Russo said.

'Come on, then.' He backed away a step or two, turned around, and started walking, obviously expecting them to close the front door and then fall in behind him. Juhle and Russo shot each other the quick secret look acknowledging that they were dealing with at the very least an eccentric and quite possibly a complete whack job. The thick, shoulder-length white hair, parted in the middle, was another clue.

They followed him a long way back down the wide Persian runner that covered the hardwood hallway, past three large open rooms on the right and a stairway and other rooms on the left that at a glance seemed devoted to cooking and eating. But the showcase moment was at the end of the hall, where Spencer had been leading them. He stopped just inside the archway and turned back to them, ushering them into a large round glass-enclosed turret, filled with a myriad of plants and even trees and featuring an impressive telescope.

'Nice room,' Juhle said.

Spencer nodded. 'I spend most of my time here. If you don't go outside a lot, and I don't, this is a good substitute. Why don't we sit down?' He drifted over to a seating area and took one of the chairs in white upholstered fabric while the inspectors sat on either end of the couch.

Russo said, 'We appreciate your agreeing to talk with us.'

'No problem. Although I don't have any idea how I can help you. I didn't know this person who was killed until I met him last night.' Spencer had one leg crossed over the other, his hands folded in his lap.

'Ivan Orloff,' Juhle said.

'All right.'

'You met him last night?' Russo asked.

'Yes, of course. I had dinner with him at Original Joe's. When I left, it must have only been a few minutes before he was shot. I'd assumed you knew that. He called me here at home last night. Which I assume is how you got my number, and why you're here now.'

'That's right,' Juhle admitted, though it wasn't strictly true. Yes, they had traced his phone number from the Hunt Club's landline, but they'd gotten his name and current address from Wyatt as soon as he'd located it on LexisNexis, and this was why Juhle and Russo were here in the first place. Hunt had also done a Google search on Lionel as soon as he'd located him that had come up maddeningly empty. The man had had no overt connection to Jonestown that Hunt had been able to find; beyond that, Lionel kept such a low general profile that the last activity noted was Lionel's high bid for a magnum of Screaming Eagle cabernet at a charity auction nearly five years before.

Due to this relative dearth of information, Juhle and Russo were reduced to taking part in the kind of interview they both hated: essentially a fishing expedition. And there was nothing for it now but for Juhle to cast the first line. 'Would you mind telling us what Mr Orloff wanted to talk to you about?'

'You don't know yourselves?'

A polite smile from Russo. 'We'd like to hear it from you, if you don't mind.'

'Do you think this might have something to do with why he got killed?'

'We're investigating the homicide,' Juhle said. 'At the moment, we don't know why he was killed. We're talking to anybody who might be able to shed light on that.'

A frown furrowed Spencer's brow. 'Am I under some kind of suspicion? I told you that we had dinner together, although I cut it a little short.'

'Why was that?' Russo asked.

'Well, after a while it became clear that he'd made the appointment with me under false pretenses.'

Juhle came in. 'And what were they?'

'He said he had some information about my ex-wife, my former wife. Evie. And my children.'

'Is she recently deceased?' Russo asked, though she knew the answer.

'No. She died in 1978. In Jonestown. Maybe you've heard of it.'

The inspectors exchanged a glance and nodded in tandem.

'Well, then.' Spencer sat back, his voice going quiet. 'It's still a difficult subject, as I hope you'll understand.'

'Of course,' Russo said. 'She went down there without you?'

'Or I would be dead, too, now, wouldn't I? Though she did take our children,' he added with what sounded like unforced bitterness. 'She ruined my life.'

After a silence, Juhle asked, 'So what did Mr Orloff tell you? About your wife?'

'Well, that was the point, you see? He didn't seem to know very much about my wife. He lured me out to talk with him saying he'd come across some new information about them. Not that it would bring any of them back. How could I resist? But that was simply untrue.'

'So what did he want to see you about, then?'

Spencer took a moment to gather himself, scanning the room, running a palm over his cheek, smoothing his hair back. 'I'm not sure, to tell you the truth. It was all a little bizarre. He asked me about some woman who evidently had been murdered in 1970 or thereabouts and who had apparently known Evie then. They were reopening that case or something like that, he said, and were looking for witnesses of some kind. I don't know – I don't think Mr Orloff really knew – what they were supposed to be witnesses to. I told him I didn't know the woman and hadn't known her then, and wished him luck, and that, essentially, was all we talked about. I can't imagine it had anything to do with his death.'

Juhle came forward on the couch. 'Did you know Jim Jones?'

Spencer's mouth twisted. 'Yes. Of course. He was a huge

part of all of our lives back then.' He scratched at the arm of his chair. 'Evie was always searching for something bigger, some ultimate meaning to life, you know. And that's what Jones was selling. It was a perfect match.'

'A huge part of all of your lives?' Russo prodded. 'Including yours?'

He nodded with a rueful look. 'At the beginning, when it seemed to be making Evie so happy, I joined up to support her. That was the way it worked. Jones got you, and if your spouse didn't want to sign on, you had to dump the spouse, or your parents and kids and anything else that wasn't part of the temple. So I stayed on at first, until I just . . . I couldn't anymore, that was all.' He fixed on the sympathetic Russo. 'This really is painful,' he said. 'I'm sorry.'

It was a dismissal. Spencer lifted himself up and out of his chair, and the two inspectors got to their feet. 'Well,' Russo said, 'thanks for your cooperation.'

He shrugged. 'For all the help I've been. But before you leave, can I ask you a question?'

'Sure.'

'This reopened murder case that Mr Orloff was talking about. Is that something you're all working on, too? I mean the real police?'

'I've looked at it a little,' Juhle said. 'And it's technically not reopened. It's still just plain open, since no one's ever been convicted. And there's no statute of limitations on murder, so it's not going away. Why?'

'Well, it just seems a little far-fetched, doesn't it? Something that happened, what, forty years ago? I can't imagine that Mr Orloff's death could have anything to do with that now after all these years.'

'Well,' Juhle said, 'that's a good point. But Orloff's death had something to do with something, and that old cold case is what he was working on, which warms it up at least a little bit, wouldn't you say?'

A resigned shrug. 'You may be right,' Spencer said. 'What do I know?'

Lieutenant Abe Glitsky had his feet up on his desk, his fingers templed in front of his mouth. As usual, his countenance was dark, his eyebrows heavy over sunken eyes. He was breathing easy and steady. The clock on his wall read 5:15. 'I'm trying to see this,' he said. 'I really am.'

'It's three homicides,' Russo said.

'Well, not exactly true. Even according to both of you, Jim Burg was a suicide.'

'But now that's been called into question,' Juhle said.

Glitsky took his hands away from his lips and faced Juhle. 'By who, Devin? Your friend Mr Hunt? And based on what evidence?'

'It's not so much specific evidence' – Russo riding to her partner's defense – 'than what's starting to look like an accumulation of connections. It's hard to dismiss them, Abe, you've got to admit. That's what we're trying to say.'

Glitsky shook his head sympathetically. 'And that's what I'm telling you. I don't have to admit them.' Now he swung his feet down and came around, elbows on the desk. 'Go with me here, both of you. Stop me when I'm wrong. We've got a domestic murder and her killer now forty – did I say *forty*? – years ago.'

'Killer never convicted,' Juhle pointed out. 'Just to be precise.'

'Noted. But I'm going to pretend the guy we put on trial twice actually did it, just for the sake of argument. Next, we have a cop suicide in, when? Nineteen seventy-five.'

Juhle wouldn't just give it to him. '*Maybe* committed suicide,

Abe. Right after he got promoted? When he was happily married? And let's not forget he was not only the arresting officer in the first murder case, he'd gone on the child-endangerment call to that same apartment, where he wrote up the victim and her friend, Evie Spencer.'

'Devin,' Glitsky said evenly. 'Those events – the calls to the apartment and the arrest, and then the suicide – are separated by four years, are they not? Four years.'

'About the time frame for the two trials,' Russo added.

'So?' Glitsky pointed at Sarah, then Devin. 'You guys are two-teaming me, and I'd appreciate if you'd just let me go on. Please? So our third victim is last night, Orloff, who is ostensibly working on the first case, the forty-year-old case, although he's also got maybe a dozen other cases he's covering, not to say that his murder had anything to do with any of them. But lo and behold, last night he finds this guy Spencer, who doesn't deny talking to him, having a meal with him, and is in all ways the picture of cooperation. Am I leaving anything out here? Isn't that about it?'

'Abe, listen.' Juhle put his hands on the edge of the desk. 'You left out that Spencer was Evie's husband. All of these dead people – even given that Burg might have been a suicide – everybody is connected with Evie Spencer.'

'Who, I might remind you, is also dead, and dead since 1978.'

'At Jonestown,' Russo said.

'And why, pray, is that relevant? Close to a thousand people died at Jonestown. Evie Spencer being one of them does not make her special.'

'It's too much to be coincidence,' Russo said. 'That's all we're saying.'

Glitsky relaxed back into his chair. 'Granted, Sarah, there's an appearance of coincidence, which we all hate. And if all this happened over the span of a couple of days, I'd be saying

"Whoa, there's got to be a connection. Look into Evie Spencer and let's find where this goes, where the pieces fit." But think about it, people: Evie's been dead thirty-two years. That's four years after Jim Burg, eight after Margie Carson, and on a different continent to boot. And now Ivan Orloff.' He spread his hands. 'I'm not exactly clear what you expect me to do. Except put much credence in this theory, which I just can't seem to make myself do.'

'Abe,' Russo said, 'if we don't get any traction with Evie Spencer, that leaves us with nothing on Orloff.'

'That's just not true, Sarah. He was a PI. He was working on other stuff. You'll just have to slog through it, that's all. There might be something there, or in his personal life, the usual. Or he might have just been randomly targeted and killed for his wallet, which I don't have to tell you both has been known to happen, especially where he was.'

Juhle and Sarah, on folding chairs in front of Glitsky's desk, exchanged a look, and Juhle, nodding, got up and walked a few steps over to the door, which he closed. When he got back to his seat, he cleared his throat and then he came forward and spoke up in a near whisper. 'Abe, what if this has got something to do with cops?'

It took Glitsky a few seconds to react and when he did, it was a blink, come and gone in an instant. 'What are you talking about? What cops? You think a cop shot Orloff? That's an amazingly offensive accusation and you'd better have some strong evidence to back it up. Do you have that?'

'Not yet, no, sir,' Juhle said. 'No evidence. And anybody might have pulled the trigger on Orloff, maybe got paid to do it.'

'You're still saying *a cop* paid somebody to do this?' Glitsky ran a hand through his hair. 'I don't believe I'm listening to this. Where is it even coming from?'

'We're not necessarily thinking a cop did it, Abe,' Russo said.

Juhle took it up. 'We think we shouldn't overlook the possibility that somehow some cops, by now probably no longer active duty, might have been involved.'

'Some cops now,' Glitsky said. 'More than one? A vast conspiracy of cops?'

'You remember that case file I had piled up out there over the last few days, the stuff Wyatt Hunt wanted to look into?'

'And that I let him. Sure.'

'Right. But then Hunt started asking questions – and not too many questions at that – and the next thing you know, Chief Lapeer gets you on the phone and she's telling you that maybe we don't want to be spending time on that.'

'And you see this as somehow ominous?'

'I think it's provocative that somebody talked to her and she came to you and had you call me and Hunt off. I think something happened back then in that first case. I think when Jim Burg became an inspector four years later, he got wind of it . . .'

'And how did he do that?'

'I don't know. Maybe he had a hunch from early on. Maybe he thought they arrested the wrong guy, which is what his wife told Hunt, and when he became an inspector, he decided to look into it.'

'This is all just fantasy, Devin. Where do you get any of this?'

'Well, not all fantasy. Jim Burg signed out the case file, all of it, in '74, a couple of weeks before he killed himself. He was the last person to look at it before Hunt and I did. I think he found something.'

'Something? Like what?'

'We don't know. Something that made sense in the context

of the case back then, which is now too far removed to see what it was.'

'Why would he have signed out the case file, Abe,' Russo asked, 'if he didn't think something was squirrelly?'

'Squirrelly how? Maybe he wanted to study how a case gets built. Maybe he thought he knew something that didn't make either trial where they could convict if they went for it a third time. Maybe, as a new inspector, he thought he could make his bones with a fresh approach. I don't really have any idea.' Over the desk, Glitsky's eyes conveyed more sadness than criticism. 'Devin. Both of you. I've given you both a good listen and I still don't know why we're having this discussion. What do you want me to do that I'm not already doing?'

This, of course, was the crux. Juhle sat back, glanced over at his partner, and came back to Glitsky. 'We just wanted you to know that this Orloff case might expose some . . . sensitivities that you might want to be aware of, and we wanted to give you a heads-up on where we're coming from.'

'I can handle sensitivities. Trust me. Sensitive, that's what I'm good at, I don't care what everybody says. And don't misunderstand me. I'm putting no restrictions – none – on how you conduct your investigation in this Orloff thing. But.' Glitsky by now had his arms folded in front of him on the desk. 'Well and good though it may be to have theories, I don't think I need to remind you that your job is getting evidence, and that theories spring from evidence rather than the other way around.'

'These Evie connections aren't theories,' Sarah said. 'They are verifiable facts.'

'Okay,' Glitsky said, 'but please remember that sometimes a fact is just a fact. It has no greater meaning. It might not rise to the level of evidence of any specific crime. What I'm telling both of you is that of course you're free to go wherever the evidence takes you – that's the job. But a bit of discretion might be advised before you go rousing any of the sensitivities we've been talking about. It better be real evidence, and it better be rock solid and airtight.'

Juhle nodded. 'That's all we're saying. If we get there.'

'Then, obviously,' Glitsky said, 'you've got to do what you've got to do.'

17

This time the housekeeper admitted Hunt to the dining room in the rectory proper. The dishes had been cleared and Bernard was sitting alone with a book facedown at the table, a half-full wine glass and half-empty bottle of cabernet in front of him.

'I'm sorry to be a bother,' Hunt began as soon as he'd crossed the threshold.

The priest held up a hand. 'Don't be ridiculous. Do I look like a man who doesn't want company? Especially from the long-lost son. Though of course I've got my book and my . . . my weakness. Can I pour you a glass? A taste?'

'I'm good, thank you, Father. I'm still more or less working.'

'So you've got more questions for me? I must say it's been a while since I've felt so . . . so useful. Are you making any progress with your search?'

'Maybe not the kind I'd want, but . . .' Hunt stood with his hands at his sides for a few seconds, then finally pulled a chair around and sat on it. 'The truth is, one of my employees was killed last night. A young guy named Ivan Orloff.'

'Killed?' Bernard's glass stopped halfway to his mouth and he put it back down on the table.

Hunt nodded. 'Shot. I think it might have had to do with my mother's case.'

'Jesus, Mary, and Joseph have mercy.' Bernard bowed his head, made the sign of the cross, and kept his eyes closed for a few seconds, apparently offering up a prayer for the soul of Ivan

Orloff. When he looked back up, he said, 'You know, Wyatt, it may be blasphemous to say this, but the longer I live, the more I understand how people can lose belief in God. What I don't see as clearly is how people can doubt the existence of the devil.' He chuckled, but there was no humor in it. 'In a twisted way, sometimes I think that's the reason I'm not an atheist. I *know* there's a devil. So then, given that, it's not unreasonable to assume there must be God. Or at least the existence of a spiritual realm, which would allow for God. You know what I'm saying?'

'I don't know if I've ever heard anyone put it like that.'

'I wouldn't go around preaching it. But don't you think there's more evidence, sometimes, of evil everywhere, than of goodness?'

'Sometimes I do, Father. Sometimes I do.'

The priest sipped at his wine. 'I'm so sorry about your employee.'

'So am I. I'm wrestling with the fact that it was my fault. That I sent him on this path that got him shot.'

'Well, if you did, it wasn't purposeful, was it? You couldn't have known.'

'No. Although that's not much comfort. Ivan's just as dead.' Hunt made a gesture in the direction of the bottle. 'Maybe I could do with a hit of that after all.'

'Certainly.' The priest pushed back, stood up, and turned to an old dark sideboard directly behind him, from which he took out a wineglass and put it in front of Wyatt, then poured. 'So how can I help you?' he asked as he sat back down.

Wyatt lifted his glass and drank. 'Well, the situation here on the ground has changed. Now, regardless of whether Ivan was working on my mother's case or not, his murder is a police matter. My best friend is a homicide inspector who's actually been assigned to the case. So whether I want to or not, I'd best be advised to keep away from their investigation, at least in an active way. I don't want to scare off witnesses or muck around the same places they're looking.'

'Yes, I can see that. So what does that leave for you?'

'Well, there are a few other things. My father, for one. I haven't been able to locate him, and I thought I'd ask you again if you could wrack your brain and try to remember any little hint about where he might have gone to when he left here.'

Bernard's face reflected his disappointment. 'I've thought about that ever since that first day you came here. He had the job offer in Texas, but he told me he might just go and keep going until he felt like he could stop. I never heard from him again.'

'All right.' Hunt turned his glass on the table. 'This may be a stretch, but what isn't, after all this time? You mentioned that you'd found him work with some of your parishioners . . .'

'Yes?'

'Well, might it be possible he stayed in touch with any of them?'

'I don't know. It might be, though I'd say it would be most unlikely.' The frustration in Bernard's expression, if anything, increased. 'It was forty-some years ago, Wyatt. If I could remember who any of them were to begin with.'

'Maybe you can, Father. That's all I'm saying. It's someplace else to look.'

'And if you found him?'

'I'll be able to go up and knock on his door. And he can then tell me who offered him the job, who else was around when all this went down. Or at least he can set me on the trail, at the end of which is my mother's killer.'

'Is that really possible?' The priest's eyes glimmered with a sudden faint hope. 'All right. Dear God. I'll find them if I can, Wyatt. I promise I'll try.'

'That's all I'm asking.' He lifted his glass in a toasting gesture, and Bernard raised his own glass and clinked it against Hunt's. Both men drank. 'Well, actually,' Hunt said, 'that's not true. It's all I'm asking about my father, but I've got a question or two about my mother as well.'

'Whatever I can do, but I think I've told you everything I know.'

'You did. But maybe we can go over again what you said about Indiana?'

Bernard pursed his lips.

Picking up on Bernard's expression, Hunt asked, 'Is something wrong?'

'No. It's just that I don't recall saying much of anything about Indiana. Other than that your mother didn't want to talk about it. She wouldn't talk about it.'

'But she'd been abused there? Somehow. Is that right? Did she say that much?'

'Yes. She said that much. I know that you have personal reasons to find out everything you can about your parents, Wyatt. But this strikes me as rather far afield. This isn't like your father, who may still be alive. What can your mother tell you about her own death?'

'I don't know. But the more I know about her life, the closer I might be to finding what it is that caused her death.'

Bernard pushed himself back from the table, his body language proclaiming his reluctance to engage any further on this topic. 'But Indiana?' he asked. 'When she was what, fifteen? How can that be any kind of help?'

Hunt sat back in his chair, gauging Bernard's response. Something had shifted in the room's dynamic, and with the priest seemingly so willing to cooperate on his father, he didn't want to lose whatever gains he'd made on that front. But though he couldn't say why, his mother's story, in Hunt's view, was more important. And suddenly he was certain that Bernard knew more than he'd earlier admitted, and it was worth any risk to find out what that was.

'Do you remember when I was here the other day, Father, asking about Evie Secrist?'

As Hunt had intended, the segue to Evie from his mother threw the priest off guard. He relaxed slightly, reached for his wine, and drank. 'Sure. Of course.'

'I found out a little more about her. Actually, quite a lot more.' He told it all in the next minute or so, ending with the dramatic punch line.

Which had its effect. 'Jonestown?'

'With her children. All of them.'

'More of the devil. God help us.' Bernard sighed heavily. 'Not that you couldn't have seen it, or even predicted it back when she knew Margie and Kevin. She was the kind of person the cults got ahold of and preyed on.'

'Do you know anything about Jim Jones, Father?'

He shrugged. 'Just pretty much what everybody knows. No real details. We in the mainstream churches didn't pay much attention to him back in the day. Until it was too late, I mean. But then afterward, I . . . I think like a lot of us, I couldn't bear to hear too much about it, or about him. Maybe it was just guilt that we didn't do something when we might have had the chance, but then again, what could we have done? He had them all brainwashed.'

'Yes, he did, Father. But you want to hear another detail about Jim Jones?'

'What's that?'

'He came from Indiana.'

A guttural sound came from Bernard's throat. Hunt could almost hear the gears working in his brain. After a bit, the priest sat back in his chair, then came forward, reached for his wine-glass. Emptying it in a gulp, he put it down on the table and poured more for both of them. At last, his eyes met Hunt's. 'She thought it was her fault,' he said. 'So many of them do.'

'What was her fault?'

'The abuse. The sexual activity. The group sex. It was with her pastor. It started when she was eleven and she wasn't the only child involved.' Bernard went back to the wine, his eyes glassy with emotion. 'I'm breaking the seal of the confessional to tell you this, Wyatt. I've never done that before in my life and I may go to hell for it, but if it helps you, I don't see how it can hurt her now. You think her pastor was Jim Jones?'

Hunt nodded. 'I don't think it's impossible. Did she ever mention a name?'

'No. Not that I recall. It was just always "him." But if it was Jones, Wyatt, what does that get you?'

'I'm not sure, Father. Maybe it just gets me someplace else to look. Someplace there might be an answer. Jones has a history. If somewhere it intersects with my mother's, that's a new truth I can work with. And I've got to believe that one of these truths is going to lead me to who killed her. And maybe killed Ivan Orloff, too.'

Hunt left Star of the Sea and made two phone calls from his car.

The first was to Tamara, who did not pick up. He left a message saying he hoped to see her when he got through with his errands tonight, whatever they might turn out to be. Would she call him back when she got the message, no matter the time?

The second call, he wasn't wild about the news from Juhle concerning Lionel Spencer. Hunt had trouble believing that the man who'd been married to Evie – in some ways the linchpin of this whole affair – was apparently a nebbish and reclusive guy who had no idea why Orloff had called him. Besides having never heard of Kevin or Margie Carson, he had offered no insight to Juhle or Russo about the People's Temple or Jim Jones or his wife or his own children, other than a corroboration of the bare facts.

Hunt also had a hard time believing that the cops had been so easy on him, given that he was clearly the last person to see Ivan alive, had in fact just eaten dinner with him! According to Juhle, he and Sarah hadn't even mentioned the names of any of the arresting or contributing officers or the lawyers involved in the trial. Spencer hadn't volunteered or expressed any knowledge or interest in Kevin Carson's trial. Essentially, Juhle and Russo had verified that Orloff had phoned, then eaten with Spencer, but hadn't pursued that any further, in spite of the fact that Orloff had met his death within minutes of Spencer leaving him.

Hunt wasn't willing to call that another coincidence. He needed better answers. His instincts told him that someone as closely connected to these dramatic events as Spencer had been must know more.

Although he had all but sworn to Devin that he would leave him and Russo to the police aspect of the investigation, that was before he'd learned that interviewing Spencer had been such a washout. Now, with a fire in his belly from the seal-of-confession revelation of Father Bernard – Hunt knew he was going to have to fly to Indiana – he didn't want to leave the city without leaning on Lionel Spencer for a few of the hard answers.

So at about 9:15, he pulled up and parked his Cooper on Larkin and walked up to the sidewalk gate at Spencer's address. He had Spencer's home number in his cell phone and could have called first, but he thought an unannounced and unexpected visit might be more productive. Pushing the button in the face of the rock wall, he waited for a click at the gate for most of a minute, then pressed the button again. When there was no answer a second time, he checked both ways to verify that he was alone on the street and vaulted over the fence into the stand of cypress.

Above him, lights shone through some of the front windows,

and he waited another minute or so, hoping to see some sign of movement, some shadow crossing in front of a source of light. Stepping back onto the path, he made it up to the front door, where there was another button and another doorbell.

The gong was audible outside where he stood. It echoed through the house as Hunt waited for the sound of approaching footsteps. In growing frustration, he knocked at the door. 'Mr Spencer!'

Hunt got out his cell phone, punched in Spencer's number, heard the ringing inside the house – one, two, three, four times – then the answering machine. He hung up without leaving a message.

Nobody home.

But all the lights were on.

And Juhle had told him that Lionel Spencer was a homebody who rarely went out. So where was he?

Four houses down the block from Spencer's gate, Hunt was sitting in his car where he'd parked earlier. He thought that the guy had probably just gone out for dinner – there was nothing if not a plethora of good restaurants within walking distance. And many people left lights on in their homes, either because they forgot to turn them off or so there'd be light on when they got back.

So he spent the time while he waited for his quarry to return flitting back and forth between his continuing guilt-ridden reaction to Ivan's death, what was going on with him and Tamara and how that was going to play out, and the line of questioning he'd try to follow when Spencer returned.

Lionel might have been a space case, Hunt thought, but had he really ignored the trial of the murder of his wife's best friend? Did that make any sense at all? And even if he hadn't paid attention, wouldn't it have been a big deal to Evie?

No, of course he'd followed the trial. How could Juhle and Russo not have pushed him harder on that, if they'd pushed him at all? The more Hunt thought about it, the more positive he was that Spencer would have to know the names of the participants and many other details of the trial itself. He'd know, if not witnesses, then other friends of Evie – and by extension of Kevin and Margie – and be able to supply some contact information on many of them, who in turn might have been aware of other conflicts, other stories, other motives.

Also, Spencer was a man who'd lost his entire family to Jonestown, who'd told Juhle that his wife had ruined his life. The fact that he hadn't gone down there with them did not absolve him from all knowledge of those events. He undoubtedly knew all about Evie's conversion, of her metamorphosis from acid-popping Jesus freak to People's Temple cultist. Had Hunt's mother been around for that? Had she been part of it? Had Jim Jones contributed to the friction between Kevin and Margie?

Hunt knew from his continuing education on Google that Jones had not moved to San Francisco until 1972, two years after Margie's death. So how could there be any connection between them? But on the other hand, if he'd been her abuser when she'd been a child, she might have been aware of what he'd been doing all along.

Tamara didn't call him back until 10:45. 'I was about to give up on you,' he said.

'You said to call whenever. Where are you?'

'I'm in hour two of an unplanned stakeout of Lionel Spencer's house, waiting for him to get back home so I can ask him some questions.'

'I thought Devin already did that.'

'He did. He just didn't ask all the right ones. Where have you been?'

Tamara's sigh came over the line. 'Mickey made a lasagna for

Ivan's parents. We took it over there. Then stayed on and I drank some vodka. It was pretty horrible. Not the vodka.'

'I haven't been able to get it out of my mind, either. I feel like I sent him to it.'

'Wyatt. Come on. We don't even know he was on the job.'

'No. I do know that. He discovered something. And Spencer stopped him.'

'How? He stole a cab?'

'I don't know.'

'Or even "if," really.'

'No. I know. Doesn't mean I can't whip myself over it, though.'

After a moment, Tamara said, 'How late are you going to be out there?'

'That depends on when Spencer gets back. I thought I'd wait for that.'

'I was thinking of coming over to your place, but Ivan's thing kept on going. So maybe I should just sleep.'

'That's all right. We'll get some time someday. Promise.'

'We're still good? I'm sorry about this. I didn't plan . . .'

'Tam. I didn't plan this, either. We're good.'

'You're sure?'

'Sure.'

'All right. Tomorrow, then?'

'Bright and early. Get some sleep.'

Hunt had lots of time to think, and the more he thought, the more he became convinced that Ivan had discovered something about Spencer that became the reason he was killed. Either Spencer had set up the last-minute dinner appointment with Ivan and gone down there to shoot him himself, or he had contacted someone else who had taken care of the wet work. And on that short a notice, it would by necessity have been someone that Spencer knew well.

How could Juhle and Russo not have recognized all this and pushed harder when they had him talking to them? Did Spencer own a gun? How did he earn his apparently significant sums of money? How could he *not* have known his wife's best friend? Did he have an explanation for that?

Ivan had been working on Hunt's mother's case.

And so the responsibility for Ivan's death lay squarely on Wyatt's shoulders. He couldn't deny it. He had sent his people out to gather information, and one of them had been killed. Ivan had gotten killed because he'd gotten close. Hunt couldn't prove it yet, but he believed it absolutely.

He had to get his people off the case, and immediately. He couldn't subject them to the risk. This was now a police matter in the present tense. Wyatt himself would talk to Juhle and Russo and keep them in the loop of his own investigation, which would be continuing, and his discoveries, if any.

And here was one more chilling certainty. Leaving out Ivan's murder, this was more or less the result that his phantom texter had engineered from the beginning. Whoever it was had wanted to stay out of the picture and at the same time to help Wyatt build a criminal case against his mother's killer, who now had been prompted to act to protect himself. And no doubt would do so again.

Hunt had a couple of guns in an underground floor safe in his house. He normally had no use for a weapon, and in fact did not have a CCW – Carry a Concealed Weapon – permit. Now, sitting in his darkened car on this empty street well after midnight, he suddenly felt the hairs on the back of his neck stand up and wished he'd thought to bring his gun along with him tonight.

He realized with a shock of adrenaline that he was a fool to be going around unarmed. He would have to be better prepared, more on his guard, until this was settled.

In his rearview mirror, a lone figure – a tall man in a trench coat, hands in his pockets – appeared, walking up the street. Coming abreast of Hunt's car, he slowed and then stopped at the passenger window, then – his curiosity either satisfied or piqued – he simply walked on. Hunt's heart, a piston in his chest, gradually found its normal rhythm again as Wyatt watched the man continue up to Spencer's gate and right past it to the corner, then around and out of sight.

Behind him, the street had reverted to its regular emptiness. Regaining his composure, Wyatt checked the time on his cell phone: 1:14.

Lionel Spencer wasn't coming home. His lights were still on. Hunt considered calling Juhle, but then thought better of it. He had nothing to give him but theories and paranoia. Instead, he hit the ignition, turned on his lights, put the Cooper in gear, and started rolling, calling it a night.

18

Hunt's home was only a few blocks from the Hall of Justice and he walked over, showing up on the fourth floor with three hot froufrou coffee drinks from the lobby as a peace offering since he knew he was about to commence being at least a pain in the ass, and maybe more, to both inspectors. Russo sat on a chair she pulled over to the back side of Juhle's desk, and when Hunt got to them, she stood up and let him take the seat.

They greeted him neutrally – he was, after all, a civilian crashing the homicide detail – and weren't exactly effusive in their thanks for the coffee. If the drinks he'd brought had been tea-based, they could have read the leaves and predicted a few true things. Even with only the coffee, they guessed pretty close.

Juhle removed the lid on his cup, slurped the scalding liquid, and said, 'Why do I get the feeling here, about ten minutes into the workday, that your earlier and admirable decision to let us handle this case and to keep yourself out of it has hit a snag?'

'I've got an easy one for you, Dev. Didn't you tell me that Lionel Spencer wasn't planning on going out last night?'

'Yes, he did.'

'Well, guess what.'

Before Juhle could answer, Sarah Russo spoke up, her morning voice raspy and her tone impatient. 'Reading between the lines here, Wyatt, you're telling us you went and saw Mr Spencer?'

'That's half right. I went there. I didn't see him.'

'All right. Even that.' She fixed him with a level gaze. 'I have to tell you you're completely out of line. You can't interfere with our investigation, period. It's obstruction, however you want to spin it, and if you keep it up, I'm not being dramatic, it might cost you your license. Am I making myself clear enough here? You . . . can . . . not . . . do . . . this.' She pushed her cup toward him. 'And I don't think I want your damn coffee, either.'

'Yeah, you do.' Hunt pushed it back toward her. 'Half the reason I'm here is to tell you that I really am out of it.'

'That'd be the good half,' Juhle said. 'What's the other half?'

Hunt reached into his jacket and pulled out a vertically folded piece of paper from his inside pocket. 'About a million questions I thought up last night while I was waiting for Mr Spencer to come home from wherever he was.'

Russo grabbed the paper and scanned it in about two seconds, a red blotch coming up her throat and into her face. 'Oh, okay, thanks a lot. No, really.' She slammed it down on the desk and threw a hot glare at Juhle. 'Jesus Christ! Do you believe this?' With a dismissive glance at Hunt, she told her partner, 'I'll be over at my desk.' Turning without looking back, she walked off halfway across the large, open room.

'She's upset,' Hunt said, 'and she forgot her coffee.'

'That's some keen observation.' Juhle shook his head in disgust. 'What did you think? Are you trying to be insulting or you just didn't take your don't-be-stupid pills?'

'He's in this,' Hunt said. 'Spencer.'

'Great. This just in. You're not.'

'I know. I know. I'm not.' He pointed to his paper again. 'But those are things you're going to want to ask him about, I promise.'

'What? You didn't think we'd get to them?'

'No. I thought you would, of course. Of course, Dev. I didn't think a cheat sheet would hurt, that's all. I've been working on this a while, too, you know. He stonewalled you yesterday. You've got to hit him harder.'

'Yeah, well. As Sarah says, thanks. We'll get to it.'

'Meanwhile, I'm calling off my people. Nobody else looks into it.'

'Nobody *else* implies somebody, though, huh? And that would be you?'

Hunt shook his head no. 'I'm leaving town.'

'That's a good idea. Keep Sarah from arresting you. Where are you going?'

'Indianapolis.'

'Of course you are. What's in Indianapolis?'

'Jim Jones.'

Juhle sat back in his chair, incredulous. 'That's your idea of not being in this?'

'I'm still looking for my mother's killer. I'm not out of that.'

'What if the same person is Orloff's killer?'

Hunt shrugged. 'If I find anything that points in that direction, I'll bring it to you and Sarah first. There doesn't have to be any conflict.'

'There'd better not be, Wyatt. If there even starts to be, you've got to back out. Sarah's not kidding about losing your license over it, if not worse, and that is no joke.'

'All right. I hear you.' Hunt reached out at last for his own cup and lifted the lid on it. 'But the fact remains, Spencer didn't answer at his house last night. Doorbell, phone, you name it. I waited around until after one and he never got home. The place was all lit up like a carnival.'

'So he went out, big deal.'

'Or didn't.'

'What do you . . .?' Juhle had to stifle a laugh. 'That imagination of yours just doesn't let up, does it? You think he's there and unable to answer the door or the phone? Unconscious? Dead?'

'Those are possibilities.'

'Well, we'll be sure to jump right on them.' Juhle lowered his voice and came forward in his chair. 'Let me ask you a question. You promise to tell me the truth?'

'If I can.'

'There's a heartening response.'

'It's what it is,' Hunt said. 'What's the question?'

'Did you let yourself in and find something?'

It was Hunt's turn to hold back his laughter. 'I would have,' he said, 'but I thought you guys would be mad at me. So my final answer, and it's the truth, is no.'

'You're sure?'

'I said "final answer," Regis. I don't know what's in the house. But I think maybe you should check it out.'

'And as I told you, we probably will as soon as we can get around to it.' He tapped a pen on his desk a few times. 'Just to let you know so you can rest easy, of course we think that Mr Spencer is a person of interest. But we don't typically want to talk too much to people like him until we've got something to talk about. So we're having his phone records checked, see if he called anybody from Original Joe's. And lest you think that we are uninterested in Mr Spencer's alibi, we have already verified that he left the restaurant alone about ten minutes before the shooting. We are trying our best to locate the cab and any other evidence that might present itself. Now, all this said, the possibility exists that Ivan was targeted for something unrelated to Mr Spencer, or to your mother's case. And we like to have an idea one way or the other before we start interrogating people so we don't get accused of harassment. Or stupidity.'

'All right.' Hunt stood up. 'Sooner would be better. That's all I'm saying.'

'Gotcha.' Juhle flashed a phony smile. 'Thanks for stopping by.'

Hunt had already packed. He had a flight to Minneapolis that left at 6:15, continuing to Indianapolis the next morning. But he stopped by the more than desultory office to underscore his directive that nobody was to do any work at all on his mother's case. If anybody – Juhle or Bernard or anybody else – called in on updates, they were to take no action. Just convey the messages to him. He understood that it had only been Tuesday – two days ago – when he'd sat them all down and included them in that investigation, but now because of what had happened to Ivan, he was taking them off it.

'But we don't even know Ivan was on that, not for sure.' Mickey sat on one of the credenzas against the windows in Hunt's office.

Hunt, on the couch next to Tamara, nodded in agreement. 'Maybe not. But I believe it with all my heart, and that's what I've got to go on, Mick. This guy's already been flushed once, and I don't think Ivan ever saw it coming. I don't want him to think this agency is somehow on his case. We're done with it, back to our regular work.'

'Except for you,' Tamara said.

'Right. Except for me. But I'm getting out of Dodge and letting Devin and Russo do their work here.' He half turned. 'Jill,' he asked, 'are you good with this?'

From the upholstered chair next to Hunt, Jill cast her gaze upward and blew out a deep sigh. Now, her eyes back on Hunt, with her fingertips she smoothed away the tears on her cheeks. 'I'm sorry,' she said. 'I'm afraid I'm not really listening. I'm still . . . I mean, I can see him sitting here just the other day.'

'I know,' Hunt said. 'It's brutal.'

Tamara reached over and placed a consoling hand over one of Jill's. 'It's all right,' she said. 'Not really listening, I mean. It's just so hard to imagine, or accept.'

Jill shook her head. 'I don't want to accept it, that's the problem. I want him back here, the way we were.'

'We all do,' Tamara said. Then again, 'We all do.'

Jill closed her eyes for a moment, gathering herself. Suddenly, she straightened her back. 'It's just so wrong,' she said.

'It is,' Hunt agreed. 'Which is why I don't want any of you out there working on any part of this, maybe giving this lunatic another target.'

Tentative, obviously coming to some kind of acceptance, Jill finally asked, 'So it's your assumption that the person who killed Ivan also killed your mother?'

'I think so. Yes.'

'We could help with this,' Jill continued.

'We want to,' Mickey added. 'Take down the son of a bitch.'

But Hunt shook his head. 'I appreciate that, both of you, I really do, but number one, Devin and Russo will have our heads if we show up around this thing at all. They promised me that this morning. I've given them all my notes. They know what we've got so far, and now the smartest thing we can do is just lie low. Make this guy think he's either scared us off or that Ivan was acting alone.'

'What's number two?' Tamara asked. 'Why we can't help?'

'Number two is it's just too risky. This madman sees any threat and he eliminates it. So I don't want any of you hitting his radar. Let the cops close in on him if they can.'

'You just said something that gave me an idea,' Jill said. 'He killed your mother because she was a threat.'

'To what?'

'I don't know. Something or somebody. At least it's a motive of some kind, and that's been missing all along, hasn't it? This is a reason she might have been killed.'

Hunt nodded. 'I'm going to keep that in mind, Jill. That's an interesting idea.'

'Okay, so what about your texter?' Mickey asked.

'What about my texter?'

Mickey shifted his position on the credenza, obviously unhappy with this whole strategy of disengagement. 'There ought to be some way we can reach out and try to make some contact again. Put an ad in the paper. Something.'

'And then what?' Hunt asked. 'This person doesn't want to go public, Mick. And because of Ivan, I think now we understand a little better why that is, don't we?'

An unsettled silence descended.

Until finally Mickey sighed. 'So what do we do, Wyatt? Just forget it?'

'That'd be best,' Hunt said. 'If the police have questions, answer them, but don't go to them and don't go out on your own. Especially don't meet with clients you don't know. Be aware if you find yourselves in sketchy areas. In fact, avoid them altogether.' He paused. 'And don't think I don't know you all think I'm paranoid. Maybe I am. But I'm still dealing with some issues about responsibility for Ivan . . .'

A small chorus of objections made Hunt raise a hand.

'Whether or not you agree with me, it's something I'm living with, okay? If I'd have known this was going to happen, I would have let my mother rest in peace, but now that it's gotten to here, I need to play it out. But none of you do.' He took a beat and met the eyes of his troops, one at a time. 'Really,' he said. 'Really really really.'

Jill and Mickey were back at their stations. Tamara closed the door to Hunt's office when they went out and now she and Hunt were both on their feet, facing each other, in the middle of a conversation.

'I just don't know what you hope to accomplish there,' Tamara said.

'I'm not too sure of that, either. Maybe nothing, but I've got to go and find out.'

'Find out what?'

'If there was any relationship between my mother and Jim Jones.'

'And what if there was? What does that get you?'

'I don't know. Knowledge. Motive. Certainty.'

'Again, Wyatt, about what?'

'About all these tenuous connections, Tam. Evie and Lionel Spencer, my mom and dad, Jonestown. Right now it's all just conjecture that all these things hook up at some point. There's a huge gap, and not just a time gap, in what happened. Everything in me is screaming for an answer to close up that gap, and I haven't been able to find it here, so I'm going there to look.'

She stood with her arms crossed, her jaw set. 'Okay, but everything in me is screaming for you not to go, Wyatt. I've got a very bad feeling about it. You should do what you ordered us all to do and just let this go. Let Devin handle it. It's his job now.'

'Maybe it's his job, but it's my mother. I've come this far. I need to know what happened to her. How it all happened. That's my job. That's my duty.'

'No, it isn't! That is just so wrong, Wyatt.' She moved a step closer to him. 'Listen. Don't you see? Your duty isn't to your mother anymore, if it ever was. She's long gone, Wyatt. Dead, dead, dead. It's Devin's duty, it's Devin's job, to find this killer, her killer.'

'Okay, but . . .'

'No "but." Your duty, your job, is to your future. If I'm going to believe everything we've said to each other in the last week, your duty is to our future, to you and me. Don't you see that? Don't you believe it?'

'I do believe it, Tam. But I've got to do this, too. I've got to find out.'

Tam's voice broke. 'What if finding out gets you killed, Wyatt? What about that? What am I supposed to do then?'

'I don't think that's going to happen.'

A bitter laugh. 'Yeah, well, Ivan didn't think it was going to happen, either. He never thought about it at all. And now look.'

Hunt hung his head, raised it back up. 'I'm not going to get killed. I'm going to go out there and find out what I need and then come back here and start our future without a killer hanging over our heads.'

She closed the last of the space between them, reached out, and grabbed him by both arms. 'Wyatt.' Her pleading voice near a whisper. 'Let's just get away from here, right now, me and you. Not someplace where you can work on this case. Just away, anywhere else. Let this whole thing work its way out, and when Devin makes his arrest in a day or a week, we come back and it's all over, just as if you'd been a part of it. Except we'd have had our time. We'd have started.'

'We have started, Tam. We're together.'

'We're not. Not yet.'

Wyatt exhaled completely, closing his eyes. 'Tam.'

'Just say yes.' Gripping his arms. 'Say yes, damn it!'

Letting out another breath, he couldn't dredge up the word.

Tamara let go of his arms, let her hands drop.

'I'm sorry,' Hunt said. 'I'll be back in a few days. We'll work this out then.'

19

Hunt landed at around midnight and checked in at his hotel in Minneapolis. When he got to his room, he dropped his bag by the bed and turned right away to go out again to the lobby bar, which was the only sign of life at the place, although it wasn't what he'd call hopping. Three men about his age, whom he took to be businessmen who'd be flying out about the same time he was next morning to another midwestern city, each sat a stool or two apart from one another, watching ESPN, eating from their little individual tray of nuts, sipping their cocktails.

Hunt picked a spot at the very end of the bar, where the TV wasn't quite facing him. A somewhat faded pretty redhead – her name tag said 'Adrienne' – placed a napkin in front of him. 'You just made it, hon. Last call's in five. What'll it be?'

Hunt didn't want a drink so much as he wanted company, although that wasn't exactly it, either. He didn't want to talk to anyone. He just didn't want to be physically alone. The entire drive down from the city to the San Francisco airport, and then during the flight out, he'd beaten himself up over his last moments with Tamara. His stomach had been knotted up back when he'd left his office, and it was knotted up now.

He'd called her when he'd landed and of course she hadn't picked up and he'd said, 'I'm sorry, but I don't think this is a mistake. I'll try to make it up to you.'

He wasn't sure he was going to be able to do that and it made him sick.

Now he gave Adrienne a weary smile and ordered a double Hendrick's on the rocks and she said, 'I don't have that. What is it?'

'Gin,' he said. 'Little round dark bottle?'

'Nope. Never heard of it. How about Beefeater?'

'An eminently fine drink,' he said. 'Beefeater would be fine.'

'Still double?'

'Sure.'

'Rocks?'

'Yep.'

'Vermouth?'

'I don't think so.'

'Olive or onion or lime?'

Hunt threw a grin at her. 'I've built model airplanes with less directions.'

She didn't take offense and smiled back at him. 'Just trying to get it right, honey. Gin drinkers can be darn persnickety.'

'I've heard about that. I'm not one of 'em.'

'Good for you. I'll breathe a little easier.' She moved off a few feet to his right, threw ice in a glass, and took the gin bottle from the well, free-pouring to the rim. 'So where you off to tomorrow?' she said as she put the drink on his napkin.

'Indianapolis.'

'Nice town. Super friendly folks.'

'That'd be nice. I could use some friendly.'

'You'll find it there,' she said. Moving off a couple of steps, she tapped on the bar. 'Last call, gentlemen.' For the next few minutes, she refilled glasses and chatted amiably with the other customers before coming back to stand in front of Wyatt. 'Top yours? Last chance.'

'Sure.'

She put the rim-filled drink back down in front of him and reached out her hand. 'Adrienne,' she said.

'I guessed.' Shaking her hand, Hunt said, 'Wyatt.'

'I love that name. I'm an OK Corral freak. I actually went to Tombstone three years ago on my vacation. You mind all this chattering?'

'No.'

'You sure?'

'Pretty much.'

''Cause I'd stop.'

'I think I just said I don't mind.'

'You did. I heard you.'

'Well, then.'

'So where you in from?'

'San Francisco.'

'And that's not a friendly town?'

Hunt shrugged. 'Sometimes not so much. It's colder than people think it is. But why do you ask that?'

'Because you just said you could use a little friendly. That sounded like you weren't getting a lot of it.'

Hunt twirled his glass. 'It's been a challenging couple of weeks,' he said. Then figured what the hell and came out with it. 'An employee of mine got killed on a job I sent him on.'

'Oh my God,' she said, 'that's awful.'

'Yeah. It is.' He paused. 'So maybe it's not so much unfriendly as just hard. If I hadn't . . . well, but I did.'

'That is hard, but these accidents happen.'

'It wasn't an accident. I'm a private investigator and he was murdered.'

The revelation backed her up a step, her hand to her mouth. 'Oh, Wyatt, honey,' she said. 'I am so sorry. That is truly terrible.'

'Yep.' He let out a long breath, sipped at his gin, forced a half smile. 'You mind all this chattering? 'Cause I'd stop.'

She patted his hand. 'You go ahead, hon. Whatever you need to say.'

'I'm out here . . . Indianapolis, I mean, I'm going there trying to run down some clues about his killer if I can. The woman I love thinks I'm a fool coming out here.'

'Why is that? 'Scuse me one sec.' The customer nearest to Hunt was pushing back his stool and she raised a hand to him. 'Thanks, hon,' she said. 'See you next time. Sleep tight.' And then he was gone and she came back to Hunt. 'So why would you be a fool doing what you're doing?'

'Because it might be dangerous. Because I feel like I need to.'

'He was your employee and you feel responsible?'

'Right. Dumb, maybe, but right.'

'But maybe not so dumb.'

'Tell that to Tamara.'

'Tamara! I just love your names out there, hon. I don't know I've ever met a Tamara. Wyatt and Tamara, I can just see the two of you together.'

'Maybe not for long. She thinks I'm betraying her. I don't know. Maybe I am. I love her, but I've got to do this.'

The two other guys tipped up their glasses and left their tips and got their good-nights from Adrienne, and when they were gone she came back down around the bar and pulled up a stool next to Hunt. 'I want to tell you a little story, Wyatt, and then I'm kicking your cute little ass out of here.

'After nine eleven, my husband, Matt, decided he had to join up. He felt it was his responsibility. I couldn't talk him out of it, and believe me, I tried. I tried and I tried and I tried. But he went anyway and sure enough got sent to Iraq and sure enough got himself killed over there.'

She sucked in a deep breath and then blew it out heavily. 'And all I can say is that I promise you, if he'd have come back, I would have forgiven him. I wouldn't have thought about it. I would have just been glad he was back. And oh, I hated him while he was gone and then for a while after, but that was who he was and I still don't regret that he was the man I picked to love. And I'd do it again, I swear.'

She sighed again, then reached over, picked up Hunt's drink, tacitly asked his permission, got a nod, and took a serious sip. 'People do what they gotta do, hon. Don't let her give up on the two of you, and don't you do it, either. Call her up. Keep her close. Goddamn it.'

Leaning over, she planted a quick kiss on his cheek. 'Now go on and get the hell out of my bar, Wyatt. And you sleep tight.'

The interrogation rooms just off the homicide detail were barely larger than closets, with room to hold only a small table and three chairs, one on one side, two on the other. A decade ago, moonlighting homicide cops had built them in their off-hours to save department budget dollars for their own overtime rather than waste that money on the city's union contractors who would probably screw up the job and take too long getting it done anyway.

Sadly, the jury-rigged version they wound up with contained some parts that did not perform as well as expected, either. For example, the video cameras, mounted at ceiling level, were supposed to record not just a voice but a suspect's face and mannerisms during interrogations. Unfortunately, the sight angle from its height was so steep that it could only capture the top of a suspect's head. In effect, the video camera was useless.

The insulation and ventilation in these rooms ranged from substandard to nonexistent. Hence, there was very little soundproofing, which not only made the audio tapes difficult to transcribe, but also created some embarrassment when inspectors in the detail, as sometimes happens, said unkind things and politically incorrect things about the folks being questioned in the booths. Or vice versa.

Finally, the rooms quickly become overheated when there

were two inspectors and hence three bodies packed inside the constrained space, but – a much worse problem from the inspectors' point of view – frequently the individuals being questioned were hygienically challenged.

Such a person was the twenty-four-year-old Hispanic male named Jesus Chavez, a.k.a. Chewey Shavez (his spelling), currently waiting for the return to the interrogation booth of either Devin Juhle or Sarah Russo. Those two inspectors had first gone into the room for the interrogation together, but within fifteen minutes, the combined heat and stench – for Chewey had apparently not bathed in at least two weeks, if then – necessitated a tactical retreat and a tag team approach that they'd been keeping up now for the past hour or so.

It was 10:15 p.m. in San Francisco.

Juhle looked at his watch, took a deep breath, and opened the interrogation room door again. Juhle was reminded of the Dumpster on the street outside of Original Joe's. 'How you holding up, Chewey? You ready to tell us something yet?'

'Hey. I already told you what I know. Everything I know. I didn't shoot no guy. He was already dead, on the ground, when I got to him.'

'But then you robbed him.'

'It was just his wallet. He didn't need it no more, now, did he?'

'And his cell phone.'

A shrug. 'Same thing.'

'The point is, Chewey, you were right there when Mr Orloff got popped and you profited from his death. Who's to say you didn't make some deal with the shooter to set it all up?'

'Aw, come on now, hey! With a cab? How's that happen?'

'I don't know, Chewey. That's why we're talking. We want you to tell us about the cab.'

'I mean, I don't know nothing about that cab. I was just sitting there like I do, chillin'. That spot, people give you their doggie bags some nights.'

'And you're just sitting there?'

'Like I said. And the cab pulls up at the curb and the window come down.'

'The passenger window?'

'Yeah.'

'The front seat passenger window?'

'Right.'

'Is there a passenger in the cab?'

'Not that I see. I mean, nobody's in the front and nobody's getting out the back.' An elaborate shrug. 'It's a cab coming to pick up somebody at the restaurant. Happens alla time.'

'So there's just the driver in the cab?'

'That I see.'

'Okay, what did he look like?'

Chewey rolled his eyes. '*Cabrón*. Do I look?'

'That's what I'm asking. Did you look?'

'I'm sitting on the sidewalk, minding my business. That's all I'm doing.'

'Yeah, but, Chewey' – Juhle putting a little edge into it – 'here's the thing. You're telling me that you're sitting there and that's all you're doing. But what that really means is that you're doing *nothing*. It's not like you're playing a video game or something. You're not into sudoku, are you?'

'That like some kind of karate?'

'Kind of,' Juhle said. 'The point is, you're not doing it – sudoku, karate, video games, whatever. You're just sitting there and a cab drives up and, what, pulls over?'

'Yeah. Like waiting for his ride, the guy who called him, you know.'

'So how long was he there, pulled over?'

'I don't know. A minute, five minutes.'

'And he's where? In front of you?'

'No. Down the street a ways.'

'Ten feet? Twenty feet?'

'Yeah.'

'Which one, Chewey?'

'I don't know. One of 'em.'

'Okay, then. Either way, here's the question: What else are you doing if you're not looking at the cab?'

'All right, I see the cab, but I'm not looking at it. I mean, it's a cab. I seen 'em before. What I look at it for?'

'You don't see the driver?'

'I must have, you just said. But I don't remember.'

'Even after the gunshot? He's ten feet away and just shot somebody almost right in front of you and you didn't happen to glance at who was doing the shooting?'

'The driver, you mean?'

Juhle cocked his head. 'Who we been talking about all this time, Chewey? The driver. Did you see the driver at any time?'

'All right, yeah.'

'There you go,' Juhle said with real satisfaction. 'How hard was that?'

'But I don't know him. I'm not, like, doing something with him.'

'No. We really didn't think you were. But the point is you saw him. What'd he look like?'

'Like a white man.'

'Old? Young?'

'Old. White hair. No beard or nothing. Just a face.'

Juhle sat back in some triumph, not just to get a little distance on the smell. 'You think you'd recognize him if you saw him again?'

'I doubt it. It was just like a second he's driving off. I wasn't really looking.'

'No, I guess you were looking at the dead guy you were fixing to rob.'

A vacant grin of sublime indifference. 'Mostly that, yeah.'

It took much if not all of Juhle's forbearance not to reach across the table and bitch slap this poor fool, and he still might have done it if there hadn't been a knock on the door. Exhaling heavily, he reached over and was looking at Russo.

'They found the cab,' she said.

20

After he left the bar downstairs, Hunt got to his room and picked up his small travel suitcase, placing it on the bed. He had just started unzipping it when he stopped and straightened up, looking around quickly from side to side, something like little bright exploding yellow lights nibbling at the edge of his vision.

Nothing there, except those pinpoints of light no matter which way he turned to focus on them.

Bringing his hands up to the sides of his head, he pushed at his temples. A sudden wave of vertigo threatened his balance for a minute and he pulled a chair up behind him and sat down on it, the back of his head suddenly struck with a searing blast of pain. Squinting against the room's dim light, he went back over how many drinks he'd had – two and a half at the most. Certainly not enough for this reaction, he knew.

Now he lay fully clothed on the bed in his dark room at the airport hotel. The pinpoints had continued to explode, even when he closed his eyes, and very much in the manner of a fireworks display, on what felt like the periphery of his vision, except that they had changed color to a dull pewter and expanded into Rorschach blobs that disintegrated with a viscosity that reminded him of motor oil.

The cab, now cordoned off by a fence of yellow crime-scene police tape, was in the last parking place on Van Ness Avenue at the end of the street near the back entrance to Fort Mason where it abutted Aquatic Park. Beyond it, the Municipal Pier jutted out into the bay. Overhead, eucalyptus and cypress branches clawed at the dark sky, silhouetted by the glow from the streetlights.

In Juhle's city-issue, he and Sarah pulled up and parked next to a lone black-and-white police car from which a couple of patrolmen emerged with flashlights. After the brief introductions and sharing of IDs, Russo nodded over toward the vehicle.

'So who reported this?' she asked.

The two patrolmen looked at one another for a second trying to decide who would do the talking.

'Anybody? Anybody?' Juhle prompted them with his best imitation of Ferris Bueller's teacher.

The tall black one, Thomas, said, 'It was a little bit roundabout. This cab here picked up three parking tickets at this same spot yesterday and today. So finally the traffic-detail guy notices it's the same cab and instead of just putting a boot on it and calling in a tow, he calls Yellow, who it turns out's been looking for this thing since it didn't check back in two nights ago.'

'We called them, didn't we?' Juhle asked.

'I vaguely remember it,' Russo said. 'And I believe they told us that all their cars came back in.'

'Except this one, which apparently they forgot.'

'Apparently. Maybe they were busy and didn't have time to check thoroughly.'

'Maybe. But we know the car, we know the last pickup, don't we?'

'I believe we could identify it, Devin. Given some time.'

Juhle turned back to the somewhat bewildered patrolmen. 'So then what?'

'Then, I think somebody at Yellow must have remembered

your call, since they called in downtown and reported that we'd found it and where. Then dispatch sent us down to watch it until you got here.'

'All right, thanks. Good job. Can I see your beam? Anybody call a tow?'

'Not yet.' Thomas handed over his flashlight. 'You want me to?'

'Give us a minute,' Juhle said, and started down to the cab.

Russo trailing by a step. 'What do you think?' she asked.

'I'm not thinking.' He shined the flashlight's beams across the windshield, over the parking tickets stuck under the wipers. Crossing in front of the car, at the driver's window he leaned over close, shading his eyes against the glare so he could see inside, and shone the light down over the front seats. 'Uh-oh,' he said, straightening up.

'What do you got?' Sarah asked.

'You tell me. Take a look.'

He shone the light in again, backing off so she could lean over and see inside. She stayed down there for a long moment, then straightened. 'That black stain?'

'Yep.'

'But that makes no sense. He didn't get shot in the car. He shot somebody from inside the car.'

'Right.' Juhle was walking, quickly now, back around the front to the other side, where he shone the light on the driver's-side window. 'You see it?'

Russo leaned down and squinted.

'On the window inside.'

Russo nodded soberly. 'It could be.'

'Give me another minute. Time for some gloves, too.'

Juhle trudged back up the street to his car, reached in, and popped open the trunk, then went back there and pulled out a strip of metal, which he brought with him back to the cab. 'Did

I ever tell you that before I was a cop I used to boost cars?' He was pulling his own latex gloves on.

Going around again to the passenger side, Juhle slid the jimmy down next to the window and jockeyed around for a minute or so until, finding the purchase he wanted, he pulled and the door's locks came up.

'Okay now.'

With great care, he pulled open the door. Again he shone the light, now without a glaring window between him and the seat. Then he brought the light up to the passenger window, the door under it. Straightening up, he blew out hard enough to puff out his cheeks. 'Patrolman Thomas,' he said over the car, 'call homicide and have them send a crime-scene unit down here right away.'

Next, leaning down now, back into the car, he reached to a point underneath the steering wheel and pulled the lever to release the trunk. Behind him, Sarah Russo was already moving, at the trunk in a couple of steps, and lifting the hood. The streetlights gave only feeble illumination, but it was enough to get the general idea, and Juhle's flashlight beam took away any vestige of doubt about what they were looking at.

'Patrolman Thomas. While you're at it, get the coroner's van down here as well.'

The man in the trunk was identified as Ahmed I. Muhammed, and he had been the driver of record. He had been shot once in the left temple at point-blank range, by someone standing outside the car. The bullet, the same size slug used with Orloff, was embedded in the car door on the passenger side.

They were hoping that the computerized dispatch records at Yellow Cab might reveal an address or phone number to which the cab had been called close to the time of Orloff's death, which was around 7:30. But the last pickup of record, to an address on

Green Street, had been at 4:48, pretty far outside of their window. And while they might have to contact that phone number and identify the caller tomorrow, neither inspector believed for a minute that it had anything to do with the crime. Apparently, Mr Muhammed preferred to troll the streets keeping an eye out for the random fare, or at least he had done that last Tuesday night. His pickup on Green put him near some high-foot-traffic real estate – Cow Hollow, the Marina, Polk Street – and he could easily have kept himself busy that way for the rest of his shift.

Or until he picked up his murderer.

'You think he picked him up?' Sarah asked Juhle as they stood around shivering in the mist, waiting for Lennard Faro, the crime-scene specialist, to finish his on-site examination before they towed the cab down to the police garage and took it apart.

'Had to. He had to get someplace quiet and secluded where he could get out, pretend to be paying him by the driver's window, and pop him. Then reach in, pull him out, and get him in the trunk. Not easy, and impossible if he's anywhere near people.'

Russo looked around. 'This is a good spot for that.'

'Yeah, but it could have been anywhere. Doesn't matter. He wound up coming here eventually.'

'So why didn't he just dump the body?'

'He wanted to buy himself a couple of days. And see? It worked. Not that I think it's going to do Mr Spencer too much good.'

Sarah stomped her feet and hugged herself. 'I'm getting tired of just standing around. You want to go get him now? I say we've got enough.'

'I'd agree. To question him with gloves off anyway. Unless you've got another old guy with white hair you want to talk to.'

'No. He'd be my favorite.'

'Good. Let's leave this party to Lennard and go wake somebody up.'

*

It was a very short, very steeply uphill drive to the Larkin Street home of Lionel Spencer. They parked at the curb in front and again rang the bell by the gate in the fence. By now it was closer to two a.m., but the lights were still on inside.

When there was no answer on the third ring, Juhle said, 'Remember he told us he often doesn't hear the bell.'

'I remember. Sometimes the delivery people have to come back twice.'

'Exactly. Talk about hell.'

'Yeah. Maybe I'll call him.'

'Sure. Do that.' After four rings, she got his answering machine and said, 'Mr Spencer. This is Inspector Russo. If you're home right now, we've been ringing your bell outside and would like to come in and talk to you. If you're not, would you please give me a call as soon as you get this message? Thanks.'

Juhle turned to her. 'So now what?'

'Call me a wimp, but I'm thinking about some sleep.'

'Wimp. But sleep would work. And tomorrow, a warrant. How's that sound?'

He held up a fist and she bumped it with one of her own. 'Winner,' she said.

21

THE INDIANAPOLIS CHILD protective services had a familiar feel, and with some reason. The same kind of people were doing the same kind of critical, frustrating, boring, dangerous, mind-numbing work that Hunt had done for most of a decade of his earlier life. Street-smart and edgy case workers and hard-core bureaucrats waged their perpetual wars on one another all in the name of what was best for the children, when in fact very few of the solutions were good ones, just better than the alternatives.

Hunt wasn't in the front door of the huge, bland office building for five minutes before he felt as though he could draw a flow chart about how the whole place worked, or didn't.

The difference to him, of course, is that he didn't have a Bettina Keck to run interference for him. He was simply an out-of-state nuisance who wasn't really part of anyone's job description. And so at a little after two o'clock, after the puddle-jumper flight to Indianapolis, after his headache had finally, mostly, passed, and after three or four stops at various CPS substations, he wound up talking to an obvious lifer in Records with a name tag that read 'John Edmonds.' And he hadn't gotten very far with him before Edmonds was shaking his bald head, peering over the tops of his half-lens glasses, an 'are you kidding me?' expression pretty much eliminating the need for Hunt to go on talking, so he wrapped it up quickly. 'No, huh?'

'I'm afraid not. No chance. All the records that far back have been destroyed.'

'That's what they told me in San Francisco, too, but it turned out nobody actually got around to doing that job, and they were stuck in the basement.'

'Yes, well, that didn't happen here. We went over to computers in the early nineties, and a command decision was made to destroy all the old records where the children would have been thirty or older. We're talking sixty years' worth of files, maybe more. And I know because I was part of the team that shredded them. It took the better part of two months full-time for six of us if you want to talk tedious. And remember, this was nearly twenty years ago, so these people, the people in those destroyed records, would be at least fifty or so now. Whatever happened to them as kids, I don't care what it was, it wouldn't matter too much anymore, would it?'

'I can appreciate that,' Hunt said. 'But I guess my question remains. Is it possible that some of these records might have fallen through the cracks?'

'Why would they? What cracks? We started at the front of the storage facility and moved through it to the back. Now the place – the old warehouse? – it's a roller derby rink, if you can believe that. So no, there weren't any cracks. We cleaned it out and the state sold the building off a couple of years later and that's all there is to it.'

Fighting his fatigue and frustration, Hunt forced a smile. 'All right, John, let me ask you just one more. This is my mother I'm talking about and I just flew two thousand miles to find out a couple of answers about her childhood. I think she had been in some trouble when she was a kid, and I think whatever it was does still matter very much in the here and now. You've been in this business a long time. If you wanted to find something about her, where would you look?'

'Well, really, then, there's only one possibility, and that's the newspapers.' Edmonds scratched behind his ear. 'Although you got a major problem with them, too. And not just the fact that there's not gonna be an index telling you where you might find something. Your eyeballs do all the walking, step by step, and that's if you're lucky and there's still copies of old editions somewhere on microfiche. So good luck with that. But the biggest problem is if your mother was a minor when she was having these problems, even if they were newsworthy events, they're not gonna have her name in the paper, now, are they?'

Hunt spent forty-five minutes driving into downtown and parking, then another hour in the redbrick multistory headquarters of *The Indianapolis Star*, getting bounced around. Adrienne had been right about the friendliness quotient of the locals; everybody he chatted with wanted to help, although nobody had any good idea about how to find what he was looking for, so they passed him along to somebody else who might.

The last of these was a woman of about sixty named Lynn Sheppard, who was in the middle of a coffee break in the staff lounge when Hunt found her, introduced himself, gave her his card, and went into the short version of his spiel, at the end of which she said, 'If you'll pardon me saying so, young man, you look exhausted.'

Hunt acknowledged the sentiment with a chuckle and a nod. 'I guess I am a little tired. It shows, does it?'

'Just a bit.' She pointed at her cup. 'The coffee in here really isn't as bad as you'd think. And the price is right.'

'You sold me.'

'You sit down, dear. I know where the mugs are.'

Two minutes later, they were sitting across from one another at a metal and plastic table, both with their hands around their steaming mugs. 'To address your main question,' Lynn said, 'you're not likely to be able to find a child in the newspaper in the late 1960s unless there was some major news story associated with her. Caylee Anthony, Casey's baby, that kind of thing? Did your mother have any kind of notoriety like that?'

'Not until she was murdered, but that was in San Francisco.'

'Oh, my dear, I am so sorry.'

Hunt shrugged. 'That, too, was a long time ago. Nineteen seventy.'

'Still.' Lynn let out a wistful breath. 'You were a baby.'

'Three years old. I really have no memory of it.'

She cocked her head to the side. 'It would be interesting if that were true.'

'It's pretty true,' he said.

'As a reporter, I've learned that pretty true and true are often not the same thing.'

Hunt hesitated, broke a small smile. 'Okay. Lately, a few things have started coming back. I think maybe I sublimated some stuff when I was young to get through it. If it would let me sleep, that's what I'd still be doing.'

'Sublimating?'

'Ignoring, maybe.'

'But it's not letting you sleep?'

A sheepish grin. 'Sleep does seem to be taking a hit. But as soon as I get to the bottom of this, everything ought to go back the way it was. That's what I keep telling myself.'

'And isn't it pretty to think so?'

'What does that mean, Mrs Hemingway?'

'It means that things don't go back to the way they were. That never happens. You learn something, you feel something, and it changes you forever. And then you adjust to the new you.'

'The new me. I can't wait.'

Lynn sat back and scrutinized him carefully. 'Wyatt. It is Wyatt, right? When you first came in here, you said you were looking for some advice on how to find information about your mother when she was a young girl. Now you tell me she was murdered and you're trying to get to the bottom of that. But that search is having more of an impact on you than you want to admit, isn't it?'

Hunt gathered his thoughts for a moment, unable to raise his eyes to look at her.

'I'm prying,' she said. 'Professional failing, I'm afraid. I'm sorry.'

'No. That's all right. You're right. It's kind of ripping me up, to tell you the truth. It's like this current, this undertow. I don't know what it is. Churning everything up. I'm just trying to do my job and it's like something is stopping me. Stopping my body. Like with the sleep thing. I can't get focused. Everything goes so far and then just shuts down and stops. I think it should be obvious by now, but I can't get my arms around it. It's like I don't really want to find out what I need to know, like I don't trust who I am.'

'Maybe it's a scary thing. Maybe you're afraid of it.'

'I can't rule that out. But if that's it, it's not conscious.'

'It sounds like your conscious and your subconscious are at war with one another.'

'That's what it feels like, too. I can't seem to get control over it.'

'And control is a big thing?'

'Are you kidding? It's the main thing.'

'Really?' She skewered him with a penetrating look. 'It sounds like some part of you doesn't want to let you believe that.'

'Now, that,' he said, 'would be scary. That is not happening.'

'All right, all right.' She shifted in her chair, reached for her coffee and sipped. 'So what are you really trying to find?'

'Really? What I said. I'm here to find my mother. The truth about my mother. Why she was murdered.'

'In San Francisco? In 1970? And you think you'll find out something about that here in Indianapolis back in the sixties? How does that happen?'

Hesitating, Hunt drummed his fingers on the table. 'This sounds far-fetched, I know, but I'm trying to verify if she had a connection to Jim Jones.'

'Jim Jones.' Lynn Sheppard went still for a long beat. 'What kind of connection? How old would she have been?'

'Eleven to fifteen, somewhere in there. I'm thinking she might have been . . . I don't know the word. Abused.'

'*Raped* would be the word, Wyatt. A grown man has sex with an eleven-year-old, it's rape. You think Jones might have killed her?'

'No. Whoever did that, he's still alive, I'm sure. I think he killed one of my associates in San Francisco the other night.'

She leveled her gaze at him, pushed farther back from the table, and crossed her legs. 'You're telling me you're working on a forty-year-old murder case that stretches down into the present that might have a tie to Jim Jones?'

'Yeah, but I can't prove any of it. It's all conjecture.'

'What would you need to prove it?'

Hunt shrugged. 'Somebody who knew my mother back then. Some kind of record. I don't know. That's what I'm here to find out. Although the trail, again, seems to stop here.'

'And if you do prove it? If Jones was raping her, then what?'

'Then we're that much closer to knowing why my mother was killed, and my associate, too, and maybe even who did it.'

Lynn, her coffee forgotten, her eyes locked on the middle distance between herself and Hunt, seemed to reach some decision and brought her hands together. 'Wyatt,' she said, 'you might not know exactly what you're looking for, but I've got to tell you that you're one hell of a motivator.'

'I am? What am I motivating?'

'Not what, who. And the answer is me.' She stood up. 'Do you realize what you've got here? You've got a long-dead case, multiple murders, a tortured private investigator, child abuse, Jim Jones and Jonestown. You know what that spells?' She waited a second. '*Pulitzer*.'

Hunt wound up talking to Lynn Sheppard at her desk in the city room for another hour or so, bringing her up to date on as many of the details of his investigation as he could remember. Taking notes on her computer, with every twist she seemed more galvanized, from the earliest text messages (But who is sending them? And why? You don't have any idea?), then Wyatt's father and the letter he'd left him, to the labyrinthine hunt for Evie See Christ/Spencer, the undoubted and verifiable correlation to Jonestown, if not to Jim Jones himself, and finally to the murder this week of Ivan Orloff.

Wyatt told her that the next day he planned to go visit the Disciples of Christ main office in Indianapolis as well as the Human Relations Commission, with both of which Jones had been closely involved. There might be some oldster or historian in or around one of those organizations who remembered his mother and her relationship, if any, to Jones. From there, Hunt would play it by ear, but if nothing substantive about his mother materialized, he would leave his card with a lot of people and hope something turned up, and then planned to fly back home in time for Ivan's memorial service on Saturday, when he would try to patch things up with Tamara and hope that Juhle had something positive to report on Ivan's murder.

Finally, realizing anew that he'd slept very little and eaten not at all last night or today, he cut things off with Lynn. She was going to go to her own collection of sources, some of them ancient, all of them confidential, and see what she could dig up, and she'd get in touch with him if she had any success.

By the time he got back to his car, it was rush hour. Hunt had turned his cell phone off while he'd been in the newspaper building, and now he checked it – he had thirty-seven e-mails, no text messages, and fourteen voice mails, including two from Juhle and none from Tamara. He punched up Juhle's first voice mail: 'Your case is solved, dude,' his friend said. 'Might as well come on home, although nobody misses you, so you could also stay away and no one would care.'

Hunt sat at the counter of the restaurant in his hotel. In front of him was a glass of milk. On his plate was what little remained of a large serving of breaded pork tenderloin, an Indianapolis specialty of which he was sure Mickey would not approve. Nevertheless, it hit the spot at the moment – hearty, bland, comforting, filling. Mashed potatoes and a really pretty good red cabbage dish as the sides rounded everything out nicely.

He felt the buzz of his cell phone at his belt before he heard its guitar-strumming ringtone. He'd played phone tag and left a message with Juhle and didn't plan to pick up for anyone except him or Tamara, and sure enough, here he was.

'What do you mean, the case is solved?'

'Is there a possible second meaning?'

'Come on. Talk to me.'

'I will. After a backbreaking day of following up leads and talking to idiots, we found the cab last night, abandoned down by Maritime Park. There was a dead guy in the trunk. Shot in the head.'

'Another dead guy.'

'Yeah. The driver. So meanwhile I'd had this scintillating discussion with a crackhead gentleman named Chewey who had seen the shooter in the cab down at Original Joe's and described him as Caucasian, old, and white-haired, which you may not know happens to fit the description of your favorite person named Spencer.'

'Lionel.'

'The very same.'

'So what happened?'

'Easy, I'm getting there. So Maritime Park is, like, just down the street from Spencer's place, and Sarah and I go up in the middle of the night and it's still lit up the way you described it. But nobody answers when we ring.'

'He ran. He killed Ivan and then ran.'

'Not really. He was busier than that. He killed the cabbie, then killed Orloff, then went home and must have gotten nervous that we were going to catch him, which we were about to, and either execute him or throw him in jail for the rest of history, not just for Orloff but for your mother, too. And the cabbie. So instead, he went into his nice telescope room and shot himself in the head.'

'Are you sure?'

'Am I sure he shot himself in the head? It's kind of a hard thing to miss, Wyatt.'

'No, are you sure it was him? A suicide.'

'Pretty much. We're running ballistics on the gun, and we've got a slug from the cabbie, which is the same caliber as Orloff. It's about as clean as you can get, dude. He killed these people because your man was getting close, and then freaked out when he realized he was going to get caught, and soon.'

Hunt forced himself to swallow. 'So he killed my mother, too.'

'That's got to be our assumption, don't you think?'

'I don't know. It's just so . . . I mean, this was fast, Dev. From nothing to done.'

'That's how it happens sometimes. You ought to feel good about it.'

'I know. But there's still Ivan and . . . the others. I don't feel like dancing.'

'No. I hear you. Of course. But still . . .'

'Still. Jesus.'

'Yeah.' Juhle took a beat. 'You fly safe,' he said.

'I will. See you.'

22

After he signed for his dinner bill, Hunt went upstairs to his generic airport hotel room. He lowered himself into the desk chair and looked out the window over the runways to the flat landscape beyond. The sun was low enough to now appear sporadically but not brightly under the cloud cover, a brooding blood-orange ball. Every few minutes, an airplane would take off or land in the foreground to an accompanying roar that the window did little to mitigate.

Hunt was so bone tired that he felt nearly tethered to the chair but paradoxically felt no urge to push himself up, cross the room, and lie down on the bed. Not only was it too early, but also he hadn't worked out the details of his deep dissatisfaction with the news that Juhle had delivered.

If Lionel Spencer had been Ivan's killer, and his mother's, then the question about Hunt's texter might forever remain unanswered, and that was profoundly unsettling. Hunt had envisioned in a nebulous way that the solution of the one mystery would somehow provide a key to the second. Instead, they now had a dead suspect and a conveniently solved case that, for Hunt, left as many questions as it resolved.

He tried calling Tamara and left a voice message when she didn't pick up.

Hunt had to go on the assumption that his texter's life would be somehow improved, and perhaps drastically, by the solution to his mother's murder. Else why bother with the whole exercise to begin with? And from all Hunt knew, Spencer lived alone. So Hunt guessed the next question would be, to whom would his death make a difference? And he had no idea, not a soul to consider.

Beyond that, Hunt had an issue with the supposed motivation for Lionel to have killed himself. Was it because the police were going to deduce, perhaps already had figured out, that he'd killed Orloff and the cabbie? Would this make a cold-blooded killer – as Lionel must have been to have wasted his two victims so mechanically – decide to take his own life? Without any kind of fight or legal battle? It seemed an untenable stretch.

And yet, apparently, that's exactly what Lionel had done. And how did you argue with uncontested facts? Hunt would, of course, find out the details from Juhle, but they must have been damn convincing if the two homicide inspectors accepted the scenario they appeared to support.

Hunt placed another call to Tamara, which again went unanswered, and this time he did not leave a message, which would have been the same as the first.

At last, as the sun settled below the horizon, Hunt opened his laptop and reserved his flights out of town for the next day. The best option, maddeningly, leaving here at eleven for Minneapolis, another couple of hours of layover there, then the flight to San Francisco that would get him in at five o'clock Saturday, thank God for the time change.

Reserving the flights took him twelve minutes.

Dusk now well advanced, Hunt broke down and texted her: *I hate not talking to you. Do you realize we've talked just about every day for the past three years? I don't know what to do without your input. I'm sorry about our disagreement. I understand why you're mad. But people who love each other can disagree and be mad and get through it, it's a proven fact. It will probably happen again sometime with us. I want to be with you. If you'd call me, I could grovel appropriately and tell you in person that I'm coming home. Juhle says the case is solved, so maybe I didn't need to come out here after all, which was, I believe, your opinion to begin with. Call me. Please.*

Hunt put his phone on the desk next to his computer and, closing his eyes, brought his hands again up to his temples. He'd been trying to ignore the onset of the little pinpoints of light that had presaged his headache the night before, but it was becoming more difficult. Popping now like flashbulbs going off at the periphery of his vision, the light show finally prodded him into movement.

In the bathroom, all the lights out in the room because lights seemed to make it worse, he swallowed four aspirin and then soaked a washcloth in cold water. Now lying on the bed in his clothes, he draped the wet cloth over his eyes and tried to will his mind into emptiness.

What the hell was this?

Last night, the pain had kicked in – a steel band tightened down over his temples and around his head – and had nearly made him black out, but there was very little of that tonight, at least not yet. Just a coming and going sense of vertigo and nausea that getting horizontal seemed to help.

He'd eventually fallen asleep, he supposed. The light show had dissipated and though still disoriented, he got over to where his cell phone was ringing on the desk, without any dizziness. The phone's clock said that three hours had passed.

'Hey.'

'Hey.'

'Thank you for calling,' he said.

'Are you all right? Did I wake you up?'

'A little.'

'That's an automatically wrong answer, Wyatt. I can call back tomorrow.'

'No. Now's good. Don't hang up.'

'I won't. You don't sound good.'

'I'm having this weird headache, though it's gone now. I was just taking a nap.'

'What's weird about the headache?'

'I don't know. It's like exploding lights and it's hugely painful.'

'You're having a migraine, Wyatt. Have you seen a doctor? No, let me guess.'

'Tam, it's just a headache.'

'Unless it's an aneurism or spinal meningitis or something.'

'Then it wouldn't go away, or I'd be dead. Anyway, it's gone now.' He paused. 'I've taken a few aspirin.'

'Oh, okay, then, we don't have to worry about it anymore.'

'Are we having another fight? I don't want another fight.'

'It's probably still part of the first one.'

'Probably. Maybe we could declare a truce.'

He heard the relief in her voice. 'A truce would be good. I'd vote for a truce.'

'All right, truce.'

'So how's it been going there?'

'Pretty much a waste of time. Nice people, decent food, no information. It's all too old. You were probably right. I shouldn't have come.'

'Except you felt you had to.'

'Yeah, except that. Stupidly.'

'Maybe not. You didn't know that then. I'm sorry I freaked out. So,' she continued, 'has Devin really got a suspect in all this?'

'Better. A suspect who killed himself rather than get arrested. Lionel Spencer.'

'Really?'

'That's the word.'

'So when are you coming home?'

'Barring unforeseen developments, I've got tickets for

tomorrow. I should be in around dinnertime, if you're going to be free.'

'I could clear my calendar.'

'That would be nice.'

'What unforeseen developments, though?'

'If I knew that, they wouldn't be unforeseen, would they? But I've got a reporter looking into a few things. Maybe she'll get lucky.'

'She?'

'Lynn.'

'Is she pretty?'

'Gorgeous. Pretty much a Reese Witherspoon look-alike. Except not.'

'And if she finds something, you'll be staying?'

'Depends on what it is. It's not impossible, but it's not very likely, either. And since Devin's already got Spencer, it would have to be pretty dramatic, don't you think?'

'I'm just saying. You're already there. If you need to stay on, just let me know, would you? We'll have a dinner date another night. Maybe a whole bunch of them before we're through. I'll understand, promise.' A short silence hung on the line. 'Why don't you call me when you're getting on the plane? Or if you're not.'

Hunt never got back to sleep. The three hours he'd crashed between dinner and Tamara's call was all he managed. Sometime in the dead dark, he'd gotten up and poured himself two miniature bottles of vodka from the honor bar in his room and drank them off neat, hoping they'd help knock him out.

They didn't.

At eight o'clock, he got the phone call from Lynn Sheppard. She had something, but didn't want to say what it was over the phone. Yes, it was substantive, possibly conclusive. Yes, he had to come down and see her, how about ten? And yes, it might take up a good portion of the rest of the day.

So Hunt left a message with Tamara and then canceled his flights.

Stretched out on his bed, hands over his eyes, he tried to control his breathing against the incessant throbbing in his head. Desperate to summon another solid block of sleep – an hour, ninety minutes, anything – he stayed in bed as long as he could before he absolutely had to get up if he was to be on time. But some internal voice had seemed to keep insisting that if he slept, he would just have another nightmare.

His brain wouldn't simply shut up and let him be.

The upshot being that when he finally gave up on sleep and got moving, he didn't have time to shave or shower or even put on a new set of clothes.

It was all right, he told himself, he'd catch up with all of that after he found out what Lynn had discovered. In his bathroom, he saw that he still looked okay, certainly presentable, if a little the worse for wear. He swallowed four aspirin, then for breakfast grabbed a to-go black coffee from the urn in the hotel's lobby.

Now, at ten o'clock, Hunt was back at the redbrick *Indianapolis Star* building, checking in at the guard desk. Lynn, who seemed herself to be running on adrenaline and caffeine, appeared from somewhere in the building and as she walked with him to her cubicle in the city room, she couldn't hold in her enthusiasm.

'I'm just so glad I caught you before you got on that plane, Wyatt. And I didn't mean to be coy with you on the phone, but things like this, you don't want to say too much to anybody, even somebody as closely involved as you are. Word gets out, and next thing you know, there's your story under somebody else's byline. Especially in today's world, you might text somebody who puts it on Facebook, and next thing you know it goes viral and then where are you? Out to lunch is where.'

'No problem,' Hunt said, though in actual fact he was truly frustrated. 'But I really wasn't out shopping this to anybody else.'

'I'm not saying you were, dear. Of course not. It's just the world we live in. And the fact that I've come to believe in this story of yours, more so now than ever. Just pull up a chair there and let me show you what I've got.'

'That's what I'm here for.'

She sat down across from him at her desk and took several sheets of paper out of her briefcase and passed them over to Wyatt.

The first was a Xerox of a portion of a newspaper page from 1964, featuring a picture of a man who appeared to be in his midthirties standing surrounded by a half dozen teenage girls in the serving line of what was identified in the caption as a soup kitchen. Four of the children were African-American, but there was one pretty white girl whom the caption identified as Margie Page.

Hunt's mother at fifteen.

To Wyatt, exhausted and wired at the same time, it felt like all the blood was draining from his face. Before he even turned to the next picture, he raised his eyes and looked across at Lynn Sheppard. 'How in the world did you find this?'

She leaned back, beaming, the pride in her work exuding from her every pore. 'Well, as we realized yesterday, the odds of finding your mother by just looking randomly through old newspapers were about zero. On the other hand, sometime late last night it occurred to me that Jim Jones really had quite a large profile in the city when he lived here. He was all over the place.' She pointed to the picture he was holding. 'That soup kitchen, for example. He set up several of them. And a couple of nursing homes. All kinds of stuff. And he was just a pure publicity junkie, in the paper for one thing or another at least every week or two.'

Hunt turned to the second page, another photograph from

another old newspaper, another picture of his teenage mother as part of a group with Jones, this time at the dedication of a teen center fostering to racial equality.

'So I thought,' Lynn went on, 'if in fact he's got a special relationship with one of these young people, with your mother, for example, Wyatt, then there'd be some chance that among all of his photo ops, she'd show up in a couple, like Monica Lewinsky somehow winding up next to Clinton in all those pictures. At least it was a shot. And, as it turned out, a good one.'

Hunt, his pulse pounding in his temples, turned to the next page. And the next. In all, there were seven of them from 1961 through 1964.

As he turned to the final page, Lynn said, 'But this last one's the real winner.'

Hunt saw nothing particularly special at first glance. As usual, Jones stood surrounded by a group that included Margie Page as one of the few white people, but this last photograph was more formal, depicting as it did the investiture of Jones as a minister in the Disciples of Christ. This time, perhaps fifteen people bore witness to Jones's charisma and popularity, and each of them – the church's lay leadership – was identified in the caption. The person standing and smiling on the left side of Margie Page, her arm around her as she stood right next to Jones, was identified as Susan Page.

'Her mother,' Hunt said.

Lynn's smile breaking again. 'Yes, I believe it is. Amazing, isn't it?'

Hunt couldn't take his eyes off the picture.

'That's not all,' Lynn said, patting her laptop in a proprietary manner. 'As soon as I got it, I looked up Susan Page on Google.'

'And found forty million of them?' Hunt asked.

'Fifty, but close enough. Then I turned to our great and true friend, LexisNexis.'

'How many did you get there?'

'Low thousands. Not too bad, but still a little inconvenient. But then look for a Susan Page who has a daughter named Margaret and you're at sixteen hundred fifty. And next you add Indianapolis to the search and that gets you down to twenty-one. Twenty-one you can actually go through the individual records line by line. A little painstaking, but possibly productive.'

'You ever want a job in California,' Hunt said with real admiration breaking through his fatigue, 'come and look me up.' He pointed at the computer. 'So we're down to twenty-one?'

Lynn shook her head, enjoying every minute. 'No, we're down to three. I figured if your mother was born around '48, '49, then her mother must have been somewhere between roughly twenty and thirty-five when she had her, so that's a fifteen-year window for Susan's date of birth. Nineteen thirteen to nineteen twenty-eight. Now we've got three living candidates. Three addresses. Three phone numbers. All here in town.' She made a show of checking her watch. 'And it's getting to be about the time of day where calling them up wouldn't be rude.'

Seventy-six-year-old Susan Wells Page loved Tuesdays and Saturdays the most because those were the days that Indy-Gardens allowed the pets in. About a year before, Susan would have said – and in fact she told anyone who would listen – that she was at the end of her life and that the only thing she had to look forward to was a full-service nursing home and then the grave. As it was, she already had moved from her sweet little brick home and now lived in this assisted-living facility where her two best friends – including Doris, her bridge partner – had just died within three months of each other.

The other people here were nice enough, the staff was efficient, the food was okay, but after Doris especially, nothing seemed to touch Susan personally anymore. It was too hard to make new connections and real friends at this age. She told Jeannette, her counselor here, that she didn't think she could open her heart to anybody new anymore. She was just done, dried up, irrelevant.

Time to go.

But then the Gardens had announced this program to bring in animals once a week. At the time, Susan, with all her wits still about her, had decided she was definitely going to boycott the whole thing. Dogs smelled bad and were dirty and stupid and Susan thought it was condescending as hell for Indy-Gardens to assume, just because the residents here were elderly and often lonely, that they would embrace the idea of temporary pets just because they were something to touch and feel an emotional connection with.

Ridiculous.

So she'd stayed in her room reading until lunchtime. When she had finally opened her door to go out to the cafeteria, Bessie had been sitting there in the hallway, all alone, unattended. She was some kind of a Lab mix, but rather small, apparently just out of puppyhood, with curiously flopping ears and a lustrous black medium-length coat.

'Shoo,' Susan had said, a brushing gesture with her hands. 'Shoo now.'

Bessie had looked up, gotten to her feet, and wagged her tail.

'I'm going around you.'

And she had.

And Bessie had fallen in beside her, walking along down the hall, sitting next to the chair Susan had pulled out for herself. Sometime during the lunch, Bessie came to rest her muzzle on Susan's thigh under the table. After a bit, Susan had broken off a small piece of bread and Bessie had taken it and licked her fingers and it hadn't seemed gross or smelly at all. Then Susan had taken her book to the lounge and Bessie followed her in there as well. She'd petted the dog and let her settle against her feet. Twice a week since then, Bessie had been dropped off by the pet people and came directly to Susan's door, where if Susan were not already waiting, she would scratch. Once. And Susan would let her in.

This morning, Bessie her savior had already been curled up in her lap in Susan's room when the telephone call had come in from the man who asked her if he could come and talk to her about her daughter Margie. He had some information that he thought she deserved to know, and of course how could she refuse? It had been so long since she had even heard her name, had even let herself think it.

When, after telling him where he could find her, she hung up, Bessie turned her head to look at her and started in with a low whimpering, then brought her face up to Susan's face to lick at the tears that overflowed onto her cheeks.

'It's okay, baby,' she said, leaning into the warmth and smell of her. 'Momma's okay.'

The private investigator, Wyatt Hunt, looked somehow vaguely familiar to Susan, which was unsettling since she'd obviously never met him before; this might be the first sign of the dementia against which she was always on her guard. Unshaven and in wrinkled clothes, he seemed rough and quite obviously tired. But she knew that this was the way many younger people went about nowadays. She wasn't going to prejudge, especially if he had something to tell her about Margie.

His friend, the reporter, looked proper enough, professional, and that was reassuring. These were serious people with something important to tell her.

They were in a little seating area in the corner of the main lounge. Bessie, bless her, somehow as always keyed to her emotional undertone, leaned up against the chair and rested her head on

Susan's leg while Susan kept her right hand moving gently up and down between the dog's ears.

After a few moments of small talk, Hunt leaned into a small pocket of silence and gave her a somewhat apologetic smile. 'I really want to thank you for agreeing to see us, but I wanted to warn you before we go too far that this conversation might be painful.'

Susan emitted a somber chortle and fixed him with her solemn hazel eyes. 'Mr Hunt,' she began, 'if your news is really about my daughter, after all this time I'd hardly expect anything else. And the very fact that you're here tells me that something has happened to her. Is she all right?'

Hunt looked over to Lynn, then came back to Susan. 'I'm afraid not, Mrs Page. She's dead.'

There it was. The words she'd been afraid of hearing for most of her life now, nevertheless hitting her with the force of a blow. Nodding, she abandoned the petting of her dog and brought a quivering hand up to her face. 'It's funny,' she said, struggling with her voice. 'You can imagine something for so long, even believe it, and then you finally hear that it's really true . . .' Her hand moved down over her heart and she let out a heavy breath. 'You're still not prepared.'

'No,' Hunt said. 'I know. I'm sorry.'

Bessie nudged her head up against Susan's leg and whimpered.

'In some ways, it's hard to believe she's lived this long,' she said. 'She was such a reckless child, so headstrong and independent. Did you know her?'

'No, ma'am. Not really.' Taking a breath, Hunt plunged on. 'Actually, this might be even harder to understand, but she didn't die recently. She died in 1970.'

'Nineteen seventy? Nineteen *seventy*? How?'

Hunt hesitated, then came out with it. 'She was murdered.'

A quizzical expression bloomed on Susan's face. 'I'm sorry? She's been dead all these years? All this time I've been hoping I might hear from her?' She closed her eyes against the awful truth. 'And murdered? Oh my God,' she said with flat matter-of-factness. 'Oh my God.'

Lynn reached over and put a hand on the elderly woman's shoulder, and for a long moment while Susan came to grips with her new reality, the tableau remained frozen. Eventually, she opened her eyes again and went back to petting Bessie, an air of reflection settling over her. Finally, she found her voice again. 'Was this in California?'

Hunt nodded. 'San Francisco.'

'Why did you think she lived in California?' Lynn asked.

'When she left here . . .' She stopped, her eyes darting back and forth between Wyatt and Lynn. 'Do you know who killed her?'

'Not yet,' Hunt said. 'That's one of the reasons I'm here. To find out.'

'You think it was someone from here?'

'I think her death might have had something to do with Jim Jones. That's about as far as I've gotten.'

At the mention of the name, Susan's face went hard. 'So she was still with the temple?'

Hunt and Lynn exchanged a look. 'Not really. She had gotten married. Her husband, who had nothing to do with the temple, was charged with the murder, but they couldn't convict him.'

She took that in and shook her head. 'But you just said you thought Jones was part of it.'

'I did. I do.'

'That wouldn't surprise me. That man, as the whole world now knows, was the pure devil.' She spoke to Lynn. 'That's why I thought she might have stayed in California. That's where they all went, Jones and all of his followers.'

'But you didn't go with them,' Lynn said.

'No. At first I was a little taken in with the man's . . . passion, I suppose is the word. He seemed to be doing really good work, important work. It was all so idealistic and beautiful in a way, and then it was also the sixties.' Her mouth tightened in distaste. 'But after I realized what he was doing with Margie . . . I mean, the girl was only what? Eleven or twelve years old when it started. I couldn't very well continue after I saw what he was really about. But to Margie, he was God. And for the longest time, he stayed God to her.'

'So the relationship was sexual?' Lynn asked.

'Yes.'

'You're sure?'

Susan snapped out her answer. 'Of course I'm sure. At first she tried to hide it. Children know this stuff is wrong. But in the end, she was brainwashed, proud of it. Out of all those other women – and believe me, there were many of them – she thought she was special. Never mind the group sex. She was the one he really loved.'

'Were there other children involved?' Lynn asked.

'I don't know. I would assume so, but I don't know. He was extremely magnetic and completely amoral. I'd be surprised if Margie was the only one taken in, but she wouldn't consider that. He loved her and he needed her and that was her life.' Again, she closed her eyes, took a few calming breaths. 'You know, when they published the list of the dead at Jonestown, I almost couldn't bring myself to look, but then of course I had to. I was sure she was going to be on it, but then when she wasn't . . . After that, for a while I had hoped . . .' The sentence trailed off into nothing.

'That was eight years after she died,' Hunt said. 'When did she leave here?'

'They all left as a group in '65. He had convinced all of them that there was going to be a nuclear war – it sounds so fantastic now, I know, but that man could sell ice to Eskimos. Anyway, that was the last I ever saw of her.'

'Excuse me, Mrs Page.' Lynn looked up from her notepad. 'But did you try to stop her? Or call the police?'

'The police here in Indianapolis? In the sixties?' Susan clearly found the idea ludicrous. 'You must remember if you're a reporter, this was the most notoriously corrupt police department in the United States back then. And Jones had all the city leaders in his pocket. Not to mention that Margie couldn't have been stopped. If the authorities, any authorities, had brought her back, she'd just have flown off again. And Jones was such a force. Terrifying, really.' She shook her head again, reliving the despair. 'It just didn't seem possible to stop them. It wasn't possible.'

'Did you stay in touch at all?' Hunt asked.

'I wrote her every few days for most of a year, until eventually the letters started getting returned unopened with no forwarding address.' Susan dabbed at her eyes and then came forward, speaking with more urgency. 'And please listen to me, both of you. I know I was wrong. There's no escaping it. I've lived with my failure about this for all of my life.

'But her father had just died two years before. I was alone, trying to raise her by myself. And I know I never should have let her go, whether she would have kept fighting with me or not. Or run away again, and again. She was only sixteen years old. I should have found a way to keep her with me. And I didn't. I just didn't. I didn't know how to do it. I wasn't strong enough, or a good enough mother. And in the end, she just disappeared off the face of the earth. If I could do any one thing in my life over again . . . but I just didn't have the strength, or the courage, or whatever. I failed her, and I failed myself.'

'It was a long time ago,' Lynn said gently. 'You don't need to beat yourself up over it anymore.'

'I sometimes feel I can never beat myself up enough.'

'I think she'd want you to forgive yourself,' Hunt said. 'She'd moved on and started a new life. She'd grown up. She was better.'

'I hope that's true.' Looking squarely at Hunt, she said, 'It's so hard to believe that she's really dead now after all this time. I don't want to believe it.'

'I know,' Hunt said. 'I'm sorry to have been the one to tell you. But I thought you deserved to know. You needed to know.'

Accepting that, Susan nodded. 'And have I helped you? In your investigation.'

'I think so. I needed to know for sure about the nature of her relationship with Jones.'

'Why? What does that get you?'

'It gets me a motive why she might have been killed.'

'And what is that?'

'She was a threat. Or at least Jones perceived her as a threat.'

'How is that? How could she possibly threaten him?'

'She could go public with her rape. A priest in San Francisco told me that there were other children involved. Never mind the criminal charges, credible evidence that he was raping eleven-year-olds would have ruined him. Obviously, Margie left the commune and came down to San Francisco, where she eventually meets a new guy named Kevin Carson and they get married. Four years later, this timing exactly works, Jones is making plans to come down and resettle in San Francisco. He'd have a much higher profile in the city, plus he'd make a ton more money. So he had feelers out to the community, City Hall, the mayor, you name it. By now she has escaped him. He doesn't know what she's thinking or who she's talking to, but he knows what she knows.'

'He was always about money,' Susan said. 'That was the other thing.'

Hunt nodded. 'That's what happens when you get a thousand

people to sign over their welfare and social security checks to you. In any event, I think that one of his recent converts was a girl named Evie Spencer, who was a friend of your daughter's. When she comes in all enthusiastic about Jones and tries to convert Margie back to the People's Temple, she's having none of it and tells Evie why. Needless to say, this is the worst possible news for Jones. Even if Margie doesn't go public with it herself, if even the rumor of it gets out, he's toast. Even in megatolerant San Francisco. He can't risk it. And he's got a soldier only too willing to do his work in the person of Evie's husband.'

'So he killed her? Evie's husband?'

'Lionel Spencer. Probably so, yes. I know the police in San Francisco think so.'

'Are they going to arrest him?'

'They don't have to. He killed himself the other night. One of my investigators made it clear he was going to be hauled in. He took another way out.'

Everyone seemed to settle back as Hunt reached his conclusion. Lynn closed her notebook. Susan gave Bessie's head a rub before she looked hard at Hunt again and straightened up. 'Can I ask you another question?'

'Sure. Anything.'

'Who is your client in all this?'

Hunt cocked his head a little to one side and offered her a tight little smile. 'At this point, I'd have to say that I'm doing it mostly on my own. With a little help from Lynn here.'

'But why? What's your interest?'

Hunt delayed another second or two. He had already loaded enough baggage onto this woman for one day and did not think it impossible that another staggering revelation would be too much for her to handle. Still, they were both here now, and she'd brought it up, asking him these last questions. Much as she deserved to know about Margie's death, she also deserved to learn about Hunt's relationship to her. 'Margie was my mother,' he said.

Susan nodded as though reassuring herself about something she already knew. Though the reaction was low-key, her eyes betrayed her – they became glassy with unspent tears. 'I knew it when I saw you,' she said. 'There is so much of her in you.' She reached out and rested her hand on his knee.

Hunt covered her hand with both of his own.

They stayed on at Indy-Gardens for about two more hours. Susan wanted to know everything about Hunt's life, how he'd grown up, his adopted family. All the details of Hunt's functional and relatively normal childhood with the Hunts seemed to bring her some solace. All her failure with her daughter had not, evidently, followed down through to the next generation. Trailing the shadow of her now-devoted Bessie, she insisted on introducing him, the 'miracle' of her grandson, to the other residents.

Hunt, for his part, was not entirely unmoved, either. This poor, lonely woman struck some atavistic chord in him to which he could not help but have some emotional response, quite possibly heightened by his fatigue and low-level but by now nearly constant head pain. Before he and Lynn left, Hunt and his grandmother were holding hands as she led them around, and they embraced – she weeping – as they said good-bye, exchanging numbers and promising to stay in touch forever.

23

HUNT AND LYNN were sitting together like conspirators in a booth at a diner around the corner from the *Star* building. Lynn had finished her burger and fries, still working on her milk shake, and something like a second or third wind had kicked in for her. 'The one thing I'm still missing,' she said, 'is the connection back to your texter.'

'Tell me about it.'

'I just did. The one thing I'm still missing . . .'

'Lynn.' Hunt held up a hand, stopping her. 'I heard you.' He'd felt hungry when he'd come in, since he hadn't eaten since the night before at his hotel, but when the food arrived he'd only been able to pick at it. Now he moved a French fry through a pool of ketchup on his plate and brought it up to his mouth. 'Which leads in a straight line to Lionel Spencer . . .' He let the thought hang. Then came back to it. 'It's just too pat.'

'What are you so mopey and negative about?' she asked. 'We just got your corroboration on your mother's connection to Jones, which is what you came all the way out here for, and you got to meet your grandmother for the first time to boot. I'd have to call that a pretty successful morning, and you're still looking like something the cat dragged in. We're winning here, Wyatt. You ought to be happy.'

Hunt shook his head. 'We're still missing the link between Lionel and Jones.'

'No, we're not. Didn't he tell your cop friends he was in

People's Temple with his wife? That puts him with Jones, does it not?'

Hunt chewed thoughtfully and swallowed. 'Jones had a thousand people with him, Lynn. It could have been any one of them. Why was it Lionel? He wasn't a Jonestown survivor. I don't think you've got your whole story, and I know I don't have mine, until we have some reason to believe that Jones could essentially have asked Lionel to kill somebody and he would just go do it.'

'We believe it because those are the kind of people Jones cultivated. That's exactly what happened at Jonestown, you recall. People who didn't want to drink the Kool-Aid got themselves shot.'

'But Lionel wasn't one of those guards. He wasn't there.'

'So he was an early incarnation of the type who happened to drop out.' Lynn slurped at her shake. 'And now he's dead and that's the end of it.'

'I don't accept it. As you say, and you're right, there's a gap between my texter and Lionel shooting himself. My texter's goal wasn't to get somebody to shoot himself. I was going to prepare a case, something the cops could use. That was the whole idea.'

'So it didn't go exactly according to plan. That happens all the time. So what?'

'So nobody's looking anymore. That's the point. Certainly not the cops. Lionel being dead ends the investigation. Doesn't that make you even a little bit suspicious? And this whole idea of killing yourself so you don't have to go to trial? For a murder that happened forty years ago? When there is no new evidence that even remotely points to you? I mean, come on. And how come Ivan is dead, then? If Lionel's going to kill himself, he kills himself. He doesn't steal a cab, assassinate the driver, shoot Ivan, then go home and kill himself a day later. What's the point of all that? If he's really that afraid of being caught, he puts the gun to his head and pulls the trigger. End of story.'

Lynn didn't agree. 'He wasn't worried about the old case, your mother, Wyatt. He thought he'd screwed up somehow with killing your guy, Ivan, and the cab driver. Didn't you say there was a witness who identified him? No, he was going to get caught for one of those and he knew it. Under those conditions, I could easily see him doing it.'

'Okay, but here's my advice. Don't write your story until . . .'

Hunt's cell phone chirped its message tone and he stopped midsentence and reached for it, reading what was on the screen. 'This,' he said, 'is the hand of God.'

And showed her the message: *It isn't Lionel.*

'So what's that supposed to mean?' Juhle asked.

'What? You think it's ambiguous?'

'No. What I think it is, is bullshit. Somebody's playing with you.'

'This isn't a joke, Dev. This is the person, this texter, who started all this.'

'You know that? You know who it is now?'

'No. But . . .'

'Did you succeed in tracing that last message?'

'No. There wasn't any time. It was just the one line.'

Juhle said, 'Look, Wyatt, since we last talked, we got ballistics on the cabbie's bullet and on Lionel's, which are a match, and which also are both consistent – same caliber – with the slug that killed Orloff. These are three gunshot deaths from the same gun, guaranteed. There is no doubt. Oh, also, three bullets missing out of the magazine.'

'Okay, but . . .'

'Also, you might be surprised to learn that we went over Lionel's place the way we do whenever there's a violent death, and there is nothing there, nada, that points to an intruder or even a second person in the room or even in the house. The dude killed himself, Wyatt, gun up against his own head. Now by extension we can perhaps infer that he also killed your mother, but if you're not happy with that, you are free to go on searching for whoever that might have been and I will try my best not to impede your continuing investigation. In fact, now that I think about it, maybe that's the only murder your texter was talking about, your mother's. Maybe Lionel didn't kill her. But I'll tell you one thing for absolute sure: Lionel's gun did kill Orloff and it did kill our cabbie and it killed him. That you can take to the bank. As for the other stuff, it's all yours.'

Juhle cut the connection and Hunt stared for a minute at the face of his cell phone, then returned it to his belt. 'You heard most of that, I presume,' he said to Lynn.

'Enough, anyway. He seems convinced. And if the ballistics are right, he's pretty persuasive.'

'I'm sure the ballistics are fine,' Hunt said. 'I'm sure there was no sign of forced entry or an invader in Lionel's house. But I'm even more sure that whoever sent me that text wasn't lying and wasn't guessing. Lionel didn't kill my mother. And he didn't kill those other guys or himself, either. That was my guy, too.'

'So who is he?'

Hunt grimaced. 'That's where I started. That's where I'm still at.' He picked up another French fry, looked at it, and placed it back on his plate. 'It's somebody who knew Lionel, still knows him. Somebody he talked to after he heard from Ivan.'

Pulling his phone back up, he drew up his Contacts list and pressed the screen to connect him. 'Callie. Wyatt . . . Can you get me the list of every call in and out to Lionel Spencer's phone from last Tuesday? Lionel's number is the last one Ivan talked to. . . . I'd ask Devin if I could see his list, if he's even run the report, but he's not sharing with me anymore. . . . You're a doll, thanks.'

Hunt put his phone away, brought his hand up and squeezed his temples.

'Are you still hurting?' Lynn asked.

'I don't know what's happening. My focus is a little off. My heart's beating about triple time and I can't seem to get a breath.' He pasted on a broken smile. 'Otherwise, I'm good.'

'Maybe you should wait for this friend of yours, Callie, to call you back and try to get some sleep?'

He shook his head. 'That might be two days, maybe more. And if Lionel got the call from Ivan on one phone and then made his call to his eventual killer on another phone, we may never find it. I've got to keep at this. There's got to be somebody who knew Lionel back . . .' Stopping, he wiped his hand down the side of his face, around the neckline of his shirt.

'What are you thinking?' she said.

'My father.' His jaw went slack at the realization. 'I've got to find my father.'

Hunt had been in Iraq for the First Gulf War, where he had been in the Criminal Investigation Command, and where the stress level was relatively high. After that, in civilian life for about ten years his job with Child Protective Services had entailed taking children away from their abusive or neglectful parents, and that career had set a standard of stress for which he had come to believe there was no equal.

Until now.

He was back in his hotel room, where he splashed water on his face and stared at himself in the bathroom mirror. The person looking back at him, with bloodshot eyes and a heavy stubble over slightly sunken cheeks, was not altogether familiar. He really should shave, he told himself, take a shower and get cleaned up. It wouldn't take him fifteen minutes, total.

But it was too much work.

Instead, he dried his face and went to lie down on his bed again. It was early afternoon and Lynn was back in her cubicle, hopefully finding something about Hunt's father that they could use.

If the man wasn't dead.

What Wyatt needed more than a shower and shave was a little snooze. He set the alarm next to the bed for four o'clock and also set his cell phone alarm as a backup.

But he was unable to get to any sort of a comfortable position. It wasn't just his brain, or his head, although he was hyperaware of the blood pulsing behind his eyes, providing a nearly subsonic backbeat in his ears.

He closed his eyes and waited for sleep to come and overtake him, but instead he flipped into frustration about what he hadn't yet figured out and then he would glance at the clock on the night table and see that twenty minutes had gone by and he still hadn't fallen asleep.

Maybe he would never sleep again.

This thought brought him to the very edge of real panic, his heart pounding now, a heavy methodic bass drum thudding in his rib cage. Rivulets of sweat dripped down his side under his shirt. His breath was starting to come in ragged gasps.

Finally, swearing in a rage, he jerked upright.

Seventeen more minutes had passed. Now he only had an hour and ten minutes of the time he'd allotted himself to get some rest before he was scheduled to show up at Lynn's desk for another brainstorming session, depending on what she'd been able to find on her computers.

He lay down, closed his eyes again, willed his breathing to slow. But now here was his grandmother in his mind's eye, standing there next to his mother with Jim Jones, and suddenly his heart just would not fall into its natural beat but took up again with the incessant drumming.

Maybe he would never sleep again.

'Could you just talk to me for a minute?'

'There is nothing I'd rather do, Wyatt,' Tamara said. 'Longer than a minute if you need. Where are you?'

'In my hotel in Indianapolis.'

'Are you all right? You don't sound good.'

'I'm not good.' Wyatt hesitated. 'I haven't slept, Tam, not in a couple of days now. I feel like I'm kind of freaking out.'

'What kind of freaking out?'

'Maybe that's not the right word. Maybe feeling a little panic, is all.'

'What kind of panic?'

'You know. Heart racing, shortness of breath.'

'Wyatt, hang up and dial nine one one.'

'No. It's not that bad. It's not an emergency or anything. It's just all this *stuff* about who I really am and where I come from that I've never dealt with before. Never really even knew about. It feels like it's all kind of punching its way up to the surface.'

'All that stuff, as you call it, is serious.'

'I'm getting that impression,' Wyatt said.

'Did you find out something new today?'

'It's just been this amazing morning, Tam. You know Lynn, this reporter I'm working with? She found my grandmother, my actual grandmother! She's alive and still vibrant and I went out and met her at this assisted-living place, which was incredible enough. But then she – her name's Susan Page – she also verified our whole theory about my mother and Jim Jones. He was in fact abusing her and she ran away to California with him when he relocated the People's Temple out there. And then I got another text saying it wasn't Lionel . . .'

'Wait a minute. New topic? You got another text?'

'Yeah. A couple of hours ago.'

'And they knew about Lionel?'

'Enough to say it wasn't him. I called Devin and told him – I mean, this is a major break in his case, right? But he's not going there. He's got his nice tight little wrapped-up package and it answers most of the questions and he's not interested in taking his investigation any further, which means it's down to us.'

A silence.

'Tam?'

'I'm here.' She paused. 'You sound pretty wound up.'

'I am pretty wound up. There's nobody left to talk to except my father, if he's still alive.'

'Talk to about what, though?'

'Who Lionel hung out with back in the day. To understand what the whole scene was really about. There's somebody else who's been involved in this all along. It's got to do with my mother and father and Spencer and Jones and all that madness, but the damn guy is just outside of my vision and he's kept his role in all this hidden for forty years now. I'm going to find the son of a bitch and take him down. I swear to God.'

Tamara's voice was soft on the phone. 'Wyatt.'

'Yeah.'

'Take a breath. Slow down.'

'I know.'

'No, I don't think you do know. I mean literally. Stop. Right now. Close your eyes. Take a breath.'

He followed orders. 'All right,' he said. 'Mission accomplished.'

'Now do it again.'

'How many times?'

'Just once more.'

'Okay. Done.'

'Now. How are you feeling?'

After a pause, Hunt said, 'Really not very good.'

'Do you want to come home?'

'More than anything, but I don't know if I can. Not yet. I think we're close.'

'That's what you said before you left. Do you remember that?'

'Closer,' he said.

'Please don't get hurt,' she said. 'Don't hurt yourself.'

'That's not in the plan.'

'Yes, but that's what seems to be happening, doesn't it?'

'It's all inside me,' he said. 'But I think I can beat it.'

'Of course you do. That's who you are. You can beat anything. But if it starts to get the better of you, do me a favor, will you? Call me again. Any time. No matter what.'

'I will.'

'Promise?'

'Promise.'

With a few more minutes to kill before he had to leave for the *Star*, and by now having completely given up on sleep, Hunt put in a call to Father Bernard. His immediate physical symptoms – racing heartbeat, difficulty getting a full breath – had somewhat subsided during and after his talk with Tamara. Now, except for the recurrent blinking aura and general lack of sleep, he nevertheless felt revitalized enough that he thought he could power through the rest of the day, whatever it might bring.

To Hunt's relief, Bernard was home at the rectory. After giving the priest a short summary of the events since they'd last spoken, Hunt asked if he had had any luck at all contacting parishioners with whom Kevin might have worked or had some relationship. The short answer was no.

'But there was one tiny bit of new information,' Bernard said, 'although I don't know what good, if any, it will do you. It's really not much.'

Hunt kept his voice neutral against the thrill of anticipation he felt. 'Anything would be welcome, Father.'

'Well, as I say, it's a small enough thing, but Joe Phelan – he's one of the people Kevin had worked for doing handyman work – I was questioning him, as you'd asked me to, if he'd ever heard from Kevin after he moved to Texas, and the question seemed to stump him for a minute before he told me that Kevin hadn't moved to Texas.'

'So where'd he move to?'

'Mexico.'

And suddenly Hunt's heart told him that this was probably true. It accounted for the lack of social security information, the complete disappearance off the grid. And, more important, with another unneeded jolt of adrenaline, Hunt realized that it left open the possibility that his father was still alive.

Bernard continued speaking over the rushing in Hunt's ears. 'He told Joe that after the two trials on his record, he just didn't think he could ever have a chance of having any kind of real life in America again. Anything criminal that ever happened near wherever he decided to settle, the police would come to look for him first. So he'd kind of lost faith in the justice system here, with some reason. And he was going to start over down there, where he knew nobody and nobody knew him.'

But another unwelcome thought surfaced. 'What about the letter he wrote to me?' Hunt didn't want to consider it but had to face the possibility that his father had lied in that letter. Because if he'd lied about planning to go to Texas, he might just as well have lied about whether he'd killed Margie.

'I don't know about that,' Bernard said. 'I know he gave the box to me pretty soon after he got released from jail. He might have stayed around a few weeks and thought about Texas and then decided that wasn't where he wanted to go, job or no job.'

Hunt would reserve judgment on that, though to his relief it was reasonably plausible. He asked Bernard, 'So did this Mr Phelan say where he was going in Mexico? Did he mention any specific place?'

'I asked him that myself,' Bernard said.

'And?'

'I'm sorry. I know this isn't the best news. But no.'

By the time Hunt got to Lynn's cubicle again, he'd come to believe that in fact Bernard's information was potentially good news that might very well at last break up the logjam. The sheer volume of hits for Kevin Carson on the LexisNexis in his office, which he'd used in his first searches, had somehow blinded him to spending much time bothering to sort and locate by limiting parameters. Of course, he'd tried several, from his father's probable age to Texas, but each search had still yielded too many hits to reasonably check out each one, or any, of them.

But while there were thousands of Kevin Carsons in the world, and without doubt the great majority of them lived in the United States, Hunt would bet that the odds of there being even hundreds in Mexico were slight. And hundreds might prove a doable number, especially if they could further limit their search with the parameters Lynn had used to locate Susan Page – notably age. How many Kevin Carsons who were sixty-three years old, born in January of 1948, and without an active U.S. social security number lived in Mexico?

The answer, as it turned out, was one.

24

In San Francisco, Tamara wasn't having her best day.

She sat in her tiny kitchen in midafternoon, gloomy outside, drinking her fourth cup of coffee of the day. Her grandfather had gone out to play bocce ball with his cronies, as he did most Saturdays. And Mickey had left early to forage at the farmers' market and hadn't yet returned, so she was alone in the apartment, fighting her own newfound concerns and worries.

Wyatt, so far away, had sounded terrible on the phone, almost like a different person. Needy, then manic, and unable to control the swing between them. For the entire time that she'd known him, most of her life, she'd never seen him lose control. That defined his personality. He was strong, rock solid, confident, self-sufficient.

But now this psychological upheaval over the search for his mother's killer had him doubting himself, his instincts, maybe the very nature of who he was. Or at least, that's what it had sounded like. It was obvious now to her that a large part of his seemingly natural resiliency had come from his denial of some of the fundamental truths of his early life.

He'd lost his mother. His father had abandoned him. Several foster homes had given up on him. And each time, he'd found some kind of strength that allowed him to go forward, to believe that something positive could come from all of this rejection, bad luck, negative karma. Thank God, she thought, for the Hunts, who had provided such stability and support and love that Wyatt, finally, could grow into the man he'd become.

But she did not have to try hard to imagine the pain he was now trying to deal with. She had felt much the same way herself, although at ten years old she'd been much older when her mother had died than Wyatt had been when he lost his. She'd had to deal with the pain and loss at the time it occurred – there was no real way of denying it. But she had shared it with her brother, no small difference from Wyatt, who had suffered it alone. She and Mickey had cried together and apart until there were no more tears left to shed. They'd worked through their anger, their fear, their abandonment not by denial but by gradual, hard-won acceptance. This was their lot. They had to deal with it.

It shocked her to think that her inner core of strength might be stronger than Wyatt's, that he might have to lean on her if all this became too much for him to bear.

Not that she was unwilling. Far from it.

But the realization that he'd called her this morning because he needed her strength frightened her on one level while it reassured her on another.

It frightened her to hear Wyatt sound this way, to realize that he was in such a weakened state that he truly could not get himself together. He needed her. The idea that Wyatt Hunt could not handle a problem – any problem – on his own was terrifying.

On the other hand, that reality brought with it a sense of calm. With their age difference, with Wyatt's far greater life experience, his unflagging confidence and adult power, she had always harbored the secret belief that any relationship between them would be doomed in the long run because of their basic inequality.

She was attractive to men. She knew that. And she had no trouble believing that Wyatt found her desirable. But that physical connection, while strong, could not be enough. Her looks would fade; he would get old before she did. If she were not his true equal in strength and security, they could never make it.

And now, suddenly, she saw with absolute clarity that this was what she had become.

His equal.

He hadn't called Gina Roake or Devin Juhle or any other of his guy friends. He'd called her because he knew that she could help him, she could calm him, get him through this. She knew what he was dealing with, who he was, in a way that maybe even he was only beginning to understand.

Perhaps she had been his equal all along, but she might never have known for certain if these convulsions over the losses and pains he'd never before acknowledged had not so shaken him.

And he might never have known, either.

She was pouring the largely untouched coffee into the sink when the phone rang in the other room, and she ran in to answer it.

'Hello.'

'Tam.' Hunt's voice, in one syllable, manic. 'Thank God you're still home. I found him.'

'Who?'

'My father. Kevin Carson. He's in Mexico. I'm sure it's him. I'm going down to talk to him.'

'Where is he?'

'A little village south of Oaxaca.'

'And you know he's there? He's still alive?'

Wyatt hesitated. 'I don't know that. But he's the last piece. I've got to go find him and talk to him. He'll know about Evie and Lionel Spencer and who they hung out with. And one of those people killed my mother.'

'If he's alive.'

'I've got to believe he's alive, Tam. He's the last chance. Which is what I'm calling you about. I need you to run down to my place and go in my safe and get my passport and FedEx it out here to me at my hotel for early-morning delivery. I've got a flight to El Paso at noon, so if you can get it here by nine, we're good.'

'And then what?' Tamara asked. 'After El Paso?'

'Then I connect to Oaxaca and I'm down there by seven or so. Then Monday morning I drive down to this village and find him and we talk and I find out what he knows.'

'Wyatt.' She stopped, swallowing her original question, and came out with another, more innocuous, one. 'How's your Spanish?'

'Adequate. Probably a little rusty. But he'll speak English, so that won't be a problem.'

'Except if he's dead. Are you thinking about that?'

'He's not dead, Tam. Lexis didn't have him dead. He was alive a couple of years ago. I need to talk to him.'

'If.'

'Okay, if. But I don't know why you're not excited. This is what I've been looking for all this time, Tam. This is the answer. I know it is.'

'It seems a little . . . desperate, don't you think? Flying all the way down there, not even knowing he's alive. To say nothing of the drug wars. Haven't something like thirty thousand people been killed down there? You want to go down into the middle of that? If they cut your head off, I'll come down and kill you again.'

'Come on, Tam. I really don't think we have to worry about that.'

'Knock on wood,' Tamara said as she tapped a knuckle against her bedstead. 'Can I ask you one other thing?'

'If you promise you'll then go get my passport.'

'All right, I promise. So here's my question: Have you thought about how you're going to handle it if your father is down there, if he's alive?'

'Sure. I'm sure I'll be fine.'

'Like you were a couple of hours ago?'

'This is different. I've gotten all that stuff out of my system.'

'All that about not sleeping? Freaking out? Panic?'

She almost heard him shrug over the line. 'It got the better of me for a minute.'

'And that's it? You're going to give it a whole minute?'

Wyatt took a beat. 'Are you mad at me?'

'No.' She hesitated. 'I'm worried about you.'

'You don't have to be. I appreciate it, but I'm okay.'

'You're in control,' she said.

'Mostly. Really.'

'Okay.' She sighed. 'So what's the address of your hotel?'

After Hunt gave it to her, she hung up and then stood in her living room/bedroom for a moment before she said, 'Clueless,' out loud, and went to get her coat.

For all of his professed certainty to Hunt about his evidence and his suspect, Devin Juhle didn't like the idea that Hunt's mysterious texter had contacted him again, this time calling into question the basic fact of Lionel Spencer's guilt in the murders. To say nothing of his own suicide. Juhle didn't forget for a second that this entire affair had gotten its start from these cell messages to Hunt, and they had never been anything but accurate. And the farthest thing in the world from frivolous. It was unnerving, to say the least, that the case, which had apparently ended with such a satisfying sense of closure, might not be solved at all.

Might, in fact, be ongoing. And with no one except Hunt even thinking now about pursuing the actual culprit.

Juhle had been pondering it all day, through the kids' soccer games, through his visit with Alexa to the Kaiser emergency room for what he hoped was just a sprained ankle and not a broken foot. He thought about it while Alexa went in after a three-hour wait to get the damn foot X-rayed (broken), and then again back at home finally at 8:30 while he reheated his now really well-done (ruined) filet mignon dinner that he was going to get to eat all alone, since everyone else, even Alexa with her cast, had gone to the pre-Halloween party at the neighbor's house down the street that Devin just hadn't had the energy to gear up for.

Try as he might, he couldn't see where his evidence was betraying him, if it was. As he'd told Hunt, he was positive about the ballistics results. True, they didn't have a slug from Ivan Orloff's murder, but they knew it matched the caliber of the bullets that had killed the cabbie and Spencer. And those two slugs had definitely come from the same gun.

Which, granted, could not be traced to anyone, so there was no absolute proof that it was Lionel's. But, Juhle knew, untraceable weapons were as common in the city as tree rats in the Presidio, maybe more so. So its presence on the floor by Lionel's outstretched hand did nothing to disprove his ownership of it.

But Hunt's call in the morning had bothered Juhle enough that he had double-checked with the lab, which had miraculously called him back on a Saturday. They told him that there was in fact gunshot residue on Lionel's right hand, which had been bagged at the scene routinely. That at least was consistent with suicide.

That left the time line for the killings, and again, here Juhle was certain that he was on solid ground. Orloff's call to Lionel had been a little over an hour before they had met for dinner. Lionel had been seen and was identified by at least three witnesses leaving Original Joe's and getting into a Yellow Cab. Orloff had stayed at the restaurant to have dessert – cheesecake with fresh fruit puree – a cappuccino, and then, afterward, an Amaretto.

(By the way, all ordered by Lionel, no doubt to give him enough time to eliminate the cabbie and return to be outside Joe's upon Orloff's exit.) Then, the following night, for whatever reason – guilt, remorse, despair, fear – he'd taken his own life. No doubt he'd already been dead when Hunt had knocked on his door.

So they had all this evidence against what other evidence?

A text message, which could have been sent by anyone in the universe, to Wyatt Hunt, saying that it wasn't Lionel. Using his first name only.

And what did that mean?

Maybe nothing.

And yet . . .

Juhle rinsed his plate and utensils and loaded them into the dishwasher. His house had a finished basement with a dilapidated old couch and a Ping-Pong table and television set, and he went down there and stretched out, hands behind his head. He gave it another fifteen minutes and then he picked up the phone and put in a call to his partner.

'Yo, Sarah. Devin. You got a minute?'

'Well, we just got the kids down, and Graham and I, we're in the middle of a video. How important is it?'

'You tell me. It's about Lionel.'

'Something new?'

He gave it to her.

On the other end of the line, she remained silent for a few seconds before she swore and told him to hang on. He heard her telling her husband the bad news and then she was back with him. 'That's all it said? "It isn't Lionel"?'

'That's the whole message.'

'So what do you want to do?'

'That's what I called you for, figuring you'd have an idea, since I've been thinking about it all day, and I don't.'

'Well, if it's not Lionel and we really want to play this game, which I don't, it had to be somebody he contacted after he heard from Orloff and . . .' She stopped. 'No.'

'No, what?'

'Just no. Period. I don't know who this person is who's tormenting your pal Wyatt or what he or she knows. But I know what *we* know, Devin, and why we know it. You give up?'

'Hit me.'

'Can you say *eyewitness*?'

As soon as he heard the word, a kind of peace settled over Juhle's heart. He couldn't believe he hadn't even put Chewey's testimony describing the shooter into the mix he'd been considering. Maybe because Chewey was a drug-befuddled thief and a total lowlife. But those character traits did not necessarily negate the truth of his testimony. Much less his later positive identification of Lionel Spencer from the six-pack of photographs (five other guys and Lionel) they'd shown him from the autopsy pictures. He had no reason to lie to them, and the fact that his description of the old guy with white hair in the Yellow Cab came before the discovery of Lionel's death dovetailed nicely into what could only be called an airtight case.

'You're right,' Juhle said. 'I'm sorry to have bothered you. I was in the ER all day today with Alexa. I think the experience must have infected my brain.'

Sarah's voice changed from cop to mom in an instant. 'Is she all right?'

'She's fine. In a soft cast for a few weeks, that's all. Soccer.'

'I know it well,' Sarah said. 'So anyway, listen, don't lose any sleep over this texting business. Somebody's screwing around with your friend. Chewey, scumbag though he is, saw Lionel pull the trigger, Dev. Firsthand and up close. Keep that in the front of your mind. I'd have to call that definitive, huh? Wouldn't you?'

'I would.'

'There you go, then. Anything else?'

'That pretty well does it. Tell Graham sorry about interrupting the video.'

'He'll get over it,' she said. 'See you Monday.'

25

On Sunday morning at 8:45, Wyatt Hunt sat on a low couch in the lobby of the Indianapolis Airport Marriott, drinking black coffee from a waxed cardboard to-go cup and, just about out of his mind with anticipation, watching the street outside for the appearance of a FedEx truck.

The sweet roll he'd wolfed down sat like a ball of lead in his stomach, and the coffee might as well have been carbolic acid, but he needed it. It was now about thirty-one hours since he'd actually slept. The last time had been the three hours of exhausted collapse back in Minneapolis. After the excitement and adrenaline of the discovery of his father's possible place of residence had worn off, he'd come back here to the hotel early to catch up on his rest if he could. The next day, he knew, was going to be a long one, and he wanted to be fresh and ready.

But in the end, last night had been a replay of earlier in the afternoon, except much, much longer. And the insomnia wasn't the result of spinning about anything specific; a good portion of the time he simply lay motionless on the bed, a dull pressure on the back of his eyes, unable to turn off the keening anxiety that seemed to course through him as though it were its own bodily system, an alternative to blood, lymph, nerve. Around midnight, he'd dumped the two airplane bottles of vodka from the honor bar onto some ice and drank it off; an hour later he put away two more of gin.

Neither had any effect.

But explicit, albeit irrational, worries plagued him, too. After he'd hung up with Tamara, it occurred to him that he wasn't one hundred percent sure that FedEx even delivered early on Sunday mornings. If they didn't, of course the ultra-reliable and efficient Tamara would call with the news, wouldn't she? And if FedEx wouldn't work, then she'd find another way to get it done – UPS, maybe, or one of the others. There must be a dozen of them.

And what if his father was dead? What if he couldn't find him anyway, even if he were alive? What if Kevin wouldn't talk to him? What if he rejected him outright again? What if he didn't get to him in time? (In time for what?) What if Wyatt never discovered the identity of his texter? What if there were other murders he hadn't stumbled upon yet? What if Ivan hadn't called Lionel Spencer? What if Wyatt got his information and made his case but Juhle wouldn't pursue it? What if?

What if?

What if . . .?

When he saw light begin to appear as a thin line under the blackout curtains in his room – the onset of dawn, a few hours ago – he'd thrown off his covers, stuffed his toiletries into his suitcase, and come downstairs to the buffet breakfast, where he'd read the Sunday *Star* from cover to cover and then had come over to this lobby couch to begin his vigil.

Now there was nothing to do but wait for his passport to arrive.

A taxi pulled into the lot and circled around, stopping at the entryway. Hunt barely gave it a glance – it wasn't the FedEx truck, after all – and then tipped back his cup, draining it. He stood up and walked over toward the reception desk to drop the cup in the trash container. When he turned around and caught sight of the cab again, the driver was going back to open the trunk as a woman emerged from the backseat.

*

Tamara finished paying the cabbie, pulled up the handle on her suitcase, and turned around, and there, an astonished though unmistakably pleased look on his face, stood Wyatt just outside the lobby door. One glance told her that her instincts had been right. She was needed here. Positively haggard, with a couple of days' growth of beard and deep purplish bags under his eyes, Wyatt, his hair tufted and unruly, looked like a homeless man.

Letting go of her suitcase, she hesitantly raised a hand. 'Hey.'

'Hey, yourself.'

'I decided I had to come.'

'I see that.'

'I brought your passport. Mine, too.'

A half smile. 'Didn't trust FedEx, huh?'

'They don't deliver on Sunday, and neither does anybody else.' She paused, then met his gaze. 'I have to be with you.'

'I can't believe I'm standing here looking at you,' he said, letting out a deep sigh of pure relief. 'I am so glad you're here.' He took a step toward her and she came forward and walked into his embrace.

On the flight to El Paso, Hunt sat by the window and finally fell into a turbulent sleep, his head on Tamara's shoulder. She held his hand the whole way and tightened her grip when he twitched or moaned or – twice – cried out 'No!' After which he would settle back against her and revert to what seemed to her to be a state of near catatonia.

He said he wasn't hungry, but she ordered and got him to eat a large burrito and drink a lemonade at the El Paso airport.

After that lunch, Wyatt excused himself for a pit stop, and when he returned, he was actually smiling as he slid in next to her. 'I caught a glimpse of myself in the mirror in there,' he said. 'I look like I got whupped with an ugly stick.'

'I wouldn't worry about it. A few days of ugly never hurt anybody. It might even strengthen the spirit.'

'How would you know? You're never ugly.'

She gave him a testy look. 'As compliments go, "You're never ugly" is quite a ways down the list.'

He reached over and took her hand. 'I didn't mean . . .'

'Shut up.' Flashing her own dazzling smile. 'I know.' She leaned over. 'Kiss me, ugly man.'

He did.

Wyatt was asleep again – in a less frenetic state – before they reached cruising altitude on the Oaxaca leg of the flight.

Tamara finished her Stieg Larsson and then pulled out of Wyatt's suitcase some of the pages he'd printed about their destination. Apparently, Kevin Carson had settled in the small village of Teotitlán del Valle, about fifteen miles south of Oaxaca. Tamara had both the LexisNexis printout – an extremely abbreviated entry listing only the subject's name, birth date by month, and last known address – and the results of another search on the regular Web, which listed a Kevin Carson and his address – matching the LexisNexis address and, to Tamara, giving further credence to the idea that Wyatt's father was still alive – in the Directory of Weavers of Teotitlán, the American surname Carson standing out in high relief among the Bautistas, Lazaros, Mendosas. Reading on, she learned that the town was famous for its woven wool rugs, or *laadi* in the local language of Zapotec, which was still in common usage in the area.

Wyatt woke up for the last couple of hours of the flight and gave Tamara a more or less complete update on everything he'd discovered over the past couple of days. He was telling her that he had no doubt that the latest unexpected text was legitimate, and that they would get to the truth at the bottom of this investigation within the next day or so, after they'd spoken with Wyatt's father.

'And how do you feel about that?' Tamara asked. 'Your father? If it is your father.'

'It is. I know it is.' He threw her a sidelong glance. 'And I don't know how I feel, or more than that, how my body will react. It's like it's out of my control completely; it just takes over, like a virus. You don't mind talking about this?'

She squeezed his hand. 'I think I brought it up, remember?'

He nodded, acknowledging that truth. 'Okay. So the truth is I don't know. I thought I was prepared to meet my grandmother in person the other day. And when I did, everything went fine talking to her. I mean, emotional, but really okay. Then I got back to the hotel, and the whole reality of it just laid me out. I don't think I'd have gotten any sleep yet if you hadn't shown up. For which thank God.' He brought her hand up to his mouth and kissed the back of it. 'And thank you, if I haven't told you yet.'

'Once more, then you've got to stop.'

'But even now, just talking about seeing my father . . .'

'We can stop.'

'I don't want to stop. But when I think about the fact that he's down here, that he might have been down here my whole life . . . one part of me wants to know how he could have done it, left his only child . . . and then last night lying awake thinking about it over and over, I couldn't get beyond this . . . this rage, this kind of curdling rage.'

'At what you didn't have? But as it turned out, you had everything with the Hunts, didn't you?'

'I did. I know. I know. As I said, it's not rational. It's silly.'

'No, it's not silly. It's real enough.'

'No. It's stupid. I've just got to suck it up.'

Tamara allowed herself a slight chuckle. 'Oh yes. That's been working very well, hasn't it? Deny it, and it ceases to exist, right? Except it does exist, Wyatt. It doesn't go away, the hurt of it all. It just goes underground. The only way to beat it is to face it head-on, let it in, accept it.'

'The pain, you mean?'

'Yes.'

'I don't know if I can do that. I don't even want to care about all this personal stuff, Tam. It happened a million years ago and I dealt with it then. And as you say, I was way better off being raised by the Hunts. I don't know why it's having all this effect on me.'

She turned to him and spoke softly. 'It's having this effect on you, Wyatt, because somebody killed your mother. That's kind of a big thing, maybe the biggest thing that can happen to anyone. Somebody stole your security and your childhood. You have to acknowledge that. Somebody made you give up believing in commitment, so you've always got one foot out the door so you can leave before they do and then you won't have to feel that pain again. But actually you're allowed to feel pain and rage and abandoned about all this. In fact, you've got to let yourself feel those things if you ever want to get it all out and be whole again.'

'Maybe I don't want that, then,' Hunt said.

'Yes, you do,' she said. 'You really do.'

It was a long flight, and picking up their rental car at the airport, they didn't get to the Holiday Inn Express in Oaxaca until nearly midnight.

Hunt unlocked the door to their room and then closed it behind them, and when he turned around, Tamara was standing right there facing him. She stepped forward and put her arms around his neck while he brought his arms up around her and they stood pressed together for a long moment until Tamara pulled back and kissed him. Getting over to the bed, she sat on it and kicked off her shoes, then looking up at him said, 'How about if we just go right to bed and get it over with.'

'I love a woman who speaks her mind.' Arms crossed, Wyatt leaned against the wall. 'Except what about if I don't think of it as something to be gotten over with?'

'The first time, I mean. And it is.'

'Even the first time. I thought maybe you'd like it if I took a shower first, got a little cleaned up.'

'I don't care about that,' she said. 'I love how you look. I love how you smell. We've put this off long enough.' Abruptly, she stood up and lifted her sweater over her head and dropped it to the floor. Her black bra connected in front, and without any hesitation she undid the clasp of that, too, and shrugged out of it. 'I'm getting way ahead of you,' she said.

Wyatt, unable to take his eyes off her, was reaching for the top button on his shirt. 'Not for long.'

'See?' She lay on her side pressed up next to him, her head nestled into his shoulder. The bedsheet partially covered her torso. Her palm rested on his chest. 'The first time.'

'I think, technically,' Hunt said, 'that would be the first two times. Not to get picky. You're right, though, I'm glad we got that out of the way. It was starting to be a distraction.'

'I think I'm still a little distracted.'

'Me, too. You might pull that sheet up a little.'

'Is that what's distracting you?'

'Maybe a little bit.'

'Well, then, I think I'll leave it. Distraction's not always a bad thing.'

'No. Not always.' Hunt ran his hand down her side from her shoulder to her waist, then turned his head and kissed her on the forehead, the side of her cheek.

She nuzzled up against his neck. 'That felt like a good-night kiss. Are you thinking about going to sleep?'

'The thought had crossed my mind.'

'You're still going to be here in the morning, right?'

'Lots of mornings,' he said.

'All right. I can live with that.' She reached down and pulled their blanket up around them. 'You know,' she whispered through a fog of half sleep, 'for an old guy, you're holding up pretty good.'

A small laugh gurgled in his throat. 'Thank you,' he said. 'And while we're complimenting each other, have I already mentioned that you're never ugly?'

'Twice now.'

He kissed her lightly. 'Still true.'

'Okay.' She turned to lie with her back against him. 'Truce again?'

'Truce.'

'Keep holding me.'

'I will.'

'Wyatt?'

'Umm?'

'I'm so glad I'm here.'

'Me, too, Tam,' he whispered. 'Me, too.'

26

All Hunt's previous time in Mexico had been spent in Baja California, and most of that on the Pacific side in the very north near Rosarito Beach, where he'd done a lot of surfing and where, to arrive, one had to navigate the lawless, poverty-stricken, godforsaken border town of Tijuana, and then forty kilometers of wasteland – abandoned, graffiti-scarred, unfinished buildings and other structures, questionable roadways, an arid and inhospitable landscape. And so while he intellectually knew that all the country could not be like this one small corner, nevertheless he was surprised when they left Oaxaca on a modern highway and headed south through some truly beautiful foothills, semiarid but well farmed and with a lot of greenery everywhere, especially on the slopes of the steeply pitched mountains that surrounded them.

Coming over the pass that led down to the valley, they had a panoramic view of the village, which from a distance seemed to have none of the chaos and poverty that Hunt had pretty much been expecting. Instead, the town appeared quaint, traditional, and altogether lovely. Tamara, although she'd spent a month after college in Greece and Italy, was far less well traveled than Hunt, and she passed the time on the drive regaling him with details and personal observations about the place: that it was no wonder it was so beautiful – the Nahuatl name *Teotitlán* meant 'land of the gods'; its elevation was nearly fifty-five hundred feet; its population topped out at around forty-five hundred, with another thousand in the immediate outlying communities; the main language was not Spanish, but Zapotec; the native people had been weaving here, paying tribute to the Aztecs in these goods, since about five hundred years before Christ.

'El Picacho,' Tamara said, pointing to one of the peaks across from them, 'is evidently sacred. The other big one is Cerro Gie Bets, which means "stone brother" in Zapotec.'

'Good to know.' Hunt looked across at her. 'Pop quiz to follow?'

'Of course.'

'You could be a tour guide down here if this whole private investigator thing doesn't work out,' Hunt said.

'I would want you to come with me.'

'That could be negotiated. If you go, I'm going with you.'

Earlier that morning, Hunt, his body suddenly and completely coming awake at around dawn, had extricated himself from the covers, kissed the shoulder of the sleeping Tamara, and gone into the bathroom to shower and shave. Nowhere nearly caught up on the sleep he had lost, he could not keep his mind from returning to the real reason they were down here, and this realization brought with it a familiar catch in his breathing, a tightening band of tension across his shoulders, a few popping points of light at the periphery of his vision.

He had taken his pounding heart back into the bed and lain there with his eyes closed until she had stirred and turned to face him, then coming all the way awake, she had rolled herself on top of him, and over most of the next hour, the two of them succeeded in driving his demons off and keeping them at bay.

Now as they drove on unpaved streets into the picturesque little village, she put her hand on his thigh. 'You sure you're okay with this?'

His jaw set, Wyatt nodded. 'This has got to happen.'

'That's not what I asked.' She hesitated. 'I could go find him and talk to him. You don't have to go.'

'Yes, I do.'

Hunt found a place to park on the edge of a square in front of a massive cathedral, close to the hotel in the center of the village at which they had a reservation in case they wound up needing a place to spend another night or two. He and Tamara got out of the car into cool, bright sunshine. It wasn't yet 10:30, several hours too early for them to check in.

Down the street a ways, several tables out in front of a restaurant named El Descanso beckoned, and holding hands, they walked over and took one of the few remaining. They were not by any stretch the only visitors to the town. In fact, although Hunt had never in his life heard the name of the village before a couple of days ago, and although it was not large at all and certainly relatively remote, Teotitlán was apparently a tourist destination, especially for Americans. All around them as they sipped their strong and delicious coffee with chocolate, people were speaking English, showing off brightly colored shawls and ponchos and rugs and other woven materials, talking about hiking and mountain biking and archeology.

They had their local map spread out on the table. Their destination looked to be about eight blocks to the west. Hunt had marked the spot with a black felt-tip X and now he finished his drink and sat back, blinking.

'You ready?' Tamara asked.

Hunt stared off around the plaza for a few seconds and then blinked again several more times. 'These damn lights. The last three or four days.' Shaking his head, he closed his eyes for a long count, then opened them and looked across at her. 'I'm all right,' he said. 'Let's go do this.'

More than a hundred and fifty families made their living doing something with weaving in the village, and Wyatt and Tamara passed thirty-five or forty businesses before they got to the address where Hunt had made his X.

The place was like all the others, a stucco structure that might sometimes double as a house, but with an open front, and with brightly colored serapes and rugs and other woven goods hanging out facing the street. In most of these establishments, the weaver did his work in the back half, and visitors were sometimes welcome but more often brought along as part of an organized tour and buying opportunity.

Wyatt put his hand out to stop Tamara and together they stood across the street in glaring sunlight. The little shop was clearly open for business and although no apparent customers were inside, there was movement in the back, in dark shadow.

Hunt couldn't will himself to move. He brought his hand to his forehead, the pain of the migraine coming on in a sudden rush into what had been the field of the aura.

Now someone called out what sounded like a command in a tongue Wyatt didn't recognize – Zapotec? – and two young boys exploded out the front of the shop into the street, laughing and running, racing one another, until they disappeared around a corner.

Tamara squeezed Wyatt's hand, and as though at that signal, he nodded to himself and crossed the five steps out of the bright sunlight and into the shadowed front of the store. His pulse exploded beat by beat in his ear. Wyatt tried to let his eyes adjust to the dimness, but the exploding balls of fire wouldn't allow him to keep them open for more than a few seconds.

To keep his balance because the force of the headache was bringing on a wave of nausea and panic, he stood holding the side of a wooden rack upon which the proprietor had draped a bunch of gaudy ponchos.

He became aware of a slow, repetitive sound, like wooden sticks slapping one another. Raising his head and opening his eyes, he saw that it was a loom – a *telar* according to Tam's lesson – behind which stood a tall, angular figure with long gray hair tied in a ponytail. He wore a green and yellow serape and was looking down through a pair of rimless glasses, concentrating, humming almost inaudibly to himself.

Hunt took a step. His breath seemed to have stopped, and he was aware that Tamara had stepped in next to him and had taken his arm. The pain in his head was suddenly, and quite literally, blinding, and he had to stop and lean into her for support.

Wyatt opened his eyes and the man looked up adjusting his spectacles and Tamara cleared her throat and said, 'Excuse me, we're looking for Kevin Carson.'

The man's expression grew quizzical, then guarded as he straightened all the way up and stopped moving his hands over his work. 'I'm Kevin Carson,' he said. 'What can I do for you?'

Tamara felt the tension in Hunt's arm as though it were an electric current.

On the walk out from the plaza, Wyatt was all grim determination. By the time they reached the Carson shop and stopped to wait across the street, it was clear that his emotions and the psychological impact of finally confronting his biological father were taking their toll on his body and mind.

When he had finally summoned the fortitude to step into the shadowed confines of the space, she could tell by the expression on his face – his brow drawn in furrows, his jaw set, the line of his mouth taut – that it was all he could do to force himself forward.

Kevin Carson was perhaps an inch shorter than Wyatt, but his face had the same clean bone structure, the same clear forehead under the same hairline, the same blue-green eyes. The merest glance eliminated any doubt that the two men were related by blood. She knew that Wyatt could not help but see the resemblance as well – there was no way to miss it.

His bicep twitched again under Tamara's grip. She looked at

his face and saw that he was not so much really blinking as consciously closing, then opening his eyes, she guessed against what last night he'd been calling his light show. His left hand still rested for balance on the rack that held the ponchos, but he moved a step or two closer so that no more than six feet separated him from the loom.

Scrunching his eyes down one last time, Hunt opened them, then took a quick breath and released all of it in a rush, his cheeks pushing out with the force of it. He leveled his gaze at the weaver. 'I'm Wyatt,' he said. 'Your son.'

The older man had already stopped his robotic working of the loom, and now in what Tamara saw as an eerie duplication of his son's behavior, he closed his eyes and raised his face to the ceiling. Taking his own long breath, when he released it his shoulders fell under the poncho. When he opened his eyes again, he had the same startling focus that Tamara had seen in Wyatt a hundred times. 'You come here to kill me?' he asked. 'I wouldn't blame you.'

'No.'

A gray-haired, heavyset woman of obvious native extraction – a little more than half Carson's height – suddenly appeared from the back of the structure and moved up next to him, saying something in Zapotec. He answered her with a few words, then came back to Wyatt. 'My wife, Maria.' He spoke to her again, a few more words in Zapotec, but they must have conveyed a sense of the moment, because she gave a quick, startled glance at Wyatt, then her hand went to her mouth before she crossed herself.

For a long moment, the two couples faced one another without a sound. Wyatt's Adam's apple bobbed up and down. His father cast his eyes to the ground, over to his wife, then settled back on Wyatt. Both men seemed to gather into themselves somehow against the onslaught of God knew what emotions.

At last, shrugging against whatever reservations he might be feeling, Carson said, 'We can sit in the back if you want to come around.' He gave what sounded like an order to Maria, who circumvented the loom, then stopped in front of Wyatt. Reaching out, she touched his hand and bowed from the waist in front of him, a greeting. Going around both of them, she pulled the large wooden doors to the street closed behind them, leaving them all now in the dim ambient light allowed by the small panes of glass in the doors and the windows high on the wall to Tamara's right.

Tamara and Wyatt followed them back into the small open rooms of the house – there was no hallway, just two rooms, one behind the other – through what looked to be a kitchen – a half-size refrigerator, a sink and counter. Here Maria peeled off to the side, and Kevin led them out to a small enclosed stucco patio with a red-tiled floor, an ornately carved wooden gate, the whole area covered by a trellis to which clung a riot of bougainvillea. A simple wooden table, surrounded on three sides by chairs, sat against a bench on the side wall. More flowers grew from sconces set into the stucco.

Tamara found the place beautiful and serene, which is what everybody seemed to need.

Wyatt's father pulled out two chairs as he passed the table and turned the third one around to straddle it backward. Wyatt took the chair closest to the house, across the table from him, with Tamara in the middle.

Under Carson's poncho, a blue work shirt peeked out, below which he wore jeans and leather sandals, no socks. Beneath his glasses, deep lines creased the skin around his eyes. He moved his mouth, pursing his lips, taking Wyatt in as he settled himself at the table. 'I guess it'd be stupid to ask how you've been,' he said.

Wyatt's shoulders heaved at the absurdity of that.

'If it's any consolation, if I had it to do over again, I'd have done it different.'

Wyatt unclasped his hands on the table, opened his palms. 'It worked out okay.'

'I see that.' Carson kept his voice flat. 'I didn't know I'd ever have a life where I could raise a kid. Never really believed I would get one. I couldn't have told you I'd have picked this place, that I'd wind up here, in a million years. And I thought, no matter what I did, you would be better off without me. And then, by the time I got finished with the trials, you were gone. Adopted out in a new life. I couldn't have found you if I wanted to.'

'I get it,' Hunt said. 'It's water under the bridge.'

'Not exactly. It was a terrible mistake. The worst mistake of my life. You should know that.'

Tamara saw Wyatt's Adam's apple rise and fall.

'You know about the trials, I presume.'

'Sure.'

'I didn't kill your mother.'

'I know that.'

Kevin's nod seemed distilled relief.

'I got the letter you left with Father Bernard,' Wyatt said. 'What about Texas?'

'Texas?'

'Your job there. That's where you said you were going.'

Kevin shook his head. 'It wasn't far enough. I wasn't sure this would be far enough, either. If I hadn't met Maria, who saved my life, and her family, who taught me how to do this work – I probably would have kept going all the way to Brazil.' He paused. 'So, let me ask, how'd you find me? I thought I'd managed to disappear.'

'And you did, pretty much.'

'Except?'

Wyatt shook his head as though it weighed a hundred pounds. 'Doesn't matter,' he said. 'You're here. I'm here.'

'He's a private investigator. He finds people,' Tamara put in, then added. 'I'm Tamara. I work with him.'

Kevin turned his head and fixed his gaze on her. 'So you're here on a job?'

Wyatt nodded and again brought his hands to his temples. 'My mother.' He closed his eyes for two or three seconds before opening them again, squinting to focus. 'We're trying to find out who killed her.'

Tamara saw him struggling and reached out to touch his arm. 'Wyatt?'

Putting his hand over hers, he said, 'I'm all right.' Then, back to his father, he repeated himself. 'We're trying to find who killed Margie. Do you have any ideas?'

Carson shook his head no. 'If I had any ideas,' he said, 'I would have told them to the police back then when it might have done some good.'

'And you haven't had any since?'

'No. There was no reason for anyone to have killed her. She was just a young mom, staying at home, taking care of you.'

'Did you know about Jim Jones?'

The question straightened Carson up in his chair. 'That was a long time before, like years. Him and her, I mean. It wasn't any part of either of the trials. How did you find out about that?'

'That doesn't matter, either. But we know it's true. That's the point.'

'Well, of course it's true. But nobody knew back then what a monster he was going to turn out to be.'

'Really?'

'Really. Honestly.'

'You don't think Margie had some inkling? Having seen what he'd done to her? How he could be?'

'Well, yes. That. But . . .'

Wyatt came forward in his chair, his hands supplicating on the table. 'But what if she told Evie Spencer?'

'Evie? How's she involved in any of this?'

'Listen. What if she told Evie she was going to tell anybody who'd listen about what Jones had done to her, and about how old she'd been when it had all happened? Did she ever tell you if she thought about doing something like that?'

Tamara's eyes went to Carson, who was frowning in concentration. 'She couldn't believe it when Evie started getting involved with the People's Temple, I know that. They were relocating down in San Francisco from wherever the hell Margie had been with them up north. And Margie tried to warn Evie not to get involved, that Jones was trouble. That's why Evie wasn't around for any part of the trials. She and Margie had had this huge fight about Jones, and she hadn't even been around the apartment for a month or more, which was fine with me. That woman was a whack job of the first order, and I was glad to see her gone out of our lives.'

'Did you know Evie's husband, Lionel?'

'Sure. We went out with them a lot – the kids, you know, playing together.'

'What'd you think of him?'

Carson shrugged. 'Not much, to tell you the truth. He was a nice enough guy, but a bit of a wimp. And how he could stand being with her I don't know.'

'What would you say,' Hunt pressed, 'if I told you that the police in San Francisco now think he killed Margie, along with one of my associates and a random cab driver, before he killed himself?'

'Lionel killed himself?'

Hunt nodded. 'Apparently. Last week. Does any of this surprise you?'

'All of it surprises me. That just doesn't sound like Lionel. I mean, killing people? Killing Margie? I can't imagine . . .' He picked at the paint on the back of his chair. 'You know,' he said, 'Lionel's the guy who offered me the job in Texas.'

Wyatt threw a look at Tamara, then came back to his father. 'Say that again.'

Carson inclined his head. 'He looked me up after the second trial and said if I wanted to get away from the city, he had some friends and maybe a job at an airfield down in Texas. He could spring for a ticket . . .'

'Why would he do that?'

'He was still with Evie and she was in the temple by then and Jones had a lot of money. They were coining money with all the social security and savings accounts they were taking in. Lionel told me they'd all followed the trials and knew I was innocent. They thought I'd been railroaded and it would be an act of Christian kindness to help get me started somewhere else, away from the heat. I could either take some travel money or he could fly me down there next time he went himself.'

'Wait a minute. You're saying Lionel was a pilot?'

'Yeah, he and his brother. They'd both been in the air force in Vietnam. The rumor was that Jones was buying them their own airplane, or had already bought it. Or maybe just the use of it.'

Maria came out from the house bearing a tray with a glass pitcher of some tropical-looking juice and three glasses. Placing it on the table in the middle of them, she said a few words to her husband before touching him on the shoulder and disappearing back inside the house.

'Guess I'd better pour some of this for you if I don't want to have her kill me,' he said. Tamara was beginning to marvel at the genetic encoding that made the father and son sound so much alike, even in tone and the rhythms of their speech. 'The key ingredient here' – he continued as he began to pour into the first glass – 'is ice. We break out the ice about twice a year.'

'Thank you,' Tamara said. 'It looks delicious.'

'It is,' he said. 'Maria's a genius.' He pushed the second glass toward Wyatt and asked, 'So where were we?'

'Lionel Spencer and his airplane.' Wyatt hadn't lost his place, spoke without hesitation. 'So did you use it? Fly down to Texas with him? Or take the money?'

'None of those,' his father said. He finished pouring his own glass and set it down untouched in front of him. 'In the end, I just split. I didn't want to owe anybody anything. If I was going to start over, and I was, it was going to be from scratch.' He adjusted his glasses and looked to Tamara again, then back to Wyatt, finally taking a drink. 'You know,' he said. 'I'm having a hard time believing that Lionel killed Margie. Did you know him?'

'No. I never met him.'

'Well, if you'd known him . . .' He shook his head against the possibility. 'I just can't see it. Especially the way she was killed, bludgeoned to death. It took a while to get it done. So it was close and personal. And Lionel was just a pure milquetoast. He didn't have it in him. If it was a gun, then maybe, but only just maybe. As it happened, no way. He was afraid of Evie, for Christ's sake.'

'Do you think Evie could have done it?' Tamara asked.

'No. She might have been crazy, but she was all about peace and love and Jesus.'

Wyatt put his own glass down after a sip. 'But she died at Jonestown. She might have even killed her own children.'

'That was a lot later. What, eight or ten years?' In another unconscious reflection of his son's mannerisms, Carson brought one hand to his forehead and squeezed at his temples. 'The news about that didn't get down here until a few weeks after it happened. When I saw her name, I couldn't believe it.'

'But she did it,' Wyatt said. 'Had her children drink the Kool-Aid, didn't she?'

'Probably,' Carson said. 'But that was years of brainwashing and drugs after Margie was killed. I can't see her hurting a flea when we knew her. In fact, and I just remembered this, if she found spiders or ladybugs or whatever in our apartment, she'd pick them up and go outside or to the window and let them go so they wouldn't be hurt.'

Wyatt sat back and crossed his arms, a study in exhaustion, the skin dark and sunken under his eyes. 'This connection to Jonestown,' he said, 'is the closest thing to a motive we've been able to come up with. It's the only thing that makes Margie's death something other than a random, totally meaningless killing.'

Carson let out a weary sigh. 'I hate to say this, but that's what I've come to believe it was.'

'Well, I'm sorry, but I can't accept that,' Wyatt replied. 'There must have been someone else. You mentioned a brother, Lionel's brother.'

'Lance.' Carson's mouth went tight for a beat, as though remembering a bad taste. 'Yeah, Lance was around. He was Lionel's older brother, couple of years older.'

Wyatt asked, 'And what was he like?'

Carson didn't answer right away. He glanced off into nothing, perhaps struck by the question, by the previously unimagined thought. 'He was a soldier,' he said at last. 'That's what he was like. A soldier.'

'And close to Jones?' Tamara asked.

'Near the top,' Carson said.

27

THEY GOT INTERRUPTED again as Maria knocked on the side of the back door and stepped into the patio, followed by a native Indian man of an indeterminate age somewhere between twenty-five and forty. Short and thick and bearded, and with a nose like Maria's, the man grew his black ponytail halfway down his back like a horse's mane. He was dressed in exactly the same manner as Kevin Carson, except that his serape was brown and yellow and he didn't wear glasses.

When Carson saw him, a cloud passed quickly over his face, but then evaporated into a mere look of exasperation. Saying 'Excuse me' to Wyatt and Tamara, he stood up and spoke sharply in Zapotec to his wife. Unmoved, she stood with her arms crossed over her chest, shaking her head in obvious disagreement.

The man said something to Carson.

The two Americans stood up as the conversation continued. 'What's happening?' Tamara whispered, but Wyatt simply shook his head – he didn't know – and reached out to take her hand.

Carson was still talking to the visitor when a couple – a tiny and very pretty young pregnant woman and another young man, this one clean-shaven, short-haired, taller, in black jeans and an Obama 'Hope' T-shirt – came up through the house and stood now in the doorway out to the patio. Taking in the situation at a glance, the younger man pulled his wife with him and crossed from the door around behind the bearded man, both of them ignoring Carson. The man extended his hand to Wyatt. 'I am

Sergio,' he said in heavily accented English, 'and this' – he pushed the pregnant woman forward – 'is Marissa. She is your sister.'

Wyatt seemed to take the news in a kind of panic, his eyes going from Marissa over to Tamara, back to his father, who had turned, apparently to try and take control before things got out of hand. 'I'm sorry,' Carson said, 'this is Maria's doing. I didn't mean . . .' He stopped, his meaning clear enough.

But Wyatt looked behind him and over to take in the first visitor. The bearded young man evidently took it as a kind of invitation and stepped around Carson and looked Wyatt up and down before extending his own hand and offering a wary smile. 'Daveed,' he said. David. *'Soy tu hermano.'*

Wyatt was shaking hands with David, introducing himself and Tamara, when the next four people, maybe the two children that they'd seen earlier, and another couple – their parents? – pressed their way out through the back door. Realizing that resistance was swiftly becoming hopeless, Kevin Carson took on the role of host and translator. Though he seemed acutely aware of Wyatt's discomfort, and in fact appeared to share a good deal of it, at this point he was mostly directing traffic. 'This is Paulo and his wife, Téadora. Paulo is my youngest. The kids are Billy, Guillermo; and Féderico, Freddy. They'd be your half nephews, I suppose.' He met Wyatt's eyes, turned to Tamara. 'I'm sorry about this. Are you all right?'

'Fine,' Wyatt said, his eyes troubled, his smile a brittle thing.

'This is amazing,' Tamara said.

'It's going to get worse,' Carson promised.

By the time Maria and the other woman started bringing out the first platters of mole and eggs and chicken and liver and tamales, for of course the return of the lost son was an unbridled cause for celebration, a total of fourteen people were circulating in and out of the patio. Another table and more chairs appeared from somewhere. David's wife, Carla, arrived, accompanied by their two toddlers, then another of Kevin's sons, another half brother, Ramon, and his wife, Gloria, showed up with their three children, coming home from school with the others' kids for their lunch.

Wyatt and Tamara stood next to their translator, all with their unrefusable beers, and tried their best to engage with the unexpected onslaught of family. Fully four of the seven youngsters would not relinquish the tight semicircle they formed in front of their newfound relative and couldn't hear enough about life in America, oohing with surprise and admiration as Tamara described Wyatt's warehouse home in San Francisco, complete with his half basketball court.

Which led to even more questions, and more answers. Yes, he had a car, a Mini Cooper. Also a Kawasaki motorcycle. Some guitars. Surfboards. He windsurfed all the time, mostly under the Golden Gate Bridge.

The breathlessness he heard in the questions didn't just come from the children. Kevin Carson, perhaps in spite of himself, couldn't keep the excitement and sense of awe at Wyatt's accomplishments and acquisitions out of his voice. And his was the voice of the multitude, everyone including Sergio speaking to Wyatt – and to Tamara – through him.

No, Tamara was not a movie star, didn't even want to be one. No, they weren't married. Well, they should be. They obviously were together and should stay together. Surely, she was at least a model. They were sure they had seen her in magazines.

All the family here made their living with the loom. After lunch, along with the mescal, they brought out samples of all the different styles they'd each come to specialize in, each in their own shop, sending the children off running to the various storefronts to bring back gifts, for of course Wyatt and Tamara must keep whatever they could carry home, and more.

And then the older children had gone back to school, the younger ones to naps, the women, including Tamara, into the kitchen to clean up. Wyatt sat on the bench against the wall under the bougainvillea, sipping mescal and ice from his juice glass with his three half brothers and his father.

Sitting around in a shaded patio in the middle of a beautiful fall afternoon, two beers and a few mescals humming in his bloodstream, Wyatt closed his eyes and put his head back against the stucco wall and listened to Kevin Carson and his three sons as they spoke in an almost dead language he would never understand about whatever it was – their families, their work, their lives, the future.

His half sister, pregnant Marissa, came out with half cups of coffee on a little tray. She let her three brothers grab theirs, but took the last two of them around the table. One, with some ceremony, she gave to Wyatt and the other she placed in front of her father, his father, pausing to lean over and sweetly kiss the top of his head.

They got checked into the hotel and Wyatt told Tamara that if she didn't mind, he was just going to lie down for a minute. If he could get a phone line to the States, maybe through the switchboard here, he was going to try to call Devin Juhle a little later and maybe see what he could find out about Lance Spencer, if he was still alive. But in the meanwhile, he could use a power nap. He was a little wrung out.

'A little?'

He shrugged, forced his lips into the semblance of a smile. 'Maybe slightly more than a little.'

'All right,' she said. 'You sleep and I'll go check my e-mails at their business center. Is your head okay?'

'A little.'

'You mean it hurts a little or it's okay a little?'

'A little of both.' He sat down on the bed. 'That's too many questions.'

'Do you want me to wake you up?'

'How 'bout in an hour?'

'You're sure that's enough?'

'It'll have to be.'

She was sitting across from him on the chair in front of the room's desk, at about his eye level. 'Wyatt,' she said. 'You can take more than an hour. The world won't end.'

'It might,' he said. Then, 'An hour would be fine. Really.'

'That's all you're going to need?'

'Not need,' he said. 'Could use, that's all.'

She took in a breath. 'Well, if you could use more, just let me know and I'll let you go.'

'I know. You're great. Thanks.'

'You're welcome.'

'I've just got to get myself a little bit together.'

She reached out and touched his knee. 'I could stay and lie here next to you. I won't get frisky, I promise.'

'No. You go ahead. I'm fine.'

'One hour alone and a quick nap and all this goes back where it needs to be, huh?'

He managed a nod and swallowed whatever he was going to say. He was staring straight ahead but not really at her. At nothing. Finally, he sighed and said, 'Oh, man,' in a tortured voice before he eased himself all the way down onto his back.

'You want to scooch up to the pillows? You'll be more comfortable.'

He didn't answer, so she shrugged and stood up to go into the bathroom for a minute. When she came out, he was still lying exactly as she'd left him, his eyes closed. But something about his body language stopped her and on closer inspection she saw that far from relaxing into sleep, he seemed to be in a state of high tension. He'd clenched his hands into fists at his sides and his breathing came in quick, shallow gasps.

'Wyatt?' She reached down and touched his leg. 'Wyatt, are you all right?'

An involuntary moan, low and deep, came up from somewhere inside him and it called forth in Tamara a stab of real fear. This was a primal sound she'd never heard from him before and she had no idea what to do with it. She sat down on the bed next to him and placed a flat palm on his chest, where she felt his heart racing under his shirt. Lying down now, her face up close next to his, she whispered to him. 'It's okay. Shhh now. It's okay.'

But clearly it wasn't okay. Wyatt turned away from her and all at once his legs were up and he was in the fetal position, and in that same moment, his whole body heaved as though from an electric shock in one great moment of release, and suddenly he was truly sobbing, gasping uncontrollably, curled up into himself, emitting unintelligible cries and a near-continuous moan.

Terrified now at this breakdown, Tamara pulled herself against him and hugged his back, trying to get her arms around him – to comfort him, to hold him down. But he showed no sign that he was even aware of her. His body shook and spasmed against her as the sobs wracked him again and again.

She held tight behind him and let it go on. She could do nothing to stop it in any event. Until finally – two minutes later? ten? – the deep, wrenching sobbing seemed to have succeeded in sapping him of all of his strength. The deep guttural moaning gave way to an exhausted mewling sound until eventually the gasping, too, subsided and at last he became still.

After the crying jag, he'd fallen into a deep sleep. Tamara pulled the covers up over him and he had stayed that way for the next four hours, occasionally calling out in an agitated fashion, but mostly on his side, curled up, silent. Tamara sat at the desk chair pretty much the whole time, thumbing through all the tourist magazines the hotel supplied to the rooms and then starting on a novel called *The Art of Racing in the Rain* that one of the earlier guests had left in the bookshelf. Given the high hurdle of disbelief she had to surmount because its narrator was a dog, she thought it was a damn good book, although because of her concerns about Wyatt, she had some trouble completely engaging with it.

When around 8:15 she looked over and saw that he had at last opened his eyes, she put her book down and went over to sit by him, gently lowering herself, touching his face, running her hand down the length of his side.

'Hey,' she whispered.

He closed his eyes and exhaled, and for a few seconds she thought that he hadn't actually woken up after all, but then he opened his eyes again.

'Everything's all right,' she said. 'You're safe here.'

No response.

His eyes were open, but he was looking more or less through her.

'Do you feel like you want to get up? I'm sure we could find some dinner somewhere. It's still not too late.'

He closed his eyes and began to rock himself back and forth.

Wyatt had come to again – if that was the word – and without much in the way of interaction had let her get him out of the bed and sitting up in the chair, where she'd put a blanket over him because he seemed to be cold. Then finally, about an hour ago, Tamara had let her mounting worries over Wyatt trump her fear that if she left him alone, he might either run away or do something else even more foolish. She had told him where she was going, then braved a run to the front desk to see if she could get some kind of help.

When Tamara brought Dr. Gutierrez, an elderly man with a

kindly manner and thank God excellent English, back to the room, Hunt was where she had left him in the armchair, sitting up with his eyes closed, his face drawn and lifeless. Gutierrez immediately crossed to him and turned on the light over his chair.

'Señor Hunt,' he said gently. 'Can you hear me?'

Wyatt opened his eyes and nodded.

'I'm a doctor. How are you feeling?'

It took a minute, but finally he dredged up a word. 'Tired.'

'Do you know where you are?'

Again, a weary nod, after which he closed his eyes again. 'Tired,' he said again.

The doctor turned back to Tamara. 'How long has he been like this?'

'I don't know exactly. A couple of hours. He kind of had a breakdown earlier in the afternoon and then went to sleep.'

'A breakdown?'

'Crying. Sobbing, really. He's been under a lot of pressure.'

'He's been drinking, too,' Gutierrez said.

'Yes. Beer and mescal.'

The doctor nodded, unsurprised. 'Not the wisest combination.'

'No. But I don't think he was drunk. We were talking all the way home, and even after we got here. And then he just kind of broke down.'

'The pressure you mentioned. It is emotional?'

'He met his biological father for the first time today. He was adopted as a small child. He's also been complaining of a migraine.'

'So this has been going on?'

'A few days at least, yes.'

'Has he been sleeping?'

'Very little. Two or three hours a day.'

Gutierrez tsked. 'Not enough. So this sounds to me like acute anxiety along with lack of sleep, which go together like beans and rice. And of course the alcohol does not help, either.'

'So you're saying he's tired and he's drunk?'

The doctor's face clouded over and he shook his head. 'Oh no, señora, much more than that. He's had what they would call in the States a nervous breakdown. He's no longer able to cope emotionally with everything that has happened to him, so his conscious mind has simply shut down.'

'So how long does this last?'

'It varies. A day, two weeks? With rest and medication, he could come out of it soon.' Gutierrez turned back and put a hand on Hunt's knee, pushing at it. He jerked back into consciousness, although his face still lacked any animation. 'Señor,' the doctor said, 'do you need to be in a hospital tonight?'

'A hospital?' Tamara asked.

Gutierrez nodded. 'In the U.S., he would be admitted to a hospital and I can arrange that here.'

'Do you think it's necessary for him to get better?'

The doctor shrugged. 'Maybe. Maybe not necessary, but it might not hurt. A hospital here in a strange place might do him more harm than good. I can't say.'

Tamara sat wringing her hands, looked over at Wyatt. 'Do you understand the doctor? Should we go to the hospital?'

Through the fog, Hunt swallowed, managed a single syllable. 'Here.'

'Can you get back over to the bed?' Gutierrez asked.

Tamara stood up. 'I can help him.'

She came over and took off the blanket, then took him by both hands and helped him rise out of the chair. A couple of steps over to the bed and it was done. 'We'll try to stay here first,' she said.

'I think and I hope,' Gutierrez said to Tamara, 'that this will pass relatively quickly. We can treat tonight as an isolated episode. He is able to talk and understand, but he is, of course, physically and emotionally exhausted. So the first thing is to sleep.' He handed her a small paper packet. 'He is to take one of these . . . how long since he stopped drinking?'

'Six hours, maybe seven.'

'All right. One and only one now. So he can sleep. Then, in the morning, if the anxiety continues, the migraine.' He gave her a small plastic container with four pills in it. 'One of these. Lorazepam. To dial down, I believe you say, the anxiety. But not until the morning, and only if he needs it. This can be addictive, so be careful and see a doctor when you get back home if he needs more. How long are you staying here?'

'Only a day or two more.'

'All right. Good. You were wise to come get me, and with sleep, the regular rhythm of sleep, this might pass quickly. Sometimes an emotional episode, a breakdown, it can be its own kind of healing. But if he does not respond by, say, tomorrow or the next day, please call me again and we will take further steps.'

'Let's hope he comes around,' she said.

'Yes, let us hope.' The doctor stood and closed his bag. Tamara walked him to the door, thanked him again, then went into the bathroom to get a glass of water so she could give Wyatt his pill.

28

Wednesday morning, two days later, Hunt opened his eyes, turned his head, and saw Tamara sitting tucked sideways into the armchair, sipping from a coffee mug and reading. She had opened the blinds and sunlight fell on her hair and across her shoulders. She wore one of the hotel's white bathrobes. A white carafe, another coffee mug, and a basket of fruit sat at her elbow on the end table.

Where had he been?

He could tell by the angle of the sun that he'd slept away most of the morning. The sky out the window was deep blue. He could smell coffee and chocolate and he stretched out in a yawn under the covers and then turned to look at her. 'You are so beautiful,' he said.

Surprise and relief seemed to hit her in a flood. She turned her book facedown, lowered her coffee mug, and turned to face him, her face etched with worry. 'I'm glad you think so,' she said. 'How are you feeling?'

'Good.' His speech came a little slowly, a trace of grogginess hanging on. 'Better,' he said, 'if I had some coffee.'

'I think I might have saved you a little.'

'That would be good, if you did.'

'Well, let's see.' She picked up the carafe – 'It's your lucky day' – and filled his mug.

He watched her add a packet of powdered chocolate and stir and then get up and come over and wait until he'd pushed himself up, stacking extra propping pillows behind him. He took the mug. 'What time is it?'

'About noon.'

'Tuesday?'

Her face relaxed into a soft smile. 'Wednesday. Last time I checked.'

'So that was two days ago?' He hesitated. Then, 'I guess that's a relief. It feels like a week ago.' Resting his mug on the sheets covering him, he patted the bed.

After a moment, she reached over and grabbed her own coffee, then came back to the bedside and sat, clutching her mug with both hands.

'I don't know what happened,' Hunt said, his voice still thick. 'I can't explain it. All I can say is I'm sorry and if you want to leave now, I wouldn't blame you.'

'Why would I want to leave you? And you don't have anything to be sorry about. You had a panic attack. The doctor said it was exhaustion and anxiety. Guess what? Real stuff. The mescal probably didn't help, either. Basically, you just shorted out for a while. That's what it was.'

'Shorted out. Nice.'

'Hey. Circuits overload. They short out. It happens.'

'All right, but it's never happened to me.'

'Sorry to say, but new reality time. Yes, it has.'

Hunt nodded wearily. 'Touché.' A pause. 'I vaguely remember a doctor. That was smart.'

'I didn't know what else to do. I didn't know what was happening. Luckily, he's on call with the hotels in town and could come right over.'

'I'm just so sorry to have put you through that.'

'Wyatt.' She dismissed the apology with a little brush of her hand. '*You're* the one who went through it. I'm just glad I was here.'

'Seeing me at my best.'

'Get over that, please, would you? Best. Worst. It doesn't matter. I'm here. You want to get rid of me, it's going to take more than that. You're going to have to kick me out.'

'I'm not doing that. The last thing I want is to get rid of you.'

'Good. It's not in my plan, either.'

'I'm just embarrassed that . . .'

She put a finger against his lips. 'What? That you're not perfect? That you've got emotions and feelings you can't control churning up in there? That sometimes life just seems too hard? This just in, Wyatt. People aren't perfect. One day – who knows? – you might even catch me on an off day. Bitchy, crabby, depressed, all of the above. That could happen, and then what? You're going to leave?'

'I'm not going to leave.'

'Me, neither. End of story. Okay?' She remembered her coffee and lifted it to her mouth. Reaching out, she touched his face and asked gently. 'So how's the light show this morning?'

Wyatt lifted his chin, seemed to scan the corners of the room, came back to her, and said with the lift of surprise, 'No sign of it.'

'Good. If it starts to come back, the doctor left another pill you can take, just so you know. Meanwhile, you might want to consider eating a little food.'

'I like the concept,' Wyatt said. 'Then I've got to call Devin.'

Hunt felt he'd gotten everything he'd come here to get. He'd followed the trail of his mother's killer forward from the first texter's message and backward to Jonestown. Evie Spencer had led him to Jones, to Indianapolis and his maternal grandmother, then from Lionel to his biological father and his happy and functional Mexican family to Lionel Spencer's brother Lance, who was now the last unturned stone. If Lance turned out to be a dry well, Wyatt had no idea of where he'd even begin to turn next. But it might not come to that, to a dead end. One faint glimmer had reoccurred to him and gave him a vestige of hope: His texter's last message had simply said that it wasn't Lionel.

First name only.

Didn't this invite the possibility that it might be another Spencer? And if another Spencer, who else could it be but Lance?

A long shot, Hunt knew, but something.

And if in the end after all his efforts he couldn't get a satisfactory conclusion to the investigation, he tried to put a good face on the possibility that he might finally have to abandon it altogether. No doubt some good had already come of it. If he wanted to look at it selfishly, it had been an incredible personal journey that had acquainted him with his long-lost origins and, he felt, had peeled off the scabs that had formed over his early life. These had opened fresh wounds that had caused some pain, but they were wounds he felt could now truly begin to heal. Perhaps had already begun to heal.

Finally, a tectonic shift had occurred with him and Tamara as well. It was far more than that they had become lovers, although that of course was part of it. A new trust flourished, a bond that hadn't been completely forged before yesterday and his breakdown, if that's what it had been, or panic attack, or whatever they wanted to call it. Now, out loud, without reservation, they were both in it, with each other, for the long haul.

So there would be compensations, yes, if he had to give up and admit defeat. But in his heart, Hunt did not want to abandon this chase. He had come this far. Each stop on the scavenger hunt had led him to the next clue. It was unfathomable for him to imagine that it would all lead nowhere.

His cell phone did not work in Teotitlán, but Wyatt managed to use the landline at his hotel after lunch to place calls to Juhle at his home and to his cell, both of which went to his voice mail.

He and Tamara made reservations to fly out of Oaxaca to Phoenix at 5:30 this afternoon.

Today, though, in their last half hour here, Hunt had an important stop to make. He pulled their car to the side of the road outside Kevin Carson's shop, which only two days ago had been so intimidating, so loaded with emotional portent, that he could barely force himself inside. Now he and Tamara knocked on the already-opened wooden door, called out a greeting, and walked together into the heavily shaded front room.

Kevin Carson stopped the work he was doing on his loom, yelled for Maria, and came around. Ostensibly, they were here to arrange to get the woven gifts from the family shipped to California. Though Tamara spoke little Spanish and Maria only token English – she was, after all, married to an American – the two women split off to tend to their business in the back of the house.

Wyatt waded into an initially awkward silence. 'I wanted to thank you for the celebration,' he began. 'That was a hell of a party.'

His father nodded. 'We don't party enough,' he said. 'Good to have an excuse, and you showing up sure was one.' He paused for a beat, then took a breath and pushed ahead. 'I don't know if it means anything – I told you I wouldn't have blamed you if you'd come to kill me, and I wouldn't've – you'd a had every right. But I can't tell you how wonderful it is to see how you turned out.'

'I've got a great family.'

'Must have.'

'So do you.'

'I know that. I'm proud of each one of them.' He met Wyatt's eyes, ran his front teeth over his lower lip. 'Not so much proud of myself, though. I don't know what I was thinking.'

'You were thinking I'd be better off. Maybe you were right.'

'I don't know about that.'

'No, of course not. You'll never know that. But you sure as hell wouldn't have wound up down here married to Maria if you'd been stuck with dragging me along. And it seems like down here is where you're meant to be.'

'I hope that's true. Though the road to get here . . .'

Hunt held up a hand. 'That's the road you had to take. I get it. That's what I'm trying to tell you. It's all right.'

Kevin Carson blinked a time or two, then cleared his throat. 'I appreciate that,' he said. 'I'm not sure I deserve it, but I appreciate it.'

'I'd like it if we tried to stay in touch,' Wyatt said.

His father nodded. 'I'm sure we can do that.'

'Good, then. Let's try to do that.'

'Deal.'

The men shook hands and nodded as their eyes met.

'It's a bitch, isn't it?' Kevin asked.

'Little bit,' Hunt replied, all the possible antecedents clear to him. 'Little bit.' It was all a bitch. That was the pure truth of it: Margie being murdered, Kevin feeling forced to abandon his only son, the two trials, running away to Mexico, building a new life in a new language from scratch, dealing with all the loss. 'I've got a plane to catch, so what say we go check on our women?' he asked. 'See what they're up to.'

Devin Juhle hated lying to his partner, but Sarah had already logically and pointedly closed the door to any other considerations concerning the guilt of Lionel Spencer, and he didn't feel as though he wanted to spin his wheels with her again on the topic, or explain to her why he was willing to waste both of their time reworking elements of a case that featured no unresolved issues. So he made up a story to Sarah about being on a witness list and possibly having to appear in court in one of his old cases, and she had bought it and went off on her own business.

But yet another call from Wyatt Hunt – two actually, and from Mexico, with the same rather urgent message about Lance, the older brother of Lionel Spencer – were, against his better judgment, nudging him along the path of doubt. Not reasonable doubt, since there wasn't anything particularly reasonable about Hunt's suggestion.

Of course the very first thing Juhle had done when he got the new name was run Lance Spencer through the criminal database, where he learned that the man had no criminal record. A quick Google search revealed that he was the CEO of an aircraft-leasing company, a pilot, a board member of three other corporations, and evidently a substantial donor to several charities. He had a home on Nob Hill in San Francisco and another one in Sonoma County. He was married with a wife and a child.

In short, the man was a pillar of the community.

So what possible reason could Juhle give Lance Spencer if he knocked on his door and told him he had some questions about his brother's death? Did Lance, by any chance, kill Lionel and try to make it look like a suicide? Well, no, Juhle would be forced to say, there wasn't any evidence to suggest such a thing, but . . .

It was ludicrous. As a cop, Juhle did not want to talk to a murder suspect without some sort of game plan. This might be his only chance to interview Lance, and certainly would be his only chance to take him by surprise. He didn't want to stumble through some vague, open-ended question-and-answer session that would accomplish nothing except to alert Lance that he was under suspicion.

It wasn't really that any of Hunt's information was immediately verifiable, led to or sprung from any hard evidence, but Juhle had a history with Hunt over the past few years. They had been involved together in three cases – twice on the same side, once more or less in opposition – and in all three, Hunt's vision and instincts had carried the day. Devin knew that Wyatt certainly understood all the subtleties that pointed to the incontrovertible guilt of Lionel Spencer, and still he remained unconvinced. So much as he might be tempted, Juhle just couldn't convince himself to discount Hunt's input.

Hunt had proven himself to be a tireless and sometimes inspired investigator. He was also by police standards a complete wild card – he didn't have to operate within the system as Juhle did, and because he didn't have to, he didn't. Hunt could operate on instinct, hunch, pique, ego, and just plain orneriness in a way that Juhle simply could not. This made him difficult both as a friend and a quasi partner. But there was no real arguing with Wyatt's success. He'd been right and Juhle had been dead wrong at least three times. Juhle knew he would be wise to remember that, and he was remembering it now as he drove out to pay a personal call on the former chief of police Dan Rigby.

Rigby had been gracious enough taking Juhle's call. He remembered their last discussion when he'd told the inspector to get back to him if he could help with the case, which at that time had been the Margie Carson murder only. Now the two men sat at Rigby's kitchen table, and the chief's cranberry juice stopped halfway to his mouth. 'You're telling me,' he said, 'that this forty-year-old case suddenly got opened and now there are three other homicides connected to it?'

'Two homicides and a suicide, but yeah.'

'That's unusual.'

'I thought so, too. Oh, and one other thing makes it more so. Kevin Carson?'

'Sure. The husband, the killer. What about him?'

'He didn't kill these latest three.'

'You know that?'

'Pretty much, yes.'

'What, is he dead?'

'No, sir. He's in Mexico. Deep Mexico. He wasn't here in San Francisco last week, guaranteed. Or last year, either. In fact, he hasn't been in this country since before the designated hitter.'

This time, the juice made it to the chief's mouth. He sloshed it around a bit, then swallowed. 'You're saying we had the wrong guy.'

'No, sir. Only that he couldn't have done the last ones. So maybe he didn't do the first one, either.'

Rigby wagged his head as though disillusioned. 'I suppose that happens. So, is that what you wanted to see me about? Tell me I screwed one up?'

'No, sir. You might remember, last time we talked I asked you about a woman named Evie Secrist. She was the other woman with Margie Carson where you and your partner Jim Burg got called out because they'd left their young kids in Margie's apartment alone together.'

'Yeah, I remember that.'

'Well, it turns out her real name was Evie Spencer. She was married at the time to the guy we've made for the two homicides last week, and who then shot himself. His name's Lionel Spencer. But I have a source who doesn't believe it's Lionel.'

'What? A snitch? A witness?'

'No. As it turns out, it's Margie Carson's son. He's a private eye in town. He's tracked down his father in Mexico, and the father thinks none of this could have been Lionel. He wouldn't have had the stomach for it.'

'So who's your friend like?'

'Lionel has a brother, Lance. The only problem is he's got no evidence for it. And Lance is some kind of big player in the corporate world, so just knocking on his door when I've got nothing specific to ask him might not be the most productive use of my time. I wonder if you remember coming across that name in the Margie Carson case?'

'Was he in the file? A witness at the trial? Anything like that?'

'No.'

The former chief grimaced. 'This was forty years ago, Inspector. I can't say the name just leaps out at me. I can tell you, though, that if he's not in the file, he wasn't part of the case. And from what you're telling me, I'm hearing that you think he should have been our prime suspect, or at least one of them.'

'I don't know that, sir. At the time, there was no way anybody could have known. Without the Jim Jones connection, and that didn't come about until a few years later, nothing connected these Spencer brothers to Margie or her death.'

Rigby straightened up in his chair. 'That's the first I've heard about Jim Jones. You mention him, you got my attention. These guys were with him?'

'Evidently. Both of them.'

'How'd they get out alive?'

'They didn't go. Evie did, though. And her and Lionel's children.'

Rigby's jaw worked as he digested this information. 'The bastard.'

'There's one other thing,' Juhle said.

'I'm listening.'

'My PI friend went and talked to Jim Burg's wife. She told him he – Burg – didn't believe Kevin Carson was guilty, either. He had just made inspector and was starting to look into the case on his own when he then suddenly committed suicide. Just like Lionel Spencer committed suicide. Bullet in the head.'

Now Rigby lowered his head, shaking it sadly at the unpleasant memory. 'Jim was a good guy,' he said. 'I couldn't believe it was true when he did that. Now you're telling me that maybe he didn't.'

'I don't know if I'm saying that exactly yet, Chief. I was going to go over to Mrs Burg's place next and ask if the name Lance

Spencer rings a bell. She couldn't name her husband's suspect last week, but if I come at it from people Burg might have known, who were in their lives somehow back then, it might spark something.'

'And then what?'

'Then maybe I've got enough to convince Glitsky and my partner that I'm not wasting all of our time.'

'And where do I fit into the picture again? Not that I'm not enjoying the visit, Inspector, but I'm not exactly on everybody's dance card lately, you may have noticed.'

Juhle shrugged. 'Where do you fit in? I don't know, sir. I needed some credibility behind me if I'm going up against somebody like who this Lance is supposed to be. Glitsky and my partner think his case is closed, and I'm just not completely sure. I thought it was possible you knew something about these guys from back in the day.'

'No,' Rigby said. 'But I'll tell you what. You're telling me we got a dead cop and maybe it wasn't a suicide. That's enough motivation for me. I'll ask around.'

Rigby obviously still had juice.

Martin Ingalls got Juhle on his cell phone and now, late in the day, the homicide inspector was sitting in another ex-cop's house, which was remarkably similar to the former chief's – or, for that matter, damn close to Juhle's own. Ingalls could have been the poster adult for the elder retired San Francisco old-school cop – weathered, punched-in face, potbelly, gin-clear eyes, with a lot of laugh lines.

They sat on two sides of a sectional sofa in the cramped but uncluttered living room, but Ingalls had been talking almost from the moment they'd shaken hands. Now he was going on. '. . . so if the chief tells me maybe I ought to talk to you, I figure that's what I've got to do.'

'Well, I appreciate it. And you said you knew Lance Spencer?'

A dry chortle. 'I don't mean know in the sense that we hung out. I knew who he was, that's all. Anybody like me working public events when Jim Jones started his voodoo magic downtown would have known who he was. He was, like, stuck to Jones's side.'

'His bodyguard?'

A shrug. 'More than that, I'd say. Maybe a little bodyguard, a lot enforcer. The guy had been in 'Nam and I'm guessing had seen action and a half. He had all the moves, anyway. Tough as nails.'

'Abusive?'

'No, no, no. Polite as they come. But, like, mess with me and I'll kill you without a thought. And I can't say he had a lot of respect for the authority of the uniform. Mine, anyway. Any of us, really. He was important, Jones was important. Everybody else, not so much.'

'Was his brother with him?'

'Oh yeah. Larry or something . . .'

'Lionel.'

'That's it. Like the train. I shoulda remembered that.' He tapped the side of his head. 'I hate when I don't remember.'

Juhle waved that off. 'What was he like? Lionel?'

'Nothing, really. Lance was the muscle. Lionel was like second string. If they weren't brothers . . .' He let the thought hang. 'And then, you know, they were both pilots. That was part of it, too. Maybe the biggest part.'

'Pilots for Jones?'

Ingalls nodded. 'Now we're moving into rumor territory. After they all left town, we heard they were his couriers.'

'Transporting what?'

'People and money or both.'

'To Guyana?'

'Not just Guyana. Europe, South America, the Caribbean. Anywhere with banks they could hide the money. That, by the way, isn't rumor. Jones had accounts everywhere.'

'So what is the rumor?'

'That they off-loaded hundreds of thousands, if not millions, of bucks in cash out of Guyana just before the slaughter. Now maybe it was just luck they weren't at Jonestown on that day, but you know the next time I saw Lance? And the last time, actually?'

'When?'

'Some fund-raiser here in town I'm working security at maybe five or six years after Jonestown. Except now he's got a fleet of private planes he and his brother are leasing out to movie stars and corporations. I'm at the door and he comes in and recognizes me and has the balls to ask me if I'd like to take a ride on one of his jets. Rubbing my face in whatever he'd done, and now he was rich and if I didn't like it, I was just a lowly cop and could bite him.'

'What'd you tell him?'

Ingalls flashed an old cop smile. 'About what you'd think.'

29

As soon as Hunt had been back in cell phone range late last night in Phoenix, he'd gotten a voice mail that Callie had left him two days before. In it, she told him that she'd downloaded Lionel Spencer's phone records from the night of Ivan Orloff's death. She had the call from Ivan to Lionel at his home and then, within two minutes, an outgoing call from Lionel to another landline number with an account under the name of Lance Spencer. That call had gone on for nearly fifteen minutes and was the last call that Lionel Spencer had made from that phone in his life.

For Hunt, this was yet more corroboration that this case was coming into clear focus. Lionel, the weak brother, had gotten the call from Orloff and he had immediately called his brother the soldier to find out what he should do.

How should he handle this sudden and unexpected threat?

And, playing the likely scenario in his mind, Hunt spun it out that Lionel had no doubt already made the appointment with Ivan at Original Joe's. So Lance knew where Ivan would be. Lionel would keep Ivan at the restaurant until Lance had time to show up out front in his hijacked cab. (Hunt would have to call Callie back and have her make sure that Lance had in fact received a call from Original Joe's number, which would have been Lionel describing Orloff and making plans for his own artful exit from the restaurant.) Then, having thought about it for the long next day after Lance had done his cold-blooded business with Ivan, he'd driven up to his brother's place, been admitted, and orchestrated the bogus suicide.

All this, Hunt knew, was far too heavily dependent on speculation. Indeed, it was almost all speculation. Maddeningly, the evidence that he would need to supply to Juhle for any chance of an arrest or trial remained elusive. Hunt had to admit that there was nothing inherently sinister about a brother calling his brother and talking for fifteen minutes. The temporal proximity to Orloff's call to Lionel might have had nothing to do with anything.

But Hunt *knew*.

He hadn't wanted to wake Juhle in the middle of the night with the new fact of the phone call from Lionel to Lance and what it might mean. And so Wyatt had waited until the morning to call him and had been more than a little pleased and surprised to hear that Devin had softened in his intransigence about Lionel. Juhle had done some footwork on his own, going back yesterday to Chief Rigby and to Elinor Burg and to another ex-cop named Martin Ingalls, trying to plug Lance Spencer into the forty-year-old equation and getting, if not solid hits, then at least provocative information.

Juhle also told Hunt that Elinor Burg, for her part, had nearly jumped out of her chair when he'd mentioned the name Lance Spencer. True, she'd never heard her husband make any connection between Lance and the investigation into Margie Carson's murder, but when Jim Jones came to the city in 1972, her husband had often been assigned to crowd control at public events where Jones was present. And he had mentioned Lance to her more than once as an officious prick who thought he had the authority to order police officers around. Martin Ingalls had basically sung the same song.

So when Hunt and Tamara landed at SFO at 10:20 on a gloriously beautiful day by the bay, he dropped Tamara off at her home and then made it to his own place to change into clean clothes, leave his car, and walk around the corner to Lou the Greek's, where he and Devin had made plans to meet for lunch.

The special on this Wednesday at Lou the Greek's broke new culinary ground even for a place that invented new Sino-Greek dishes on a regular basis. Today's masterpiece featured eggplant and octopus layered as a kind of moussaka over a bed of sticky rice, heavily seasoned with garlic and Mae Ploy sweet/hot sauce under the cheese-laden béchamel that covered the whole thing. Lou told everybody who came in that it was going to be such a giant hit that it needed an easily remembered catchy name like Yeanling Clay Bowl and he was holding a contest to come up with a winner. Grand prize: a lifetime of free eating whenever it was the featured special.

So far, he had three names written on the blackboard behind the bar: Pulpo Diablo, Lulu's Delight, and Fishegg, all of which Hunt thought were pretty weak, especially the last one: 'Where do they get "Fishegg"?'

Juhle chewed and swallowed. 'Octopus, fish, egg, eggplant. Fishegg.'

Hunt shook his head. 'Nobody's going to get it. You don't see the word *fishegg* and think of what we're eating here. You're thinking of fish eggs. Way different than this stuff.'

Juhle shrugged.

'Also,' Hunt went on, 'what if you come up with the winning name and don't like this actual dish?'

'I'm sure Lou would let you work something out. Maybe trade for something you like better.' Not liking the dish was clearly not Juhle's problem. He was shoveling food with enthusiasm. 'Or maybe you could have a raffle or an auction or something and sell off the rights, make yourself a lot of money. But who wouldn't like this? Lou's right. This thing's an instant classic.'

'That wouldn't be a bad name.'

'What wouldn't be a bad name?'

'Instant Classic,' Hunt said. 'The only problem being who'd get credit for it, you or me.'

'I would, obviously.' Juhle forked in another bite. 'I'm the one who said it.'

'Yeah, but you didn't recognize it for what it was. That was me.'

'We could split the prize.'

'Then how would Lou keep track? He'd have to make a punch card or something, and then we'd have to remember to carry it around in our wallets and pass it back and forth whenever we used it and it was the other guy's turn.'

'That would be a hassle,' Juhle said. 'Maybe we should forget the whole name thing. Let somebody else get all the glory.'

Just at this moment, Lou was passing their table on the way to the kitchen and Juhle snagged him, pointing down at the dish. 'Instant Classic. That's the name, Lou. Instant Classic.'

The proprietor nodded in approval. 'I'll put it on the board,' he said.

'Wyatt and me. We both came up with it.'

Lou shook his head no. 'One winner only. You can flip for it.'

'Who decides who wins anyway?' Hunt asked.

'Everybody. I'm passing ballots around next week.'

'What day?' Juhle asked.

'I don't know yet. It's a secret until I pass 'em out. Otherwise, everybody brings their friends on the day, you know, and they stuff the ballot box. That wouldn't be fair.'

'Rampant voter fraud,' Hunt agreed, 'could be a huge problem.'

'I'm trying to avoid it,' Lou allowed. 'What was your name again?'

'Still Wyatt,' Hunt said.

Lou rolled his eyes. 'The dish. The name of the dish.'

'Instant Classic.'

He nodded. 'I like it. I'll put it on the board.'

'No, I haven't talked to Lance,' Juhle was saying over his coffee. 'It's been forty years. I think it could go another couple of days without too much harm.'

'If he doesn't kill somebody else first.'

'And let's hope he doesn't. Which is a good bet, since the Spencer-Orloff-cabbie hat trick is a closed circle. So Lance isn't threatened by us or anybody else just now. But there's also the point that before I go and knock on his door, I wanted to have something substantive to talk to him about. And by substantive, I mean evidence to connect him to any one of these five murders. Of which, let me remind you, we have none.'

'Five? So you're thinking he killed Burg, too.'

'Not impossible. Same m.o. as Lionel Spencer. If it worked so well once . . .'

Hunt scratched at the table for a moment. 'All right,' he said. 'We've got the phone call to him from Lionel right after the Orloff call. If we get the other call that Lionel must have made from Original Joe's . . .'

'Which we don't have.'

'Yet. We'll get it.'

'Okay, but even if we did, then we've got two phone calls from one brother to another. So what?' Juhle wasn't having any of it. 'Fatally weak. Not even worth considering.'

'Devin. The guy did it.'

Juhle swallowed his coffee and nodded. 'He might have. I even agree with you. But the sad truth is that there's no case. At least not yet. And you might have noticed that I'm severely constrained in trying to build one, what with both my partner and my boss going on the assumption that there are no questions left unanswered.'

'Of course there are. What do you think we're talking about here?'

'Name one. A question, I mean.'

'Okay, where did Lance get his money?'

'From Jones. He smuggled it out of Jonestown a hundred years ago. So what? Everything you can say about him you can say about Lionel, too. Any other questions?'

'I'm thinking.'

'I can hear the gears turning. Take your time.'

Hunt stared off across the restaurant. 'I could go rattle his cage, piss him off, wear a wire, get him to admit something.'

'What?'

'I don't know. Something. Anything. I could tell him I'm Margie's kid, out for revenge. Tell him I know he did it.'

'And this would accomplish what, exactly?' Juhle's tolerance for this conversation was clearly wearing thin. 'Except maybe get you arrested, get him lawyered up, maybe lose your license while you're at it. Yeah, that's a swell plan.'

'So what do you suggest?'

Chewing on the question, Juhle finally spoke. 'What about your texter?'

'What about her?'

Juhle straightened. His eyebrows went up. 'Why do you say it's a her?'

'Because it is a her.'

'How do you know that? You know who she is?'

'Pretty much, yes.'

'When did this happen?'

'Over the last few days.'

'So who is she?'

'You're going to hate this, but I can't tell you.'

Juhle's indignation couldn't have been more thorough or more immediate. Eyes blazing, he leaned in across the table. 'Bullshit, Wyatt. Of course you can tell me. You have to tell me.'

'No, I don't. I can't. Not until I talk to her first anyway. I've got to make sure it's her.'

'And then what?'

'Then I find out what she knows, what got this whole thing started.'

Juhle, disgusted, settled back into his chair, his arms crossed over his chest. 'And at what point do you deign it appropriate to include the police, if I may ask?'

'When I've got something you can use.'

'You don't think we're capable of determining that?'

'That's not it, Devin.' He blew out in frustration. 'I've got to go on the belief that the deal we've had all along is that she stays out of it. I build the case, then pass it off to you guys, then you bring him in.'

'That's all well and good if we're talking about your mother forty years ago, Wyatt. But this is two, maybe three homicides last week. If she knows something about those, whatever it is, it's not up to her to decide if she wants to be involved. We get to make that call. You see that?'

'I understand why you see it like that,' Hunt replied evenly. 'But I've got to play this my way. I owe her.'

'You owe her? Please.'

'She's filled in my whole life story, Devin. You might not think that's such a big thing, but it's pretty major to me. And the deal is she stays out of it.'

'You sign a contract, did you?'

'We have an understanding.'

'Really? Well, understand this: If we figure out a way to get to this guy, and it turns out you withheld information that could have allowed us to get him sooner, or God forbid he kills somebody else in the interim, including your texter . . .'

Hunt held up a hand, stopping him. 'You'll get any information I get as soon as I can get it to you, Devin. I just can't give you the source of it.'

Juhle sat with a stony visage for the better part of a minute. Then, abruptly, he pushed his chair back and stood up. 'Lunch is on you,' he said. 'See you when I do.'

30

The Sassafras room at the Mission Club on Nob Hill was not much more than a closet featuring two doors and one window to outdoors, with every inch of the minimal wall space covered with framed old random black-and-white photographs of San Francisco – the earthquake and fire, Coit Tower as it was going up and again finally completed, both bridges during their construction, Market Street in 1913, Ghirardelli Square, various photos of women who had presumably once been household names among the social set.

Too nervous to sit still for long, Hunt paced in front of the small and empty fireplace, back and forth about three steps each way between the two Queen Anne chairs that comprised the room's only furniture. It was 4:45 and he'd been here for fifteen minutes or so; after leaving Juhle, he first checked in at the office, where he had done a little fence-mend marketing with the clients he'd been ignoring for the past week or more. He then went back home to change again into suitable garb for this appointment – a charcoal pinstripe suit, white dress shirt, muted cranberry tie, Italian lace-ups.

She was at least fifteen minutes late and he was starting to worry that she might not appear at all, despite the urgency of his request to her, albeit under false pretenses. He had told her on the phone that in following up his investigation of Judith Black's suitability for membership in the club, he had come upon some possible bookkeeping improprieties that he thought she would want to know about and address as quickly as possible. They were quite sensitive and he didn't feel comfortable talking about them on the telephone – perhaps they could meet quietly in one of the club's private rooms?

Hunt checked his watch for the tenth time, sick that she must have seen through the makeshift ruse, when at last there was a soft knock on the door just before it opened and she came in. Closing the door behind her, she turned with her radiant Grace Kelly smile, advancing toward him, hand outstretched. 'Wyatt. You're getting to be a regular here. A woman could get used to seeing your face.'

Here it was again, that flirtatious persona that she seemed to employ as a matter of course, at once flattering, irresistible, and untouchable. So, Hunt thought, either she believed the nonsense he'd made up about the club, or she was going to try to brazen it and pretend to be ignorant, or he was wrong and she was not his texter.

Except that Hunt knew he wasn't wrong. It was she.

Dodie Spencer, the wife of Lance Spencer, CEO of Execujet.

He took her hand and told her he was glad that she was able to meet him on such short notice.

'Well, you made it sound so mysterious I couldn't very well refuse, could I?'

'I don't suppose you could,' Hunt said. 'Why don't we sit down?'

'Why don't we?'

But as soon as they had, Hunt flashed a grin at her and then found it impossible to keep up the charade. It must have showed on his face.

'That's an awful solemn look, Mr Hunt. Is it that serious?'

'It's very serious,' he said, 'and it's not about the club.' He met her eyes. 'As I believe you know.'

He had to admire her control. She fell into a mild expression of confusion, cocked her lovely head to one side, then increased the wattage on her smile. 'I'm sorry, but I'm afraid I really don't know what you're talking about.'

'Yes, you do, Dodie.' Hunt drew a breath. 'I understand why you're afraid. You've got every reason to be afraid. But the fact that you've come down here to meet me tells me that you know there's only one way out of this, and that's for you to come out of hiding.'

She eyed him uncertainly. 'No,' she said ambiguously.

'Is that why you were so late getting here?' he asked her. 'Deciding yes, you were going to come down and meet me, then changing your mind? How many times did you go back and forth?' He leaned forward, his elbows on his knees. 'Dodie, look at me. Listen to me.'

She sat with her back straight, her lips pursed, casting her eyes to the corners of the room, still controlled enough that she did not convey any sign of panic. She was biding time. Until she said something, until she admitted that she knew what Hunt was talking about, she could tell herself that she still had plausible deniability. Any small deviation from her plan now, any break in the facade she was presenting to Hunt, would be a full capitulation, and she was hanging on lest she do something irrevocable before she consciously decided that this was what she had to do.

Hunt spoke in his most soothing voice. 'The fact that you're still sitting here, you realize, is an answer in itself.'

Still she didn't break. She came back to him with that quizzical look for a brief flash, her lips quivering, wavering between a smile and an apology. At last, she seemed to come to her decision. 'I'm afraid I'm going to have to speak to someone about this,' she said, getting to her feet. 'I'm sorry you've felt the need to do something like this. You're frightening me, getting me here under a false pretext. I don't think we'll be able to use your services here anymore. I'll just let myself out.'

She turned around, stepped toward the door.

'Dodie, please.'

Her hand was on the doorknob – Hunt heard the meshing gears as she started to turn it.

'No one can hear us in here.' He was speaking to her back. 'That's why I picked this place. No one will ever know. I will never tell, I swear on my mother's grave, on everything that's sacred. But he has to be stopped.'

Her shoulders rose, then fell. Rose, then fell. Finally, she lowered her head and went still.

Hunt did not trust himself to speak again. Without even realizing it, he'd gotten to his feet as well and now he stood, hanging in anticipation, waiting for her to commit.

At last, she shook her head slightly from side to side, then turned around with a half smile and spoke conversationally. 'He really is evil incarnate, you know. No one has any idea.'

The tension bled from Hunt's body as he lowered himself back into his chair. He didn't want to push her. He said nothing and waited.

She finally took her own seat and fixed him with a look of surpassing calm and condescension. 'And while of course I was hoping you could stop him, you must understand there is no way I'm going to jeopardize myself any more than I have. How did you find me?'

'When you texted and said it wasn't Lionel and I learned there was a Lance, there weren't many other options. I think on some level you knew that if you left off the name Spencer, you were telling me it was another Spencer, just not Lionel. I think that's when you started wanting me to find you.'

She gave a brief and chilling tinkle of laughter. 'No. I never wanted that. I don't want it now. I'm just not entirely sure what to do about it.'

Hunt was suddenly aware that he'd become an inconvenience

and that if she could simply wish him away, he'd be gone in an instant. 'All right,' he said. 'Why didn't you just originally go to the police? When you suspected about my mother?'

'I didn't suspect.' Her voice now measured and low. 'I knew,' she said. 'He told me.'

'He told you?'

She nodded. 'Three years ago, maybe four. He'd hit me, beat me really. I could barely walk afterward. I couldn't go out anywhere for a couple of weeks.' She paused and took a breath, then another. 'Anyway, it was the third time he'd done that and I made up my mind I was going to leave him, just take Jamie and move out and sue him for everything I could get my hands on.'

'Jamie?'

'My son. Not Lance's son, my first husband's son. James died. Jamie's fourteen now. He's my joy.' Glancing at each of the two doors – were they locked? Were they safe in here? – she came back to Hunt. 'So where was I?'

'You were going to leave your husband.'

'Right. Right. But then Lance took me aside and told me if I ever tried to leave, he'd never let us. He would kill us both. Jamie first.' She brought her hands to her face. 'Oh my God, did this really happen? In any event, I told him I didn't believe him. He'd never do that. He just laughed at me and told me if I thought I knew what he was capable of, I had a different think coming.'

She glanced around at the doors again.

'No one's coming in here,' Hunt said.

'No, I know. It's just . . .' She blew out heavily. 'Okay, so the next day he leaves for work, I think, and I start packing. I'm going to go to school and pick up Jamie after and we're getting away.

'But then it turned out that Lance hadn't gone to work. In

the middle of my packing he comes back in and sits down, calm as you please, and starts telling me that, really, killing isn't any big deal for him. It was important that I believe that. He'd killed at least a hundred gooks – he called them gooks – in Vietnam, and a couple of his own officers over there, too. Laughing about it. Friendly fire. Hah!

'If I thought it was any different killing women, maybe I should look up a woman named Margie Carson who got herself killed here in the city back in 1970. That was to him, plain and simple, just a job.

'He really didn't want to kill me, he said. He loved me, whatever that means to him. But he'd do it in a heartbeat if I really was going to go. He'd hunt me down and find us both and kill us. Jamie first.'

Hunt swallowed. 'So you stayed?'

'I didn't think I had a choice. So I negotiated. He couldn't hit me anymore. He couldn't hit Jamie ever. We could start over. I can't believe I'm telling you this.'

'You're doing fine,' Hunt said. 'Go on. Margie Carson.'

'It's an easy name to remember,' she said. 'One day I looked it up. The murder. The family. The trials. The whole thing. One of the details that stuck was that her child was named Wyatt, a fact I never really thought about until about four months ago or whatever it was, when I met you.'

'I remember.'

'And in the interview I learned that you had been adopted. It just came up in the conversation. And after that, remember how personal I got? Did you remember your birth parents? How old were you? All that. I was starting to get a feeling you might have been him. Margie's son.'

'I am,' Hunt said.

'I know.' She took another short break, pulling out of the

reverie for a moment. 'I didn't know how all of this was going to turn out.'

'People generally don't,' Wyatt said.

'I mean, the other murders . . .'

Hunt nodded. 'We still don't know how it's going to turn out, Dodie. It's not done yet. And I'm afraid I still don't understand why you didn't just go to the police. Why you don't go even now.'

'You don't?' She chirped out a small little laugh. 'Do you really believe that once I did that, they could keep me out of it?'

'Why would they have to? You'd be their star witness. If he confessed to you, that's direct testimony, not hearsay. That could be enough, all by itself.'

'And what about me and Jamie?'

Hunt shrugged. 'They put you in witness protection. Your husband goes away forever. You're free of him.'

Again, Dodie seemed to find Hunt's worldview slightly amusing. 'Do you really not see this?' she asked.

'See what?'

She came forward in her chair and spoke in a condescending tone, almost as if she were explaining to a child. 'I'm not going to change my identity, Wyatt. I'm not putting me and my son through that. After all I've worked for and achieved to become who I am? To support Jamie in what he wants to become? You've got to be kidding me. Witness protection? At the mercy of idiot government bureaucrats who think they can tell me where I need to live and how I need to act? For the rest of my life? Do you really think I'd put myself in that position? Never. Never. It's simply out of the question. And also . . .'

'Also?'

She paused. 'Oh, come, you must realize you're forgetting a crucial element in all this.'

'What's that?'

'The money, Wyatt. The money.'

Hunt shook his head. 'I'm sorry?'

'The minute Lance finds out I'm involved, even if they hide me away for my protection, the first thing he does is cut me and Jamie out of his estate. We're talking like fifty million dollars, Wyatt, give or take. Do you know how much money that is? If I do anything that Lance gets wind of, I lose access to any part of the estate and, with his lawyers, I never get any of it back. And after all I've been through with him, the time I've put in, the personal sacrifices I've made – as I think you can imagine – I'm not willing to let that happen. And if I go to the police, that's exactly what would happen. Beyond which, as I believe I already said, I don't for a second think that the police would be able to keep me and Jamie physically safe.'

Hunt sat back, incredulous at the baldness of her rationale. Crossing an ankle over his knee, feigning nonchalance, he asked, 'So you chose me?'

Apparently, Dodie saw no issue, moral or otherwise, with this decision. She even nodded with some enthusiasm. 'It was the ideal solution. I hope you see that.'

'Not too clearly, I'm afraid.'

'Come on, Wyatt. If there was a case to be brought against Lance, you were a professional investigator. You could build it. It was your own mother's death, after all, so your motivation would be off the charts. And if you succeeded and Lance got arrested and then even convicted, from his perspective, I'm still his loyal wife.'

'Still on the payroll.'

She gave him a disapproving little moue. 'I don't know if I'd put it like that. This is millions and millions of dollars we're talking about here, Wyatt, not some allowance I'd get if I were nice. This is my son's future. Mine, too.'

Hunt struggled to keep his tone civil. 'It was also, it turns out, the end of the future for one of my people.'

She let her head drop as though she did in fact feel perhaps a pang of sympathy for Ivan Orloff. 'I've already told you I didn't know what was going to happen. I do feel sorry for that boy, for his family, but it wasn't anything anyone could have predicted, and it certainly wasn't my fault. This all began with Lance, and a good way to look at it is that your friend was just another one of his victims. In fact, literally one of his victims.'

'You know that absolutely?'

'As much as anybody can know anything.'

'You want to tell me how you're so sure?'

'Well, he got the call from Lionel – two of them, actually – and went out in a rush at dinnertime that night. He was gone till midnight. Then, the next night – the night he went back and killed Lionel – I saw him take the gun out of the bed board and it wasn't there the next morning and hasn't been since. He killed them all. How's that?'

'That's a good start, but we're left facing the same problem you started with, Dodie. Plus a brand-new one.'

'What are those?'

Hunt heaved a sigh. 'Well, the first one is evidence. I may believe everything you do, but I still don't have anything to bring to the police. You yourself admit he's gotten rid of the gun. The only real evidence left here is you. If you're not willing to testify, there's no case. Do you realize that?'

Now visibly impatient, Dodie brushed that off. 'That's nonnegotiable,' she said with a small shake of her head. 'I'm not testifying. That's not happening, period.' Then, moving on, 'What's the new problem?'

'It's one that hits a little closer to home, Dodie. How long do you think before your husband realizes that Ivan Orloff wasn't working alone when he called Lionel?'

This pretty much unassailable interpretation hit Dodie with some force – perhaps she realized, as Wyatt intended, that her own anonymity and safety would be in jeopardy once Lance came to understand or intuit her connection to Hunt. She opened her mouth to say something but couldn't get anything to come out.

'Ivan was working for me,' Hunt went on. 'He wasn't the real threat. I'm the real threat. And here's the fun part. I still am.'

'If he thought that, he would have already done something about it.'

'Except I've been out of the state, out of the country. He couldn't get to me because nobody knew where I was. He can now.'

'Well, it appears you have a real problem, then.' She looked down at her bejeweled fingers. 'I don't suppose you'd like to solve that problem proactively. That would keep you safe and leave me comfortable. And you would find that I am both grateful and generous.' She raised her eyes and locked them on his. 'We're talking *fifty million dollars* here, Wyatt.'

Hunt came right back at her. 'We're talking about *my life*, Dodie.'

She shrugged her shoulders dismissively. 'Well, if you're not willing to help yourself, then I don't know what to tell you.'

Hunt pulled at the knot in his tie, which suddenly seemed to be choking him. He uncrossed his legs and moved forward to the edge of his chair, leveling his gaze at her. 'Dodie, please. You've got to go to the police. I can take you right now. They can pick up Jamie at school and have Lance in custody by tonight. It's multiple murders, which is special circumstances. He won't be able to get bail. This is doable. More than that, it's the only way. And if you can't do it, I may have to go to the cops myself.'

Her nostrils flared in righteous anger. 'You can't do that. You gave me your word. You swore on your mother's grave. But beyond that, I'll deny everything you say. Then what? You'll look like a fool.'

'I've looked like a fool before. At least it would be a chip to play against Lance. If the cops know that he's my suspect and I wind up dead, now he's really got a problem, doesn't he? At least it might slow him down.'

She shook her head emphatically. 'You don't know Lance. Slowing him down isn't stopping him. You'll still wind up dead.'

'And you're willing to let that happen?'

'It wouldn't be my fault. Not if you go to the police about me. I'm telling you not to do that. I will not testify, and I'm his wife, they can't make me. You simply need to find something else.'

'You don't think I've been looking?'

'You'll have to look harder.'

Hunt sat back and grabbed a breath, shocked in spite of himself at the power of greed in the form of this beautiful woman, perfectly willing to continue in the lie that was her life, and even perhaps to let him die, just so long as she got to keep her money.

Hunt got to his feet. Dodie stood, too, and, astoundingly, came up and placed a chaste kiss on his cheek. 'I know you'll do the right thing,' she said, as though she would recognize the right thing if it were writ large in the clouds by the hand of the Almighty Himself. 'For now, though, if you'd just give me a minute to let me get out first, it might be good if people didn't see us leaving together and start to talk.'

31

The Hunt club office had been running on fumes for the past couple of weeks, with their real work pretty much on hold while Wyatt checked out of his everyday job to work on his mother's case and then, much more disruptively, while they all dealt with the aftereffects of Ivan's death. Tamara and Wyatt missing most of this week hadn't helped matters, either.

So Tamara spent the afternoon catching up on paperwork, trying to get a handle on what Jill and Mickey had been able to accomplish alone over the past few days – really a gratifying amount, as it turned out – and reassuring sometimes gnarly clients about scheduling, billing, deadlines, and the reasons things had been so relatively unstable lately. She told one and all that they were hoping to bring on two or three new staff in the next few weeks and had in fact already begun interviewing, not an absolute lie since Wyatt had solicited Juhle on that topic a couple of weeks before.

The law firms with whom they did most of their work all had heard about Ivan and expressed their understanding and sympathy, but they were, after all, law firms, and as such not particularly given to accepting excuses – except possibly death – for lack of performance. And even death could be suspect, Tamara knew, depending on the circumstances. So the calls, one after another all afternoon, tended to be lengthy, friendly, apologetic, and – especially after a day that had started while it was still dark that morning in Phoenix – exhausting.

At 5:30, she shut off her computer, made sure Jill and Mickey weren't hiding back in their offices but had really gone for the day, turned out the lights, and walked out into the corridor, locking the office door behind her. She knew that Wyatt had scheduled a secret appointment at 4:30, and he'd told her he didn't know how long it would go on. She shouldn't wait for him, but depending on how the meeting went, if he didn't check in by close of business, he would call her later at home and maybe they could go out to dinner. Or stay in.

Taking the elevator down to the ground floor, she thought about stopping in for a glass of wine at Boulevard but realized that in her state of fatigue it would probably be smarter to keep all her wits about her and wait until she got home before she had anything to drink, so she turned and walked out the back door, on the sidewalk by the Embarcadero. Daylight saving time had ended the previous weekend, but she and Wyatt had missed it in their travels, and now the dusk felt unusually disorienting.

She looked at her watch, still set at 6:18, an hour late.

On the spur of the moment, she decided to surprise Wyatt and go directly to his place instead of her own, meet him perhaps with a light supper foraged from his refrigerator and a cocktail when he got home. Or maybe they'd just go to bed, order some Chinese afterward. She still had his keys from when she'd gone to get his passport, and after the time they'd spent together over the past few days, she knew he would be happy to see her.

She caught the jammed Muni at the corner and it let her off two dark and desolate blocks up from Hunt's warehouse. When she got to it, she opened the Brannan Street door and hit the light switch next to it. The basketball court and the high lights shining down from the ceiling illuminated the rest of the fantastic place. She stood still for a moment, taking it in with a different eye. It wasn't impossible to think that this place might someday in the not too distant future be part of her everyday life.

The idea seemed to wash away her fatigue with a jolt of contentment. What she was feeling here, she recognized, was pride of ownership. Maybe a little bit prematurely, all right, but this whole thing with Wyatt could really work out, she believed. It was already working out.

She cast her eyes over the space – the motorcycle, the surfboards, the baseball mitts and bats and other sports stuff everywhere, the guitars and amps and computers, and hell, don't forget the damned basketball court! – and loved the fact that he was such a *guy*, and yet a guy who had allowed himself, and trusted her enough, to break down in her presence, to lay bare his soul.

Closing the door and locking it behind her, she actually half skipped over the concrete until she got to the wood of the court, where she put down her purse and picked up one of the three basketballs just sitting there. She took a shot from behind the free throw line and when it went in without even touching the rim, she allowed herself a surge of hope that would have been unimaginable only a few weeks before.

But she wasn't going to push her luck. She'd made the one shot, now she'd go in on the residence side of the warehouse and see what the refrigerator might yield . . . or maybe she'd just take off her clothes, get in the shower, go back to bed, and wait for him.

She opened the connecting door and hit the light switch.

The doorknob suddenly got jerked out of her hands and somebody spun her around and pushed her, slamming her up against the wall, one hand to her throat and the other holding – the hole of the barrel centered on the middle of her face – a black handgun.

Reflexively, stupidly, Tamara reached up with one hand and slapped the gun aside while she clawed at the man's eyes with her other one. The grip on her throat loosened and she raised a leg, trying to get a knee into his groin. Grunting with the exertion, she swung a fist at his face.

The gunshot was deafening in the narrow hallway.

She felt a physical blow, almost as though she'd been hit with a baseball bat. Then a searing pain.

Badly shaken by his interview with Dodie Spencer, Hunt waited in the Sassafras Room for a lot longer than the minute she'd recommended so that people wouldn't gossip about them. He sat in his ornate chair surrounded by the photo images that spoke of mankind's progress through adversity and setbacks. Bridges and monuments going up. A city rising from its ashes. More than a hundred years of matriarchs gazing out serenely into the world of culture and resurrection and beauty they'd helped create.

The thought that educated, graceful, well-spoken, impeccably tasteful, and physically stunning Dodie Spencer, all things being equal, would in all probability one day be enshrined here as a beacon of probity was deeply unsettling. In fact, he realized, she was nothing but a whore – heartless, charming, amoral, and totally driven by greed and her own comfort.

But then he remembered that he was sitting in a room on Nob Hill, a neighborhood settled in the late 1800s by the railroad robber barons, who had raped and pillaged and cheated their way into fortune and the appearance of respectability.

What else did he expect? For certain people, it was and always would be all about money. And more money. Gobs of it, never enough, unending amounts of money against which all honor and beauty and morality paled to insignificance.

Finally, thoroughly sick at heart, after dusk had begun to descend, he let himself out of the club. The Top of the Mark sparkled above him in the still-warm air. He put his hands in his pockets and walked up to the Fairmont Hotel, then along

California Street past the Flood Mansion, over to Grace Cathedral. This was Gina Roake's neighborhood and he knew it well.

Venticello, the romantic restaurant he and Tamara had eaten at last week, was only a few blocks away. It suddenly struck him that he could use a shot of Tamara's levelheaded goodness, her common sense, her decency. Herself.

Together they'd decide what he was going to do about Lance Spencer. About Dodie.

She didn't answer at work or on her cell phone, which he thought was a little strange, but not unheard of. After leaving a message on her cell, he then called at her home. Her grandfather told him that she wasn't home yet, but he'd give her the message when she got in. All dressed up anyway, Hunt decided to cross the street, stop at the bar of the Huntington Hotel, and kill some time until he heard back from her.

Where are you? Come home. I'm here.

Hunt heard the message tone and, enduring a disapproving look from the Huntington's bartender, took his phone from his belt and read the message from Tamara.

He wasn't making much of a dent in his beer anyway, so he pushed his glass away and dropped a ten on the bar, saying, 'Keep it.' Then he got up and walked through the well-dressed and buzzing crowd out again to the street, punching up Tamara's number.

'You don't look like Wyatt Hunt to me.' The white-haired older man was growling at her. 'Now what the hell am I supposed to do with you?'

One of the secrets to his success was adhering to the mantra: Do your business and get out.

You waited around, even for seconds, and you invited all kinds of problems. People hear a noise. Somebody gets a glimpse of you. Not good.

No. You struck and you struck fast. And then you were gone.

That had been the plan and the execution for Margie Carson, for Jim Burg, and then those fools from last week, including his clown of a brother, the gutless wonder who'd gone from zero to a state of high panic at the very first sign of trouble. Trouble that was way off on the horizon.

But just hearing his brother's voice on the phone, Lance had known that Lionel would crack under even the slightest interrogation pressure from the police. So Lance had made up his mind: Lionel would have to be eliminated, and in the same way as Jim Burg, those many years ago. No one would miss him. No one would even care. Lionel had lived as a lonely and worried hermit for the past five years or more. It was time for him to go, especially when his death would serve Lance's purpose so perfectly.

The symmetry of apparent suicide was beautiful – it explained away so much, especially in the absence of any other forensic evidence.

But now, suddenly, with this girl showing up out of the blue, doing his business and getting out wasn't going to be an option.

His business, in this case, was straightforward, as it always was in these situations. This time, he was here to cut off the head of the snake, and that was this guy Wyatt Hunt, Orloff's boss. He had some suspicions as to how Hunt and his minions had come to start looking into the Margie Carson murder, and he'd deal with them in good time. No, make that in short order. Was Dodie really so naïve as to believe that he wouldn't have kept a close eye on her as soon it became clear that someone was looking into the events around Margie Carson's death? Apparently so.

She didn't just pick up and 'go to the club,' as she had this afternoon, for 'a meeting I forgot all about.' Ha! Her life was as orchestrated as an opera. Did she think her nerves weren't betraying her? Did she really believe he wouldn't see it and put things together? Didn't she know he would have already been aware of this Wyatt Hunt through the Orloff matter? Wouldn't have done his homework? Find out where he lived, what he looked like, learn his routines.

Did she think he was an idiot?

Bragging about Margie Carson to her had been a mistake. He saw that now. He should have cut his losses and just let her go. But her physical goddamn beauty, he thought. Strongest force on the earth. You couldn't help but want it, touch it, own it. Well, at least he'd had it for a few more years than he would have otherwise. He'd go find some more when all this was done.

But in the meanwhile, here at Hunt's warehouse home, the bullet seemed to have gone through the girl's leg, maybe hit a bone, maybe not. Considering what had to happen to her anyway, it didn't really matter. Nevertheless, he'd stopped the bleeding with a towel. No use in having her bleed out in case he needed her alive later.

Now in the bedroom he had her trussed hands and feet with clothesline rope he'd found in the kitchen closet, with a pair of socks stuffed into her mouth. What was he supposed to do with her?

If he simply killed her now in Hunt's house and left – the obvious solution if he kept to his mantra – it would prompt another investigation, far more serious than any he'd yet weathered. He could make it look like a botched burglary or a sexual assault, but with Hunt's suspicions about him already probably part of the record somewhere, that investigation could not help but come back to him.

In fact, killing Hunt by itself posed that risk, but not as great as the one the private eye posed by remaining alive. As long as Hunt breathed, and especially if this girl got herself killed at

Hunt's home, Lance knew he would be on the defensive at best, and the ongoing target of Hunt's own investigation in any event.

He also knew he could buy an alibi for tonight if he had to, as he had for last Tuesday and Wednesday, but this whole business was getting old – you could only buy so much alibi, and trusting whoever you bought it from never ceased to be a problem. He might very well become a suspect, *the* suspect. The fabric of his life was all this close, he knew, to unraveling, to coming undone.

He swore out loud.

He wasn't really aware that he'd said anything, but the girl moaned on the bed.

He pointed the gun at her and said, 'Shut up or I'll shoot you in the face.'

Her damn cell phone rang again in her purse, the third time in the forty-five minutes they'd been here.

Twice before, he'd decided he would just have to shoot her and be done with it. Find out a way to come back and take care of Hunt later if he still needed to at that point. The police would investigate this girl's death, of course, but he'd proven time and again – the whole time that Kevin Carson had been on both trials, for example – that he was smarter than the cops. He'd covered his tracks with Margie and never wasted a second worrying that any of those losers would get wise to him. And they never had.

So nobody could say he couldn't take the heat. But there was no reason to put yourself in a difficult position voluntarily.

He wasn't really as worried about the police as he was about Hunt. If Lance killed this girl, he had the feeling that Hunt would never rest. The police? Give them a week or two and a lack of physical evidence – which Lance had pretty much mastered by now – and they would move on to the next homicide.

There was always another homicide, the fresher ones becoming the low-hanging fruit.

Hunt, he knew, would be a different proposition.

The girl unexpectedly stopping by here was not ideal. No question, her showing up was a problem. But by far, the best solution now would be if Hunt simply got here, too. Then two quick shots point-blank and Lance would be gone, leaving the cops to sort out what had happened. Lance would have an alibi. He'd have permanently ditched the gun and his clothes before he even got back home. Hunt himself, a private investigator, would undoubtedly have other cases with an element of personal risk. Eventually, this case would cool down and go stone-cold.

Lance could tough it out.

But he had to have Hunt.

Lance was prepared to wait all night, but the longer he waited, the more time he'd have to account for. Best would be for Hunt to show up soon. Get it over with.

If Lance could somehow . . .

He'd been sitting, thinking, the gun in his lap, across from where the girl lay bound on the bed. Suddenly, he got up and in a few steps reached down to pick her purse off the floor. The girl was staring up at him wild-eyed either with fright or perhaps believing she could do him some damage since he was, for a moment, so close.

He pointed the gun at her head. 'Don't even think about it,' he said.

Back at his chair, he rummaged through the purse and came out with a cell phone. The gun trained on the girl, he punched the voice mail button and listened to the three messages, two from Wyatt Hunt just trying to get in touch and one from somebody named Mickey telling her Hunt was trying to reach her. She should call him.

Or at least text.

Good idea, he thought. Text from Tamara's phone.

He sat holding the instrument on his lap for a long moment. Then he started tapping the phone's face.

In Lance Spencer's hand, the cell phone rang with an old-fashioned telephone ringtone. It announced itself on the screen as Hunt's return call. For a moment, he froze.

Another jarring ring.

Screw it, he thought. This isn't going to work. Too much hassle. Time to cut his losses and get out of here.

But there was so much advantage if he could just get Hunt here. Wherever Hunt was now, Lance could still do the girl before he got home. And even if he was just outside the door, coming up Brannan Street right now, then Lance would prevail anyway. Blow him away as he came inside. Then disappear.

Brrriinnngg!

As the connection flipped over to voice mail, Lance put down the gun for a second so he could punch in a text with both thumbs, as fast as he could. He still had a chance to lure Hunt in here. *Can't talk right now. Busy. Come home.*

Can't talk right now. Busy. Come home.

Hunt stared down at the message. What the hell? What was she doing that she couldn't talk to him? Cooking? Tasting stuff?

How about surprising him by being at his place, he berated himself, making him a special dinner, which would be their first one together alone at his home? Venticello would keep for another night. He should be able to recognize this for what it was, the spontaneous gesture of a woman aiming to please and delight.

Cut her a little slack, would you, Wyatt.

He had to remember that he was the one having the supremely difficult last few days here, the one suffering from the revelations he'd discovered. He had the angst. From all indications, Tamara was blooming in the sunshine of their love and he would be well advised to cherish those moments and even try to get in the spirit of them himself.

Pulling up his text screen to reply, suddenly another thought brought him up short. He looked back down at the last two messages.

Where are you? Come home. I'm here.

Can't talk right now. Busy. Come home.

Both unusually terse. And both with neither a sign-off of any kind – she almost always wrote 'Love' or 'Luv,' then 'T' – nor with a smiley-face emoticon, which she would almost invariably use, especially when the message had an apologetic cast, such as 'Can't talk now.'

Wyatt flashed back to his interview with Dodie Spencer. He didn't like to dwell on the sometimes dangerous nature of his work, and neither did he think he was paranoid. But the plain fact of what he'd told Dodie was undeniable: Ivan Orloff had never been Lance's biggest problem; Ivan had been doing Hunt's work. And now in Ivan's absence, that work would devolve back to Hunt.

Which made Wyatt the threat now.

And given the apparent acceptance of Lionel's guilt by the police, Hunt was the only person left standing between Lance and his freedom. Of course, if Hunt bought the Lionel story, then Lance was safe. But what if Lance had followed his wife today, or was having her followed? What if he'd somehow discovered that she'd met with him at the club? A bribe to Taylor the footman would accomplish that nicely. Then Hunt was truly back in the danger zone.

How likely was that? Not very, he realized.

But impossible? No.

And even 'possible' was almost too disturbing to bear.

He stood out on the sidewalk on California Street, just in front of the Huntington. Suddenly, his blood rushed in his ears and a wave of nausea washed over him as he realized that though the text messages came from Tamara's phone, that did not necessarily mean it was her sending them, did it?

Still clutching his cell phone, Wyatt leaned back against a streetlamp, trying to slow down his thoughts, the swiftly creeping onset of panic. Maybe he should have taken another dose or two of Dr. Gutierrez's pills. But he had not. He hadn't felt he needed them.

Should he try to call her, not text her, again? Or text her again with an urgent message to call him back, or . . .?

Easy, he told himself. Think it through. Easy.

He needed time. He needed time. All at once, this became the imperative. With time, he could consider possibilities, evaluate, plan, decide.

I'll be there in an hour. His finger paused over the 'Send' button. He added, *Love, Wyatt.*

He sent the text.

Before he made any other phone calls, he needed more evidence that he was not suffering from paranoid delusions. He didn't need absolute certainty, but another hint would not be unwelcome. So he punched up his home landline telephone number and listened as the kitchen phone rang four times, then kicked over to his answering machine. He heard his voice telling callers that he wasn't able to get to the phone, but they should leave a message and he'd get right back to them.

If Tamara were cooking in the kitchen, she might choose to monitor calls and not pick up under normal circumstances, but if she heard his voice, that was a different story. Even if – especially if – the message was clearly false. 'Hey, Wyatt,' he said. 'This is Mario. I'm stuck down at the Marina on this Tucker matter and I need to know what you want me to do. So if you're monitoring calls . . .' After a reasonable pause and a theatrical sigh, he went on. 'Okay, I'll try your cell.'

He hung up.

If Tamara was in the house as she'd texted him she was, there was no way she would not have picked up the phone on that call.

The unlikely possibility moved inexorably toward the terrifying probability.

The clock was now ticking and Wyatt could not allow himself the luxury of second-guessing himself. He had to gather as much information as quickly as he could, and then make what might be split-second decisions based on what he'd learned. Almost without conscious thought, he was searching his Contacts list and selecting a number. First things first: Determine where Lance was not.

Dodie picked up on the second ring, her voice tinged with a whispered urgency. 'Wyatt, what are you doing calling me at home? You can't call here.'

'Don't hang up. I just have some quick questions: Is Lance there with you?'

'No. He hasn't come home from work yet.'

'Do you know he's at work?'

'Not for sure, no. He doesn't check in with me.'

'Have you heard from him in the last hour or so?'

'No, but what is this about?'

'Do you know where he is for a fact?'

'No.'

'Does he have a cell phone?'

'Of course.'

In the moment, an idea surfaced. He had originally planned to ask Dodie to call Lance and try to locate him. Make up some excuse to find out, at least, where he was not. But suddenly a much more elegant solution occurred to him. 'Will you give me the number for it?' he asked.

'I don't think so. What for?'

'I need to know where he is.'

'How can knowing his phone number tell you that?'

'You'll have to trust me. It can. Please. It's extremely urgent.' He lowered his voice. 'This can get you everything you want. Everything you talked about today. This could be the end game, Dodie. Please.'

A pause. 'All right,' she said, and gave him the number.

32

After their less than amicable parting at lunch, Hunt wasn't at all sure that Juhle would even pick up when he saw who the call was from. So when Devin did answer, Wyatt laid it on thick. If he was correct about what was happening right now, Juhle's initial reaction to him wouldn't matter. Also if he was wrong, it wouldn't matter. So he had nothing to lose.

'You were right and I apologize,' he began. 'If I'm going to get you involved in my stuff, I've got to include you in whatever I find out. I don't know what got into me. I was a horse's ass, okay. I'm sorry.'

'So who's your texter?'

'Dodie Spencer. Lance's wife. It's Lance.'

'Your mother's murderer, you mean?'

'And Orloff, and the cabbie, and Lionel Spencer.'

'And you know this how?'

'Because right now Lance is at my place, holding Tamara captive.'

Hunt could almost hear Juhle come bolt upright.

'What?'

Giving him the short version, Hunt nevertheless didn't want to leave anything out. Twenty-five valuable minutes had already been lost since he'd talked to Dodie while Callie Lucente triangulated her 'ping' of Lance Spencer's phone. So far she had picked up the signal from his cell phone on two towers south of Brannan, and it would take a third tower for a dead-on GPS read of exactly where the phone was located. But the two towers made it clear that he was within no more than a two-hundred-yard radius of Hunt's warehouse, close enough for Wyatt to be certain. '. . . so I'm calling you, and you know how badly I hate to say this, because this now is clearly a police matter. You need to get some troops and surround the place. And I mean now.'

'Just like that, huh?'

'As soon as you can, Dev. This is no joke. He's there with her, there's no doubt. He's waiting for me to show up so he can kill me when I open the door.'

'You say no doubt. Do you know this for sure? This is a damn serious matter, Wyatt. You can't be wrong.'

'I understand that, but this isn't a hunch. I promise.'

Lance Spencer checked his wristwatch.

It had been nearly another forty minutes since Hunt had texted back that he would be here within an hour.

The girl had stopped her whimpering and now just lay there on her side. He'd secured her in the manner he'd learned in Vietnam: got her on her stomach, bound her hands tightly behind her, then brought the rope down to her feet, pulled them up and wrapped the rope around her ankles five times, tying it off when he was done. She wasn't going anywhere.

He'd pulled the bedroom chair out into the hallway, where he could keep a better eye on the door to the garage and with an ear to the lock turning in the kitchen door. Either way, he was covered.

He'd gotten up twice: once to use the bathroom, after which he carefully wiped down the toilet and all around it; and once going down to the kitchen to make sure the door there was locked back up the way he'd found it before he'd broken in. Although Hunt would almost certainly enter the building by driving his Mini through his garage door on Brannan, there was some small possibility that he might leave the car somewhere else and come in through the kitchen. Given that the place was an industrial warehouse in a fairly dicey area of town, he couldn't believe it didn't have an alarm system. But sometimes, he knew, you just got lucky.

Both times he'd gotten up, Lance had returned to find the girl exactly how he'd left her, facing away from him on her side on the bed, the knots holding nicely.

She really wasn't much in the way of company, was she?

Lance realized that Hunt couldn't be too far away and thought he might as well get rid of the girl now and avoid any potential source of drama or hassle later. He'd thought about the volume of the gun's report earlier, and that had slowed him down in his execution – he didn't feel good about hanging around after the noise of another shot – so he figured he would simply get a knife from the kitchen and cut her throat. Quiet and effective, one less detail to worry about.

He got up from his chair and started to move toward the kitchen, when the telephone rang again in the kitchen. He stopped – it would only delay things here for a second – and listened. It might be Hunt with an explanation or a change in his timing, and that would be worth knowing about.

Four rings, and then the answering machine.

Lance Spencer took a step down the hallway that extended in a straight line to the kitchen.

Hunt's machine played out its message. A pause. The beep.

'Lance Spencer,' he heard. 'You need to pick up the telephone. This is Inspector Juhle of the San Francisco police. We have the building surrounded. There are only two exits and we have them both covered. You need to come outside right now with your hands in the air.'

Lance Spencer picked up the telephone's receiver. 'You can kiss my ass,' he said. 'I've got a hostage and I want a car.'

'Look, Lance,' Devin said. 'This isn't going to work out for you. You know you're not going to get away from here. Let the girl go and we can talk about how to end this so nobody gets hurt.'

'I'll tell you how nobody gets hurt. You get me a car or I'll blow her head off. Right now.'

'You don't want to kill her, Lance. What would that get you?'

'Satisfaction, if nothing else. But that's not really the question, which is, Who is more screwed if I kill her, you or me? And I think we both know the answer to that, don't we? Especially when killing her is so easily avoidable. You get me a car, I'm going to the airport to get on a plane. I leave the girl on the tarmac and fly away. It's an easy deal.'

'Lance. I just can't do that.'

'Really? Maybe you want to talk to someone else about that before you get too committed to a bad idea. Your chief, or maybe the mayor. Or Wyatt Hunt. You know who he is?'

'We know him. You're in his house.'

'That's right. And you know what's special about this place? It's a goddamn fortress. All the windows are high up, you notice. No seeing inside, no telling where I am. You say you've got the entrances covered? Well, so do I. And nobody's even *trying* to get in here, or I shoot the girl. You teargas the place, I shoot the girl. Is that clear? And you haven't got all the time in the world. And oh, did I mention I had to shoot her already? She caught a bullet in the leg. She's already lost a lot of blood. So you're going to have to move on this. You still there?'

'I'm here.'

'All right, Inspector. So here's what going to happen, and it's going to happen exactly as I say, or I finish the girl.'

The first SWAT unit mobilized in about an hour from Juhle's first call. They cordoned off the block of Fifth Street where it abutted the alley behind Hunt's place, and also all of Brannan

Street between Fourth and Fifth. Four police cars and the SWAT team van lined the bigger main streets, while a patrol car and two SWAT members had pulled down into the alley behind Hunt's place all the way to where it ended at the shipping entrance to another warehouse, and a final patrol car with its two SWAT members blocked the mouth of the alley at Fifth. The alley, normally ill lit with only one streetlight, now glowed with the banks of kliegs they'd set up to illuminate the back entrance. Three television mobile units with their crews were strung along the street back up toward the Hall of Justice.

Out front on Brannan, they had a command post with Glitsky, Juhle, and Sarah Russo and some SWAT officers set up behind the SWAT van. Though not remotely a member of that unit, Wyatt Hunt hung in the close periphery, largely ignored, but since he'd been the one to sound this particular alarm, and since it was his domicile and his girlfriend, he was tolerated. It also didn't hurt that he had been right about Lance, and not Lionel, as the perpetrator of the three homicides last week.

Now the city's hostage negotiator, Cyril Jarvik – an ex-SEAL psychologist with a quiet, friendly demeanor – was making another phone call to Hunt's number inside with instructions to tell Lance Spencer that they'd located and reserved his airplane and were preparing it for flight.

Lance picked up on the first ring, heard him out, then said, 'I've been watching all you fools on television, and I want all those cop cars out of here – off the street and out of the alley – when we're getting ready to come out. Is that understood?'

'Perfectly,' Jarvik said. 'No problem. But before we go further here, Lance, I want to tell you that it's not too late to change your mind. At any time. If you want to end this, just let us know and we'll take care of you.'

'There is slim and no chance of that. Who the hell are you? Where's the other guy I was talking to, Juhle?'

Jarvik pointed at Juhle, motioned him forward. 'He's right here if you'd like to talk to him. Should I put him on?'

'I don't give a shit who I'm talking to. I just want to get this done.'

'That's our intention, too. We do, however, have a request for you.'

'Not a chance. I've told you what I want.'

'Right. We know that. But before we give you your car, we'd like to talk to the girl and be sure that she's okay.'

'Not gonna happen,' Lance said. 'In fact, we've got a new problem. While you morons were screwing around, she's passing in and out of consciousness. She can't drive me anyplace now and I need a driver. And before you even say it, I'm not taking a cop. And that means I'm not taking anybody I don't know. So here's the new deal. I'll trade you the girl for a car and Wyatt Hunt to drive it.'

Jarvik paused. 'You know we can't do that. We can't trade you one civilian for another. What difference does it make if we send in a cop? Either way you've got your hostage. Either way you've got your plane.'

'You heard my offer,' Spencer said. 'And you better take it in a hell of a hurry. I don't know how much longer she's going to last.'

Jarvik looked at Juhle. Juhle looked at Hunt, who nodded his head.

'We're out of time,' Wyatt pleaded. 'Let's just do this.'

Jarvik nodded, spoke into the phone. 'Okay, you got a deal.'

At last Lance said, 'He comes alone to the alley door. No Kevlar, and his hands are behind his back in handcuffs. Handcuff key in a shirt pocket or somewhere I can get it.'

'You want the handcuff key?'

'You heard me.' Lance, impatient, explained. 'Think about it. How's he going to drive with his hands behind his back? He gets in the driver's seat, I cuff him to the steering wheel. Also, he's all the way in before she goes out.'

'Nope,' Jarvik said. 'He goes halfway. Then the girl comes outside the door.'

Lance considered for a second, then said, 'I need a few minutes to get her set. Call again when Hunt's ready.'

They removed the squad cars from the alley and drove the van around so the command team had a view of Hunt's back door. The plan Jarvik and Lance had agreed on was that once Tamara was out of the house, and the police had hustled her to safety, Hunt would walk down the alley and come in the back door to the kitchen. Meanwhile, an officer would back the van down the alley to a spot where the side entrance opened directly in front of Hunt's back door, right up against the building. Lance wasn't going to give some sharpshooter on a nearby rooftop the opportunity to get him in his sights. When the van was in position, the driver would get out and Lance and his hostage would emerge from the warehouse, enter the van by the side door, and close the door behind them. When Hunt was cuffed to the steering wheel, the van would start driving toward the airport.

En route, they would keep in contact through Lance's cell phone. When they reached the Gulfstream on the tarmac at SFO, there were to be no police. The van would come to the bottom on the stairs that led into the plane – again, close in – and both men would enter the aircraft. Only after Lance had determined to his satisfaction that he had a clear runway, that the plane was prepped, fully gassed up, and flight ready, would he release the hostage.

Except, of course, everybody knew that wasn't what he was going to do to the hostage at all.

Hunt passed the officer carrying Tamara in the alley. She was nearly unconscious but opened her eyes when he said her name, giving him a weak and terrified smile.

Now, his hands bound behind his back by Juhle's handcuffs

and his shirtsleeves rolled up, he walked down the familiar stretch of asphalt behind his warehouse until he came to the small step that led up to his kitchen door, where he waited. Suddenly the door opened and he was looking at a man about his own size dressed in black jeans, tennis shoes, and a black T-shirt that hugged a well-developed body. A cold slab of a face, deathless eyes.

He might be in his sixties, but Lance Spencer kept himself in excellent shape.

He held a handgun centered on Hunt's chest.

'Get in. Close the door.'

Hunt stepped up and into the kitchen, kicking the door closed behind him.

'Women, huh?' Spencer said. 'What a pain in the ass.'

Hunt leaned back against the door and looked flat into Spencer's eyes. 'Why'd you kill Margie Carson?'

'What do you care?'

'She was my mother.'

Spencer allowed himself the ghost of a smile as though a sudden revelation had just come to him. 'Oh yeah, that's right. Wyatt. The name. That's how Dodie started to put all this together, isn't it?'

'Why'd you kill her?'

'Who gives a shit?' He shrugged at the triviality of it. 'Because I was ordered to. I had a boss who considered her a threat.'

'Jim Jones?'

He nodded. 'As a matter of fact.'

'A twenty-year-old mother of a baby was a threat?'

Another shrug. 'Threats are what they are. Age doesn't come into it. Jones needed her gone, so she had to go.'

'And what about Jim Burg?'

'What is this, twenty questions? The cop, right? See if you can guess.'

'He found something.'

'Not yet, but Burg was already talking to Lionel, who was freaking out, so it was only a matter of time. I should've taken care of my brother back then, too, while I was at it. He was always the weak link.'

Spencer pointed the gun at Hunt and said, 'Turn around. Now. I told them to send in the cuff key with you. Where is it?'

Hunt gestured to his shirt pocket.

'Here's how it goes. When we get in the van, you get in the front seat and I cuff you to the steering wheel. Make any little move in the meantime, I put a bullet in your head. Now turn around.'

Spencer uncuffed one of Hunt's hands, keeping the key, stepping back away. Pointing the gun at Wyatt, he said, 'Don't try anything clever with those free hands. Put 'em behind you. Get on the floor, now. Feet straight in front of you, back against the wall, hands behind.'

The phone jangled again and Spencer picked up the receiver. 'Talk,' he said. Then, 'You're making my day. Yeah, I'll stay on; just bring that van down and tell me when it's here.' Coming back to Hunt, he motioned with the gun and said, 'Get up. Slow. We're moving. When I give the word, you get the door.'

Hunt half rolled to get to where he could maneuver himself upright. Through the door, he heard what sounded like the van backing its way into its place. He got to his feet, found the knob, held his hands on it.

Spencer was aware of him, of course, but Lance's greater attention was focused on the telephone he held to his left ear.

The gun, its presence well established, hung down, pointing to the floor somewhere in the area between where the two men stood maybe eight feet apart.

Ten seconds passed. Twenty.

'All right,' Spencer said into the phone, then hung up and

turned back to Hunt. 'Let's do this. Get the door, then wait for me. We're going out together.'

Hunt turned the knob, got himself another step closer to Spencer, then pulled the door open, in toward him, bracing a foot against it, reaching one free hand out as far as he could through the crack.

Two seconds later, halfway to Hunt's bedroom, a huge crash shook the walls as someone in the basketball court side tried to break down the hallway door to that side of the house.

For a mere instant, the noise diverted Spencer's attention. His head turned a fraction of an inch at the unexpected explosion of sound, and for Hunt, watching and waiting for that moment of distraction, that was enough.

Hunt brought his hands around as he threw himself forward. After two quick steps, he slammed into Spencer's body with all his force, pinning him up to the wall.

The gun went off.

His arms now wrapped around Lance, Hunt tried to throw him sideways to the ground, but his dress shoes slipped on the kitchen tile and he couldn't get any purchase, so he came up all elbows and arms, knocking the gun free.

It clattered to the floor behind him.

Another tremendous crash got to the kitchen now from the door in the hallway just as Spencer managed to throw Hunt backward off balance and down onto the floor. Diving over him for the gun, scrambling, Spencer got his hand on the barrel and swung to bring it down.

Hunt reached up and stopped the blow, grabbing the gun by its grip and rolling on his side to get away.

Spencer dove at it and Hunt dodged, spun, realized he was still holding the gun.

Lance had suddenly, somehow, gotten to his feet and lunged one more time.

Wyatt's arm came up, the gun in his hand, and he pulled the trigger.

The shot drove Spencer back against the wall, where he stood staring down at Hunt with a quizzical look in his eye.

Hunt wasted no more time. 'Here's for my mother,' he said, as he took careful two-handed aim and shot him twice more – *Bam! Bam!* – a double tap in the center of his chest.

The two SWAT team officers, finally having broken down the hallway door with their battering ram, got to the entry to the kitchen a half second after the last shot, their own weapons drawn. 'Drop it! Drop it!'

Hunt threw the gun out onto the floor, where it skittered against the tile and came to rest against the wall under the telephone. His breath coming in ragged gasps, Wyatt raised his hands and held them above his head.

He saw Spencer slide down the wall to the floor, a corona of red blossoming in the black of the T-shirt. As Hunt watched, Lance's chest rose, then fell.

Then rose. Then fell another time.

And then his chest did not rise again.

'But what if . . .?'

Hunt put a finger up to Tamara's lips. She lay on the gurney in the back of the ambulance, wrapped in a couple of blankets, an IV with pain meds hooked up to her left arm. They'd bandaged her upper leg where the bullet had passed through her thigh, missing her femur and each one of the major blood vessels, and now she was sitting up, holding Hunt's hand in both of hers on top of the blankets.

Wyatt, still coming down from his own adrenaline rush, was blown away by Tamara's resilience. An hour ago she had been a captive, tied, wounded, and held at gunpoint, but once they were together again and out of danger, she had allowed herself a five-minute crying jag, holding Hunt possessively, but now, still groggy, her face drawn and blotched, just wanted to know what had happened, how Hunt had pulled it off.

'"What if" didn't happen,' he said gently. 'It worked.'

'I know it worked, but . . .'

'Look,' Hunt said. 'The first thing was I had to get you out of there. And once I knew he wanted a handcuff key, it was a no-brainer. It meant at some point he was going to take the cuffs off. And I figured that would be my chance.'

'Okay, but how'd you know you'd be able to rush him?'

'Improvise, adapt, overcome. I didn't know. But I figured it would be my best shot. Which, if I do say so myself, wasn't a bad idea.' He brushed a strand of hair from her face. 'The crucial element was the wall telephone in the kitchen. We were already controlling the conversation, calling him on that phone, right? As long as he's on that phone, he can't be watching the Brannan Street door, can he? No, he can't. It's impossible. So while I'm standing by the kitchen door, he's on that phone with Jarvik. Meanwhile, the SWAT guys use the key I've given them to let themselves into the courtside half with the ram for the inside door.'

'But what if they hit that door and you weren't ready?'

'That would have been bad,' Hunt said, 'which is why I had them wait until I gave them the sign.'

'You had a sign?'

'Gotta have a sign, Tam. It's one of the rules.'

'And what was it, this sign?'

'Opening the alley door. If I open it and stick one hand out, either cuffed or my free hand, it doesn't matter, the cop on the roof with binoculars knows my hands are free and signals the SWAT guys waiting outside to go, they hit the hall door full force with their ram, and at that moment I jump Spencer.'

'But what if . . .?' she started to ask.

'Tam,' he said. 'He'd already killed at least five people connected to my mother. He wasn't going to let me go at the airport. It had to work.'

'But . . .'

'Hey, hey, hey. Easy.' He leaned in with a soft kiss. '"What if" didn't happen, Tam. It worked.'

33

Susan Page and Lynn Sheppard had developed something of a personal relationship over the past few weeks as Lynn had worked the background details of her story. Now the two women sat in the Indy-Gardens dining room having lunch together, Bessie the dog nestling quietly on Susan's feet under the table. When they had finished their salads and caught up on some personal gossip – Lynn was seeing a new man, Wyatt Hunt had invited Susan to his family Thanksgiving and was paying her way out and putting her up at the St. Francis Hotel – Susan finally got around to asking how Lynn's story was coming along.

'I've pretty well gotten the whole thing written. They're talking about running it in seven parts starting next Sunday, so it will at least get a lot of visibility.'

'That's good.'

'It is. But . . .'

'But what?'

Lynn fussed with her napkin, pushed some food around on her plate. Finally, she smiled with a little air of embarrassment. 'If I tell you, I might blow my reputation as a hard-hitting investigative journalist.'

'That's not the way I think of you anyway. I think of you as my new best friend.'

'Well, thank you. I'm starting to think of you the same way. But the truth is, I'm a little scared.'

'What of?'

'That's the scariest part. It's all nebulous and really makes no sense, since the story itself, Wyatt's story looking for your daughter and his father, has great closure. We know what this man Lance Spencer did and pretty much how he did it, and he's dead, so there shouldn't be any further issues.'

'But there are?'

Again, Lynn hesitated. 'It's the money.'

Susan nodded. 'It's always the money, isn't it?'

'Often enough,' Lynn said. 'But in this case, maybe even more so.'

'You mean still? After all this time?'

'You know how much we're talking about, dear? When I first started looking into this, I was thinking the People's Temple's total worth came to somewhere around the realm of one or two million dollars, possibly as much as five.'

'But there was more.'

Lynn might have been scared, but she was clearly proud of her research. 'Estimates go as high or higher than fifty million, and this is in 1978 dollars, remember. Of which only about thirty-five million has been recovered or accounted for to this day. So clearly the Spencer boys weren't the only ones moving money around and siphoning off the occasional suitcase of cash for their own use.'

'The Spencer boys? So it was both of them?'

'Oh yes. Lionel and Lance were both pilots for Jones and his people. They just never settled in Jonestown permanently and weren't there during its last days, so they never even made the survivors' lists. Essentially, they'd become invisible.'

'So what did Jones need these private planes for?'

'Well, to transport people and money, of course.'

'But to where?'

Lynn put a hand on Susan's arm. 'This is what is so amazing to me. This money turned up in banks in San Francisco of course, but also L.A., Switzerland, France, the Bahamas, Venezuela, and five or six other countries. Curaçao, Grenada, Guyana. Oh, and don't forget the Vatican, which set up like a dozen ghost companies in Panama to transfer Temple money. And that's just the money the court-appointed receivers actually found. The point is that this was mostly a huge, global, money-laundering racket, which makes the tragedy there even greater, since the average person in Jonestown thought this was about saving their souls, when that was barely even incidental to the real work.'

'It is so sad,' Susan said.

'More than that, though,' Lynn said, 'it's frightening. There's still a ton of money out there, and all the people who stole it. They're not going to want to get all this stirred up again. And my editors are already asking me if I could run down another of the money trails and see where it's gotten to today. Find out if the story's still alive. Which, as we learned from the Spencers, it is.'

'You can always refuse, can't you?'

'And then what kind of a reporter would I be?'

'A live one.'

Lynn again patted her companion's arm. 'When you say it like that, it sounds so melodramatic. I'm probably just getting the heebie-jeebies waiting for the story to run. I don't really have a choice, anyway, do I? It's about those people who died down in Jonestown. It's up to us to remember, and it's up to me to help fill in the rest of the story, at least as much as I can. There's no statute of limitations on something like that, not morally anyway.'

'But you will be careful, won't you?'

'Of course, dear. Don't you worry,' Lynn said. 'Careful is my middle name.'

Elinor Burg did not want an elaborate ceremony, so it was a relatively small group that assembled in the back room of the

Fior d'Italia on the Wednesday a week before Thanksgiving. Besides Elinor, her three children, and their spouses and children, the guests seated at the long table included the chief of police Vi Lapeer and homicide chief Abe Glitsky (both in full dress uniform), Devin Juhle, Wyatt Hunt, and the PD's press secretary Donna Gigliani.

After the lunch dishes had been cleared and the coffee poured, Vi Lapeer stood up at the head of the table, and Devin Juhle tapped his water glass a few times to signal for quiet. When she had everyone's attention, Lapeer began:

'We are here today in some small way to help correct an injustice that occurred thirty-six years ago. At that time, James A. Burg, a recently coined inspector for this city's police department, decided on his own initiative to pursue an investigation into the murder of a young woman named Margie Carson. Margie's husband, Kevin, had already been tried twice for this killing, and twice a jury of his peers had declined to convict him.

'Jim Burg had known Kevin Carson and he, too, believed that Mr Carson was not guilty. In a short time, Inspector Burg's investigation came to center on a pair of brothers, Lionel and Lance Spencer, who were acquaintances of the victim and who had become involved as self-styled soldiers in Jim Jones's People's Temple, which had in the past couple of years relocated to the city.

'Shortly after his interrogations of Lionel Spencer, Inspector James Burg died of an apparent, though inexplicable, suicide. San Francisco homicide conducted an investigation into Inspector Burg's death and regrettably failed to uncover the evidence that demonstrated that Inspector Burg died in the line of duty while investigating an open murder case. Because of this, Inspector Burg has never before been publicly acknowledged among the ranks of his brother and sister officers who have fallen in the line of duty, their names inscribed in granite on the Memorial Wall of Honor in the Hall of Justice.

'Today we are gathered to present to you, Mrs Burg, a commemorative plaque from the city, approved by myself and the Board of Supervisors, and signed by the mayor, stating that your husband, Inspector James A. Burg, died gallantly in the line of duty, and directing that his name be added to the Memorial Wall of Honor.'

As Elinor Burg stood up with tears in her eyes to thank the chief, Juhle turned toward Hunt and rolled his eyes.

'Don't be so cynical,' Hunt whispered to him. 'Look at her. This is all she's ever wanted.'

'Wyatt. Hey, it's Lynn Sheppard. Out in Indianapolis?'

'As opposed to the Lynn Sheppard I know in Albuquerque?'

He heard her chuckle.

'I guess so. Am I interrupting you? Is this a good time?'

He was in the office at 5:30. 'It's always a good time for you, Lynn. How's it going?' And then, a thought occurring, 'Is Susan all right?'

'Susan's fine. In fact, I just saw her the other day. She told me you'd asked her out for Thanksgiving. That was very nice.'

'It was pure selfishness,' Hunt said. 'I love that woman.'

'I think she feels the same way.'

'I know. It's kind of a miracle. So what can I do for you?'

After a beat, she said, 'I mentioned this to Susan, but then I realized that it's you I ought to be talking to.'

'About what?'

She let out a heavy breath. 'Well, this Jonestown stuff. The money.'

'What about it?'

'There's still a lot of it out there, is what. I mean, possibly in the millions. And my editors are kind of pushing me to dig around a little more since we hit such pay dirt on the Spencers. They think maybe I've barely scratched the surface.'

Hunt paused. 'I think maybe they're right. Have you come across anything specific yet?'

'Nothing more than what you started me with a few weeks ago, but look where that led.'

'It led to the bad guy being dead, Lynn.'

'Right. That was one.'

'What are you saying?'

'I'm saying that this Spencer story has kind of blown the lid off this thing – I mean the whole Jonestown lost-money angle – and I'm going to still be writing about it and maybe you should be a little hyperaware for a while and watch your back. If there are more Spencer types out there, they're probably not going to be nice people, either.'

'But, I notice, you're still looking for them, too.'

'That's my job, Wyatt. But I'd be lying if I told you I wasn't a little concerned. And maybe you should be, too.'

'But I'm not looking for anybody.'

'I know that and you know it, but maybe they – whoever they may be – maybe they don't. Or maybe they wouldn't care.'

Hunt hesitated again. 'Could you stop digging?'

She laughed a brittle laugh. 'That's like saying could I stop breathing. But I will keep you informed if I stumble onto anything like a real bite. I just wanted to give you a little bit of a heads-up in the meantime. Just be aware, okay?'

'Always.'

'A little more than normally aware.'

'I will be. Promise.'

'Maybe I *should* just stop.'

'Breathing?'

She laughed again. 'I'm just being paranoid, aren't I? But I felt I had to tell you.'

'I'm glad you did. And maybe you're not being paranoid. Somebody out there has that money, and they probably want to keep it. I hear what you're saying, though. I'll be extra vigilant.'

He heard the relief in her voice. 'For a while, anyway.'

'For a while,' he said. 'Or forever.' Then added, 'Whichever comes first.'

In the workout clothes he slept in, in the dim glow of the screen-savers on the court side of his warehouse, Hunt slumped in his ergonomic chair, his hands templed at his mouth. Very occasionally, he registered a vehicle passing by outside, or the house heating cycling on and then off on the residence side. By these nearly subliminal signals, he was aware that time was passing, but he couldn't have given any length to the amount of it he'd been sitting there – an hour, three?

He knew that when he had jerked awake it had been 1:15. In the bed next to Tamara, he'd tossed until nearly two, then gave up and came out here, shot a few hoops, then simply had sat down on the court, finally stretched out full length.

Uncounted minutes passed. Cars droned by outside. A siren wailed somewhere in the distance. At last he got himself up, intending – no, determined! – to go and give sleep another try, but when he got to the door, he couldn't make himself turn the knob. Instead, he switched off the lights on this side and made his way over to his computer area, where he lowered himself into his chair and tried to will himself into a state of calm, of acceptance, of grace.

It wasn't happening.

Tamara knocked gently on the connecting door and pushed it open, whispering as though afraid that she might wake him. 'Wyatt?'

'I'm here.'

She pushed open the door and started to make her awkward way forward – she'd be limping for at least another few weeks – when Wyatt pushed himself up from his chair.

'Whoa,' he said. 'If anybody is going to be walking around here, it should be me.'

'I can walk.'

'Of course you can. It's just that I can walk without pain.' By this time, he'd crossed to where she stood and put an arm around her. 'I didn't mean for you to have to get up and go searching for me. Let's go back in.'

'Only if you want to.'

'Why wouldn't I want to?'

'Because you came out here. Maybe this is where you really want to be.'

'As opposed to?'

'In your bed.' She paused. 'In our bed.'

Hunt let a breath escape. 'I was thrashing around and didn't want to wake you up.'

'I know. But are you sure that's it?'

'Yes. What else would it be?'

'It might be that this thing we've just been through together went too fast, pushed us together when we might not have gotten there on our own.'

'Yes, we . . .'

She put her hand up against his lips. 'No. Let me say this. So now I'm basically living here or at work, limping around both places, half disabled, and it's like you're my caretaker, which is maybe not what you had in mind about all this. And then you get in bed with me and wake up every couple of nights to go sit by yourself. And you say it's because you don't want to wake me up, but I don't think it's that. Or I don't think that's all it is, at least. What do you think?'

Hunt stood for a long beat in silence. Finally, his voice husky, he said, 'You talk about yourself being disabled. How about if the disabled one is really me and I don't want you to see me this way?'

'Wyatt,' she whispered, 'do you remember how you were in Mexico?'

He shook his head with a kind of restrained violence. 'That's done. I got that way for a few days and then got out of it. That problem's over. Lance is dead, Tam. The whole thing's in the past. I don't know why I can't just put this behind me and get on with my life. And meanwhile, I risk losing . . . I mean, if you . . . if this is the way I'm going to be, I wouldn't blame you if you didn't want any part of it. I don't even want you to see it. I'm trying not to blow things here with you and instead, every night or two it's this . . . this whatever it is. It's wiping me out. To say nothing of driving you away.'

'Hey! Listen to me. It won't drive me away. Nothing's going to drive me away, you understand? Except maybe you not sharing this stuff with me. This real stuff.'

'This real stuff,' Hunt said. 'I don't know how long it's going to go on, Tam. I can't guarantee a damn thing. It just wells up, doesn't let me sleep, gives me these goddamn headaches . . .' He shook his head in fatigue and frustration. 'I don't need to put anybody else through that.'

She put her head up against his and held him close against her. 'Wyatt,' she said. 'It's been what? Three weeks? Five weeks? Versus your whole life before all this started? You can't expect this to go away for a while, maybe even a long while, and that's okay. Don't you see that? In fact, facing all this real stuff, as we're calling it, may be the best thing that could happen for you. Get the decks cleared so you can start moving ahead on the next stage of your life, whatever that might be. And all I really want is that you let me be part of it, too. Be part of you. You think you can do that?'

'I hate it,' Hunt said.

'I know you do. But you don't have to face it alone. Really. I'm here. I want to be here.'

'I'm afraid I'm going to scare . . .'

Again, she touched her hand to his lips. 'Stop right there. Okay, you're afraid. It's okay to be afraid. You being afraid, me seeing you afraid, isn't going to scare me away. I'm here until you kick me out.' She kissed him. 'You hear me?'

He held her tightly against himself, his breath coming heavily.

'Come back to bed,' she said.

Dodie hadn't expected that Lance would be killed.

She told herself that that had never been her idea. Her plan had been only that the law catch up to him, take him away, and leave her free, unencumbered, and financially comfortable. When she got the news that he was dead, it completely and unexpectedly hollowed her out.

So she had no trouble playing the grieving widow – in many ways it wasn't even an act.

To have someone you're living with suddenly die was traumatic, even if you felt nothing like love for him. Still, they'd had sex within the last week. For the past three years, he'd treated her with reasonable respect, following their rules. Her part of their deal was being available for him. And it wasn't that he was unattractive, or unskilled. Rather the contrary, in fact. She had her needs in that direction, too, and he more or less satisfied them.

But now she'd been three weeks in black. She'd done the endless press interviews, then the funeral, the lunches with her friends, the meetings with her attorneys, her accountants, the Execujet staff, now all her underlings.

She was carrying on, bearing up.

Wyatt Hunt, to his credit, said nothing about the role she'd played in giving him Lance's cell number. She still didn't understand how knowing that could pinpoint a location, but apparently it was possible.

In any event, enough!

Today, the Friday before Thanksgiving, she rang Execujet when she woke up and ordered the Gulfstream for ten o'clock. By dinnertime she had checked into the Ritz-Carlton in Kapalua – twenty-five hundred square feet with wraparound ocean views. If you would have asked her, she would have said she needed the space because Jamie would be coming over on Wednesday for the weekend. But to herself, really, what did it matter? She had the money.

She had all the money.

She opened the complimentary bottle of champagne and ordered a dozen oysters, a platter of sushi, and a lobster tail from room service. When she'd had enough of all that, she went in and took a bath.

The sun was just going down as she stepped out of the tub. The night was balmy, with a light trade, so she didn't bother drying off. Instead, she poured the last of the champagne into her fluted glass and walked out, naked, onto the patio.

Looking out over the grounds and the ocean beyond, she rested her champagne glass on the railing and spread her arms out as if to embrace the whole world, her eyes sparkling with avarice and delight.

The question of where to celebrate Thanksgiving every year was ongoing in the greater Hunt family. The clan consisted of five kids, four with their respective spouses, plus the parents, Bob and Charlene, and the possibilities seemed almost endless. Until this year, Wyatt had always been a guest at someone else's house, but suddenly, with a newfound appreciation for the importance of family, he felt it was time to step up and host the day himself.

He'd had the place professionally cleaned, got the inner door fixed and painted, and rented three large circular tables, setting them up beside the basketball court. Besides his natural grandmother from Indianapolis, he had invited all seventeen members of the extended Hunt family, plus Tamara, Mickey and Alicia, and their grandfather, Jim Parr.

Mickey, of course, was honchoing the cooking for all twenty-three of them, loving every minute of it. Tamara – bad leg and all – and Alicia were sous-chefing. The seven young cousins – ages four months to eight years – pretty much thought they'd all died and gone to heaven with the basketball court and all the various toys that Uncle Wyatt allowed them to touch and play with.

He had Pandora hooked up to his terrific speaker system, and it was playing the Tony Bennett channel, mostly classics from Bennett himself, along with a decent smattering of Sinatra, Billie Holliday, Steve Tyrell, Mel Tormé, Steve Lawrence, and Eydie Gormé. Great sounds.

Hunt was helping out in the kitchen whenever Mickey asked for it. Otherwise, he was making the rounds playing the host, shooting the occasional hoop, playing some guitar, giving mock surfing lessons and real motorcycle rides around the room's periphery – not a big hit with the parents, but he was the eldest brother, he never exceeded ten miles per hour, and they were all pretty much helpless against him.

The four oldsters – Bob, Charlene, Jim, and Susan – sat at one of the tables with their Old Fashioneds, enjoying the bedlam around them, chattering like they were the oldest friends in the world. At one point, Hunt looked over and was pretty sure he saw Jim Parr, the dog, holding hands with Susan, who looked about twenty years younger than she had the day they'd met in Indianapolis.

When Hunt walked into the kitchen to see how things were coming along on the food front, Mickey pointed up to a hole in the wall above the kitchen door. 'When did that get here?'

'Guess. I thought I'd leave it as a souvenir. Not everybody has a bullet hole in their kitchen.'

'That's odd,' Alicia said, 'when you think about how many people want one.'

Hunt gave her a smile and asked Mickey, 'How long till dinner?'

'Forty-five minutes or so.'

'Can I borrow your sister for a minute? Tam?'

They walked down the hallway and out the door into the courtside space, then picked their way through the maelstrom of kids and their parents, and finally made their way outside onto Brannan.

'Where are we going?' Tamara asked.

'It's a surprise,' Hunt said. 'I can't tell you yet.'

Holding her hand, he led her up to the corner, then around to where the alley came out behind his building, then into the alley itself.

'What's that on your stoop?' she asked.

'Hmm,' Hunt said. 'Looks like flowers.'

And in fact, it was a large mixed bouquet of roses and nearly everything else the flower shop had available.

'When did this get here?' Tamara asked. 'We've been in the kitchen all along. I don't know why they didn't just knock.'

'Maybe it was here earlier. Maybe it got here this morning.' Or actually, as Hunt knew, Mickey had gotten the signal when Hunt had left the kitchen with Tamara, and had just put it out there from its hiding place in his closet, where it had been since yesterday.

Hunt went to a knee and pulled the card out from the middle of the bouquet. 'It says it's for you. Must be an admirer.' He handed the bouquet up to her. 'We can just take it inside, if you want. It can be a centerpiece.'

'Or three centerpieces. It's big enough.' She smiled down at him. 'Wyatt, you are so sweet. Was this the surprise?'

'Most of it,' he said. 'The other part I'm a little nervous about.'

'What's that?'

He swung around to sit on the back stoop and patted the concrete next to him. 'Here,' he said. 'Sit a minute. Take some of the pressure off that leg.'

Hesitating briefly, she finally set the flowers down, then lowered herself and said, 'Okay. I'm sitting. Now what?'

'Now I need to ask you something.'

'Butterfly wings,' she said.

'That's amazing,' Hunt replied. 'I was going to ask you the main ingredient in butterfly-wing soup.'

'Great minds,' she said. And took his hand. 'Are you really nervous?'

'Somewhat.'

'What about?'

He drew in a breath. 'Change. The future.' Squeezing her hand, he continued, 'You know, when I heard you were shot, the first thing I thought is that he'd killed you. And just like that, you were gone out of my life forever.'

'Which, as you can see, I'm not.'

'No, thank God. But the point is you might have been. Easily. And the last few weeks I keep coming back to that moment, and every time, the idea of going on without you gets more and more impossible to imagine.'

'I am with you, Wyatt. Completely.' She brought their clasped hands together in her lap and now held his hand in both of hers. 'That's what you're nervous about? You don't need to be. We've already been through this, babe, in one version or another. I'm not going to die. You're not, either. Neither of us is going away, or breaking up with each other very soon, either.'

Wyatt sat a minute, then reached into his pocket and withdrew a small fuzzy black box. Opening it to reveal the ring, he said, 'I was thinking maybe we should make it a little more formal, if you want to.'

Her eyes went down to the ring, up to his eyes. She brought his hand up to her lips and kissed it. 'This is what you were nervous about? You thought there was any small chance that I'd say no?'

'I didn't know for sure. A small one, maybe.'

Now her own eyes glistened with joyful tears. 'How about maybe no chance at all, you idiot? How about never, no how, no way could I tell you no?'

'Okay.' He let out a breath. 'I realize this might be a little soon, but . . .'

'Wyatt, we've known each other for fifteen years. That's a fair start.'

'Right. I know. But since we really got together, I mean. I don't want you to feel rushed, or any pressure, or . . .'

Reaching out, she wiped a tear from her cheek with her fingertip, then pressed that fingertip against his lips. 'Shhh. I say yes. Get it? Yes.' She leaned over, tight against him. 'Now, in the immortal words of Mary Chapin Carpenter,' she said, 'shut up and kiss me.'

Acknowledgments

This book's genesis came about because of a discussion with a former e-mail correspondent, now friend of mine, Dr. Jack Crary. Jack had been helpful before on issues related to traumatic brain injury in both *Betrayal* and *A Plague of Secrets*. At a dinner we were having in San Francisco, Wyatt Hunt's adoption came up, and Jack mentioned that he thought it would be fascinating to explore commitment and abandonment issues in adults in light of time spent as children in foster homes and with an adoption background. He was right – it's fascinating stuff – and I thank Jack for pointing me down this path and helping to show me the way.

Because I am not the most technologically savvy person on the face of the earth, when I began the general outline for this book, I knew I would need an expert in all things cell-phonic, and I was extremely fortunate to make the acquaintance of RJ Reynolds, a long-time employee of AT&T who was working at the company's retail shop in my hometown. Over several meetings, RJ opened my eyes to many of the common realities of our tech-driven culture that I had never known about or even considered. Our privacy is, it turns out, not as sacrosanct as many of us think. RJ's contribution to this book was seminal and I am grateful for his time, knowledge, and advice.

For their knowledge of the changing protocols of adoption in California over the past generation or two, I'd like to thank Karen Erickson of Catholic Charities CYO in San Francisco and Don Mencarini, California State Department of Social Services,

Adoption Support Unit, both of whom accepted my cold calls for information with good humor and cooperation.

This is, after all, a book about a private investigator, yet another arena in which I have no firsthand experience. In my research, I reached out to several real-life private investigators to find out what life feels like in this profession, and all these people were extremely forthcoming and helpful. These include: Larry DeMates, Marcel Myres of Submar Investigations, and Rick Fuller. Thanks, guys – I'm planning to call you again next time, too, so be warned!

Some books write themselves, and some want to wrestle. For some reason, in spite of my clearest outline yet and tremendous faith in the story, this one is of the latter category, and two wonderful writers, Paul McHugh and Max Byrd, familiar with the process, showed up regularly with well-timed bonhomie and support. Also, in the good friends rooting things along category, are Spring and Louis Warren, Eileen Randahl and Andy Watson, Bob Zaro, Don Matheson, Tom Hedtke, and Vicki Lorini.

Dr. Mark Detzer (and of course, his lovely wife – my sister – Kathryn) was tremendously helpful in walking me through the pathology and psychology of nervous breakdowns and panic attacks. On another major plot point, I would never have known where Wyatt Hunt needed to go in Mexico without the nudge from Karin Nieves that I look into the exotic and beautiful weaving village of Teotitlán del Valle. This turned out to be a brilliant suggestion.

In this as in all my other books, Al Giannini remains a true collaborator – pitch-perfect sounding board, legal vetting expert, sensitive student of the human condition. These books gain immeasurably in depth, verisimilitude, and complexity by Al's involvement in them. From the first notes of the outline until the completion of the manuscript, Al's input was and is, as always, immeasurable.

On the home office front, I've been blessed for many years now with the perfect coworker and administrative assistant, Anita Boone. Day to day, year to year, Anita coordinates all of the logistical and promotional endeavors that make up the business of the working author, all the while retaining a sunny optimism and can-do demeanor. She is truly a treasure. I am also lucky with my freelance editors – it seems like no matter how many times you read your book, you miss something. Even the pros at the publishers miss something. So to keep the flow of these books from being interrupted by typos, redundancies, or just plain stupidity, my proofreaders are without peer: thanks to Peggy Nauts and Doug Kelly.

For the title, I'd like to thank my son, Jack, with a little help from my wife, Lisa.

Several people have generously contributed to charitable organizations by purchasing the right to name a character in this book. These people and their respective organizations are: Jim Burg (Special Olympics); Gary and Debbie Dennis (Big Brothers and Big Sisters); Carol Davis (CASA of Humboldt); Tim Phillips (Heart Association); and Lynn Manger (National Association for Drug Abuse Prevention).

We are all living more and more in the world of social networking, and this is especially true in the book business, the landscape of which seems to change under our feet every day or so. Navigating through the shoals of Web-based marketing, Twitter, Facebook, and so on is not a job for sissies. I got on the boards with this stuff a few years ago with expert help from Maddee James on my Web page and Aryn DeSantis on Facebook, and now they've handed off these and other duties to Eager Mondays – Dr. Andy Jones and Briony Gylgayton. I love hearing from my readers and urge you to visit my Web site (www.johnlescroart.com), become a fan on Facebook (www.facebook.com/johnlescroart), and/or follow along with the always lively interaction on Twitter (www.twitter.com/johnlescroart).

I am very fortunate to have such a hardworking and talented team at Dutton helping to publish these books with such taste and commitment. Brian Tart is simply a publisher par excellence; Ben Sevier is the editor every writer dreams that one day he'll be lucky enough to work with. Christine Ball and Carrie Swetonic are tireless and creative in their marketing efforts. The rest of the team is nothing short of outstanding: Jess Horvath, Stephanie Kelly, Susan Schwartz, Rachael Hicks, Signet/NAL paperback publisher Kara Welsh, Phil Budnick, Rick Pascocello, and Rich Hasselberger, jacket cover guru extraordinaire.

Last but by no means least – in fact, in many ways most – Barney Karpfinger remains a great friend, an insightful advisor, a tireless advocate, and in all ways a superb literary agent. It is no exaggeration to say that I owe my career largely to Barney's efforts, and I can not thank him enough. Thanks, man. You are the greatest!

The Hunt Club

John Lescroart

A federal judge is murdered, found shot in his home together with the body of his mistress. To homicide inspector Devin Juhle, it looks like a case of a wife's jealousy and rage. But the judge had some powerful enemies . . .

Meanwhile, Private Investigator Wyatt Hunt finds himself smitten with the beautiful and enigmatic Andrea Parisi, a celebrity television lawyer. But Andrea, too, had a connection to the judge, along with a client that had everything to gain from the judge's death. And then she suddenly disappears . . .

Andrea becomes Juhle's prime suspect. Wyatt Hunt thinks she may be a kidnap victim, or worse, another murder victim. And far more than that, she's someone with whom he believes he may have a future.

As the search for Andrea intensifies, Hunt gathers a loose band of friends and associates willing to bend and even break the rules, leading to a chilling confrontation from which none of them might escape.

Praise for John Lescroart:

'Grisham and Turow remain the two best-known writers in the genre. There is, however, a third novelist at work today who deserves to be considered alongside Turow and Grisham. His name is John Lescroart' *Chicago Sun-Times*

978 0 7553 9317 6

headline

Treasure Hunt

John Lescroart

When Mickey Dade discovers the body of Dominic Como, he sees this as his chance to prove himself. He's been stuck behind a desk at Wyatt Hunt's private investigative service, The Hunt Club, but now seizes the opportunity to work on a real case.

Como was one of San Francisco's most high-profile fundraisers and one suspect in the case is Como's business associate, Alicia Thorpe – young, gorgeous, and the sister of one of Mickey's friends.

As Mickey and Hunt are pulled into the case, they soon learn that Como was involved in some highly suspect deals. And the lovely Alicia knows more about this – and more about Como – than she's letting on.

As the case reaches its nail-biting conclusion, Mickey Dade finds his world crumbling around him as he learns the hard lessons Hunt knows only too well.

Praise for John Lescroart:

'The real star of *Treasure Hunt* is San Francisco in all its social and political complexity . . . Bay Area details permeate the story like the local fog, and the city becomes an integral character, complete with secrets of its own' *Entertainment Weekly*

978 0 7553 9319 0

headline